GREEK
BOUND BY THE

GREEK BACHELORS COLLECTION

January 2018

February 2018

March 2018

April 2018

May 2018

June 2018

GREEK BACHELORS: BOUND BY HIS HEIR

SHARON
KENDRICK

DANI
COLLINS

REBECCA
WINTERS

MILLS & BOON

Published in Great Britain 2017
By Mills & Boon, an imprint of HarperCollins*Publishers*
1 London Bridge Street, London, SE1 9GF

GREEK BACHELORS: BOUND BY HIS HEIR © 2017 Harlequin Books S.A.

Carrying the Greek's Heir © 2015 Sharon Kendrick
An Heir to Bind Them © 2014 Dani Collins
The Greek's Tiny Miracle © 2014 Rebecca Winters

ISBN: 978-0-263-93187-7

09-0118

MIX
Paper from
responsible sources
FSC **FSC® C007454**
www.fsc.org

This book is produced from independently certified FSC™ paper to ensure responsible forest management.

For more information visit: www.harpercollins.co.uk/green

Printed and bound in Spain
by CPI, Barcelona

CARRYING THE GREEK'S HEIR

SHARON KENDRICK

With special thanks to Iona Grey (Letters to the Lost) *who makes discussing characters such fun.*

And to Peter Cottee for giving me a glimpse into a businessman's mind.

Sharon Kendrick started story-telling at the age of eleven, and has never really stopped. She likes to write fast-paced, feel-good romances with heroes who are so sexy they'll make your toes curl!

Born in west London, she now lives in the beautiful city of Winchester – where she can see the cathedral from her window (but only if she stands on tiptoe). She has two children, Celia and Patrick, and her passions include music, books, cooking and eating – and drifting off into wonderful daydreams while she works out new plots!

CHAPTER ONE

HE WANTED HER. He wanted her so badly he could almost taste it.

Alek Sarantos felt the heavy jerk of lust as he drummed his fingers against the linen tablecloth. Tall candles flickered in the breeze and the rich perfume of roses scented the air. He shifted his position slightly but still he couldn't get comfortable.

He was…restless. More than restless.

Maybe it was the thought of returning to the crazy pace of his London life which had heightened his sexual hunger, so that it pulsed through his veins like thick, sweet honey. His throat tightened. Or maybe it was just her.

He watched as the woman walked through the long grass towards him, brushing past meadow flowers which gleamed like pale discs in the dying light of the summer evening. The rising moon illuminated a body showcased by a plain white shirt, tucked into a dark skirt which looked at least a size too small. A tightly tied apron emphasised her hips. Everything about her was soft, he thought. Soft skin. Soft body. The thick hair which was plaited in a heavy rope and fell down to the middle of her back was silky soft.

His lust was insistent—his groin the opposite of soft—yet she wasn't his type. Definitely not. He didn't usually get turned on by curvy waitresses who greeted you with an uncomplicated, friendly smile. He liked his women lean and independent, not gently rounded and wholesome. Hard-eyed women who dropped their panties with ease and without question. Who took him on his terms—which had no room for manoeuvre. Terms which had helped carve out his position as a man of influence and given him a lifestyle free of domestic tie or encumbrance. Because he didn't want either. He avoided anyone he suspected might be soft, or needy or—heaven forbid—*sweet*. Sweet wasn't a quality he required in a bed partner.

So why was he lusting after someone who'd been drifting around the periphery of his vision all week, like a ripe plum waiting to fall from the tree? Something to do with her apron, perhaps—some late-onset uniform fetish, which was playing some very erotic fantasies in his head?

'Your coffee, sir.'

Even her voice was soft. He remembered hearing its low, musical cadence when she'd been comforting a child who had cut open his knee on one of the gravel paths. Alek had been returning from a game of tennis with the hotel pro when he'd seen her crouching down beside the boy, exuding a general air of unflappability. She'd stemmed the flow of blood with her handkerchief as an ashen-faced nanny had stood shaking nearby and, turning her head, had seen Alek. She'd told him to 'Go inside and get a first-aid kit' in the calmest voice he'd ever heard. And he had. A man more used to issuing orders than taking them, he'd returned with the kit and

felt a savage twist of pain in his gut to see the boy looking up at her with such trust shining from his teary eyes.

She was leaning forward now as she placed the cup
of coffee in front of him, drawing his attention to her
breasts, which were straining tightly against her shirt.
Oh, God. Her breasts. He found himself wondering what
her nipples might look like if they were peaking towards
his lips. As she straightened up he saw pewter-grey eyes
framed by a pale and heavy fringe. She wore no adorn-
ment other than a thin gold chain around her neck and
a name badge which said *Ellie*.

Ellie.

As well as being cool and unflappable towards small
boys, she'd spent the week anticipating his every need—
and while that was nothing new to someone like him,
her presence had been surprisingly unobtrusive. She
hadn't tried to engage him in conversation, or wow
him with wisecracks. She'd been pleasant and friendly
but hadn't hinted about her evenings off, or offered to
show him around. In short, she hadn't come onto him
like any other woman would have done. She had treated
him with the same quiet civility she'd exhibited towards
every other guest in the discreet New Forest hotel—
and maybe that's what was bugging him. His mouth
hardened—for it was almost unheard of for Alek Sarantos to be treated like other people.

But it wasn't just that which had captured his interest. She had an air about her which he couldn't quite put
his finger on. Ambition maybe, or just some quiet professional pride. Was it that which made his gaze linger
for a heartbeat too long—or the fact that she reminded
him of himself, more years ago than he cared to remember? He'd once had that same raw ambition—back in

the days when he'd started out with nothing and waited
tables, just like her. When money had been tight and
the future uncertain. He had worked hard to escape his
past and to forge a new future and had learnt plenty of
lessons along the way. He'd thought that success was
the answer to every problem in life, but he had been
wrong. Success made the pill sweeter, but you still had
to swallow the pill all the same.

Wasn't he realising that now—when he'd achieved
every single thing he'd set out to achieve? When every
hurdle had been leapt over and unimaginable riches
were stuffed into his various bank accounts. Didn't
seem to matter how much he gave away to charity, he
still kept making more. And sometimes that left him
with a question which made him feel uncomfortable—
a question he couldn't seem to answer, but which he'd
been asking himself more and more lately.

Was this all there was?

'Will there be anything else, Mr Sarantos?' she was
asking him.

The waitress's voice washed over him like balm.
'I'm not sure,' he drawled and lifted his eyes to the sky.
Above him, stars were spattering the darkening sky—
as if some celestial artist had sprayed the canvas silver.
He thought of returning to London the following day
and a sudden, inexplicable yearning made him lower
his head and meet her gaze. 'The night is still young,'
he observed.

She gave him a quick smile. 'When you've been waiting tables all evening, eleven-thirty doesn't really feel
young.'

'I guess not.' He dropped a lump of sugar in his coffee. 'What time do you finish?'

Her smile wavered, as if the question wasn't one she'd been anticipating. 'In about ten minutes' time.'

Alek leant back in his chair and studied her some more. Her legs were faintly tanned and the smoothness of her skin made you almost forget how cheap her shoes were. 'Perfect,' he murmured. 'The gods must be smiling on us. So why don't you join me for a drink?'

'I can't.' She shrugged as if in answer to his raised eyebrows. 'I'm not really supposed to fraternise with customers.'

Alek gave a hard smile. Wasn't *fraternise* an old-fashioned word, which had its roots in *brotherly*? An irrelevant word as far as he was concerned, because he'd never had brothers. Never had anyone. Well, nobody that mattered, that was for sure. He'd always been alone in the world and that was the way he liked it. The way he intended to keep it. Except maybe for this star-lit night, which was crying out for a little female company. 'I'm just asking you to join me for a drink, *poulaki mou*,' he said softly. 'Not to drag you off to some dark corner and have my wicked way with you.'

'Better not,' she said. 'It's against hotel policy. Sorry.'

Alek felt the stir of something unknown whispering down his spine. Was it the sensation of being refused something—no matter how small—which had started his heart racing? *How long since he had been refused anything and felt this corresponding frisson of excitement? A heady feeling that you might actually have to make an effort—instead of the outcome being entirely predictable.*

'But I'm leaving tomorrow evening,' he said.

Ellie nodded. She knew that. Everyone in the hotel did. They knew plenty about the Greek billionaire who had been creating a stir since he'd arrived at The Hog last week. As the most luxurious hotel in the south of England, they were used to rich and demanding guests—but Alek Sarantos was richer and more demanding than most. His personal assistant had actually sent a list of his likes and dislikes before he'd arrived and all the staff had been advised to study it. And even though she'd considered it slightly over the top, Ellie had got stuck right in, because if a job was worth doing—it was worth doing well.

She knew he liked his eggs 'over easy' because he'd lived in America for a while. That he drank red wine, or sometimes whisky. His clothes had arrived before he did—delivered by special courier and carefully wrapped in layers of filmy tissue paper. There had even been a special staff pep talk just before he'd arrived.

'Mr Sarantos must be given space,' they'd been told. *'Under no circumstances must he be disturbed unless he shows signs of wanting to be disturbed. It's a coup for someone like him to stay in this hotel, so we must make him feel as if it's his own home.'*

Ellie had taken the instructions literally because The Hog's training scheme had given her stability and hope for the future. For someone who'd never been any good at exams, it had offered a career ladder she was determined to climb, because she wanted to make something of herself. To be strong and independent.

Which meant that, unlike every other female in the place, she had tried to regard the Greek tycoon with a certain impartiality. She hadn't attempted to flirt with him, as everyone else had been doing. She was practical enough to know her limitations and Alek Sarantos would never be interested in someone like *her*. Too curvy and too ordinary—she was never going to be the preferred choice of an international playboy, so why pretend otherwise?

But of course she had looked at him. She suspected that even a nun might have given him a second glance because men like Alek Sarantos didn't stray onto the average person's radar more than a couple of times in a lifetime.

His rugged face was too hard to be described as handsome and his sensual lips were marred by a twist of ruthlessness. His hair was ebony, his skin like polished bronze, but it was his dark-fringed eyes which captured your attention and made it difficult to look away. Unexpectedly blue eyes, which made her think of those sunlit seas you always saw in travel brochures. Sardonic eyes which seemed to have the ability to make her feel…

What?

Ellie shook her head slightly. She wasn't sure. As if she sensed something lost in him? As if, on some incomprehensible level, they were kindred spirits? Stupid crazy stuff she shouldn't be feeling, that was for sure. Her fingers tightened around the tray. It was definitely time to excuse herself and go home.

But Alek Sarantos was still staring as if he was waiting for her to change her mind and as those blue eyes seared into her she felt a brief wobble of temptation. Because it wasn't every day a Greek billionaire asked you to have a drink with him.

'It's getting on for twelve,' she said doubtfully.

'I'm perfectly capable of telling the time,' he said with a touch of impatience. 'What happens if you stay out past midnight—does your car turn into a pumpkin?'

Ellie jerked back her head in surprise. She was

amazed he knew the story of Cinderella—did that mean they had the same fairy tales in Greece?—though rather less surprised that he'd associated her with the famous skivvy.

'I don't have a car,' she said. 'Just a bicycle.'

'You live out in the middle of nowhere and you don't have a car?'

'No.' She rested the tray against her hip and smiled, as if she were explaining elementary subtraction to a five-year-old. 'A bike is much more practical round here.'

'So what happens when you go to London—or the coast?'

'I don't go to London very often. And we do have such things as trains and buses, you know. It's called public transport.'

He dropped another cube of sugar in his coffee. 'I didn't use any kind of public system until I was fifteen.'

'Seriously?'

'Absolutely.' He glanced up at her. 'Not a train or a bus—not even a scheduled airline.'

She stared at him. What kind of life had he led? For a moment she was tempted to offer him a glimpse of hers. Maybe she should suggest meeting tomorrow morning and taking the bus to nearby Milmouth-on-Sea. Or catching a train somewhere—anywhere. They could drink scalding tea from paper cups as the countryside sped by—she'd bet he'd never done *that*.

Until she realised that would be overstepping the mark, big time. He was a hotshot billionaire and she was a waitress and while guests sometimes pretended to staff that they were equals, everyone knew they weren't. Rich people liked to play at being ordinary, but for them it was nothing but a game. He'd asked her to stay for a drink but, really, what possible interest could a tycoon like him have in someone like her? His unusually expansive mood might evaporate the moment she sat down. She knew he could be impatient and demanding. Didn't the staff on Reception say he'd given them hell whenever he'd lost his internet connection—even though he was supposed to be on holiday and, in her opinion, people on holiday shouldn't be working.

But then Ellie remembered something the general manager had told her when she'd first joined the hotel's training scheme. That powerful guests sometimes wanted to talk—and if they did, you should let them.

So she looked into his blue eyes and tried to ignore the little shiver of awareness which had started whispering over her skin. 'How come,' she questioned, trying to make her voice sound cool and casual, 'it took until the age of fifteen before you went on public transport?'

Alek leant back in his chair and considered her question and wondered whether now might be the right time to change the subject, no matter how easy he found it to talk to her. Because the reality of his past was something he usually kept off-limits. He had grown up in a pampered palace of a home—with every luxury known to man.

And he had hated every minute of it.

The place had been a fortress, surrounded by high walls and snarling dogs. A place which had kept people out as well as in. The most lowly of staff were vetted before being offered employment, and paid obscenely well to turn a blind eye to his father's behaviour. Even family holidays were tainted by the old man's paranoia about security. He was haunted by the threat of stories about his lifestyle getting into the papers—terrified that anything would be allowed to tarnish his outward veneer of respectability.

Crack teams of guards were employed to keep rubberneckers, journalists and ex-lovers at bay. Frogmen would swim silently in reconnaissance missions around foreign jetties, before their luxury yacht was given the all-clear to sail into harbour. When he was growing up, Alek didn't know what it was like not to be tailed by the shadowy presence of some burly bodyguard. And then one day he had escaped. At fifteen, he had walked away, leaving his home and his past behind and cutting his ties with them completely. He had gone from fabulous wealth to near penury but had embraced his new lifestyle with eagerness and hunger. No longer would he be tainted by his father's fortune. Everything he owned, he would earn for himself and that was exactly what he'd done. It was the one thing in life he could be proud of. His mouth hardened. Maybe the only thing.

He realised that the waitress was still waiting for an answer to his question and that she no longer seemed to be in any hurry to get off duty. He smiled, expectation making his heart beat a little faster. 'Because I grew up on a Greek island where there were no trains and few buses.'

'Sounds idyllic,' she said.

Alek's smile faded. It was such a cliché. The moment you said *Greek island*, everyone thought you were talking about paradise, because that was the image they'd been fed. But serpents lurked in paradise, didn't they? There were any number of tortured souls living in those blindingly white houses which overlooked the deep blue sea. There were all kinds of dark secrets which lay hidden at the heart of seemingly normal lives. *Hadn't he found that out, the hard way?* 'It looked very idyllic from the outside,' he said. 'But things are rarely what they seem when you dig a little deeper.'

'I suppose not,' she said. She transferred the tray to her other hand. 'And does your family still live there?'

His smile was slow—like a knife sinking into wet concrete. His *family*? That wouldn't be his word of choice to describe the people who had raised him. His father's whores had done their best, with limited success—but surely even they were better than no mother at all. Than one who'd run out on you and never cared enough to lift the phone to find out how you were.

'No,' he said. 'The island was sold after my father died.'

'A whole island?' Her lips parted. 'You mean your father actually *owned an island*?'

Another stab of lust went kicking to his groin as her lips parted. If he'd announced that he had a home on Mars, she couldn't have looked more shocked. But then, it was easy to forget how isolating wealth could be—especially to someone like her. If she didn't even own a car, then she might have trouble getting her head around someone having their own island. He glanced at her hands and, for some reason, the sight of her unmanicured nails only intensified his desire and he realised that he hadn't been entirely honest when he'd told her he wasn't planning to drag her away to a dark corner. He thought he'd like that very much.

'You've been standing there so long that you've probably come to the end of your shift,' he said drily. 'You could have had that drink with me after all.'

'I suppose I could.' Ellie hesitated. He was so persistent. Flatteringly so. She wondered why. Because he'd been almost *friendly* since he'd helped with the little boy who'd cut his knee? Or because she'd displayed a degree of reluctance to spend time with him and he wasn't used to that? Probably. She wondered what it must be like, to be Alek Sarantos—so sure of yourself that nobody ever turned you down.

'What are you so scared of?' he taunted. 'Don't you think I'm capable of behaving like a gentleman?'

It was one of those life-defining moments. Sensible Ellie would have shaken her head and said no thanks. She would have carried the tray back to the kitchen, unlocked her bike and cycled home to her room in the nearby village. But the moonlight and the powerful scent of the roses were making her feel the opposite of sensible. The last time a man had asked her on a date—and you couldn't really call this a date—was over a year ago. She'd been working such unsociable hours that there hadn't been a lot of opportunity for down time.

She looked into his eyes. 'I hadn't really thought about it.'

'Well, think about it now. You've been waiting on me all week, so why not let me wait on you for a change? I have a fridge stocked with liquor I haven't touched. If you're hungry, I can feed you chocolate or apricots.' He rose to his feet and raised his eyebrows. 'So why don't I pour you a glass of champagne?'

'Why? Are you celebrating something?'

He gave a low laugh. 'Celebration isn't mandatory. I thought all women liked champagne.'

'Not me.' She shook her head. 'The bubbles make me sneeze. And I'm cycling home—I don't want to run over some poor, unsuspecting pony who's wandered out into the middle of the road. I think I'd prefer something soft.'

'Of course you would.' He slanted her an odd kind of smile. 'Sit down and let me see what I can find.'

He went inside the self-contained villa which stood within the extensive hotel grounds and Ellie perched awkwardly on one of the cane chairs, praying nobody would see her, because she shouldn't be sitting on a guest's veranda as if she had every right to do so.

She glanced across the silent lawn, where a huge oak tree was casting an enormous shadow. The wild flowers which edged the grass swayed gently in the breeze and, in the background, lights blazed brightly from the hotel. The dining room was still lit with candles and she could see people lingering over coffee. In the kitchen, staff would be frantically washing up and longing to get home. Upstairs, couples would be removing complimentary chocolates from on top of the Egyptian linen pillows, before getting into bed. Or maybe they would be sampling the deep, twin baths for which The Hog was so famous.

She thought she saw something glinting from behind the oak tree and instinctively she shrank back into the shadows, but before she could work out exactly what it was—Alek had returned with a frosted glass of cola for her, and what looked like whisky, for him.

'I guess I should have put them on a tray,' he said.

She took a sip. 'And worn an apron.'

He raised his eyebrows. 'Perhaps I could borrow yours?'

The implication being that she remove her apron… Ellie put her glass down, glad that the darkness disguised her suddenly hot cheeks because the thought of removing anything was making her heart race. Suddenly, the moonlight and the roses and the glint in his eyes was making her feel way too vulnerable.

'I can't stay long,' she said quickly.

'Somehow I wasn't expecting you to. How's your cola?'

'Delicious.'

He leant back in his chair. 'So tell me why a young woman of twenty…?' He raised his eyebrows.

'I'm twenty-five,' she supplied.

'Twenty-five.' He took a sip of whisky. 'Ends up working in a place like this.'

'It's a great hotel.'

'Quiet location.'

'I like that. And it has a training scheme which is world famous.'

'But what about…' he paused '…nightlife? Clubs and boyfriends and parties? The kind of thing most twenty-five-year-olds enjoy.'

Ellie watched the bubbles fizzing around the ice cubes he'd put in her cola. Should she explain that she'd deliberately opted for a quiet life which contrasted with the chaos which had defined her childhood? Somewhere where she could concentrate on her work, because she didn't want to end up like her mother, who thought a woman's ambition should be to acquire a man who was a meal ticket. Ellie had quickly learnt how she *didn't* want to live. She was never going to trawl the internet, or hang around nightclubs. She had never owned a thigh-skimming skirt or push-up bra. She was never going to date someone just because of what they had in their wallet.

'Because I'm concentrating on my career,' she said. 'My ambition is to travel and I'm going to make that happen. One day I'm hoping to be a general manager— if not here, then in one of the group's other hotels. Competition is pretty fierce, but there's no harm in aiming high.' She sipped her cola and looked at him. 'So that's me. What about you?'

Alek swirled the whisky around in his glass. Usually he would have changed the subject, because he didn't like talking about himself. But she had a way of asking questions which made him want to answer and he still couldn't work out why.

He shrugged. 'I'm a self-made man.'

'But you said—'

'That my father owned an island? He did. But he didn't leave his money to me.' And if he had, Alek would have thrown it back in his face. He would sooner have embraced a deadly viper than taken a single drachma of the old man's fortune. He felt his gut tighten. 'Everything I own, I earned for myself.'

'And was that…difficult?'

The softness of her voice was hypnotic. It felt like balm being smoothed over a wound which had never really healed. And wasn't this what men had done since the beginning of time? Drunk a little too much whisky and then offloaded on some random woman they would never see again?

'It was a liberation,' he said truthfully. 'To cut my ties with the past.'

She nodded, as if she understood. 'And start over?'

'Exactly that. To know that every decision I make is one I can live with.'

His cell phone chose precisely that moment to start

ringing and automatically he reached into his pocket, glancing at the small screen.

Work, he mouthed as he took the call.

He launched into a long torrent of Greek, before breaking into English—so that Ellie couldn't help but sit there and listen. Though if she was being honest, it was very interesting listening to a conversation, which seemed to involve some high-powered forthcoming deal with the Chinese. And then he said other stuff, too— which was even more interesting.

'I *am* taking a holiday. You know I am. I just thought it wise to check with the New York office first.' He tapped his finger impatiently against the arm of the chair. 'Okay. I take your point. *Okay.*'

He cut the connection and saw her staring at him. 'What is it?' he demanded.

She shrugged. 'It's none of my business.'

'No, I'm interested.'

She put her drink down. 'Don't you ever stop working?'

His irritated look gave way to a faint smile which seemed to tug reluctantly at the corners of his lips. 'Ironically, that's just what my assistant was saying. He said I couldn't really nag other people to take holidays if I wasn't prepared to do so myself. They've been pushing me towards this one for ages.'

'So how come you're taking business calls at this time of night?'

'It was an important call.'

'So important that it couldn't have waited until the morning?'

'Actually, yes,' he said coolly, but Alek's heart had begun beating very fast. He told himself he should be irritated with her for butting in where she wasn't wanted, yet right then he saw it as nothing but a rather disarming honesty. Was this why people went on vacation—because it took you right out of your normal environment and shook you up? In his daily life, nobody like Ellie would have got near him for long enough to deliver a damning judgement on his inability to relax. He was always surrounded by *people*—people who kept the rest of the world at arm's length.

But the protective nucleus of his business life suddenly seemed unimportant and it was as if everything was centred on the soft face in front of him. He wondered what her hair would look like if he shook it free from its ponytail and laid it over his pillow. How that soft flesh would feel beneath him as he parted her legs. He drained the last of his whisky and put the glass down, intending to walk across the veranda and take her into his arms.

But she chose that moment to push the heavy fringe away from her eyes and the jerky gesture suddenly brought him to his senses. He frowned, like someone wakening from a sleep. Had he really been planning to seduce her? He looked at the cheap shoes and unvarnished nails. At the heavy fringe, which looked as if she might trim it herself. *Was he insane?* She was much too sweet for someone like him.

'It's getting late,' he said roughly, rising to his feet. 'Where's your bike?'

She blinked at him in surprise, as if the question wasn't one she had been expecting. 'In the bike shed.'

'Come on,' he said. 'I'll walk you there.'

He could see the faint tremble of her lips as she shook her head.

'Honestly, there's no need. I see myself home every night,' she said. 'And it's probably best if I'm not seen with you.'

'I am walking you back,' he said stubbornly. 'And I won't take no for an answer.'

He could sense her disappointment as they walked over the moonlit grass and he told himself that he was doing the right thing. There were a million women who could be his for the taking—better steer clear of the sweet and sensible waitress.

They reached the hotel and she gave him an awkward smile. 'I have to go and change and fetch my bag,' she said. 'So I'd better say goodnight. Thanks for the drink.'

Alek nodded. 'Goodnight, Ellie,' he said and leant towards her, intending to give her a quick kiss on either cheek, but somehow that didn't happen.

Did she turn her head, or did he? Was that why their mouths met and melded, in a proper kiss? He saw her eyes widen. He felt the warmth of her breath. He could taste the sweetness of cola and it reminded him of a youth and an innocence which had never been his. It was purely reflex which made him pull her into his arms and deepen the kiss and her tiny gasp of pleasure was one he'd heard countless times before.

And that was all he needed. All his frustration and hunger broke free; his hands skimmed hungrily over her body as he moved her further into the shadows and pressed her up against a wall. He groaned as he felt the softness of her belly and it made him want to imprint his hardness against her. To show her just what he had and demonstrate how good it would feel if he were deep inside her. Circling his palm over one peaking nipple, he closed his eyes. Should he slip his hand beneath her uniform skirt and discover whether she was as wet as he suspected? Slide her panties down her legs and take her right here, where they stood?

The tiny moan she made in response to the increased pressure of his lips was almost enough for him to act out his erotic thoughts.

Almost, but not quite.

Reason seeped into his brain like the cold drip of a tap and he drew back, even though his body was screaming out its protest. Somehow he ignored the siren call of his senses, just as he ignored the silent plea in her eyes. Because didn't he value his reputation too much to make out with some anonymous waitress?

It was several moments before he could trust himself to speak and he shook his head in faint disbelief. 'That should never have happened.'

Ellie felt as if he'd thrown ice-cold water over her and she wondered why he had stopped. Surely he had felt it, too? That amazing chemistry. That sheer *magic*. Nobody had ever kissed her quite like that before and she wanted him to carry on doing it. And somehow her bold words tumbled out before she could stop them.

'Why not?'

There was a pause. 'Because you deserve more than I can ever offer. Because I'm the last kind of man you need. You're much too sweet and I'm nothing but a big bad wolf.'

'Surely I should be the judge of that?'

He gave a bitter smile. 'Go home, Ellie. Get out of here before I change my mind.'

Something dark came over his face—something

which shut her out completely. He said something abrupt, which sounded like *'Goodbye,'* before turning his back on her and walking back over the starlit grass.

CHAPTER TWO

'WAS THAT YOUR boyfriend I saw you with last night?' The question came out of nowhere and Ellie had to force herself to concentrate on what the guest was saying, instead of the frustrated thoughts which were circling like crows in her mind. Because of the recent heat wave, the restaurant had been fully booked and she'd been rushed off her feet all day. The lobster salad and summer pudding had sold out, and there had been a run on the cocktail of the month—an innocuous-tasting strawberry punch with a definite kick to it.

But now there was only one person left, a wafer-thin blonde who was lingering over her third glass of wine. Not that Ellie was counting. Well, actually, she was. She just wanted the woman to hurry up so that she could finish her shift in peace. Her head was pounding and she was exhausted—probably because she hadn't slept a wink last night. She'd just lain on her narrow bed, staring up at the ceiling—wide-eyed and restless and thinking about what had happened. Or rather, what hadn't happened. Telling herself that it was insane to get herself worked up about one kiss with a man who shouldn't really have been kissing her.

He was a billionaire Greek who was *way* off limits. She didn't know him, he hadn't even taken her on a date and yet… She licked her lips, which had suddenly grown very dry. Things had got pretty hot, pretty quickly, hadn't they? She could still recall his hands cupping her breasts and making them ache. She remembered wriggling with frustration as he pushed her up against the wall—his rock-hard groin pressing flagrantly against her. For a few seconds she'd thought he was going to try and have sex with her right there, and hadn't part of her wanted that? It might have been insanely wrong and completely out of character—but in the darkness of the summer night, she had wanted him more badly than she'd ever wanted anyone. She'd seen a side of herself she didn't recognise and didn't like very much. She bit her lip. A side like her *mother*?

The blonde was still looking at her with the expression of a hungry bird who had just noticed a worm wriggling up through the soil. 'So he *is* your boyfriend?' she prompted.

'No,' said Ellie quickly. 'He's not.'

'But you were kissing him.'

Nervously, Ellie's fingers slid along the frosted surface of the wine bottle before she recovered herself enough to shove it back in the ice bucket. She glanced around, terrified that another member of staff might have overheard, because although The Hog was famously laid-back and didn't have rules just for the sake of it—there was one which had been drummed into her on her very first day… And that was: you didn't get intimate with the guests.

Ever.

Awkwardly, she shrugged. 'Was I?' she questioned weakly.

The blonde's glacial eyes were alight with curiosity. 'You know you were,' she said slyly. 'I was having a cigarette behind that big tree and I spotted you. Then I saw him walk you back to the hotel—you weren't exactly being discreet.'

Briefly, Ellie closed her eyes as suddenly it all made sense. So that was the brief flare of light she'd seen from behind the tree trunk and the sense that somebody was watching them. She should have done the sensible thing and left then. 'Oh,' she said.

'Yes, *oh*. You *do* know who he is, don't you?'

Ellie stiffened as a pair of lake-blue eyes swam into her memory and her heart missed a beat. *Yes, the most gorgeous man I've ever seen. A man who made me believe all the fairy-tale stuff I never believed before.* 'Of course I do. He's…he's…'

'One of the world's richest men man who usually hangs out with supermodels and heiresses,' said the blonde impatiently. 'Which makes me wonder, what was he doing with you?'

Ellie drew back her shoulders. The woman's line of questioning was battering her at a time when she was already feeling emotionally vulnerable, but surely she didn't have to stand here and take these snide insinuations—guest or no guest. 'I don't really see how that's relevant.'

'Don't you? But you liked him, didn't you?' The blonde smiled. 'You liked him a lot.'

'I don't kiss men I don't like,' said Ellie defensively, aware of the irony of her remark, considering it was over a year since she'd kissed *anyone*.

The blonde sipped her wine. 'You do realise he has a reputation? He's known as a man of steel, with a heart to match. Actually, he's a bit of a *bastard* where women are concerned. So what have you got to say to that…' there was a pause as she leant forward to peer at Ellie's name badge '…Ellie?'

Ellie's instinct was to tell the woman that her thoughts about Alek Sarantos were strictly confidential, but the memory of his hands moving with such sweet precision over her body was still so vivid that it was hard not to blush. Suddenly it was easy to forget that at times he'd been a demanding and difficult workaholic of a guest, with an impatience he hadn't bothered to hide.

Because now all she could think about was the way she'd responded so helplessly to him and if he hadn't pulled away and done the decent thing, there was no saying what might have happened. Well, that wasn't quite true. She had a very good idea what might have happened.

She chewed on her lip, remembering the chivalrous way he'd told her to go home and the way she'd practically begged him not to leave her. Why *shouldn't* she defend him?

'I think people may have him all wrong,' she said. 'He's a bit of a pussycat, actually.'

'A pussycat?' The blonde nearly choked on her wine. 'Are you serious?'

'Very,' said Ellie. 'He's actually very sweet—and very good company.'

'I bet he was. He'd obviously been flirting with you all week.'

'Not really,' said Ellie, her cheeks growing pink again. What was it with all this blushing? 'We'd just chatted and stuff over the week. It wasn't until…' Her voice trailed away.

'Until?'

Ellie stared into the woman's glacial eyes. It all seemed slightly unreal now. As if she'd imagined the whole thing. Like a particularly vivid dream, which started to fade the moment you woke up. 'He asked me to join him for a drink because it was his last night here.'

'And so you did?'

Ellie shrugged. 'I don't think there's a woman alive who would have turned him down,' she said truthfully. 'He's…well, he's gorgeous.'

'I'll concur with that. And a brilliant kisser, I bet?' suggested the blonde softly.

Ellie remembered the way his tongue had slipped inside her mouth and how deliciously intimate that had felt. How, for a few brief moments, she'd felt as if someone had sprinkled her with stardust. It had only been a kiss, but still… 'The best,' she said, her voice growing husky.

The blonde didn't answer for a moment and when eventually she did there was an ugly note in her voice. 'And what would you say if I told you he had a girlfriend? That she was waiting for him back in London, while he was busy making out with you?'

Ellie's initial disbelief was followed by a stab of disappointment and the dawning realisation that she'd behaved like a fool. What did she think—that someone like Alek Sarantos was free and looking to start a relationship with someone like *her*? Had she imagined that he was going to come sprinting across the hotel lawn to sweep her off her feet—still in her waitress uniform—just like in that old film which always used to make her blub? Hadn't part of her hoped he hadn't meant it when he'd said *goodbye*—and that he might come back and find her?

A wave of recrimination washed over her. Of course he wasn't coming back and *of course* he had a girlfriend. Someone beautiful and thin and rich, probably. The sort of woman who could run for a bus without wearing a bra. Did she really imagine that *she*—the much too curvy Ellie Brooks—would be any kind of competition for someone like that?

And suddenly she felt not just stupid, but *hurt*. She tried to imagine his girlfriend's reaction if she'd seen them together. Didn't he care about loyalty or trampling over other people's feelings?

'He never said anything to me about a girlfriend.'

'Well, he wouldn't, would he?' said the blonde. 'Not in the circumstances. It's never a good move if a man mentions his lover while making out with someone else.'

'But nothing happened!'

'But you would have liked it to, wouldn't you, Ellie? From where I was standing, it looked pretty passionate.'

Ellie felt sick. She'd been a few minutes away from providing a live sex show! She wanted to walk away. To start clearing the other tables and pretend this conversation had never happened. But what if the blonde went storming into the general manager's office to tell her what she'd seen? There would be only one route they could take and that would be to fire her for unprofessional behaviour. *And she couldn't afford to lose her job and the career opportunity of a lifetime, could she? Not for one stupid kiss.*

'If I'd had any idea that he was involved with someone else, then I would never—'

'Do you often make out with the guests?'

'Never,' croaked Ellie.

'Just him, huh?' The blonde raised her brow. 'Did he say why he was keeping such a low profile?'

Ellie hesitated. She remembered the way he'd smiled at her—almost wistfully—when the little boy with the cut knee had flung his arms around her neck. She remembered how ridiculously *flattered* she'd felt when he insisted on that drink. She'd thought they'd had a special bond—when all the time he was just *using* her, as if she were one of the hotel's special offers. Angrily, her mind flitted back to what he had told her. 'He's been working day and night on some big new deal with the Chinese which is all top secret. And he said his staff had been nagging him for ages to take a vacation.'

'Really?' The blonde smiled, before dabbing at her lips with a napkin. 'Well, well. So he's human, after all. Stop looking so scared, Ellie—I'm not going to tell your boss, but I will give you a bit of advice. I'd stay away from men like Alek Sarantos in future, if I were you. Men like that could eat someone like you for breakfast.'

Alek sensed that something was amiss from the minute he walked into the boardroom but, try as he might, he couldn't quite put his finger on it. The deal went well—his deals always went well—although the Chinese delegation haggled his asking price rather more than he had been anticipating. But he pronounced himself pleased when the final figure was agreed, even if he saw a couple of members of the delegation smirking behind their files. Not a bad day's work, all told. He'd bought a company for peanuts, he'd turned it around—and had now sold it on for a more than healthy profit.

It wasn't until they all were exiting the boardroom when the redhead who'd been interpreting for them sashayed in his direction and said, 'Hello, pussycat,' before giving a fake growl and miming a clawing action.

Alek looked at her. He'd had a thing with her last year and had even taken her to his friend Murat's place in Umbria. But it seemed she hadn't believed him when he'd told her that theirs was no more than a casual fling. When the relationship had fizzled out, she'd taken it badly, as sometimes happened. The recriminatory emails had stopped and so had the phone calls, but as he met the expression in her eyes he could tell that she was still angry.

'And just what's that supposed to mean?' he questioned coolly.

She winked. 'Read the papers, tiger,' she murmured, before adding, 'Scraping the barrel a bit, aren't you?'

And that wasn't all. As he left the building he noticed one of the receptionists biting her lip, as if she was trying to repress a smile, and when he got back to his office he rang straight through to his male assistant.

'What's going on, Vasos?'

'With regard to…?' his assistant enquired cautiously.

'With regard to *me*!'

'Plenty of stuff in the papers about the deal with the Chinese.'

'Obviously,' Alek said impatiently. 'Anything else?'

His assistant's hesitation was illuminating. Did he hear Vasos actually *sigh*?

'I'll bring it in,' he said heavily.

Alek sat as motionless as a piece of rock as Vasos placed the article down on the desk in front of him so that he could scan the offending piece. It was an innocuous enough diary article, featuring a two-year-old library photo, which publications still delighted in using—probably because it made him look particularly forbidding.

Splashed above his unsmiling face were the words: Has Alek Sarantos Struck Gold?

His hands knuckled as he read it.

One of London's most eligible bachelors may be off the market before too long. The Midas touch billionaire, known for his love of supermodels and heiresses, was spotted in a passionate embrace with a waitress last weekend, following candlelit drinks on the terrace of his luxury New Forest hotel.

Ellie Brooks isn't Alek's usual type but the shapely waitress declared herself smitten by the workaholic tycoon, who told her he needed a vacation before his latest eye-wateringly big deal. Seems the Greek tycoon takes relaxation quite seriously!

And, according to Ellie, Alek doesn't always live up to his Man Of Steel nickname. 'He's a pussycat,' she purred.

Perhaps business associates should keep a saucer of milk at the ready in future...

Alek glanced up to see Vasos looking ill at ease, nervously running his finger along the inside of his shirt collar as he gave Alek an apologetic shrug.

'I'm sorry, boss,' he said.

'Unless you actually wrote the piece, I see no reason

for you to apologise. Did they ring here first to check the facts before they went to press?' snapped Alek.

'No.' Vasos cleared his throat. 'I'm assuming they didn't need to.'

Alek glared. 'Meaning?'

Vasos looked him straight in the eye. 'They would only have printed this without verification if it were true.'

Alek crumpled the newspaper angrily before hurling it towards the bin as if it were contaminated. He watched as it bounced uselessly off the window and the fact that he had missed made him angrier still.

Yes, it was true. He had been making out with some waitress in a public place. He'd thought with his groin instead of his brain. He'd done something completely out of character and now the readers of a downmarket rag knew all about it. His famously private life wasn't so private any more, was it?

But worst of all was the realisation that he'd taken his eye off the ball. He'd completely misjudged her. Maybe he'd been suffering from a little temporary sunstroke. Why else would he have thought there was something special about her—or credited her with *softness* or *honesty*, when in reality she was simply on the make? The reputation he'd built up, brick by careful brick, had been compromised by some ambitious little blonde with dollar signs in her eyes.

A slow rage began to smoulder inside him. A lot of good his enforced rest had done him. All those spa treatments and massages had been for nothing if his blood pressure was now shooting through the ceiling. Those solemn therapists telling him he must relax had been wasting their time. He must be more burnt out than he'd thought if he'd seriously thought about having sex with some little nobody like her.

His mood stayed dark for the remainder of the day, though it didn't stop him driving a particularly hard bargain on his latest acquisition. He would show the world that he was most definitely *not* a pussycat! He spent the day tied up with conference calls and had early evening drinks with a Greek politician who wanted his advice.

Back in his penthouse, he listened moodily to the messages which had been left on his phone and thought about how to spend the evening. Any number of beautiful women could have been his and all he had to do was call. He thought of the aristocratic faces and bony bodies which were always available to him and found himself comparing them with the curvaceous body of Ellie. The one whose face had inexplicably made him feel…

What?

As if he could trust her?

What a fool he was. A hormone-crazed, stupid fool. Hadn't he learnt his lesson a long time ago? That women were the last species on the planet who could be trusted?

He'd spent years building up a fierce but fair persona in the business world. His reputation was of someone who was tough, assertive and professional. He was known for his vision and his dependability. He despised the 'celebrity' culture and valued his privacy. He chose his friends and lovers carefully. He didn't let them get too close and nobody ever gave interviews about him. Ever. Even the redhead—supposedly broken-hearted at the time—had possessed enough sense to go away and lick her wounds in private.

But Ellie Brooks had betrayed him. A waitress he'd treated as an equal and then made the mistake of kissing had given some cheap little interview to a journalist. How much had she made? His heart pounded because he hadn't even had the pleasure of losing himself in that soft body of hers. He'd mistakenly thought she was *too sweet* and then she'd gone and sold him down the river. He'd behaved decently and honourably by sending her chastely on her way and look at all the thanks he'd got.

His mouth hardened in conjunction with the exquisite aching in his groin.

Maybe it wasn't too late to do something about that.

CHAPTER THREE

I'M SORRY, ELLIE—but we have no choice other than to let you go.

The words still resonating painfully round in her head, Ellie cycled through the thundery weather towards the staff hostel and thought about the excruciating interview she'd just had with the personnel manager of The Hog. Of *course* they'd had a choice—they'd just chosen not to take it, that was all. Surely they could have just let her lie low and all the fuss would have died down.

Negotiating her bike along the narrow road, she tried to take in what they'd just told her. She would be paid a month's salary in lieu of notice, although she would be allowed to keep her room at the hostel for another four weeks.

'We don't want to be seen as completely heartless by kicking you out on the street,' the HR woman had told her with a look of genuine regret on her face. 'If you hadn't chosen to be indiscreet with such a high-profile guest, then we might have been able to brush over the whole incident and keep you on. But as it is, I'm afraid we can't. Not after Mr Sarantos made such a blistering complaint about the question of guest confidentiality.

My hands are tied—and it's a pity, Ellie, because you showed such promise.'

And Ellie had found herself nodding as she'd left the office, because, despite her shock, hadn't she agreed with pretty much every word the manager had said? She'd even felt a bit sorry for the woman who had looked so uncomfortable while terminating her employment.

She couldn't *believe* she'd been so stupid. She had behaved inappropriately with a guest and had then compounded her transgression by talking about it to a woman who had turned out to be a journalist for some low-end tabloid. A journalist! Clutching on to the handlebars with sticky palms, she stared fixedly at the road ahead.

And that had been at the root of her sacking, apparently. The fact that she had broken trust with a valued client. She had blabbed—and Alek Sarantos was *seething*. Apparently, the telephone wires had been practically smoking when he'd rung up to complain about the diary piece which had found its way into a national newspaper.

The day was heavy and overcast and she heard the distant rumble of thunder as she brought her bike to a halt outside the hostel which was home to The Hog's junior staff. Ellie locked her bike to the railings and opened the front door. Next to one of the ten individual doorbells was her name—but not for very much longer. She had a month to find somewhere new to live. A month to find herself a new job. It was a daunting prospect in the current job market and it looked as if she'd gone straight back to square one. Who would employ her now?

A louder rumble of thunder sounded ominously as she made her way along the corridor to her small room. The day was so dark that she clicked on the light and the atmosphere was so muggy that strands of her ponytail were sticking to the back of her neck. The day yawned ahead as she filled the kettle and sat down heavily on the bed to wait for it to boil.

Now what did she do?

She stared at the posters she'd hung on the walls—giant photos of Paris and New York and Athens. All those places she'd planned to visit when she was a hot-shot hotelier, which was probably never going to happen now. She should have asked about a reference. She wondered if the hotel would still give her one. One which emphasised her best qualities—or would they make her sound like some kind of desperado who spent her time trying it on with wealthy guests?

Her doorbell shrilled and she gave a start, but the sense that none of this was really happening gave her renewed hope. Was it inconceivable to think that the big boss of the hotel might have overridden his HR boss's decision? Realised that it had been nothing but a foolish one-off and that she was too valuable a member of staff to lose?

Smoothing her hands over her hair, she ran along the corridor and opened the front door—her heart clenching with an emotion she was too dazed to analyse when she saw who was standing there. She blinked as if she'd somehow managed to conjure up the brooding figure from her fevered imagination. She must have done—because why else would Alek Sarantos be outside *her* home?

A few giant droplets of rain had splashed onto the

blackness of his hair and his bronze skin gleamed as
if someone had spent the morning polishing it. She'd
forgotten how startlingly blue his eyes looked, but now
she could see something faintly unsettling glinting from
their sapphire depths.

And even in the midst of her confusion—*why was he
here?*—she could feel her body's instinctive response
to him. Her skin prickled with a powerful recognition
and her breasts began to ache, as if realising that here
was the man who was capable of giving her so much
pleasure when he touched them. She could feel colour
rushing into her cheeks.

'Mr Sarantos,' she said, more out of habit than anything else—but the cynical twist of his lips told her that
he found her words not only inappropriate, but somehow insulting.

'Oh, please,' he said softly. 'I think we know each
other well enough for you to call me Alek, don't you?'

The suggestion of intimacy unnerved her even more
than his presence and her fingers curled nervelessly
around the door handle she was clutching for support.
Now the rumble of thunder was closer and never had a
sound seemed more fitting. 'What…what are you doing
here?'

'No ideas?' he questioned silkily.

'To rub in the fact that you've lost me my job?'

'Oh, but I haven't,' he contradicted softly. 'You managed to do that all by yourself. Now, are you going to
let me in?'

Ellie told herself she didn't have to. She could slam
the door in his face and that would be that. She doubted
he would batter the door down—even though he looked
perfectly capable of doing it. But she was curious about

what had brought him here and the rest of the day stretched in front of her like an empty void. She was going to have to start looking for a new job—she knew that. But not today.

'If you insist,' she said, turning her back on him and retracing her steps down the corridor. She could hear him closing the front door and following her. But it wasn't until he was standing in her room that she began to wonder why she had been daft enough to let him invade her space.

Because he looked all wrong here. With his towering physique and jewelled eyes, he dominated the small space like some living, breathing treasure. He seemed larger than life and twice as intimidating— like the most outrageously alpha man she had ever set eyes on. And that was making her feel uncomfortable in all kinds of ways. There was that honeyed ache deep down in her belly again and a crazy desire to kiss him. Her body's reaction was making her thoughts go haywire and her lips felt like parchment instead of flesh. She licked them, but that only made the aching worse.

The kettle was reaching its usual ear-splitting crescendo just before reaching boiling point and the great belches of steam meant that the room now resembled a sauna. Ellie could feel a trickle of sweat running down her back. Her shirt was sticking to her skin and her jeans were clinging to her thighs and once again she became horribly aware of her own body.

She cleared her throat. 'What do you want?' she said.

Alek didn't answer. Not immediately. His anger—a slow, simmering concoction of an emotion—had been momentarily eclipsed by finding himself in the kind of environment he hadn't seen in a long time.

He looked around. The room was small and clean and she had the requisite plant growing on the windowsill, but there was a whiff of institutionalisation about the place which the cheap posters couldn't quite disguise. The bed was narrower than any he'd seen in years and an unwilling flicker of desire was his reward for having allowed his concentration to focus on *that*. But he had once lived in a room like this, hadn't he? When he'd started out—much younger than she was now—he'd been given all kinds of dark and inhospitable places to sleep. He'd worked long hours for very little money in order to earn money and get a roof over his head.

He lifted his eyes to her face, remembering the powerful way his body had reacted to her the other night and trying to tell himself that it had been a momentary aberration. Because she was plain. *Ordinary.* If he'd passed her in the street, he wouldn't have given her a second glance. Her jeans weren't particularly flattering and neither was her shirt. But her eyes looked like silver and wavy strands of pale hair were escaping from her ponytail and the ends were curling, so that in the harshness of the artificial light she looked as if she were surrounded by a faint blonde halo.

A *halo*. His mouth twisted. He couldn't think of a less likely candidate for angelic status.

'You sold your story,' he accused.

'I didn't *sell* anything,' she contradicted. 'No money exchanged hands.'

'So the journalist is clairvoyant, is that what you're saying? She just guessed we were making out?'

She shook her head. 'That's not what I'm saying at

all. She saw us. She was standing behind a tree having a cigarette and saw us kissing.'

'You mean it was a set-up?' he questioned, his tone flat.

'Of course it wasn't a set-up!' She glared at him. 'You think I deliberately arranged to get myself the sack? Rather a convoluted way to go about it, don't you think? I think being caught dipping your fingers in the till is the more traditional way to go.'

He raised his eyebrows in disbelief. 'So she just *happened* to be there—'

'Yes!' she interrupted angrily. 'She did. She was a guest, staying at the hotel. And the next day she cornered me in the restaurant while I was serving her and there was no way I could have avoided talking to her.'

'You still could have just said *no comment* when she started quizzing you,' he accused. 'You didn't have to gush and call me a pussycat—to damage my business reputation and any credibility I've managed to build up. You didn't have to disclose what you'd overheard when you'd clearly been *listening in to my telephone conversation*.'

'How could I help but listen in, when you broke off to take a call in front of me?'

He glared at her. 'What right did you have to repeat *any* of it?'

'And what right do you have to come here, hurling all these accusations at me?'

'You're skirting round the issue. I asked you a question, Ellie. Are you going to answer it?'

There was an odd kind of silence before eventually she spoke.

'She told me you had a girlfriend,' she said.

He raised his eyebrows. 'So you felt that gave you the right to gossip about me, knowing it might find its way into the press?'

'How could I, when I didn't know what her job was?'

'You mean you're just habitually indiscreet?'

'Or that you're just sexually incontinent?'

He sucked in an angry breath. 'As it happens, I don't have a girlfriend at the moment and if I did, then I certainly wouldn't have been making out with you. You see, I place great store on loyalty, Ellie—in fact, I value it above everything else. While you, on the other hand, don't seem to know the meaning of the word.'

Ellie was taken aback by the coldness in his eyes. She had made a mistake, yes—but it had been a genuine one. She hadn't set out to deliberately tarnish his precious reputation.

'Okay,' she conceded. 'I spoke about you when maybe I shouldn't have done and, because of that, you've managed to get me the sack. I'd say we were quits now, wouldn't you?'

He met her gaze.

'Not quite,' he said softly.

A shiver of something unknowable whispered over her skin as she stared at him. There was something unsettling in his eyes. Something distracting about the sudden tension in his hard body. She stared at him, knowing what he was planning to do and knowing it was wrong. *So why didn't she ask him to leave?*

Because she *couldn't*. She'd dreamed about just such a moment—playing it out in her mind, when it had been little more than a fantasy. She had wanted Alek Sarantos more than she had thought it possible to want anyone and that feeling hadn't changed. If anything, it had grown even stronger. She could feel herself trembling as he reached out and hauled her against him. The angry expression on his face made it seem as if he was doing something he didn't really want to do and she felt a brief flicker of rebellion. How dare he look that way? She told herself to pull away, but the need to have him kiss her again was dominating every other consideration. And maybe this was inevitable—like the thunder which had been rumbling all day through the heavy sky. Sooner or later you just knew the storm was going to break.

His mouth came down on hers—hard—and the hands which should have been pushing him away were gripping his shoulder, as she kissed him back—just as hard. It felt like heaven and it felt like hell. She wanted to hurt him for making her lose her job. She wanted him to take back all those horrible accusations he'd made. And she wanted him to take away this terrible aching deep inside her.

Alek shuddered as he heard the little moan she made and he told himself to tug her jeans down and just *do* it. To give into what they both wanted and feed this damned hunger so that it would go away and leave him. Or maybe he should just turn around and walk out of that door and go find someone else. Someone immaculate and cool—not someone all hot and untidy from cycling on the hottest day of the year.

But she was soft in his arms. So unbelievably soft. She was like Turkish Delight when you pressed your finger against it, anticipating that first sweet, delicious mouthful. He pulled his lips away from hers and slowly raised his head, meeting a gaze which gleamed silver.

'I want you,' he said.

He saw her lips tremble as they opened, as if she was about to list every reason why he couldn't have her and he guessed there might be quite a long list. And then he saw something change—the moment when her eyes darkened and her skin started to flush. The *what-the-hell?* moment as she looked at him with naked invitation in her eyes.

'And I want you, too,' she said.

It was like dynamite. Like nothing he'd ever known as he drove his lips back down on hers. A kiss which made him feel almost savage with need. It went on and on until they were both breathless, until he drew his mouth away from hers and could suck in a ragged breath of air. Her eyes were wide and very dark and her lips were trembling. With a sense of being slightly out of control, he tugged open her shirt to reveal the spill of her breasts and stared at them in disbelief.

'Theo,' he said softly. 'Your breasts are magnificent.'

'A-are they?'

'They are everything I dreamed they would be. And more.'

'Have you been dreaming about my breasts?'

'Every night.'

He drew a finger over one generous curve and he heard her moan as he bent to touch his lips to the same spot. And that was when she chose to press her palm over the tight curve of his denim-covered buttock, as if tacitly giving him her permission to continue.

He groaned as he straightened up to kiss her again and once he'd started he couldn't seem to stop. It was only when she began to writhe frustratedly that he tugged off the elastic band so that her pale hair spilled free, and suddenly she managed to look both wholesome and wanton. She looked…like a *woman*, he thought longingly. Soft and curving; warm and giving.

His hands were shaking as he stripped her bare, then laid her down on the narrow bed as he removed his own clothes, his eyes not leaving her face. With shaking hands he groped for his wallet and found a condom. Thank God. Slipping it on as clumsily as if it had been his first time, he moved over her, smoothing back her thick hair with hands which were still unsteady. And as he entered her a savage cry was torn from his throat.

He moved inside her and it felt pretty close to heaven. Sweet heaven. He had to keep thinking about random stuff about mergers and acquisitions to stop himself from coming and it seemed like an eternity until at last her body began to tense beneath him. Until she stiffened and her back arched and, inexplicably—she started to cry.

Only then did Alek let go himself, although the salty wetness of her tears against his cheek gave him a moment of disquiet. Outside, the thunder seemed to split the sky. The rain began to teem down against the window. And his body was torn apart by the longest orgasm of his life.

CHAPTER FOUR

ELLIE TURNED THE sign to Closed and started clearing away stray currants and dollops of frosting from the glass counters which lined the cake shop. She stacked cardboard boxes, swept the floor and took off her frilly apron.

And then she went and stood at the back of the little store, and wept.

The tears came swiftly and heavily and she tried to think of them as cathartic as she covered her face with her hands. But as they dripped through her fingers all she could think was: *How had this happened? How had her life suddenly become a living nightmare?*

She knew she'd been lucky finding work and accommodation at Candy's Cupcakes so soon after leaving the hotel. She'd been doubly lucky that the kindly Bridget Brody had taken a shine to her, and not cared about her ignominious sacking. But it was hard to focus on gratitude right now. In fact, it was hard to focus on anything except the one thing she couldn't keep ignoring. *But you couldn't make something go away, just because you wanted it to—no matter how hard you wished it would.* Her feet were heavy as she made her way up to the small, furnished apartment above the shop, but not nearly as heavy as her heart.

The mirror in the sitting room was hung in a position you couldn't avoid, unless you walked into the room with your eyes shut, which was never a good idea with such uneven floorboards. The healthy tan she'd acquired while working in the garden restaurant of The Hog had long since faded. Her face was pasty, her breasts were swollen and her skin seemed too loose for her body. And she'd lost weight. She couldn't eat anything before midday because she kept throwing up. She hadn't needed to see the double blue stripes on the little plastic stick to confirm what she already knew.

That she was pregnant with Alek Sarantos's baby and didn't know what she was going to do about it.

Slumping down in one of the overstuffed armchairs, she stared blankly into space. Actually, that wasn't quite true. There was only one thing she *could* do. She had to tell him.

She had to.

It didn't matter what her personal feelings were, or that fact that there had been a deafening silence ever since the Greek billionaire had walked out of her bedroom, leaving her naked in bed. This was about more than *her.* She knew what it was like not to have a father and no real identity. To feel invisible—as if she were only half a person. And that wasn't going to happen to her baby. She hugged her arms tightly around her chest. *She wouldn't allow it to happen.*

But how did you tell someone you were having his baby when he had withdrawn from you in more ways than one as soon as he'd had his orgasm?

Her mind drifted back to that awful moment when

she'd opened her eyes to find Alek Sarantos lying on top of her in the narrow bed in the staff hostel. His warm skin had been sticking to hers and his breathing sounded as if he'd been in a race. On a purely physical level, her own body was glowing with the aftermath of the most incredible sexual experience of her life—although she didn't exactly have a lot to compare it with. Her body felt as if she were floating and she wanted to stay exactly where she was—to capture and hold on to the moment, so that it would never end.

But unfortunately, life wasn't like that.

She wasn't sure what changed everything. They were lying there so close and so quiet while the rain bashed hard against the windows. It felt as if their entire lives were cocooned in that little room. She could feel the slowing beat of his heart and the warmth of his breath as it fanned against the side of her neck. She wanted to fizz over with sheer joy. She'd had a relationship before—of course she had—but she had never known such a feeling of completeness. Did he feel it, too? She remembered reaching up to whisper her fingertips over his hair with soft and rhythmical strokes. And that was the moment when she read something unmistakable on his face. The sense that he'd just made the biggest mistake of his life. She could see it in his eyes—those compelling blue eyes, which went from smoky satisfaction through to ice-cold disbelief as he realised just where he was. And with whom.

With a wince he didn't even bother disguising, he carefully eased himself away from her, making sure the condom was still intact as he withdrew. She remembered the burning of her cheeks and feeling completely out of her depth. Her mind was racing as she thought how best to handle the situation, but her experience of men was scant and of Greek billionaires, even scanter. She decided that coolness would be the way to go. She needed to reassure him that she wasn't fantasising about walking up the aisle wearing a big white dress, just because they'd had sex. To act as if making love to a man who was little more than a stranger was no big deal.

She reminded herself that what they'd done had been driven by anger and perhaps it might have been better if it had stayed that way. Because if it hadn't suddenly morphed into a disconcerting whoosh of passion, then she might not be lying there wishing he would stay and never leave. She might not be starting to understand her own mother a bit more and to wonder if this was what *she* had felt. Had she lain beside her married lover like this, and lost a little bit of her heart to him, even though she must have known that he was the wrong man?

She remembered feigning sleepiness. Letting her lashes flutter down over her eyes as if the lids were too heavy to stay open. She could hear him moving around as he picked up his clothes from the floor and began pulling them on and she risked a little peep from between her lashes, to find him looking anywhere except at her. As if he couldn't bear to look at her. But she guessed it was a measure of how skewed her thinking was that she was still prepared to give him the benefit of the doubt.

'Alek?' she said—casual enough to let him know she wouldn't mind seeing him again, but not so friendly that it could be interpreted as pushy.

He was fully dressed by now—although he looked dishevelled. It was strange to see the powerful billionaire in *her* room, his shirt all creased from where it had been lying on the floor. He was running his fingers through his ruffled hair and his skin gleamed with the exertion of sex, but it was his eyes which got to her. His eyes were cold. Cold as ice. She saw him checking in his pocket for his car keys. Or maybe he was just checking that his wallet was safe.

'That was amazing,' he said, and her suddenly happy heart wanted to burst out of her chest, until his next words killed the dream for ever.

'But a mistake,' he finished with a quick, careful smile. 'I think we both realise that. Goodbye, Ellie.'

And then he was gone and Ellie was left feeling like a fool. He didn't even slam the door and for some reason that only added to her humiliation. As if the quiet click as he shut it behind him was all he could be bothered with.

She didn't move for ages. She lay in that rumpled bed watching the rain running in rivulets over the window, like giant tears. Why had she cried afterwards? Because it had been so perfect? And that was the most stupid thing of all. It *had*. It had felt like everything her faintly cynical self had never believed in. He'd made her feel stuff she'd never felt before. As if she was gorgeous. Precious. Beautiful. Did he do that with everyone woman he had sex with? *Of course he did.* It was like tennis, or playing poker. If you practised something often enough, you got very accomplished at doing it.

She went straight to shower in the shared bathroom along the corridor in an attempt to wash away her memories, but it wasn't that easy. Vivid images of Alek seemed to have stamped themselves indelibly on her mind. She found herself thinking about him at inconvenient times of the day and night and remembering the way he had touched her. And although time would probably have faded those memories away she'd never had a chance to find out because her period had been late.

What was she talking about? Her period hadn't been *late*. It just hadn't arrived and she was normally as regular as clockwork. Waves of nausea had begun striking her at the most inopportune times and she knew she couldn't keep putting it off.

She was going to have to tell him. Not next week, nor next month—but now.

Firing her ancient computer into life, she tapped in the name of the Sarantos organisation, which seemed to have offices all over the world. She prayed he was still in London and as the distinctive blue logo flashed up on the screen, it seemed he was. According to the company website, he'd given a speech about 'Acquisitions & Mergers' at some high-profile City conference, just the evening before.

Even if she'd known his home address—which of course she didn't—it made much more sense to go to his office. She remembered him telling her that he always stayed late. She would go there and explain that she had something of vital importance to tell him and—even if it was only curiosity—she was certain he would listen.

And if he didn't?

Then her conscience would be clear, because at least she would have tried.

Wednesday was her day off and she travelled by train to London, on another of the sticky and humid days which had been dominating the English summer. Her best cotton dress felt like a rag by the time she left the train at Waterloo and she had a nightmare journey on the Underground before emerging close to St Paul's cathedral.

She found the Sarantos building without too much difficulty—a giant steel and glass monolith soaring up into the cloudless blue sky. Lots of people were emerging from the revolving doors and Ellie shrank into the shadows as she watched them heading for the local bars and Tube. How did the women manage to look so cool in this sweltering heat, she wondered—and how could they walk so quickly on those skyscraper heels they all seemed to wear?

She walked into the reception area, where the blessed cool of the air conditioning hit her like a welcome fan. She could see a sleek woman behind the desk staring at her, but she brazened it out and walked over to one of the squidgy leather sofas which were grouped in the far corner of the lobby, sinking down onto it with a feeling of relief.

A security guard she hadn't seen until that moment walked over to her.

'Can I help you, miss?'

Ellie pushed her fringe out of her eyes and forced a smile. 'I'm just waiting for my…friend.'

'And your friend's name is?'

Did she dare? And yet, wasn't the reality that in her belly was growing a son or daughter who might one day be the boss of this mighty corporation? She sucked in a deep breath, telling herself that she had every right to be here.

'His name is Alek Sarantos,' she blurted out, but not before she had seen a wary look entering the guard's eyes.

To his credit—and Ellie's surprise—he didn't offer any judgement or try to move her on, he simply nodded.

'I'll let his office know you're here,' he said, and started to walk towards the reception desk.

He's going to tell him, thought Ellie as the reality of her situation hit her. *He's going to ring up to Alek's office and say that some mad, overheated woman is waiting downstairs for him in Reception.* It wasn't too late to make a run for it. She could be gone by the time Alek got down here. She could go back to the New Forest and carry on working for the owner of Candy's Cupcakes— who wasn't called Candy at all—and somehow scrape by, doing the best she could for her baby.

But that wasn't good enough, was it? She didn't want to bring up a child who had to *make do*. She didn't want to have to shop at thrift stores or learn a hundred ways to be inventive with a packet of lentils. She wanted her child to thrive. To have new shoes whenever he or she needed them and not have to worry about whether there was enough money to pay the rent. Because she knew how miserable that could be.

'Ellie?'

A deep Greek accent broke into her thoughts and Ellie looked up to see Alek Sarantos directly in front of her with the guard a few protective steps away. There was a note of surprise in the way he said her name, and a distinct note of unfriendliness, too.

She supposed she ought to get to her feet. To do something rather than just sit there, like a sack of potatoes which had been dumped. She licked her lips and tried to smile, but a smile was stubbornly refusing to come. And wasn't it crazy that she could look at someone who was glaring at her and *still* want him? Hadn't her body already betrayed her once, without now shamefully prickling with excited recognition—even though she'd never seen him looking quite so intimidating in an immaculately cut business suit?

Keep calm, she told herself. *Act like a grown-up.*

'Hello, Alek,' she said, even managing what she hoped was a friendly smile.

He didn't react. His blue eyes were cool. No. Cool was the wrong temperature. Icy would be more accurate.

'What are you doing here?' he questioned, almost pleasantly—but it didn't quite conceal the undertone of steel in his voice and she could see the guard stiffen, as if anticipating that some unpleasantness was about to reveal itself.

She wondered what would happen if she just came out and said it. *I'm having your baby. You're going to be a daddy, Alek!* That would certainly wipe that cold look from his face! But something stopped her. Something which felt like self-preservation. And pride. She couldn't afford to just *react*—she had to *think*. Not just for herself, but for her baby. In his eyes she'd already betrayed him to the journalist and that had made him go ballistic. She couldn't tell him about impending fatherhood when there was a brick-house of a guard standing there, flexing his muscles. She ought to give him the opportunity to hear the news in private. She owed him that much.

She kept her gaze and her voice steady—though that wasn't particularly easy in the light of that forbidding blue stare. 'I'd prefer to talk to you in private, if you don't mind.'

Alek felt a sudden darkness envelop his heart as the expression on her face told him everything. He tried to tell himself that it was the shock of finding her here which had sent his thoughts haywire, but he knew that wasn't true. Because he'd thought about her. Of course he had. He'd even wondered idly about seeing her again—and why wouldn't he? Why wouldn't he want a repeat of what had been the best sex he could remember? If only it had been that straightforward, but life rarely was.

He remembered the way he'd lain there afterwards, with his head cradled on her shoulder as he drifted in and out of a dreamy sleep. And her fingers—her soft fingers—had been stroking his hair. It had felt soothing and strangely intimate. It had kick-started something unknown inside him—something threatening enough to freak him out. He had felt the walls closing in on him—just as they were closing in on him right now.

He tried to tell himself that maybe he was mistaken— that it couldn't possibly be what he most feared. But what else could it be? No woman in her situation would turn up like this and be so unflappable when challenged—not unless she had a trump card to play. Not when he'd left her without so much as a kiss or a promise to call her again. Somehow he sensed that Ellie had more pride than to come here begging him to see her again. She'd been strong, hadn't she? An equal in his arms and out of them, despite the disparity of their individual circumstances.

He noted the shadows on her face, which suddenly seemed as grey as her eyes, and thought how *drained* she looked. His mouth tightened and a flare of anger and self-recrimination flooded through him. He was going to have to listen to her. He needed to hear what she had to say. *To find out whether what he dreaded was true.*

His mind raced. He thought about taking her to a

nearby coffee shop. No. Much too public. Should he take her upstairs to his office? That might be easier. Easier to get rid of her afterwards than if he took her home. And he had no desire to take her home. He just wanted her out of his life. To forget that he'd ever met her. 'You'd better come up to my office.'

'Okay,' she said, her voice sounding brittle.

It felt bizarre to ride up in the elevator in silence but he didn't want to open any kind of discussion in such a confined space, and she seemed to feel the same. When the doors opened she followed him through the outer office and he looked across at Vasos.

'Hold all my calls,' he said—catching the flicker of surprise in his assistant's eyes.

'Yes, boss.'

Soon they were in his cool suite of offices, which overlooked the city skyline, and he thought how out of place she looked, with her flower-sprigged cotton dress and pale legs. And yet despite a face which was almost bare of make-up and the fact that her hair was hanging down her back in that thick ponytail—there was still something about her which made his body tense with a primitive recognition he didn't understand. Even though she looked pasty and had obviously lost weight, part of him still wanted to pin her down against that leather couch, which stood in the corner, and to lose himself deep inside her honeyed softness. His mouth flattened.

'Sit down,' he said.

'There's no need.' She hesitated, like a guest who had turned up at the wrong party and wasn't quite sure how to explain herself to the host. 'You probably want to know why I've turned up like this—'

'I know exactly why.' Never had it been more of an

ordeal to keep his voice steady, but he knew that psychologically it was better to tell than to be told. To remain in control. His words came out calmly, belying the sudden flare of fear deep in his gut. 'You're pregnant, aren't you?'

She swayed. She actually swayed—reaching out to grab the edge of his desk. And despite his anger, Alek strode across the office and took hold of her shoulders and he could feel his fingers sinking into her soft flesh as he levered her down onto a chair.

'Sit down,' he repeated.

Her voice was wobbly. 'I don't want to sit down.'

'And I don't want the responsibility of you passing out on the floor of my office,' he snapped. But he pulled his hands away from her—as if continuing to touch her might risk him behaving like the biggest of all fools for a second time. He didn't want the responsibility of her, full stop. He wanted her to be nothing but a fast-fading memory of an interlude he'd rather forget—but that wasn't going to happen. Not now. Raising his voice, he called for his assistant. 'Vasos!'

Vasos appeared at the door immediately—unable to hide his look of surprise as he saw his boss leaning over the woman who was sitting slumped on a chair.

'Get me some water.' Alek spoke in Greek. 'Quickly.'

The assistant returned seconds later with a glass, his eyes still curious. 'Will there be anything else, boss?'

'Nothing else.' Alek took the water from him. 'Just leave us. And hold all my calls.'

As Vasos closed the door behind him Alek held the glass to her lips. Her eyes were suspicious and her body tense. She reminded him of a stray kitten he'd once brought into the house as a child. The animal had been a flea-ridden bag of bones and Alek had painstakingly brought it back to full and gleaming health. It had been something he'd felt proud of. Something in that cold mausoleum of a house for him to care about. And then his father had discovered it, and…and…

His throat suddenly felt as if it had nails in it. *Why remember something like that now?* 'Drink it,' he said harshly. 'It isn't poison.'

She raised her eyes to his and the suspicion in them had been replaced by a flicker of defiance.

'But you'd probably like it to be,' she answered quietly.

He didn't answer—he didn't trust himself to. He blocked out the maelstrom of emotions which seemed to be hovering like dark spectres and waited until a little colour had returned to her cheeks. Then he walked over to his desk and put the glass down, before positioning himself in front of the vast expanse of window, his arms crossed.

'You'd better start explaining,' he said.

Ellie stared up at him. The water had restored some of her strength, but one glance at the angry sizzle from his blue eyes was enough to remind her that she was here on a mission. She wasn't trying to win friends or influence people, or because she hoped for a repeat of the passion which had got her into this situation in the first place. *So keep emotion out of it*, she told herself fiercely. *Keep to the plain and brutal facts and then you can deal with them.*

'There isn't really a lot to explain. I'm having a baby.'

'We used a condom,' he iced back. 'You know we did.'

Stupidly, that made her blush. As if discussing contraception in his place of work was hopelessly inappropriate. But while it might be inappropriate, it was also *necessary*, she reminded herself grimly. And she was not going to let him intimidate her. It had taken two of them to get into this situation—therefore they both needed to accept responsibility.

'I also know that condoms aren't one hundred per cent reliable,' she said.

'So. You're an expert, are you?' He looked at her with distaste. 'Perhaps there are other men to whom you've taken this tale of woe. How many more in the running, I wonder—could you tell me my position on the list, just so I know?'

Ellie clenched her fists as a wave of fury washed over her. She didn't *need* this—not in any circumstances but especially not now. She made to rise to her feet, but her legs were stubbornly refusing to obey her brain. And even though at that moment she wanted to run out of there and never return, she knew that flight was an indulgence she simply couldn't afford.

'There's nobody else in the running,' she spat out. 'Maybe you're different, but I don't have sex with more than one person at the same time. So why don't you keep your unfounded accusations to yourself? I didn't come here to be your punchbag!'

'No? Then what did you come for?' The brief savagery of his dark features realigned themselves into a quizzical expression. 'Is it money you want?'

'*Money?*'

'That's what I said.'

Ellie's anger intensified but somehow that seemed to help, because it was giving her focus. It was making her want to fight. Not for herself, but for the tiny life growing inside her. Because *that* was what was important. *That* was the reason she had come here today, even though she'd known it was going to be an ordeal. *So think before you answer. Don't make cheap retorts just for the sake of trying to score points. Show him you mean business. Because you* do.

'I'm here to give you the facts,' she said. 'Because I thought it was your right to have them. That you needed to be aware that there were consequences to what happened that afternoon.'

'A little dramatic, isn't it? Just turning up here like this. Couldn't you have called first to warn me?'

'You think I should have done that? Really?' She tipped her head to one side and looked at him. 'I didn't have your number because you deliberately didn't give it to me, but even if I'd managed to get hold of it—would you have spoken to me? I don't think so.'

Alek considered her words. No, he probably wouldn't, despite his faintly irrational desire to see her again. Through Vasos, he would have demanded she put everything down in an email. He would have kept her at an emotional distance, as he did with all women. But he was beginning to realise that the whys and wherefores of what had happened between them were irrelevant. Didn't matter that she'd broken a cardinal rule and invaded his workspace. There was only one thing which mattered and that was what she had just told him.

And this was one reality he couldn't just walk away from. He asked the question as if he were following some ancient male-female rule book, but if his question sounded lifeless it was because deep down he knew the answer. 'How do I know it's mine?'

'You think I'd be here if it wasn't? That I'd be putting myself through this kind of aggravation if it was someone else's baby?'

He tried telling himself that she might be calling his bluff and that he could demand a DNA test, which would have to wait until the child was born. And yet, once again something told him that no such test would be needed, and he wasn't sure why. Was it the certainty on her pale face which told him that he was the father of her child, or something more subtly complex, which defied all logic? He could hear the door of the prison swinging shut and the sound of the key being turned. He was trapped. Again. And it was the worst feeling in the world. He remembered that distant fortress and his voice sounded gritty. Like it was coming from a long way away. 'What do you want from me?'

There was a pause as those shadowed grey eyes met his.

'I want you to marry me,' she said.

CHAPTER FIVE

WITH NARROWED EYES, Alek looked at her. 'Or what?' he questioned with soft venom. 'Marry you or you'll run blabbing to your journalist friend again? This would be a real scoop, wouldn't it? Pregnant With the Greek's Child.'

Meeting the accusation on his face, Ellie tried to stay calm. She hadn't meant to blurt it out like that—in fact, she hadn't really been planning to say that at all. She had meant to tell him that she was planning to have the baby and would respect whatever decision he made about his own involvement. She had intended to imply that she wasn't bothered one way or another—and she certainly wasn't intending to control or manipulate what was happening.

But something had happened to her during the awkward conversation which had just taken place in the alien surroundings of his penthouse office. With the air-conditioning freezing tiny beads of sweat to her forehead and her cotton dress clinging to her like a dishcloth she had felt worse than ugly. Surrounded by the unbelievable wealth of Alek's penthouse office suite, she had felt *invisible*.

She thought about all the women she'd seen leaving the building—clipping along in their high-heeled shoes with not a hair out of place. Those were the kind of women he dealt with on a daily basis, with their air of purpose and their slim, toned figures. Where did she fit into that world, with her cheap dress and a growing belly and a feeling that she had no real place of her own?

Because she didn't have any real place of her own. This was *his* world and neither she nor her baby belonged in it. How long before he conveniently forgot he had sired a child in a moment of ill-thought-out passion? How long before he married someone classy and had legitimate children who would inherit everything he owned, while her own child shrank into the shadows, forgotten and overlooked? Didn't she know better than anyone that unwanted children usually stayed that way? *She knew what it was like to be rejected by her own father.*

And that was her light-bulb moment. The moment when she knew exactly what she was going to ask for. Her ego didn't matter and neither did her pride, because this was more important than both those things. *This was for her baby.*

'I'm not threatening to blackmail you,' she said quietly. 'I've told you until I was blue in the face that the whole journalist thing was a stupid mistake, which I don't intend on repeating. I just want you to marry me, that's all.'

'That's all?' he echoed with a cruel replica of a smile. 'Why?'

'Because you're so charming, of course,' she snapped. 'And so thoughtful and—'

'Why?' he repeated, a note of steel entering his

voice—as if he suspected that behind her flippancy she was teetering perilously on the brink of hysteria.

'Isn't it obvious?' With an effort she kept her gaze steady, but inside her heart was pounding so loudly she was certain he must be able to hear it. 'Because I want my baby to have some kind of security.'

'Which doesn't need to involve marriage,' he said coldly. 'If the baby really is mine, then I will accept responsibility. I can give you money. A house.' He shrugged. 'Some baubles for yourself, if that's what you're angling for.'

Baubles? *Baubles?* Did he really think her so shallow that he thought jewels might be her motivation? 'It isn't,' she said, her cheeks growing pink, 'just about the money.'

'Really? Woman claims money isn't her sole motivation.' He gave a cynical laugh. 'Wow! That must be a first. So if it isn't about the money—then what *is* it about?'

Distractedly, she rubbed at her forehead. 'I want him—or her—to know who they are—to have a real identity. I want them to bear their father's name.'

She saw the darkness which passed over his face like a cloud crossing the sun.

'And I might not have the kind of name you would want to associate with your baby,' he said harshly.

'What's that supposed to mean?'

But Alek shook his head as the old familiar shutters came slamming down—effectively sealing him off from her questions. Because marriage was a no-no for him—right at the very top of things he was never going to do. And although he'd shaken off his past a long time ago—he could never entirely escape its long tentacles. They reached out and whipped him when he wasn't expecting it. In the darkness of the night they sometimes slithered over his skin, reminding him of things he'd rather forget.

His parents' marriage had been the dark canker at the heart of his life, whose poison had spilled over into so many places. The union between a cruel man and a woman he despised so much that he couldn't even bear to say her name. His mouth hardened. Why the hell would *he* ever want to marry?

Alek's success had been public, but he'd managed to keep his life private. He had locked himself within an emotional shell in order to protect himself and he rarely let anyone get close. And hadn't that been another reason for his anger with Ellie? Not just because her indiscretion had tarnished his hard-won business reputation, but because she'd broken his foolishly misplaced trust in her.

'Maybe I'm not great husband material,' he told her. 'Ask any of the women I've dated and I'm sure they'd be happy to list all my failings. I'm selfish. I'm intolerant. I work too hard and have a low boredom threshold—especially where women are concerned.' He raised his eyebrows. 'Shall I continue?'

She shook her head, so that her ponytail swung from side to side. 'I'm not talking about a real marriage. I'm talking about a legal contract with a finite time limit.'

His eyes narrowed. 'Because?'

'Because I don't want my baby to be born illegitimate—I'm illegitimate myself. But neither do I want to spend the rest of my life with someone who doesn't even seem to like me. I'm not a complete masochist—'

'Just a partial one?' he put in mockingly.

'I must have been,' she said bitterly, 'to have had sex with you.'

'Pretty amazing sex, though,' he said, almost as an aside.

Deliberately, Ellie pushed that thought away, even though just the mention of it was enough to start her body tingling. Yes, it had been amazing. It had started out in anger but it had turned into something else. Something passionate and all consuming, which had completely blown her away. Had he felt it, too—that incredible connection? Or was she doing that thing women were so good at doing? Believing something to be true because you *wanted* it to be true.

'It doesn't matter now what the sex was like,' she said slowly. 'Because the only thing that matters now is the baby.'

He flinched as she said the word. She could see his jaw harden so that it looked as if it were carved from granite.

'Cut to the chase and tell me exactly what you're proposing,' he said.

The combination of heat, emotion and a lack of food was making her feel dizzy but Ellie knew she mustn't crumple now. The thought of having Alek in her life didn't exactly make her want to jump for joy—but it was still better than going it alone.

'We have a small wedding,' she said. 'No doubt your lawyers will want to draw up some kind of contract and that's fine by me.'

'Good of you,' he said sardonically.

'We don't even have to live together,' she continued. 'You just acknowledge paternity and provide support for the future. The baby gets your name and a share of your inheritance.' She shrugged, because the words sounded so bizarre. A few short weeks ago she'd been thinking no further than her next promotion and here she was talking about *paternity*. 'And after the birth, we can get ourselves a no-blame divorce. I think that's fair.'

'Fair?' He gave a short laugh. 'You mean I'm to play the tame benefactor? Sitting on the sidelines, just doling out money?'

'I'm not intending to be greedy.'

He narrowed his eyes. 'And you don't think people are going to be suspicious? To wonder why we aren't living together and why I haven't spent any time with the mother of my baby?'

'Given the way you've reacted to the news, I was assuming that being given a get-out clause would be your dream scenario.'

'Well, don't,' he snapped. 'Don't ever *assume* anything about me, Ellie. That was the first mistake you made. I am not a "pussycat" as you seem to think, not by any stretch of the imagination.'

'Don't worry. I've changed my mind about that!'

'I'm pleased to hear it.' His gaze raked over her, lingering almost reluctantly on her belly. 'I didn't plan a baby and I certainly didn't want marriage. But if these are the cards fate has dealt me—then these are the cards I'm going to have to play. And I play to win.'

She pushed her fringe out of her eyes. 'Is that supposed to be a threat?'

'Not a threat, no. But you haven't yet heard my side of the bargain.' Alek stared at her mutinous face. He knew what he had to do. No matter how much it flew in the face of everything he believed in, he was going to have to make sacrifices for his child in a way nobody had ever done for him. He was going to have to marry her. Because it was far better to have her by his side as his wife, than to leave her free to behave like a loose cannon, with his child helpless and without his protection.

His heart clenched. 'If you want my ring on your finger, then you're going to have to act like a wife,' he said. 'You will live with me—'

'I told you that wasn't—'

'I don't care what you told me,' he interrupted impatiently. 'If we're going to do this, we're going to do it properly. I want this wedding to mimic all the traditions of what a wedding should be.'

'M-mimic?' she echoed, in confusion. 'What do you mean?'

'Can't you guess?' His mouth twisted into a bitter smile. 'We will pretend. You will wear a white dress and look deep into my eyes and play the part of my adoring bride. Do you think you can manage that, Ellie?'

Ellie's stomach began to rumble and she wondered if he could hear it in the strange silence which had descended. It seemed a long time since she'd eaten that apple on the train. In fact, it seemed a long time since she'd done anything which felt remotely *normal*. One minute she'd been waiting tables and the next she was standing discussing marriage with a cold-eyed billionaire who was telling her to pretend to care about him. Suddenly she felt like a feather which had found itself bouncing around on a jet stream.

'You want to make it into some sort of farce,' she breathed.

'Not a farce. Just a performance credible enough to convince the outside world that we have fallen in love.'

'But why?' she questioned. 'Why not just treat it like the contract we both know it is?'

He flexed his fingers and she saw the whitening of his knuckles through the deep olive skin.

'Because I want my child to have *memories*,' he said harshly. 'To be able to look at photos of their mother and father on their wedding day, and even if they are no longer together—which obviously, we won't be—then at least there will be the consolation that once we were an item.'

'But that's...that's a lie!'

'Or just illusionary?' he questioned bitterly. 'Isn't that what life is? An illusion? People see what others want them to see. And I don't want my child hurt. Let him believe that once his parents loved one another.'

Ellie watched his face become ravaged by a pain he couldn't hide. It clouded the brilliance of his blue eyes and darkened his features into a rugged mask. And despite everything, she wanted to reach out and ask him what had caused him a hurt so palpable that just witnessing it seemed intrusive. She wanted to put her arms around him and cradle him.

But he looked so remote in his beautifully cut suit, with its dark fabric moulding his powerful limbs and the white shirt collar which contrasted against his gleaming skin. He looked so proud and patrician that he seemed almost *untouchable*, which was pretty ironic when you thought about it. She cleared her throat. 'And when should this *marriage* take place?'

'I think as soon as possible, don't you? There's something a little in your face about a bride who is so *obviously* pregnant. I'll have my lawyers draw up a contract and you will move into my London apartment. We can discuss buying you a property after the birth.'

Ellie felt as if her old life was already fading. As if she'd been plucked from obscurity and placed in the spotlight of Alek's glamorous existence and she was suddenly beginning to realise just how powerful that spotlight could be. But when she stopped to think about it, what did she imagine would happen next? That she'd carry on selling cupcakes while wearing his ring on her finger? 'I suppose so,' she agreed.

His blue gaze raked over her. 'You've lost weight,' he observed.

'I get sick in the mornings, but it usually wears off by mid-afternoon.'

'Yet you're expecting to carry on working?'

'I'll manage,' she said stubbornly. 'Most women do.'

'And after the birth—what then? Will your baby take second place to your career?'

'I can't say what will happen,' she said quietly. 'All I do know is that a child shouldn't have to take second place to anything.'

They stared at one another and for a moment Ellie thought he was actually going to say something *nice*, but she was wrong.

'You're going to have to update your wardrobe if you're to make a convincing bride, but that shouldn't be a problem. As the future Mrs Sarantos, you'll get unlimited access to my credit card. Does that turn you on?'

Ellie glared as she met his sardonic smile. 'Will you please stop making me sound like some kind of gold-digger?'

'Oh, come on, Ellie,' he said, and briefly some of the

harshness left his voice. 'Didn't you ever learn to make the best out of a bad situation?'

She felt a twist of pain as she turned away. Didn't he realise he was talking to the queen of the positive spin? That she'd spent her life trying not to be influenced by a mother who was steeped in bitterness and regret. And hadn't she vowed that her own life would be different? That she would make something of herself? She would be strong and most of all…*independent*. And now here she was, tying herself to a cold and unfeeling man because she needed security.

But that didn't matter. None of it did. She was going to do whatever it took to give her baby a better life than the one she'd known.

Her heart clenched.

Even if it meant marrying someone who seemed to despise her.

CHAPTER SIX

ELLIE'S NEW LIFE began the minute Alek agreed to marry her and it felt like waking up in a parallel universe.

No more travelling across London, or a sticky train journey home to the New Forest. He didn't do public transport, did he? And neither would the woman who was carrying his child. A sleek limo was ordered to take her home, but not before Alek insisted she eat something. Her attempts to tell him she wasn't hungry fell on deaf ears and he sent Vasos out for warm bread, tiny purple grapes and a rich chickpea spread, which Ellie fell on with a moan of greed. She ate the lot and looked up to find him studying her.

'You're obviously not looking after yourself properly,' he said repressively. 'Forget working out your notice and move up here straight away. It makes perfect sense.'

'I can't leave Bridget in the lurch. She's been very kind to me. I'll need to give her a month's notice.'

He hadn't been happy about that, just as he hadn't been happy when she'd refused the wad of banknotes he'd tried to press on her for any *expenses*.

'Please don't try to give me money in the street,

Alek,' she hissed. 'I'm not some kind of hooker. And while we're on the subject, I'm going to want my own room when I move into your apartment.' The look of surprise on his face had been almost comical. 'And that's a requirement,' she added tartly. 'Not a request.'

It was late when the car eventually dropped her off in the New Forest—too late to speak to Bridget, but Ellie's plan of telling her boss the following day was blown when Bridget walked into the shop with an expression Ellie had never seen before. The fifty-something widow who had treated her like the daughter she'd never had looked as if she was about to burst with excitement.

'Sweet saints in all heaven—why didn't you tell me?' Bridget demanded, her Irish accent still discernible, even after three decades of living in England.

'Tell you what?' questioned Ellie, her skin prickling with an instinctive dread.

'That you're going to be married! And to a handsome Greek, no less! My, but you're a secretive one, Miss Brooks.'

Ellie gripped the glass counter, forgetting the smudgy marks her fingers would leave behind. 'But how—?' She swallowed as she asked a question to which she already knew the answer. 'How did you find out?'

'How do you think?' questioned Bridget, followed by a quick demonstration of her explosive laugh. 'I got a call from the man himself late last night. He woke me out of a deep sleep, but he's so full of the Greek blarney that I told him I didn't mind a bit! He said he needs you at his side and he's offering to compensate me so that you can leave early. Why, I can get ten shop assistants for the money he's giving me—and still have plenty left over for the extension for the tea room! He's a very generous man, Ellie—and you're a very lucky woman.'

Ellie felt sick. Lucky? She felt about as lucky as someone who'd just tossed their winning lottery ticket onto a roaring fire. But she wasn't stupid. Bridget didn't care about her giving a full four weeks' notice, because Alek's offer had wiped out all other considerations. What price is friendship or loyalty in the face of all that hard cash? Was that what made him so cynical? she wondered—knowing everything had a price tag and if he paid enough, he could get exactly what he wanted?

'I've got a girl coming in from the village tomorrow,' continued Bridget chattily. 'It's all sorted.'

Ellie wondered how her boss would react if she told her the truth. *We've only had sex the once and we weren't supposed to see each other again. He's only marrying me because there's a baby on the way.*

But what good would that do? Why disillusion someone for the sake of it? Surely it would be best to repay Bridget's kindness by letting her think this was what she really wanted. Oughtn't she at least act out the fairy tale—even if she didn't believe in it herself?

'It's very sweet of you to be so understanding, Bridget,' she said.

'Nonsense. It's an absolute pleasure to see you so settled and happy. Come round to the cottage tonight and we'll have a slap-up meal, to celebrate.'

After work, Ellie went upstairs to her little flat and, sure enough, there was a text message waiting on her phone.

I've sorted things out with your boss. Car arriving for you at eleven tomorrow morning. Make sure you're ready to leave. Alek.

If she'd thought it would make any difference, she might have been tempted to ping back a stinging reply, but Ellie was too tired to try. Why waste energy fighting the inevitable?

She packed up her meagre wardrobe, then went round to Bridget's hobbit-sized cottage for a vegetarian goulash. Afterwards, as she walked home in the warm summer evening, she looked up at the star-spangled sky with a feeling of wistfulness. She was going to miss the beauty of the forest—with all those cute ponies which wandered around and then stood in the middle of the road, regularly bringing all the traffic to a standstill as they swished their feathery tails. She'd always dreamed she might one day live in a big city, but never in circumstances like this. Her future lay ahead like a big uncharted map, and she felt scared.

Yet the sleep she fell into was deep and she was startled awake by the sound of a car horn beeping from beneath her open window. She staggered out of bed and hastily pulled on a robe. She had overslept and the driver was obviously here.

Except that it wasn't the driver. Ellie waited until the sickness had passed before poking her head out of the window, her breath catching in her throat when she saw Alek himself. He was leaning against a dark green sports car and it was just like the first time she'd seen him—when he'd been off duty in the spa hotel and she'd been trying very hard not to stare.

Dark shades covered his eyes and faded jeans clung

to the muscular contours of his long legs. His shirt-sleeves were rolled up to display powerful forearms and his hair glinted blue-black in the bright sunshine. Liquid desire began to unfold in the base of her belly—warm and unwanted and much too potent.

'Oh,' she said coolly, because she didn't want to feel this way when she looked at him. She wanted to feel *nothing*. 'It's you.'

Lifting up his shades, he narrowed his eyes against the bright light. 'I've had better greetings,' he said drily. 'Why don't you open the door and I'll come up and collect your stuff?'

'There's a key on the top ledge,' she said, withdrawing her head and grabbing some clothes as she headed for the bathroom. By the time she emerged, washed and dressed—he was standing in the middle of her sitting room, not looking in the least bit repentant.

She slammed her soap bag onto the table and turned on him, her growing temper fuelled by the arrogant look on his face. 'How dare you ring up my boss and offer her money to release me from my contract, when I told you I wanted to work out my notice?' she demanded. 'Does it give you a kick to be so *controlling*?'

'If you can give me a single valid objection,' he drawled, 'other than the mild wounding to your ego—then I'll listen. But you can't, can you, Ellie? You've been sick every morning and you look like hell, but you still want to carry on. Not the greatest advertisement for a cake shop, is it—unless you're trying to drive away the customers?' He glanced down at the two battered suitcases which were standing in the middle of the floor. 'This all you've got?'

'No, there are several Louis Vuitton trunks next door,' she said sarcastically.

He picked them up as easily as if they were full of feathers, rather than the entire contents of her world. 'Come on. The car's waiting.'

She took the keys downstairs to the shop, where Bridget was showing the new assistant all the different cupcakes. The Strawberry Shortcake and the Lemon Lovely. The Chocolate Nemesis and the bestselling Cherry Whirl. It was farewell to a simple life and a great leap into a sophisticated unknown, and Ellie's chest felt tight with emotion as the Irishwoman hugged her, before waving her off in the shiny car.

The car roof was down and the noise of the traffic made conversation difficult but that was a relief because Ellie had no desire to talk and, besides, what would she say? How did you start a conversation with a man you barely knew in circumstances such as these? Staring out of the window, she watched as trees and fields gave way to tall buildings which shimmered in the summer sunshine like distant citadels.

Their journey took them through South Kensington, a place she'd once visited on a school trip. Thirty-five boisterous children had spent the morning in the Natural History Museum and afterwards had been allowed to descend on the museum shop. Ellie had used all her pocket money to buy her mother an expensive little bar of soap in the shape of a dinosaur. But the gift had failed to please. Apparently, it had reminded her—yet again—of all the things which were missing in her life. Ellie remembered her mother staring at the tiny bar as if it had been contaminated. Her voice had been bitter, her face contorted with a rage which was never far from the surface. *If your father had married me, you could have afforded to buy me something which was bigger than a walnut!*

And wasn't that memory reason enough to be grateful that Alek wasn't washing his hands of his responsibilities? Despite his authoritarian attitude, he was stepping up to the mark and shouldering his share of the life they had inadvertently created. He wasn't planning to never pay a penny towards his baby's upkeep, or never bother keeping in touch, was he? She stole a glance at his rugged profile. He wasn't *all* bad. And following on from that wave of appreciation came another, which was rather more unwelcome, especially when his thigh tensed over the accelerator. He was so unbelievably *hot* and she hadn't really stopped to think about what the reality of that might be, when she was closeted together with him in his apartment. Could desire be switched off, like a tap? Or would close contact only increase her awareness of just how gorgeous the father of her unborn child was?

Alek lived in Knightsbridge and his apartment was everything Ellie had expected and more, although nothing could have prepared her for its sheer size and opulence. Even the relative luxury of The Hog paled into insignificance when compared to each high-ceilinged room which seemed to flow effortlessly into the next. Squashy velvet sofas stood on faded silken rugs and everywhere you looked were beautiful objects. On a small table was a box inlaid with mother-of-pearl and a small gilded egg studded with stones of emerald and blue. She blinked at it as it sparkled brightly in the sunshine. Surely those stones weren't *real*? She wanted to ask, but it seemed rude—as if she were sizing up the place and trying to work out its worth. But it wasn't the value so much as the beauty which took her breath away. Everywhere she looked were paintings of places she'd longed to visit—upmarket versions of the posters she'd had hanging in her room at the hostel. Leafy streets in Paris and iconic churches in Rome, as well as the unbelievable architecture of Venice reflected in the dappled water of the canals.

She looked at them longingly. 'Your paintings are amazing.'

'Thank you.' He inclined his head—the tone of his voice altering slightly, as if her comment had surprised him. 'It's something of a hobby of mine. You are fond of art?'

She bit back the defensive remark which hovered on her lips. Did he think someone who worked in the service industry was incapable of appreciating art, or that you had to be wealthy to enjoy it? 'I enjoy visiting galleries when I get the chance,' she said stiffly. 'Though I've never seen stuff like this in someone's home.'

But then she'd never been in a home like this. She walked over to one of the windows which framed a stunning view of the park and when she turned round it was to find him watching her, his blue eyes giving nothing away.

'I take it you approve?'

'How could I not?' She shrugged, trying not to be affected by the intensity of that sapphire gaze. 'It's remarkable. Did you design it yourself?'

'I can't take any of the credit, I'm afraid.' His smile was bland. 'I had someone do that for me. A woman called Alannah Collins.'

Ellie nodded. Of course he did. Men like Alek didn't choose their own wallpaper or spend ages deliberating where to position the sofas. They paid for someone else to do it. Just as he paid shop owners to release their staff early from a contract. He could do what the hell he liked, couldn't he? All he had to do was to take out his chequebook. 'She's a very talented designer,' she said.

'She is.' He narrowed his eyes. 'So I take it you'll be able to tolerate living here for a while?'

'Who knows?' she answered lightly. 'We might be wanting to kill each before the week is out.'

'We might.' There was a heartbeat of a pause. 'Or we might find infinitely more satisfying ways to sublimate our…frustrations. What do you think, Ellie?'

His words were edged with mockery but there was a very real sense of sexual challenge sparking beneath that cool stare, and of course she was tempted by that look.

But even stronger than temptation was Ellie's overwhelming sense of *disorientation* as he flirted with her. Seeing him in his fancy home made it hard to believe the circumstances which had brought her here. Had he really arrived at her humble room in the staff hostel and then had sex with her on that single bed? It seemed like a muddled dream to remember him pulling urgently at her clothing, like a man out of control. She remembered the anger on his face and then the sudden transformation as his rage had given way to a passion which had left her crying in his arms afterwards.

But men could feel passion in the heat of the moment and then turn it off once their appetite had been satisfied, couldn't they? She didn't know a whole heap about sex, but she knew that much and she had to remember that she was vulnerable as far as Alek was concerned. They might have come together as equals that day, but they weren't really equals. She might soon be wearing his wedding ring but that was only a symbol. It didn't *mean* anything. It certainly didn't mean any of the things a wedding band was *supposed* to mean. She needed to keep her emotional distance. She *had* to, if she wanted to protect herself from getting hurt.

'Just to be clear.' She met the blue gleam of his eyes. 'I meant what I said about wanting my own room. So if you're thinking of trying to persuade me otherwise, I'm afraid you'll be wasting your time.'

He gave a wry smile. 'On balance, I think I agree with you. I'm beginning to think that sharing a room with you would only complicate an already complicated situation.'

Ellie felt a wave of something very feminine and contrary flaring through her as she followed him from the huge reception room. Couldn't he at least have *pretended* to be disappointed, rather than appearing almost *relieved*? With difficulty she dragged her gaze away from his powerful back and forced herself to look at all the different things he was showing her. The plush cinema with its huge screen. The black marble fittings in the shamelessly masculine kitchen. The modern dining room, which didn't look as if it was used very much—with tall silver candlesticks standing on a beautiful gleaming table. On the wall of his study, different clocks were lined up to show the time zones of all the world's major cities and his desk contained a serious amount of paperwork. He explained that there was a swimming pool in the basement of the building, as well as a fully equipped gym.

The bedroom she was allocated wasn't soft or girly—and why would it be?—but at least it was restful. The

bed was big, the view spectacular. The en-suite bathroom had snowy towels and expensive bottles of bath oil
and she thought about how perfect everything looked.
And then there was her. Standing there in her jeans and
T-shirt, she felt like a cobweb which had blown onto a
line of clean washing.

'Do you like it?' he questioned.

'I can't imagine anyone not liking it. It's beautiful.'
She ran her fingertip along a delicate twist of coloured
glass which served no useful purpose other than to cap-
ture the light and reflect it back in rainbow rays. 'I just
can't imagine how a baby is going to fit in here.'

His gaze followed the line of her fingers. 'Neither
can I. But I wasn't planning on having a baby when I
bought this place.'

'You didn't think that one day you might have a family of your own? I don't mean like this, obviously—'

'Obviously,' he interrupted tightly. 'And the answer
is no. Not every man feels the need to lock himself
into family life—particularly when so few families are
happy.'

'That's a very cynical point of view, Alek.'

'You think so? Why, was your own childhood so
happy?' His gaze bore into her. 'Let me guess. A cosy
English village where everyone knew each other? A
cottage with roses growing around the door?'

'Hardly.' She gave a short laugh. 'I didn't meet my
father until I was eighteen and when I did I wished I
hadn't bothered.'

His eyes had narrowed. 'Why not?'

It was a story she wasn't proud of. Correction. It
was one she was almost ashamed of. She knew it was
illogical, but if you were unloved, then didn't that au-

tomatically make you unlovable? *Didn't the fault lie within her?* But she pushed that rogue thought away as she had been trying to do for most of her adult life. And there was no reason to keep secrets from Alek. She wasn't trying to impress him, because he'd already made it clear that he no longer wanted her. And if you moved past that rather insulting fact—didn't that mean she could be herself, instead of trying to be the person she thought she *ought* to be?

'I'd hate to shock you,' she said flippantly.

His voice was dry. 'Believe me, I am not easily shocked.'

She watched as the filmy drapes moved in a cloud-like blur at the edges of the giant windows. 'My father was a businessman—quite a successful one by all accounts—and my mother worked as his secretary, but she was also his…' She shrugged as she met his quizzical expression. 'It sounds so old-fashioned now, but she was his mistress.'

'Ah,' he said, in the tone of a man addressing a subject on which he was already an expert. 'His mistress.'

'That's right. It was the usual thing. He set her up in a flat. He bought her clothes and in particular—underwear. They used to go out for what was euphemistically known as "lunch," which I gather didn't make her very popular back at the office. Sometimes he even managed to get away for part of a weekend with her, though of course she was always on her own at Christmas and during vacations. She told me all this one night when she'd been drinking.'

'So what happened?' he questioned, diplomatically ignoring the sudden tremble in her voice. 'How come you came along?'

Caught up in a tale she hadn't thought about in a long

time, Ellie sat down heavily on the bed. The Egyptian cotton felt soft as she rested her palms against it and met the cool curiosity in Alek's eyes. 'She wanted him to divorce his wife, but he wouldn't. He kept telling her that he'd have to wait for his children to leave home— again, the usual story. So she thought she'd give him a little encouragement.'

'And she got pregnant?'

'She got pregnant,' she repeated and saw the look on his face. 'And before you say anything—I did not set out to repeat history. Believe me, the last thing I wanted was to recreate my own childhood. What happened between us was—'

'An accident,' he said, almost roughly. 'Yes, I know that. Go on.'

She'd lost the thread of what she'd been saying and it took her a couple of seconds to pick it up again. 'I think she mistakenly thought that he'd get used to having a baby. That he might even be pleased…evidence of his virility…that kind of thing. But he wasn't. He already had three children he was putting through school and a wife with an expensive jewellery habit. He told her…'

Ellie's voice tailed off. She remembered that awful night of her birthday when her mother had seen off the best part of a bottle of gin and started blubbing—telling her stuff which no child should ever hear. She had buried it deep in the recesses of her own mind, but now it swam to the surface—like dark scum which had been submerged too long.

'He told her to get rid of it. Or rather…to get rid of me,' she said, her bright, pointless smile fading as her mother's words reverberated round her head. *And I should have listened to him! If I'd known what lay ahead, I damned well would have listened to him!* 'I think she thought he'd change his mind, but he didn't. He stopped paying the rent on my mother's apartment and told his wife about the affair—thus effectively curtailing any thoughts of blackmail. Then they moved to another part of the country and that was the end of that.'

'He didn't keep in contact?'

'Nope. It was different in those days, before social media really took off—it's easy to lose touch with someone. There was no maintenance—and my mother was too proud to take him to court. She said she'd already lost so much that she wouldn't give him the satisfaction of seeing her begging. She said we would manage just fine, but of course—it's never that simple.'

'But you said you saw him? When you were eighteen?'

Ellie didn't answer for a moment, because this territory was not only forbidden—it was unmarked. She wondered whether she should tell him—but how could she not? She hadn't talked about it with anyone before because she didn't want to look as if she was drowning in self-pity, but maybe Alek had a right to know.

'I did see him,' she said slowly. 'After my mother died, I tracked him down and wrote to him. Said I'd like to meet him. I was slightly surprised when he agreed.' And slightly scared, too, because she'd built him up in her head to be some kind of hero. Maybe she'd been longing for the closeness she'd never had with her mother. Perhaps she had been as guilty as the next person of wanting a fairy tale which didn't exist. The big reunion which was going to make everything in her life better.

'What happened?'

She narrowed her eyes. 'You really want to know?'

'I do. You tell a good story,' he said, surprisingly.

She wanted to tell him that it wasn't a *story*, but when she stopped to think about it—maybe it was. Life was a never-ending story—wasn't that how the old cliché went? She cleared her throat. 'There was no psychic connection between us. No sense that here was the person whose genes I shared. We didn't even look alike. He sat on the other side of a noisy table in a café at Waterloo station and told me that my mother was a conniving bitch who had almost ruined his life.'

'And that was it?' he asked after a long moment.

'Pretty much. I tried asking about my half-sister and half-brothers and anyone would have thought I'd asked him for the PIN number for his savings account, from the way he reacted.' He had stood up then with an ugly look on his face, but the look had been tinged with satisfaction—as if he'd been *glad* of an excuse to be angry with her. She remembered him knocking against the table and her untouched cappuccino slopping everywhere in a frothy puddle. 'He told me never to contact him again. And then he left.'

Alek heard the determinedly nonchalant note in her voice and something twisted darkly in his gut. Was it recognition? A realisation that everyone carried their own kind of pain, but that most of it was hidden away? Suddenly her fierce ambition became understandable—an ambition which had been forced into second place by the baby. He felt a pang of guilt as he recalled how cavalier he'd been about her losing her job. Suddenly, he could understand her insistence on marriage—a request which must have been fuelled by the uncertainty of her own formative years. Not because she wanted the cachet of being his wife, but because she wanted to give her own baby the security she'd never had.

But recognising something didn't change anything. He needed to be clear about the facts and so did she—and the most important fact she needed to realise was that he could never do the normal stuff that women seemed to want. He might be capable of honouring his responsibility to her and the baby—but, emotionally, wasn't he cut from exactly the same cloth as her father? Hadn't he walked away from women in the past—blind to their tears and their needs?

Ellie Brooks wasn't his type, but even if she were he was the last man she needed. She needed his name on a birth certificate and she needed his money, and he could manage that. *Neh.* A bitter smile curved his lips. He could manage that very well. But if she wanted someone to provide the love and support her father had never given her, then he was the wrong person.

She had pushed the heavy fringe away from her eyebrows. Her face was pale, he thought. And now that she no longer had those generous curves, there was a kind of fragility about her which gave her skin a curious luminosity. And suddenly, all his certainties seemed to fade away. He forgot that it was infinitely more sensible to keep his distance from her as he was overcome by a powerful desire to take her in his arms and offer her comfort.

He swallowed, his feelings confusing him. And angering him. He didn't *want* to be in thrall to anyone, but certainly not to her. Because he recognised that Ellie possessed something which no woman before her had ever possessed. *A part of him.* And didn't that give her a special kind of power? A power she could so easily abuse if he wasn't careful.

He walked quickly towards the door, realising that he needed to get the hell out of there. 'You'd better unpack,' he said abruptly. 'And then we need to sit down and discuss the practicalities of you living here.'

CHAPTER SEVEN

WITH A SPEED which left her slightly dazed, Alek took over Ellie's life. He organised a doctor and a credit card. He filled in all the requisite forms required for their upcoming wedding and booked the register office. But it quickly dawned on Ellie that the most important *practicality* of living with the Greek tycoon was an ability to be happy with her own company.

'I work long hours,' he told her. 'And I travel. A lot. You'll need to be able to amuse yourself and not come running to me because you're bored. Understand?'

Biting back her indignation at being spoken to as if she were some kind of mindless puppet, Ellie told herself that snapping at him was only going to make a difficult situation worse. Bad enough that he prowled around the place looking like a sex god, without taking him to task over his patronising comments. She was trying very hard to give him the benefit of the doubt— telling herself that perhaps he didn't mean to be quite so insulting. That he was a powerful man who was clearly used to issuing orders which he expected to be obeyed. And at first, she did exactly that.

During those early days in his Knightsbridge penthouse, she was still too disorientated by the speed at which her life had changed to object to his steamroller-ing approach to life. She was introduced as his fiancée to the confusingly large number of staff who worked for him both in and outside his organisation and she tried to remember everyone's name.

There were cleaners who moved noiselessly around the vast apartment—like ghosts carrying buckets—and a woman whose job was to keep his fridge and wine cellar stocked. There was the doctor who insisted on visiting her at home—unheard of!—and told her she should take it easy, and these instructions she followed to the letter. She made the most of her free time. She realised it was the first time she'd ever had a prolonged break—or enjoyed a guilt-free session of relaxation— and she concentrated on settling into her new habitat like a cuckoo finding its way round a new and very luxurious nest.

But the baby still felt as if it weren't happening, even though she was now in possession of a glossy black and white photo showing what looked like a cashew nut, attached to the edge of a dark lake. And when she looked into the icy beauty of Alek's eyes, it was hard to believe that the tiny life growing inside her was some-how connected with him. Would he love his baby? she found herself wondering. Was he even *capable* of love?

He's capable of sex, prompted a whispering voice inside her head—but determinedly she blocked out the thought. She wasn't going to think of him that way. She just wasn't.

The friendly concierge in the lobby gave her a street map and she started exploring Kensington and Chel-sea, as well as the nearby park, where the leaves on the trees were showing the first hints of gold. She began visiting the capital's galleries with enough time on her hands to really make the most of them, which she'd never had before.

Each morning, Alek left early for the office and would return late, a pair of dark-rimmed reading glasses giving him a surprisingly sexy, geeky look as he carried in the sheaf of papers he'd been studying in the car. He would disappear into his room to shower and change and then—surprisingly—disappear into the kitchen to cook them both dinner. An extensive repertoire of dishes began to appear each evening—one involving aubergine and cheese, which quickly became Ellie's favourite. He told her that he'd learnt to cook at sixteen, when he'd been working in a restaurant and the chef had told him that a man who could feed himself was a man who would survive.

His skill in the kitchen wasn't what she had been expecting and it took some getting used to—sitting and politely discussing the day's happenings over dinner, like two people on a first date who were on their best behaviour. It was like being in some kind of dream. As if it were all happening to someone else.

It was just unfortunate that Ellie's body didn't feel a bit dreamlike, but uncomfortably real. Her reservations about living with him had been realised and she was achingly aware of him. How could she not be? His presence was impossible to ignore. Much as she tried to deny it, he was her every fantasy come to life. Worse still, she'd had a brief taste of what lovemaking could be like in Alek's arms, and it had left her hungry and wanting more. And daily exposure to him was only reinforcing that hunger.

She saw him first thing when he was newly showered

and dressed, with his dark hair slicked back and his skin smelling of lemon. She saw him sitting at the breakfast bar, sliding heavy gold cufflinks through one of his pristine shirts—and her heart would give a powerful contraction of blatant longing. Did he know that? Did he realise that inside she was berating herself for having insisted on a stupid no-sex rule? Had she imagined a hint of amusement dancing in the depths of those sapphire eyes when he looked at her? As if he was enjoying some private joke at her expense—silently taunting her with the knowledge that he could cope with sensual deprivation far better than her.

It was weekends which were hardest, when his failure to leave for the office left a gaping hole in the day ahead, along with the distraction of having him around without a break. This was when breakfast became a more awkward meal than usual. Was she imagining him staring at her intently, or was that just wishful thinking on her part? Had he deliberately left a button of his silk shirt unbuttoned, so that a smooth golden triangle of skin was revealed? Ellie would feel her breasts tingling with a hateful kind of hunger as he slid a jar of marmalade across the table towards her. She remembered what he'd said about faking affection for the wedding photos. No. She definitely wasn't going to have a problem with that.

On the third weekend, she was as edgy as an exam candidate and glad to get out of the apartment for Alek's suggested trip to the Victoria and Albert. It was a museum she'd longed to visit again, even though this time the statues were wasted on her. She kept looking at the carved and stony features of various kings and dignitaries and comparing them unfavourably with the beautiful features of the man by her side. Afterwards, they walked to an open-air restaurant for a late lunch and she had to fight to quash her stupid desire to have him touch her again. She thought about their wedding and their wedding night, and wondered how she was going to cope with *that*.

This time next month I'll be his wife, she thought. *Even though both of us seem determined not to talk about it.*

The sun was dipping lower in the sky as they walked back across the park, but when she got back to the apartment she found herself unable to get comfortable. Her feet were aching and she was wriggling around restlessly on the sofa.

She didn't know what she was expecting when Alek walked across the room and sat down next to her, lifting her bare feet into his lap and beginning to massage each one in turn. It was the first time he'd touched her in a long time and, despite her thoughts of earlier, her instinctive reaction was to freeze, even though her heart had started hammering. Could he hear its wild beat or maybe even see it, beneath her thin T-shirt? Was that why he gave that slow half-smile?

But her initial tension dissolved the instant the warm pad of his thumb started caressing her insole and once she realised that this wasn't a seduction but simply a foot massage, she just lay back and enjoyed it. It felt like bliss and she found herself thinking how ironic it was that all his money couldn't buy something as good as this. Did he realise how much she loved the thoughtful gesture, even though she'd done her best to conceal her squirming pleasure from him? Was he aware that small kindnesses like these were the dangerous blocks which made her start building impossible dreams?

The following Monday, she was drinking ginger tea at the kitchen table when he glanced up from his newspaper and narrowed his eyes.

'About these new clothes you're supposed to be buying,' he said.

'Maternity clothes?'

'Not quite yet. I meant pretty clothes,' he said. 'Isn't that what we agreed? Something to make you look the part of a Sarantos bride. Not long to go now.'

'I know that.'

'You haven't shown very much interest in your wedding so far.'

'It's difficult to get enthusiastic about a ceremony which feels fake.'

He didn't rise to the taunt. 'I thought you'd be itching to get your hands on my chequebook.'

'Sorry to disappoint you,' she said in a hollow voice, thinking about the foot massage. Didn't he realise that something that simple and intimate was worth far more to her than his money? Of course he didn't. It suited him much more to imagine her salivating over his credit card.

He put his newspaper down. 'Well, there's no point in putting it off any longer. I can arrange for Alannah to take you shopping and you can choose your wedding dress at the same time, if you like. You'll find she has a superb eye.'

'You mean I don't?'

He frowned. 'That wasn't what I said.'

'But that's what you implied, isn't it? Poor little Ellie—snatched up from rural Hampshire with no idea how to shop for clothes which might make her believable as the wife of the powerful Greek!' She stood up quickly—too quickly—and had to steady herself. 'Well, I'm perfectly capable of buying my own clothes—and my own wedding dress. So why don't you give me your precious credit card and I'll see if I can do it justice? I'll go out this morning and just spend, spend, spend like the stereotypical gold-digger you're so fond of portraying!'

'Ellie—'

She stalked off into her room and slammed the door very noisily, but when she came out again sometime later it was to find him still sitting there—the pile of newspapers almost completely read.

'I thought you were going into the office this morning,' she said.

'Not any more,' he said. 'I'm taking you shopping.'

'I don't want you to…' Her voice faltered, because when his blue eyes softened like that, he was making her feel stuff she didn't want to feel.

'Don't want me to what?'

She didn't want him standing on the other side of a curtain while she tried to cram her awkward-looking body into suitable clothes. She didn't want to see the disbelieving faces of the sales assistants as they wondered what someone like him was doing with someone like her. Shopping for clothes was a nightmare experience at the best of times, but throwing the arrogant Alek into the mix would make it a million times worse. 'Hang around outside the changing room,' she said.

'Why not?'

She shrugged. Why not tell him the truth? 'I'm self-conscious about my body.'

He poured himself a cup of coffee. 'Why?'

'Because I *am*, that's why.' She glared at him. 'Most women are—especially when they're pregnant.'

His gaze slid over her navel, his expression suggesting he wasn't used to looking at a woman in a way which wasn't sexual. 'I should have thought that my own reaction to your body would have been enough to reassure you that I find it very attractive indeed.'

'That isn't the point,' she said, unwilling to point out that lately he hadn't shown the slightest interest in her body, because wouldn't that make her seem *vulnerable*? 'I'm not willing to do a Cinderella transformation scene with you as an audience.'

He opened his mouth and then, shutting it again, he sighed. 'Okay. So what if I act as your chauffeur for the day? I'll drive you to a department store and park up somewhere and wait. And you can text me when you're done. How does that sound?'

It sounded so reasonable that Ellie couldn't come up with a single objection and soon she was seated beside him in the car as he negotiated the morning traffic. She was slightly terrified when he dropped her off outside the store, but she'd read enough magazines to know that she was perfectly entitled to request the services of a personal shopper. And it didn't seem to matter that she was wearing jeans and a T-shirt or that her untrimmed fringe was flopping into her eyes like a sheepdog— because the elegant woman assigned to her made no judgements. She delicately enquired what Ellie's upper price limit was. And although Ellie's instinct was to go for the cheapest option, she knew Alek wouldn't thank her for shopping on a budget. He'd once drawlingly told her that it was the dream of every woman to get her hands on his credit card, so why disappoint him? Why not try to become the woman that he and his fancy friends would obviously expect her to be?

She quickly discovered how easy shopping was when you had money. You could buy the best. You could complement your outfits with soft leather shoes and pick up a delicate twist of a silk scarf which echoed the detail in a fabric. And expensive clothes really could transform, she decided. The luscious fabrics seemed to flatter her shape, rather than highlight her defects.

The shopper persuaded her into the dresses she usually rejected on the grounds that jeans were more practical, and Ellie found she liked the swish of the delicate fabrics brushing against her skin. She bought all the basic clothes she needed and then picked out a silvery-white wedding gown which did amazing things for her eyes as well as her figure. On impulse, the personal shopper draped a scarlet pashmina around her shoulders—a stole so fine it was almost transparent, and it was that addition which brought glowing life to her skin. Ellie stared at herself in the long mirror.

'It's perfect,' she said slowly.

By the time she emerged from the store wearing some of her purchases, she felt like a new woman.

She saw Alek's face change as she approached the car, accompanied by two doormen who were weighed down with armfuls of packages. His arm brushed over her back with proprietary courtesy as he held open the car door for her and she stiffened, because just that brief touch felt as if he'd branded her with the heat of his flesh. Was that why he stiffened, too? Why his eyes narrowed and a nerve began to work at his temple? She thought he might be about to touch her again—and wasn't she longing for him to do just that?—but some car had begun sounding its horn and the noise seemed to snap him out of his uncharacteristic hesitation.

He didn't say much as they drove to Bond Street, not until they were standing in front of a jeweller's window which was ablaze with the glitter of a thousand gems. And suddenly he turned to her and his face had that expression she'd seen once before, when all the cool arrogance which defined him had been replaced by a raw and naked hunger.

His finger wasn't quite steady as it drifted a slow path down over her cheek and he must have felt her shiver in response, because his eyes narrowed.

'You look…different,' he said.

'I thought that was the whole point of the exercise?' she said, more archly than she had intended. 'I have to look *credible*, don't I, as the future Mrs Sarantos?'

'But you don't, Ellie—that's the thing.' He gave her an odd kind of smile. 'You don't look credible at all. Not with that uptight expression on your face. It's not the look one might expect from a woman who is just about to marry one of the world's most eligible bachelors. There's no real joy or pleasure there, and I think we might have to remedy that. Shall we make a statement to the world about our relationship, *poulaki mou*? To show them we really do mean business?'

And before Ellie realised what was happening, he was kissing her. Kissing her in full view of the traffic and the security guard and all the upmarket shoppers who were passing them on the pavement. He had wrapped his arms tightly around her and was making her feel as if he *owned her*. The man who was so famously private was making a very public declaration.

And even though her heart was pounding with joy, suddenly she felt like a possession. A woman he was putting his stamp on. *His* woman; *his* property.

She tried keeping her lips clamped shut to prevent his tongue from entering her mouth—to let him know that she was *not* a possession. That he couldn't just pick her up and put her down when he felt like it. But there was only so much resistance she could put up when he was this determined. When he was splaying his fingers over the bare skin of her back and making it tingle. His hard body was so close that a cigarette paper couldn't have come between them, and, beneath her delicate new bra, her breasts were growing heavy.

His lips were still brushing against hers and her eyelids fluttered to a close. She thought how crazy it was that so many emotions could be stimulated by a single kiss. Did he realise that she found being in his arms satisfying in all kinds of ways? Ways which were about so much more than sex? She felt safe and secure. Like nothing could ever hurt her while Alek was around. And it was his strength rather than his sensuality which finally melted the last of her reservations. She kissed him back with fervour and passion and, in the process, completely forgot where she was. Her hands reached up to frame his head and she moaned softly as she circled her hips against him, so that in the end it was Alek who pulled back—his eyes smouldering with blue fire.

'Oh, my,' he said softly, and a distinctive twang of North Atlantic entered his gravelly Greek accent. 'Maybe I should have kissed you back at the apartment, if I'd known that this was the reaction I was going to get.'

His words broke the spell and Ellie jerked away with

a bitter feeling of self-recrimination. She had allowed herself to be seduced again when this was nothing but a game to him. A stupid, meaningless game. He had kissed her to make a point and she wasn't sure if it had been a demonstration of power, or just payback time for her expensive new wardrobe. But either way, she was going to get hurt if she wasn't careful. Badly hurt. She rose up on tiptoe in her new leather pumps, placing her lips to his ear.

'What was that all about?' she hissed.

'Want me to draw a diagram for you?' he murmured back.

'That won't be necessary.' She moved her mouth closer to his ear, tempted to take a nip at its perfect lobe. 'Sex just *complicates* matters. That was the deal— remember?'

'I think I might be prepared to overlook the deal in view of the response I just got.'

'Well, I wouldn't—and there's something you'd better understand, Alek.' She swallowed, trying to inject conviction into her voice. 'Which is that I wouldn't go to bed with you if you were the last man standing.'

He tipped his head back so that she was caught in the crossfire of his eyes, the darkened blue hue backlit by the definite glitter of amusement. He lifted his fingertip to her mouth and traced it thoughtfully along the line of her lips. 'I don't think that's entirely true, do you, Ellie?'

'Yes,' she said fiercely, resisting the urge to bite his finger, afraid that if she did she might just start sucking it. 'It's true.'

He took her hand in his and she wanted to snatch it away like a sulky child. But the doorman was still watching them and she knew that if she was to play the part of fiancée convincingly, then she had no choice other than to let him carry on stroking her fingers like that and pretend it wasn't turning her on.

'Let's go and buy your wedding ring,' he said.

CHAPTER EIGHT

THE RING WAS a glittering band of diamonds and the silvery shoes which matched her wedding dress had racy scarlet soles. Ellie touched her fingertips to her professionally styled hair, which had been snipped and blow-dried. She looked like a bride, all right, but a magazine version of a bride—untraditional and slightly edgy. The silver dress and scarlet pashmina gave her a sophisticated patina she wasn't used to and projected an image which wasn't really *her*. But the unfamiliar sleekness of her appearance did nothing to subdue the butterflies which were swarming in her stomach. They'd been building in numbers ever since she and Alek had said their vows earlier, with Vasos and another Sarantos employee standing as their only witnesses.

Strange to believe they were now man and wife—and that fifty of Alek's closest friends were assembling at the upmarket restaurant they'd chosen to stage their wedding party. And if it felt like a sham, that's because it was.

And yet...

Yet...

She stared down at her sparkling wedding band. When he'd kissed her so passionately in Bond Street—

hadn't that felt like something? Even though she'd tried telling herself that he'd only done it to make a point, that hadn't been enough to dull her reaction to him. She had nearly gone up in flames as sexual hunger had overpowered her and a wave of emotion had crashed over her with such force that she'd felt positively weak afterwards. It was as if the rest of the world hadn't existed in those few minutes afterwards, and wasn't that... *dangerous*?

The peremptory knock on her bedroom door broke into her thoughts and she opened it to find Alek standing there—broodingly handsome in his beautifully cut wedding suit, with a tie the colour of storm clouds.

'Ready?' he questioned.

She told herself she wasn't waiting for him to comment on her appearance—but what else would account for the sudden plummeting of her heart? She'd blamed pre-wedding jitters for his failure to compliment her the first time he'd seen her in her wedding dress. But now that they were man and wife, surely he could have said *something*. Had she secretly been longing for his eyes to light up and him to tell her that she made a halfway passable bride? Or was she hoping he'd make another pass at her, only this time she might not get so angry with him? She might just let him carry on...and they could consummate their marriage and satisfy the law, as well as their hungry bodies.

She swallowed. Yes. If the truth be known, she had wanted exactly that. From the time they'd returned from that shopping trip right up to the brief civil ceremony this morning, she'd been like a cat on a hot tin roof. She'd been convinced he would try to renegotiate the separate bedrooms rule, but she had been wrong. Despite her feisty words, he must have known from the way she'd responded to his kiss that she'd changed her mind. That all he needed to do was to kiss her one more time and she would be his. But Alek wasn't a man whose behaviour you could predict. It felt as if he had been deliberately keeping his distance from her ever since. Skirting around her as if she were some unexploded device he didn't dare approach. Even when he'd put the ring on her finger this morning in front of the registrar, she had received nothing more than a cool and perfunctory kiss on each cheek.

She gave him her best waitress smile. 'Yes, I'm ready.'

'Then let's go.'

She felt sick with nerves at the thought of meeting all his friends, especially since the only person she'd invited was Bridget, who wasn't able to attend because the new assistant still wasn't confident enough to be left on her own. Ellie picked up her handbag. She'd thought about inviting some of her New Forest friends, but how to go about explaining why she was marrying a man who was little more than a stranger to her? Wouldn't one of her girlfriends quickly suss that it was odd not to be giggling and cuddling up to a man you were planning to spend the rest of your life with? No. She didn't want pity or a well-meaning mate trying to talk her out of what was the only sensible solution to her predicament. She was going to have to go it alone. To be at her sparkling best and not let any of her insecurities show. She was going to have to make the marriage look as real as possible to *his* friends—and surely that wasn't beyond her capabilities to play a convincing part in front of people who didn't know her?

'Remind me again who's going,' she said as their car began to slip through the early evening traffic.

'Niccolò and Alannah—property tycoon and interior designer,' he said. 'Luis and Carly—he's the ex world champion racing driver and she's his medic wife. Oh, and Murat.'

Ellie forced a smile. Didn't he know any *normal* people? 'The Sultan?'

'That's right. And because of that, security will be tight.'

'You mean, I'll be frisked going into my own wedding party?'

He'd been staring out of the window and drumming his fingertips over one taut thigh and Ellie wished he'd say something equally flippant—anything to dispel this weird *atmosphere* between them. But when he spoke it was merely to resume a clipped tally of the guest list. 'There are people flying in from Paris, New York, Rome, Sicily—'

'And Greece, of course?' she prompted.

He shook his head. 'No. Not Greece.'

'But…that's where you come from.'

'So what? I left there a long time ago, and rarely visit these days.'

'But—'

'Look, can we just dispense with the interrogation, Ellie?' he interrupted coolly. 'I'm not really inclined to answer any more questions and, anyway, we're here.'

'Of course,' she said, quickly turning her head to look out of the window.

Alek felt a pang of guilt as he saw her silvery shoulders tense up. Okay, maybe he *had* been short with her but she needed to realise that being questioned like that wasn't his idea of fun. His mouth flattened. But what had he expected? Wasn't this what happened when you spent prolonged time with a woman? They felt it gave them the right to chip away at things. To quiz you about stuff you didn't want to talk about, even when you made it clear that a subject was deliberately off limits.

He'd never lived with anyone before Ellie. He'd never given a home to a second toothbrush, nor had to clear out space in his closet. Even though they had their own rooms, sometimes it felt as if it were impossible to get away from her. And the stupid thing was that he didn't want to get away from her. He wanted to get closer, even though instinct was telling him that was a bad idea. She was a constant temptation. She made him want her all the time, even though she didn't flirt with him. And wasn't even *that* a turn on? She was there in the morning before he left for work, all bright-eyed and smiling as she sat drinking her ginger tea. Just as she was there at night when he got home, offering to pour him a drink, telling him that she'd started experimenting with cooking and would he like to try some? She'd asked him for tips on how to cook the aubergine dish and he had found himself leaning dangerously close to her while she stirred something in a pot, tempted to kiss the bare neck which was a few tempting inches away from him. Slowly and very subtly her presence was driving him mad. Mostly, it was driving him mad because he wanted her—and he had no one to blame but himself.

That hot-headed kiss outside the jewellers had been intended as nothing more than a distraction. If he was being honest, it had also been intended as an arrogant demonstration of his sexual mastery. To show her that he was boss and always would be. But somehow it had backfired on him. It had reactivated his desire and now he was stuck with a raging sexual hunger which kept him awake most nights, staring at the ceiling and imagining all the different things he wanted to do to her.

He knew there was nothing stopping him from acting on it. From stealing into her room when darkness had fallen. From pulling back a crisp sheet and finding her, what…naked? Or wearing some slinky little nightgown she might have bought at the same time as the killer heels and new clothes. Those occasional longing looks and accidental touches had reinforced what he'd already known…that she wanted him as much as he wanted her. Physically, at least. He was confident enough to know he could be inside her in minutes if he put his mind to it, tangling his fingers in the soft spill of her pale hair and staring down at her beautiful pale curves.

And then what?

He felt another unwanted and unfamiliar stab of his conscience, which was enough to kill his desire stone-dead. Make her fall in love with him? Break her heart as he had broken so many in the past and leave her bitter and upset? Some good that would do when Ellie, above all others, was someone he needed to keep onside. She was carrying his baby and he needed her as a friend, not as a lover.

Because something inside him had changed. He'd imagined he would feel nothing about the new life growing inside her and that he would feel disconnected from her pregnancy. But he had been wrong. Hadn't his heart clenched savagely in his chest the first time he'd seen her fingertips drift almost reflectively over her still-flat belly?

With a fascination which seemed beyond his control, he had found himself watching her when she wasn't looking. When she was curled up in an armchair reading a book and making his life seem almost…*normal.* He'd never had normal before. And hadn't he been filled with an unbearable sense of longing for the family life which had been nothing but a dark void during his own childhood? Hadn't he started wondering again whether he could give this child what he'd never had himself? And one thing was for sure: he could not break the heart of his child's mother…

The car stopped outside the restaurant and as she draped the scarlet shawl around her shoulders he found he couldn't look away. He wanted to pull her into his arms and kiss all that shiny lipstick away from her beautiful lips, but why start the evening on a false promise?

'You look…great,' he said neutrally as the driver opened the limousine door for her.

'Thanks.'

Ellie's fingers tightened around the gilt chain of her handbag. First he'd shot her down in flames and then he'd told her she looked *great*? Was that the best he could do? Why, she'd had more praise from her science teacher at school—and she was hopeless at science. Cautiously, she stepped onto the pavement, balancing carefully on her high heels, thinking how unlike the Ellie of old she must look with enough diamonds glittering on her finger to have bought her an apartment outright.

She was grateful for the armour of her expensive new clothes in a room where every other woman looked amazing—but it wasn't that which made her feel suddenly wistful. All the wives and girlfriends looked so *happy.* Did she? Did she look how a new bride was supposed to look—all dewy-eyed and serene? She wondered if anyone guessed that inside she felt as if she were clinging onto this strange new reality by the tips of her fingers.

But sometimes you built things up in your head and they weren't nearly as bad as you'd feared. The woman who'd designed Alek's apartment—Alannah—turned out to be a lot less scary than Ellie had imagined. Maybe because she was married to Niccolò da Conti, a stunningly handsome man who seemed to command almost as much attention as Alek and who clearly adored his wife.

Some of the guests were more memorable than others. Ellie stood for ages talking to Luis and Carly and discovered they were all friends going back years. When the sultan arrived—last—Ellie was overcome with nerves because she'd never met a royal before and might not have bought such high heels if she'd thought about having to curtsey in them. But Murat was charming and quickly put her at her ease, and his Welsh wife was lovely.

Ellie watched the exalted group of men joshing and laughing with one another and as she listened to their wives eagerly discussing their social calendars she tried not to feel like the outsider in their midst.

'Let me see your ring, Ellie,' said Alannah, catching hold of Ellie's hand and peering down at the glittering band. 'Gosh, it's beautiful. Those diamonds look almost blue—they're so bright.' She raised her eyes and smiled. 'So tell us about Alek's proposal—was it romantic?'

Ellie wished she'd anticipated this perfectly understandable question so that she could have prepped an answer. She didn't know how honest to be. She didn't know how much he'd already told them. She knew that apart from the faint swell of her breasts, there was no outward sign of her pregnancy. Maybe some of the women had already guessed the reason why the world's most reluctant groom had put a ring on her finger, but for some reason she didn't want to tell them. Not right now. Couldn't tonight be her fantasy? Couldn't she play the part of the shiny-eyed new bride and pretend, just this once?

So she curved a smile—and found it was stupidly easy to let her voice tremble with excitement as she allowed herself to be caught up in the memory. 'He kissed me in Bond Street and almost stopped the traffic.'

'Really?' Alannah smiled. 'Not *another* "get a room" moment from the famously private Alek Sarantos? Didn't I read something about him kissing you while you were working as a waitress?'

A sudden lump in her throat was making words difficult and Ellie just nodded. She wondered if Alek ever thought about that moment of passion beneath the starry sky. That split second of thoughtlessness, setting off the domino effect which had brought them to this moment. Did he regret it?

Yet as she glanced over to see him deep in conversation with Murat, she found that she *couldn't* regret what had happened, because sometimes your feelings defied logic. Something incredible had happened when she'd lain with him and she couldn't seem to scrub that memory away. He could be arrogant and cold, but there was something about him which drew her to him like a magnet, no matter how hard she tried to resist. It might be senseless to care about him, but did that mean it was wrong? Could you stop yourself from falling in love with someone, even if you knew it was a mistake?

She saw him smile at something Murat said and he responded by gesturing expansively with his hands in a way an Englishman would never do. She'd never been to Greece, but in that moment he seemed to sum up everything about that sun-washed land with its ancient history and its passions.

Yet that side of his life remained a mystery to her. He'd clammed up when she'd mentioned his birthplace on the way here. He had snapped and changed the subject and done that not very subtle thing of letting her know who had all the power in this relationship. How much did she really know about the father of her baby? She stared down at the slice of lime which was bobbing around in her tonic water. Probably as much as she knew about her own father.

But she pushed the troublesome thoughts away and tried to enter into the spirit of the evening. She nibbled on a few canapés and stood beside Alek as he made a short speech about love and marriage, with just the right touch of lightness and solemnity.

And that was the bit she found hardest. The moment when she wanted to shake off the hand which was resting lightly on her shoulders, because it was kick-starting all kinds of reactions. It was making her want to feel that extraordinary *connection* with him again. To lie with him and feel him deep inside her. To wonder why the hell she'd insisted on separate rooms—not realising that denial would only feed the hunger she felt for him.

She spoke to all the guests with just the right amount of interest and pretended she was Ellie the trainee hotel manager again—chatting away with smiling attention.

People were never terrifying if you got them on a one-to-one basis, no matter how initially intimidating they were. She met a judge, a Hollywood actress and a Spaniard named Vicente de Castilla, whose buccaneering appearance was attracting plenty of covert glances. But gorgeous as Vicente was, there was only one man who commanded Ellie's attention and she knew exactly where he was at any given point in the evening. He seemed to command all her attention and it was difficult not to stare. Beneath the fractured rainbow light of the chandeliers, his hair gleamed like jet. At one point he slowly turned his head to look at her, his blue eyes blazing as they held her in their spotlight. And she turned away, feeling curiously *exposed*…stiffening slightly when he came to stand beside her, sliding his arm around her waist with easy possession. As if he touched her like that all the time, when they both knew he didn't touch her at all.

She knew it was done to add authenticity to their marriage. She *knew* his touch meant nothing, but unfortunately her body didn't. It was sending frantic messages to her brain. It was making her want more. It was making her wish it were all real. That he'd married her because he loved her and not because there was a baby on the way.

Quickly excusing herself, she made her way to the restroom where Alannah was standing in front of the mirror, brushing her long black hair.

'Enjoying your wedding party?' she questioned.

Ellie pulled out a convincing smile as she met the other woman's denim-blue eyes. 'It's wonderful. Such a gorgeous place. And all Alek's friends seem lovely and very welcoming,' she added.

Alannah laughed. 'You don't *have* to say that—but thanks very much all the same. We're just all very happy for him, that's all. Nobody thought he would ever settle down. I expect you know that he's never really committed to anyone before? Mind you, Niccolò was exactly the same. They just need to find the right woman,' she said, pulling open the door and wiggling her fingers in a little wave of farewell.

Ellie watched the door swing closed again.

The right woman.

If only they knew. Would they all be choking into their champagne if they realised that the newlyweds were about as far apart as two people could be?

But *she* had been the one who insisted on having separate rooms, hadn't she? She'd been the one who had thought that keeping distance between them would help protect her against emotional pain. And it didn't. Because she found herself wanting Alek no matter how hard she tried not to want him.

She gazed at her reflection, thinking that her appearance betrayed nothing of her turmoil. The silvery silk dress gleamed and her professionally blow-dried hair fell in a soft cascade over her shoulders. She didn't look like herself, and she didn't feel like herself either. All she could feel was a longing so powerful that it felt like a physical pain. It might be crazy but she wasn't going to lie…and the truth was that she wanted Alek.

She closed her eyes.

She wanted more than that single encounter which had resulted in this pregnancy. She wanted something slow and precious because everything else had happened so *fast*. She'd become pregnant after that one time. She had demanded marriage and moved in with him. She'd attended doctor's appointments, taken care of herself and tried to keep busy. But she wasn't a cardboard cut-out. She still had feelings—feelings she'd tried to put on ice, only somewhere along the way they had started to melt.

So what was she going to do about it? Was she brave enough to go after what she really wanted and to hell with the consequences? Did she dare risk pain for another moment of passion?

Picking up her handbag, she walked out into the corridor where Alek's shadow fell over her and instantly she froze.

'Oh,' she said, attempting a smile. 'You startled me.'

Alek felt a pulse hammering away at his temple as he stared at her. She was close enough to touch and it was distracting. *Theos*, but it was distracting. Her hair was tumbling down over her shoulders and she had that slightly untouchable beauty of all brides. But all he could think about was the creaminess of her skin and the scent of something which smelt like roses, or cinnamon. Maybe both. He felt his throat thicken. 'I was looking for you.'

'Well…here I am,' she said, and as she met his eyes her lips parted. 'What exactly do you want?'

Alek went very still. He saw the darkening of her eyes and heard the dip of her voice, but it was more than that which told him what was on her mind. He'd been around enough women to realise when they were sending out messages of sexual availability—it was just that he hadn't been expecting it with Ellie. Not tonight. He knew that she considered the wedding a farce. That they hadn't been honest with anyone, least of all themselves. Nobody knew the real reason for this wedding,

but he'd justified not telling his friends about the baby
by remembering what the doctor had said—that there
was a slightly higher risk of miscarriage until after the
twelve-week mark. And something about those caution-
ary words had made him realise how much he wanted
this baby—for reasons he didn't care to fathom. He
realised that the life she carried inside her *mattered*.
Should he tell her that? Should he?

But suddenly he wasn't thinking about the baby and
neither, it seemed, was she. He could almost *see* the invitation glinting from her eyes and although he wanted
her more badly than he'd ever wanted anyone—one
last stab of conscience told him to hang fire. That the
most sensible option would be if they ended the night
as they'd begun it. Separately.

But sometimes the right decision was the wrong decision when it went against everything your body was
crying out for. The ache in his groin was unbearable
as he reached for her hand, which was trembling, just
like his.

He studied the sheen of her fingernails before lifting his head in a clashing of eyes. 'I want you,' he said
unsteadily. 'Do you have any idea how much?'

'I think I'm getting the general idea.'

'But I'm not going to do this if it's not what *you*
want.' He stared at her intently. 'Do you understand?'

'Alek.' One of the silvery straps of her dress slipped
off one shoulder and she pushed it back again with fingers which were trembling and her grey eyes looked
wary. As if she was suddenly out of her depth. As if
the words she was about to say were difficult. 'You...
you're an experienced man. You must know how much
I want you.'

He shook his head. 'I know that your body wants me and that physically we're very compatible. But if you're going to wake up in the morning with tears all over my pillow because you're regretting what happened, then I'll back off right now and we'll act like this conversation never happened.'

There was silence. A silence which seemed to go on for countless minutes.

'I don't want you to back off,' she whispered at last.

His heart pounded and his body grew hard. He raised her hand to his lips and although the now faint voice of his conscience made one last, weak appeal, ruthlessly he brushed it aside. 'Then let's get home,' he said roughly. 'So I can take you to bed.'

CHAPTER NINE

ALEK FELT AS if he wanted to explode but he knew he
had to take it slowly.

He and Ellie had left the party almost immediately—
smiling through the rose petals and rice showering
down on their heads. But the journey home had been
tense and silent, in direct contrast to their teasing ban-
ter at the wedding reception. He hadn't trusted himself
to touch her and maybe Ellie had felt the same because
she'd sat apart from him, her shoulders stiff. The tension in the car had grown and grown until it had felt
as if he was having difficulty breathing. *And wasn't he
terrified that she'd changed her mind?*

Her face had been paler than usual as they'd ridden
up in the elevator. The space had seemed to close in
on them until the ping announcing their arrival at the
penthouse had broken into the silence like the chime
of a mighty bell. He'd convinced himself that she *had*
changed her mind as he'd unlocked the door to his apartment. But it seemed she hadn't. *Oh.* She…had…*not*—
and the minute the door had closed behind them they
had been all over each other.

Their first kiss had been hungry—almost clumsy.
They'd reached blindly for each other in the hall as

some ornament had gone crashing to the ground, and he'd ended up pushing her up against the wall with his hand halfway up her dress until he'd realised that he hadn't wanted to do it to her like that. Not on her wedding night. Not after last time. He wanted to show her he knew the meaning of the word *consideration*. He wanted to make love to her slowly—very slowly. And so she had allowed him to lead her to his bedroom where now she stood, looking around her with a slightly nervous expression on her face.

'I suppose this must be the scene of a thousand seductions?'

'A rather inflated estimate,' he responded drily. 'You don't want me to lie to you? To say you're the first woman I've brought here?'

She gave a funny little smile. 'No, of course not.'

'I haven't asked you about any of *your* former lovers, have I?'

'No, that's right. You haven't.'

He wondered what he was trying to do—whether he was trying to sabotage things before they'd even got started. Why the hell hadn't he just told her that in her silvery gown she eclipsed every other woman he'd ever known? That she was beautiful and soft and completely desirable? With a small growl of anger directed mainly at himself, he pulled her into his arms and kissed her again and he heard the gasping little sound she made as she caught hold of his shoulders. He kissed her for a long time, until she started to relax—until she began to press herself against his body and the barrier of their clothes suddenly seemed like something he couldn't endure for a second longer. He led her over to the bed and sat her down on the edge, before getting down on his knees in front of her.

'What are you doing?' she joked weakly as he began to unstrap one of her shoes. 'You've already made the proposal.'

He lifted his gaze; his expression mocking. 'I thought it was you who did the proposing?'

'Oh, yes.' She tipped her head back and expelled a breath as he started rubbing the pad of his thumb over her instep. 'So I did.'

He removed both shoes and peeled off her silvery wedding dress before laying her back on the bed and kicking off his shoes and socks. He lay down next to her, pushing the hair from her face and brushing his lips over hers, taking his time. 'You are very beautiful,' he said.

'I'm—'

He silenced her with the press of his forefinger over her mouth. 'The correct response is, thank you, Alek.'

She swallowed. 'Thank you, Alek.'

'But I'm afraid of hurting you.'

She reached her hand up to brush a strand of hair off his forehead and suddenly her face looked very tender. He felt his heart clench.

'Because of the baby?' she asked softly.

He nodded, still wary around that shining tenderness which instinctively put him on his guard. 'Because of the baby,' he repeated.

'The doctor said it was okay.' She leant forward and kissed him. 'But that maybe we should avoid swinging from the chandeliers.'

'I don't have any…chandeliers,' he said indistinctly, but suddenly the flirting word games of foreplay became swamped by a far more primitive need to possess. Refocusing his attention, he began to explore her properly—touching the coolness of her flesh above her stocking tops as she began to make soft little sounds of pleasure. Did she feel his uncharacteristic hesitation as his fingers tiptoed upwards? Could she hear the loud pounding of his heart? Did she know that suddenly—ridiculously—this felt completely new?

'It's no different from how it was before,' she whispered. 'I'm still me.'

He kissed her again. But it *was* different. She was like a ship carrying a precious cargo. His baby. He swallowed as his finger trailed over her navel and he could tell she was holding her breath, expelling it only when he eased his hand beneath the elastic of her panties and cupped her where she was warm and wet.

'Oh,' she said.

His mouth hovered over hers. 'Oh,' he echoed indistinctly as, blindly, he reached for his belt and suddenly she was unbuttoning his shirt, making a low sound of pleasure as she slipped it away from his shoulders. And he stopped thinking. He just gave himself up to every erotic second. There was a snap as he released her bra and her breasts tumbled into his eager hands. He felt the slide of her bare thigh against his as she used her foot to push his trousers down his legs. He could smell the musky aroma of her sex as he peeled off her panties and threw them aside.

Their eyes met in a long moment and he felt shaken by the sudden unexpected intimacy of that.

He slid the flat of his hand over her hip. 'I don't want to hurt you—'

She bit her lip, as if she was about to say something

controversial but had thought better of it at the last moment. 'Just make love to me, Alek,' she said with a simple sincerity which tore through him like a flame.

Slowly he eased himself inside her, uttering something guttural in Greek, which wasn't like him. But none of this was *like* him. He'd never felt this close to a woman before, nor so aware of her as a person rather than as just a body. It rocked him to the core and, yes, it intimidated him, too—and he didn't like that. He wasn't used to being out of control. To feeling as if he were putty in a woman's hands. He groaned. Maybe not putty. Because putty was soft, wasn't it? And he was hard. Ah, *neh*. He was very hard. Harder than he could ever remember. And if he wasn't careful, he was going to come too soon.

This is sex, he told himself fiercely. *Sex which you both want. So treat it like sex.* Breaking eye contact, he buried his face in her neck as he began to take command, each slow and deliberate thrust demonstrating his power and control. He smiled against her skin when she moaned his name and smiled some more when she began to gasp in a rising crescendo. 'Oh, yes…*yes*!'

He raised his head and watched as she came. Saw her tip her head back and her eyes close. He saw her body shudder and heard the disbelieving little cry which followed. And then he saw the first big fat tear which rolled down her cheek to be quickly followed by another, and he frowned. Because hadn't she cried last time—and wasn't the deal supposed to be that this time there were no tears? No regrets. His mouth twisted. No nothing—only pleasure.

'Alek,' she whispered and he could no longer hold

back—letting go in a great burst of seed which pumped from his body as if it was never going to stop.

He must have fallen asleep, and when eventually he opened his eyes again he found her sleeping, too. Rolling away, he stared up at the ceiling, but although his heart was still pounding with post-orgasmic euphoria he felt confusion slide a cold and bewildering trail across his skin.

He glanced around the room. Her wedding dress lay on the floor along with his own discarded trousers and shirt. His usually pristine bedroom looked as if someone had ransacked it and he found himself remembering the ornament breaking in the hall—a priceless piece of porcelain shattered into a hundred pieces which had crunched beneath his feet.

What was it about her which made him lose control like that? He turned his head to look at her again—a pale Venus rising from the crumpled white waves of the sheets. His gaze shifted to her belly—still flat— and his heart clenched as he thought about the reality of being a father.

The fears he'd been trying to silence now crowded darkly in his mind. What if certain traits were inherited rather than learnt? Wasn't that one of the reasons why he'd always ruled out fatherhood as a life choice, not daring to take the risk of failing as miserably at the task as his own father had done?

She began to stir and opened her eyes and he thought how bright and clear they looked, with no hint of tears now.

'Why do you cry?' he asked suddenly. 'When I make love to you?'

Ellie brushed her fringe out of her eyes, more as

a stalling mechanism than anything else. His question suggested a layer of intimacy she hadn't been expecting and that surprised her. This was supposed to be about sex, wasn't it? That was what she thought his agenda was. The only agenda there could possibly be—no matter what her feelings for him were. If she suddenly came out and told him the reason she'd cried was because he made her feel *complete*, then wouldn't he laugh, or run screaming in the opposite direction? If she told him that when he was deep inside her, it felt as if she'd been waiting her whole life for that moment, wouldn't it come over as fanciful, or—worse—needy? If she told him she was crying for all the things she would never have from him—like his *love*—wouldn't that make her seem like just another woman greedily trying to take from him something she knew he would never give?

She told him part of the truth. 'Because you are an amazing lover.'

'And that makes you cry?'

'Blame my hormones.'

'I suppose I should be flattered,' he drawled. 'Though, of course, that would depend on how experienced you are.'

She pushed her hair out of her eyes and narrowed her eyes. 'Are you fishing to find out how many lovers I've had before you?'

'Is it unreasonable of me to want to know?'

She sat up and looked down at his dark body outlined against the tumbled bedding. 'I've had one long-term relationship before this and that's all I'm going to say on the subject, because I think it's distasteful to discuss it, especially at a time like this. Is that acceptable?'

'Completely acceptable would be for there to have been no one before me.' He smiled, but it was a smile tinged with intent rather than humour. 'And since I intend to drive the memory of anyone else from your mind for ever, you'd better come back over here and kiss me right now.'

His hand starfished over her breast and, even though his questioning was unfair and his attitude outrageously macho, Ellie couldn't seem to stop herself from reacting to him. She wondered what he'd say if she told him he'd banished every other man from her mind the first time he'd kissed her. Would he be surprised? Probably not. Women probably told him that kind of thing all the time.

It hadn't been her plan to have him parting her legs again quite so soon, and certainly not to cry his name out like a kind of prayer as he entered her a second time. But she did. And afterwards she was left feeling exposed and naked in all kinds of ways, while he remained as much of an enigma as he'd always done.

She lay there wrapped in his arms and although his lips pressing against her shoulder were making his words muffled, they were still clear enough to hear.

'I'm thinking that we ought to start sleeping together from now on—what about you?' he said. 'Because it would be crazy not to.'

It was a strangely emotionless conclusion to their lovemaking and Ellie didn't know why she was so disappointed, because he was only behaving true to form. But she made sure her smile didn't slip and show her disappointment. She kept her expression as neutral as his. He wanted to treat sex as simply another appetite to be fed, did he?

Well, then, so would she.

She lay back against the pillow and coiled her arms around his neck. 'Absolutely crazy,' she agreed huskily.

CHAPTER TEN

HER WEDDING RING no longer mocked her and neither did the closed door of Alek's room. Because Ellie now shared that room, just as she shared the bed within and the man who slept in it.

Pulling on a tea dress, Ellie began to brush her hair. To all intents and purposes, she and Alek now had a 'full' marriage. Ever since the night of their wedding—when they'd broken the sexual drought—they had been enjoying the pleasures of the marital bed in a way which had surpassed her every expectation.

He could turn her on with a single smile. He could have her naked in his arms in seconds. Even when she told herself she ought to resist him—in a futile attempt to regain some control over her shattered equilibrium—she would fail time and time again.

'But you can't resist me, *poulaki mou*,' he would murmur, as if he guessed exactly what she was trying to do. 'You know you really want me.'

And that was the trouble. She did. She couldn't seem to stop wanting him, no matter how much she tried to tell herself that she was getting in too deep. And if sometimes she lay looking wistfully at the ceiling after he'd made love to her, she made sure it was while Alek was asleep. She tried to stop herself from caring for him too much—and certainly to hide her feelings for him. Because that wasn't what he wanted. This was as close to a business arrangement as a personal relationship could be.

But her life had changed in other ways, too. They started going out more as a couple, so that at times the marriage felt almost authentic. He took her to the theatre, which she loved. They watched films and ate in fancy restaurants and explored all the tiny backstreets of the city. They drove down to the south coast, to visit Luis and Carly in their amazing house which overlooked a beautiful river.

And yet, despite the increased richness of their day-to-day existence, it was difficult to get to know the real man behind the steely image, despite the external thaw between them. He could do that thoughtful stuff of massaging her feet when she was tired, but if his fingers hadn't been made of flesh and blood she might have thought she was being administered to by some sort of robot. Sometimes it felt as if she didn't know him any better than when that list of his likes and dislikes had been circulated to staff at The Hog before his arrival. She still wasn't sure what motivated him, or what made him sometimes wake her in the night when he'd had a dream which had clearly been a bad one. She would turn to find his eyes open but not really seeing, his body tense—suspended between the two worlds of sleeping and waking. But when she gently shook him awake, his face would become guarded and he would deflect her concerns with something sensual enough to send any questions scuttling from her mind.

He was a master at concealing the real man who

lay beneath; adept at avoiding questions. His cool blue eyes would narrow if she tried to probe more deeply; his gaze becoming one of sapphire ice. *Don't push me*, those eyes seemed to say. But that didn't stop Ellie from trying, even though he would deflect her questions by sliding his hand beneath her skirt and starting to make love to her. He'd leave her breathless and panting as all her questions dissolved and nothing was left but the pleasure he gave her, time after time. And she didn't give up. She just lowered her sights a little. She stopped expecting big revelations and just concentrated on the little ones.

And every time she discovered something about him, it felt like a major victory—like another little missing bit of the jigsaw. In those sleepy moments after making love, he told her about how he'd worked his way up from being a kitchen boy in Athens, to owning an entire chain of restaurants. He told her about working on a fancy vineyard in California, so that he knew all about the wine trade. He made a wistful face when he described his friend Murat's beautiful country of Qurhah and told her how big the stars looked when you were out in the middle of the desert. He explained how life was just one great big learning experience and everything he knew, he had taught himself.

And one thing she was learning faster than any other was that it wasn't so easy to put the brakes on her own emotions. She wasn't sure if it was her fluctuating hormones which were changing her feelings towards her Greek husband, or just that sex had removed the protective shield from her heart. No matter how hard she tried, she couldn't seem to stop herself from caring for him in a way that went bone-deep. Her heart was stubbornly refusing to listen to all the logic her head tried to throw at it.

Yet she *knew* what happened to women who were stupid enough to love men who didn't love them back. She'd watched her mother's life become diminished because she had wanted something she was never going to have. She'd wasted years on bitterness and resentment, because she'd refused to accept that you couldn't make another person do what you wanted them to.

And that was not going to happen to her.

She wouldn't let it.

Smoothing down the folds of her tea dress, she walked into the kitchen to find Alek seated at the table, a half-full coffee pot beside him as he worked his way through a stack of financial newspapers. He glanced up as she walked in, his eyes following her every step, like a snake bewitched by a charmer. She had become used to his very macho appraisal of her appearance and, with a certain amount of guilt, had grown to enjoy it.

He put the newspaper down as she sat down opposite him and his eyes glinted as she reached for the honeypot.

'I enjoyed licking my favourite honey last night,' he murmured.

Her eyes widened. 'Alek!'

'Are you blushing, Ellie?'

'Certainly not. It's just the steam from the coffee making me hot.'

'Would you like to come to Italy?' he questioned.

Ellie dropped the little wooden spatula back in the pot. 'You mean, with you?' she said.

'Of course with me. Unless you had someone else in mind?' He smiled and gave a lazy shrug. 'We can treat it as a kind of honeymoon, if you like. I thought we could go to Lucca. I have business in Pisa and I can go there afterwards while you fly home. And Lucca is an extraordinarily pretty city. They call it the hidden gem of Tuscany. It has an oval piazza instead of a square one and a tower with trees growing out of the top. Lots of dark and winding streets and iconic churches. You've never been there?'

She shook her head. 'I've never been anywhere apart from a day trip to Calais with my mother.'

'Well, then.' He raised his eyebrows. 'Didn't you once tell me how much you longed to travel?'

Yes, she'd told him that, but that had been when she'd still had ambition burning big in her heart. When travelling had been part of her work plan and independence had been a believable dream which seemed to have fallen by the wayside since she'd discovered she was pregnant. She thought of Italy—with its green hills and terracotta roofs. All those famous churches and marble statues she'd only ever seen in pictures.

Wouldn't it be good to go on an unexpected honeymoon for some sunshine and culture—even if it was the most unconventional honeymoon in the history of the world? And yet, just the fact that Alek had suggested it brightened her mood. Wasn't this a bit of a breakthrough from her enigmatic husband? Could she possibly make it a *real* honeymoon—as if they were people who genuinely cared about one another, rather than two people who were just trying to make the best of a bad situation?

She began to spread the thick, golden honey on her toast and smiled at him. 'I'd like that,' she said. 'I'd like that very much.'

'*Thavmassios.* We will fly the day after tomorrow.'

* * *

Two days later their flight touched down in Pisa where Alek had arranged for a car to take them to Lucca. The drive took less than an hour and they arrived in the late afternoon, when all the shops were closed and the place had a drowsy feel about it. Ellie looked up at the high city walls and thought she'd never seen anywhere more beautiful. Alek had rented an old-fashioned apartment overlooking a sheltered courtyard, where geraniums tumbled brightly from terracotta pots. The wooden frame of their bed was dark and worn and the sheets were crisp and scented with lavender.

She knew that they weren't like other traditional honeymooners, and yet as he closed the apartment door behind them Ellie was filled with something which felt awfully like *hope*. She thought: *We're in a city where nobody knows us. Two strangers blending with all the other strangers.* Mightn't there be a chance that here the man she had married would let his mask slip for once, when there was only her to see?

They made love, unpacked and showered and then Alek took her out to dinner in a garden shimmering with candlelight where they ate the local delicacy of *tortelli lucchese*—a bright yellow stuffed pasta, topped with a rich ragu sauce. Afterwards, they sat beneath the star-spangled sky and drank their coffee—their fingers linking together on the table, and for once it felt real. As if they really were genuine honeymooners and not just a pair of actors acting out the parts. When he took her home, she put her arms around his neck and kissed him passionately and he picked her up and carried her to the bedroom with a look on his face which made her tremble.

The following morning Ellie awoke alone. For a minute she lay there as sensual memories of the previous night filtered into her mind, then she pulled on a robe, splashed cold water over her sleepy face and went off to find Alek. He was sitting on their balcony with breakfast laid out on the small table and the aroma of coffee vying with the powerful scent of jasmine.

'Where did all this come from?' she questioned as she looked at the crisp bread, the buttery pastries and the rich red jam.

'I got up early and you looked much too peaceful to wake. I went for a walk around the city walls and called in at the *panificio* on the way back.' He poured out two cups of coffee and pushed one across the table and smiled. 'So what would you like to do today?'

And suddenly—she had no idea what caused it— the perfect scene before her began to disintegrate. It was like tugging at a tiny nick on a delicate piece of fabric which suddenly ripped open. It all seemed so *false*. There was Alek—looking ruggedly handsome in an open-necked white shirt and dark trousers, his blue eyes gleaming like jewels. Yet his polite distance made her feel as if she were just another item to be ticked off on his agenda. His smile seemed more automatic than genuine and she found herself resenting his control and his inbuilt detachment. *This has nothing to do with reality*, she thought, as a feeling of rebellion began to bubble up inside her.

She sat down and looked at him. 'Actually, I'd like to talk about the baby.'

He stilled. 'The baby?'

'That's right. Our baby. You know. The one we never talk about.' She paused and laid her hand over her stomach. 'Because although it's growing inside me, we never discuss it, do we? We always seem to skirt around the subject. I mean, I go to the doctor and report back with a clean bill of health—and you manage to look pleased. And once or twice you've even come with me and you nod your head in all the right places, but you still act like nothing's happening, or as if it's happening to someone else. As if none of this is real.'

A shuttered look came over his face and he shrugged. 'I suppose we could sit around having hypothetical discussions about what we're going to do and how we're going to react when the baby arrives, but why bother when it's impossible to predict?'

'So you just want to ignore it until it happens?'

His eyes became hooded and suddenly he didn't look quite so detached. 'Isn't that what I've just said?'

And Ellie heard the distortion in his words—the crack of bitterness he couldn't quite hide. She saw the way his body had grown hard and tense and wondered what had caused it. And she wondered why she didn't have the guts to come right out and ask him, and keep on asking him until he finally gave her an answer. What was she so afraid of? Scared that if she unlocked his secrets, she'd discover something to kill off the dormant hope which lingered so foolishly in her heart? Surely it was better to know and to face up to the truth, no matter how grim it was… Better that than building dreams which were never going to materialise.

'You know, through all the time we've been together, you've never spoken about your childhood,' she said. 'Apart from a throwaway comment about never having used public transport because your father owned an island.'

'And why do you think that is?' he questioned. 'If somebody doesn't want to talk about something, there's usually a reason why.'

'You've never told me anything about your family,' she continued stubbornly. 'Not a single thing. I don't even know if you've got any brothers or sisters—'

'I don't.'

'And you've never mentioned your parents.'

Unsmilingly, he looked into her eyes. 'Maybe that's because I don't want to.'

'Alek.' She leant forward. 'You need to tell me.'

'Why?' he snapped.

'Because this baby is going to share your parents' genes. Your father—'

'Is dead,' he said flatly. 'And believe me, you'd better hope that our baby doesn't share many of his genes.'

A shiver ran down her spine. 'And what about your mother?'

For a moment there was silence. 'What about her?'

Ellie was unprepared for the savage note in his voice or the bunching of his powerful shoulders. Everything about his reaction told her she was entering dangerous territory—but she knew she couldn't let up. Not this time. If she backtracked now she might win his temporary approval, but then what? She would simply be signing up to a life of half-truths. Bringing up a baby in a world of ignorance, where nothing was what it really seemed. Because knowledge was power. *And wasn't the balance of power in this relationship already hopelessly unequal?*

'Is she still alive?'

'I don't know,' he snapped, his voice as cold as ice. 'I don't know a damned thing about her. Do you want me to spell it out for you in words of one syllable, Ellie? She walked out on me when I was a baby. And while I'm known for my amazing sense of recall—not even I can remember that. Are you satisfied now?'

Ellie's head was spinning. *His mother had walked out on him.* Wasn't that the worst thing that could happen to someone? Hadn't she read somewhere that it was better to be abused than abandoned, and wondered at the time if that was true? She supposed you could always challenge your abuser—but if you were deserted, wouldn't that leave you with no choice except to feel empty and bewildered? She imagined a tiny baby waking up one morning crying for his mother—only that mother never came. How would that feel, to miss the comfort of a maternal embrace and never know it again? Even if the bond wasn't strong, a cuddle would still feel like safety to a helpless infant. On some primitive and subliminal level—would that make it impossible for you to put your trust in a woman afterwards? Would that explain his coldness and his lack of real intimacy, no matter how many times they had sex?

'What…what happened?'

'I just told you.'

'But you didn't.' She met his gaze, determined not to be cowed by the fury sparking from those cold blue depths. 'You only gave me the bare facts.'

'And didn't it occur to you that maybe that's all I wanted to give you?' Pushing back his chair, he got up from the table and began to pace around the veranda like a man in a cell. 'Why don't you learn when enough is enough?'

She'd never seen him so angry and a few weeks ago Ellie might have backed down, but not any more. She wasn't someone who was trying to win his affection or keep the peace, no matter what. She was a mother-to-be and she wanted to be the best mother she possibly could be—and that meant decoding her baby's father, even if he didn't want her to. Even if it pushed them further apart, it was a risk she had to take.

'Because it's not enough,' she said stubbornly.

'What difference does it make that a woman walked out of a house on a Greek island over thirty years ago?'

'It makes all kinds of difference. I want to know about *her*. I want to know whether she was artistic, or good at math. I'm trying to join up all the dots, Alek—to imagine what kind of characteristics our baby might inherit. Maybe it's extra important to me because I don't know much about my own father. If things were different, I'd have learnt the answers to some of these questions already.'

Alek stared at her as her passionate words broke into the quiet Italian morning. Her own upbringing hadn't been much of a picnic but, despite all that, her mother had stuck by her, hadn't she? Ellie hadn't been rejected by the one person you were supposed to be able to rely on. Behind her the jasmine and miniature lemon trees made her look like a character in a painting. In her silky robe she looked fresh and young, and nothing could disguise the flicker of hope in her eyes. Did she think there was going to be some fairy-tale ending, that he could soothe everything over and make everything okay with a few carefully chosen words?

His jaw tightened. Maybe he *should* tell her the truth. Let her understand the kind of man he really was—and why. Let her know that his emotional coldness wasn't something he'd just invented to pass the time. It had been ground into him from the start—embedded too deeply for him to be any other way. Maybe knowing that would nip any rosy dreams she was in danger of nurturing. Show her why the barriers he'd erected around himself were impenetrable. *And why he wouldn't want them any other way.*

'There were no custody visits or vacations,' he said. 'For a long time, I knew nothing about my mother. Or indeed, any mother. When you grow up without something, you don't even realise you're missing it. Her name was never mentioned in front of me, and the only women I knew were my father's whores.'

She flinched at his use of the word and he saw her compose her face into an expression of understanding. 'It's perfectly reasonable not to like the women who supplanted your mother—'

'Oh, please. Quit the amateur psychology,' he interrupted, pushing his fingers impatiently through his hair. 'I'm not making a prudish judgement because it makes me feel better. They *were* whores. They looked like whores and acted like whores. He paid them for sex. They were the only women I came in contact with. I grew up thinking that all females caked their face in make-up and wore skirts short enough for you to see their knickers.' And one in particular who had invited a boy of twelve to take her knickers down so that she could *show him a good time.*

Did she believe him now? Was that why she was biting her lip? He could almost see her mind working overtime as she searched for something to say—as if trying to find a positive spin to put on what he'd just told her. He could have saved her the trouble and told her there was none.

'But…you must have had friends,' she said, a touch of desperation in her voice now. 'You must have looked at *their* mothers, and wondered what had happened to yours.'

'I had no friends,' he said flatly. 'My life was carefully controlled. I might as well have had a prison as a house. I saw no one except for the servants—my father liked childless, unmarried servants who could devote all their time to him. And if you have nothing with which to compare, then no comparisons can be made. His island was remote and inaccessible. He ran everything and owned everything. I lived in a vast complex which was more like a palace and I was tutored at home. I didn't find out anything about my mother until I was seven years old and when I did—the boy who told me was beaten.'

He stared into space. Should he tell her that the boy's injuries had been so bad that he'd been airlifted to the hospital on the mainland and had never returned? And that the boy's parents—even though they had been extremely poor—had threatened to go to the police? Alek had only been young but he remembered the panic which had swirled around the complex as a result. He remembered the fearful faces of his father's aides, as if the old man really *had* overstepped the mark this time. But he'd wriggled out of it, just as he always did. Money had been offered, and accepted. Money got you whatever it was you wanted. It bought silence as well as sex—and another catastrophe had been averted. *And hadn't he done that, too? Hadn't he paid off Ellie's contract with the Irishwoman with the same ruthlessness which his father would have employed?*

He saw the distress on her face and tried to imagine how this must sound through her ears. Incredible, probably. Like one of those porn films his father's body-guards used to watch, late into the night. He wondered if he stopped the story now, whether it would be enough to make her understand why he was not like other men. But she had demanded the truth and perhaps she would continue to demand it. To niggle away at it, as women invariably did. He realised that for the first time in his life he couldn't just block her out, or refuse to take her calls. To fade her into the background as if she had never existed, which was what he'd always done be-fore. Whether he liked it or not, he was stuck with Ellie Brooks, or Ellie Sarantos as she was now. And maybe she ought to learn that it was better not to ask questions in case you didn't like the answers.

'Anything else you want to know?' he demanded. 'Any other stone you've left unturned?'

'What did the boy tell you about your mother?'

'He told me the truth. That she'd left in the middle of the night with one of the island's fishermen.' He leant back against the intricate wrought-iron tracings of the balustrade. Somewhere in the distance he could hear a woman call out in Italian and a child answered. 'It was convenient that she chose a lover with his own boat, for there would have been no other way of her leaving the island without my father knowing about it. But I guess her main achievement was in managing to conduct an affair right under his nose, without the old man find-ing out. And the fact that she was prepared to risk his rage.' His mouth twisted. 'She must have been quite some woman.'

He felt a pain he hadn't felt in a long time. A hot, unwelcome pain which excluded everything else. It stabbed at his heart like a rusty knife and he wished he'd told her to mind her own business, but now he was on a roll and somehow he couldn't stop—pain or no pain. 'My father was completely humiliated by her desertion and determined to wipe away all traces of her. Something he found surprisingly easy to accomplish.' He looked into her bright eyes and then he said it. He'd never admitted it before. Never told anyone. Not the therapist he'd half-heartedly consulted when he'd been living in New York, not any of his friends, nor the women who'd shared his bed in the intervening years and tried to dig away to get at the truth. No one. Not until now. He swallowed as the bitterness rose up inside him like a dark tide. 'I never even saw a photo of her. He destroyed them all. My mother is a stranger to me. I don't even know what she looks like.'

She didn't gasp or utter some meaningless platitude. She just sat there and nodded—as if she was absorbing everything he'd told her. 'But…didn't you ever think about tracking her down and hearing her side of the story?'

He stared at her. 'Why would I want to find a woman who left me behind?'

'Oh, Alek. Because she's your mum, that's why.' She got up and walked across the sun-dappled balcony until she'd reached him. And then she put her arms tightly around his back and held him, as if she never wanted to let him go.

He felt her fingers wrapping themselves around him—like one of those speeded-up documentaries of a fast-growing vine which covered everything in seconds. He tried to move away. He didn't need her softness or her sympathy. He didn't need a thing from her.

He had learnt to live with pain and abandonment and to normalise them. He had pushed his memories into a place of restricted access and had slammed the door on them…what right did she have to make him open the door and stare at all those dark spectres? Did she get some kind of *kick* out of making him confront stuff that was dead and buried?

He wanted to push her away, but her soft body was melting against his. Her fingers were burying themselves in his hair and suddenly he was kissing her like a man who had finally lost control. Losing himself in a kiss as sweet as honey and being sucked into a sensation which was making him feel…

He jerked away from her, his heart pounding. He didn't want to *feel* anything. She'd stirred up stuff which was better left alone and she needed to learn that he was not prepared to tolerate such an intrusion. She'd done it once, but it would not happen again. With an effort, he steadied his breath.

'I don't really want to provide some sort of erotic floor show for the surrounding apartments,' he said, his voice cold as he walked over to the table and poured himself a glass of juice. 'So why don't you sit down and eat your breakfast, before we start sightseeing? You wanted to travel, didn't you, Ellie? Better not waste this golden opportunity.'

CHAPTER ELEVEN

IT WAS NOT a successful honeymoon.

Yes, Lucca was completely gorgeous, and, with her brand-new sun hat crammed down over her hair, Ellie accompanied Alek to every iconic destination the beautiful city had to offer. She saw the tower with the trees growing from the top and drank cappuccino in the famous oval piazza. They visited so many churches that she lost count, and ate their meals in leafy squares and hidden courtyards. There were marble statues in beautiful gardens, where roses grew beside lemon trees. And when the sun became too fierce there were shady streets to walk down, with the rich smell of leather purses and handbags wafting out from the tiny shops which lined them.

But a new *froideur* had settled over Alek. It didn't seem to matter that her first instincts on meeting him had been correct—and that on some level they *were* kindred spirits. They'd both known pretty awful childhoods but had just chosen to deal with them in different ways. And yes, she'd managed at last to extract the truth about his past. She now knew him better…but at what price? It hadn't made them closer, or brought them together in some magical kind of way.

It was as if the confidences she'd forced him to share had ruptured the tentative truce which had existed between them. As if he'd closed right down and shut her out—only this time she sensed there was no going back. No chink of light coming from behind the steely door he had retreated behind. The anger had gone and in its place was a consideration and cool courtesy which made him seem even further away. He spoke to her as if he were her doctor. Was she too hot? Too tired? A little hungry, perhaps? And she would assure him that she felt absolutely fine, because what was the alternative?

But she didn't feel fine. She felt headachey and out of sorts—with a kind of heaviness which seemed to have entered her limbs and which she put down to the new tension which had sprung up between them. She understood now why he was emotionally distant, but she still didn't know how to solve it.

Vasos called several times from London but instead of saying something like, *sorry, but I'm on my honeymoon*—Alek took every call and spent as much time as possible on it. Or so it seemed to Ellie. She would be left sitting on the terrace, her book stuck on the same page while he spoke in a torrent of Greek she couldn't understand.

She stared at the unread pages of her novel. Had she thought this was going to be easy? Had she been naive enough to think that extracting information about his painful childhood might make him warm and open towards her? If she'd known that the opposite would be true, she might have thought twice before quizzing him about the mother who had deserted him. She slammed the book shut. No wonder he was so closed off. So lacklustre about *their* baby.

Feeling queasy, she glanced up to see him standing framed by the miniature orange trees which grew on their leafy terrace and frowning as he slid his cell phone back into his pocket.

'That was Vasos,' he said.

'Again?'

'The new deal on the Rafael building seems to be nearing completion earlier than planned and the architect is flying into London later this evening.'

'And let me guess.' Her voice was light. 'You need to get back?'

'I'm afraid I do. My business in Pisa will have to wait.' His frown deepened as he seemed to look at her properly for the first time. 'You're sweating, Ellie. Are you okay?'

No, she was not okay. She felt hot and dizzy and disillusioned. Maybe it was time to stop grabbing at rainbows and settle for reality.

'I'm fine,' she said tightly. 'I'd better go and pack.'

Something dark and unwanted rose up inside him as Alek watched her go, her shoulders tight with tension. Something which clutched at his heart and made it twist with pain. *Damn her*, he thought. Why hadn't he slapped her down? Why hadn't he refused to answer all those intrusive questions which had done nothing but open up a dark can of worms?

And yet now that he had pushed her away, the sense of relief he'd been anticipating hadn't happened. They'd been doing that thing of sleeping on opposite sides of the bed—their breathing sounding unnaturally loud in the darkness of the night—each knowing the other was awake and yet not speaking. *Because they had nothing left to say.*

Was it some cruel twist of fate which had left him feeling so lost without the softness of her arms around him? A taunting reminder of just how empty and alone rejection could make you feel. And yet wasn't it better this way? For him to do the rejecting rather than risk being pushed away for a second time?

When she returned from packing, he thought her face looked almost translucent beneath the brim of her straw hat, which she had worn during most of the trip. The Italian sun had barely touched her skin and her grey eyes seemed shadowed, and even though he knew he ought to say something he could think of nothing which would fall easily into the empty silence. She was quiet all during the journey back to London and the moment their plane touched down and he turned on his phone, it began to vibrate with a flurry of calls. And deep down, wasn't he glad to have the opportunity to lose himself in the infinitely more straightforward problems of work? Far better than having to confront the silent reproach or the lip she kept biting as if she was trying to hold back tears. He had the car drop her off at the apartment while he went straight to the office.

'You don't mind?' he questioned.

She gave an unconvincing laugh, as if she recognised the question for what it was—a meaningless platitude. 'And if I do? Would you be prepared to put your precious work aside and spend the afternoon with me, if I asked you to?'

'Ellie—'

'I'll take that as a no,' she said with another brittle smile. 'Anyway, I want to have a lie-down. I'm tired.'

After he'd gone she closed the bedroom curtains and, switching her phone to Silent, left it in her handbag on the far side of the room. But she could hear it vibrating like a persistent fly as she lay on the bed drifting in and out of an uncomfortable doze—too lazy to get up and switch it off completely.

By five o'clock she forced herself to get up and saw there were three missed calls from a number she didn't recognise. Muzzily, she took a shower but her mood was still flat as she pulled on a pair of linen trousers and a T-shirt. She was drinking a glass of water when the doorbell rang.

Touching her fingertips to her belly, she went to answer the door to find a blonde woman standing on the step—someone she didn't recognise but who looked oddly familiar.

'Can I help you?' questioned Ellie.

'You don't remember me?'

Ellie shook her head. 'Should I?'

'Probably. I knew you before you were married. I was staying at The Hog when you were working there. Remember now?'

And suddenly the mist cleared. Of course. It was the journalist. The sneaky blonde who had asked those questions which Ellie had stupidly answered, and which had ended up with her getting the sack. She looked into the woman's glacial eyes.

'I've got nothing to say to you,' said Ellie.

'Maybe not. But you might be interested in what I have to say to you.'

'I don't think so.' She started to close the door. 'My husband doesn't like journalists and neither do I.'

'Does your husband realise he has a brother?'

Sweat broke out on her forehead as Ellie leant against the door. She thought about what Alek had told her about his childhood. And amid all the pain and the heartbreak of his upbringing, he hadn't mentioned his father having any more children. *But maybe his mother had gone on to have more children. If he'd never met her, he wouldn't actually know, would he?* 'You're lying,' she croaked.

'Why would I lie? Actually, he has a *twin* brother. Yeah, I thought you'd be interested.'

Yes, she was interested but that didn't stop Ellie from shaking her head, because the dramatic words seemed to make no sense. 'But if what you say is true, how come you know and he doesn't?'

The woman shrugged. 'His brother asked me to track him down and speak to him. He wanted to know whether Alek would be receptive to a meeting. The first part wasn't difficult but the second part was, because I could never get close enough to ask him. Men like Alek Sarantos are never easy to get close to. He doesn't do interviews and he's not the kind of man who drinks alone in bars, so trying to pick him up was never going to work. And as you say, he doesn't like journalists.'

'Are you surprised?'

'Nothing surprises me any more,' said the woman cynically. 'That's why I couldn't believe my luck when I saw him with you that night. A waitress who was way out of his league and you were making out like two teenagers at a school disco! I thought I had the perfect opportunity to smoke him out, and I was right.'

'Smoke him out?' echoed Ellie in horror.

'Sure. Put a woman into a man's life and immediately you've got another way in.'

'You're disgusting.'

'No, honey. I'm just doing my job.' The journalist

leant forward and tucked a business card into Ellie's free hand. 'Why don't you tell him to call me?'

After she'd gone, Ellie shut the door, leaning back against it and trying very hard to steady her breathing.

A brother.

A *twin* brother.

How could that be? Did Alek know about this explosive fact and was this just one more thing he had deliberately omitted to tell her? She felt so spaced out that she couldn't seem to take it in. Had the journalist being doing what journalists did so well…inventing a story to try to get some sort of reaction? Her heart was pounding and a weird kind of pain was spearing through her and she wasn't sure how long she stood there, only that she couldn't stay there. She couldn't let Alek come home from work and find her slumped there like a zombie.

She forced herself to dress, but the silky tea dress seemed only to mock her. She remembered the day she'd gone shopping, when she'd felt so proud of herself. So stupidly proud. As if managing to run up a massive bill on a man's credit card all by herself was some sort of mega achievement. She remembered how easy she'd found it to spend his money. For all her feisty words, was she really any different from the other women who adored his wealth? He hated gold-diggers. He seemed to hate women in general and now she could understand why.

Never had that famous saying seemed more appropriate.

Give me the child until he is seven and I will give you the man.

Wasn't that just the truth?

Alek had spent the first years of his life deserted by his mother and left alone with a cruel father. Was it any wonder that he'd locked his emotions away and thrown away the key?

She got more and more nervy as time wore on but when eventually Alek arrived home and walked into the sitting room, she thought how weary he looked. She'd been intending to break it to him gently but maybe something in her expression alerted him, because he frowned the minute he saw her.

'What's wrong?'

She'd been racking her brain to come up with the right way of telling him, but maybe there was no *right* way. There were only facts. She couldn't protect him from what she was about to tell him, no matter how much she wanted to.

'You remember that journalist who wrote the diary piece about us?'

He tensed. 'I'm not likely to forget her.'

'Well, she was here today.'

He scowled. 'How the hell did she find out where I lived?'

'I don't think that's really the issue here.'

'No?' His mouth twisted. 'Well, my privacy *is* an issue, something which I thought you might have re-alised by now. What did you tell her this time?' He gave a bitter laugh. 'Did you give her a blow-by-blow account of your husband's tragic childhood?'

'I would *never*—'

'Or maybe you thought you'd announce the baby news.' His words cut over hers. 'Even though we agreed not to say anything before the twelve weeks is up?'

'Actually, she was the one with the news.' She hesitated and then drew a deep breath. 'She told me that you've got a brother.'

His eyes narrowed. 'What the hell are you talking about?'

'Actually, a twin brother.' She licked her lips. 'You didn't know?'

'I don't know what you're talking about,' he said coldly.

'He asked her to contact you, to see if you'd be receptive to a meeting.'

I do not have a brother!' he thundered.

'Alek…' But her words were forgotten as her body was racked by the most piercing pain Ellie had ever felt. Hot knives were chasing through her belly and stabbing deeper and deeper. All the strength was draining from her legs. Shakily, she reached out to grab the edge of the window seat as Alek strode across the room, his face criss-crossed with concern as he caught hold of her.

But she didn't want his concern. She just wanted something to stop the pain. Not just the one in her belly—but the one in her heart.

'Go away!' she mumbled, lashing out at him ineffectively—but she could see something else in his eyes now. Something which scared her. Why was he looking like that? And why had his face gone so white? Following the direction of his gaze, she saw the shocking scarlet contrast of blood as it began to drip onto the polished gleam of the wooden floorboards.

And that must have been when she passed out.

CHAPTER TWELVE

ALEK FELT THE clench of pain around his heart—icy-cold and constricting. He couldn't breathe. He couldn't think. He was powerless to help her and even if he'd been capable of helping her—it seemed he wasn't going to get the chance to try. Ellie didn't want him in the ambulance with her, or so one of the paramedics told him, a faintly embarrassed look on his face as he didn't quite dare look him in the eye.

For the first time in his adult life, Alek discovered the feeling of powerlessness. He couldn't insist on doing things *his* way, or overrule what was happening by the sheer force of his personality or financial clout. He was being forced to accept the bitter facts. That Ellie was sick and their baby's life was in danger. That she was being rushed through the London streets with blue lights flashing and sirens blaring and she didn't want him anywhere near her.

A bitter taste stained his mouth.

Who could blame her?

He drove to the hospital as quickly as he could but his usual unerring sense of direction failed him and he found himself lost in the maze of hospital corridors, until a kindly nurse took pity on him and showed him the way to the unit. His heart was in his mouth as he approached that white and sterile place. And still they wouldn't let him see her.

'But I'm her husband,' he said, wondering if the words sounded as fake as they felt. What right did he have to call himself her husband? Was that why the ward sister was fixing him with a disapproving look? Had Ellie blurted out the truth to her in a moment of weakness, begging the nurses not to allow him anywhere near her—this man who had brought her nothing but pain?

'The doctor is with her right now.'

'Please…' His voice broke. It sounded cracked and hollow. Not like his voice at all. But then he'd never asked anyone for anything, had he? Not since those air-conditioned nights in his father's miserable fortress of a house, when he'd lain awake, the pillow clasped tightly over his head but too scared to cry. To the background sound of the night herons which had called across the island, he had silently begged an uncaring god to bring his mother back to him. And then, just like now, events had been completely outside his control. Things didn't happen just because you wanted them to. He saw now that maybe the reason he'd always turned his back on relationships was because, ultimately, he was unable to control them and that control had become his security in an uncertain world. His heart slammed against his ribcage. Or maybe it was just because, until Ellie, he'd never had a real relationship with anyone.

He looked into the ward sister's eyes. 'How is she?'

'She's being stabilised right now.'

'And…the baby?'

His voice cracked again. He hadn't expected that

question to hurt so much, nor for it to mean as much as it did. When had been the critical moment that this unborn life had crept into his heart and taken residence there? The world seemed to tip on its axis as the woman's face assumed an expression of careful calm—as if she was attempting to reassure him without raising false hopes. He guessed she must have been asked that question a million times before.

'I'm afraid it's too early to say.'

He could do nothing but accept her words and he nodded grimly as he was shown into a waiting room which looked onto an ugly brick wall. There was a stack of old magazines on a chipped table and—all too poignantly—a little heap of plastic bricks piled in one corner, presumably for any accompanying children to play with.

Children.

He hadn't wanted any of his own—that had always been a given. He hadn't wanted to risk any child of his having to go through what he had gone through. But now, suddenly, he wanted this baby so bad. He wanted to nurture the child that the baby would grow into.

I will never abandon my baby or hurt or punish him, he thought fiercely. *He will know nothing but love from me—even if I have to learn how to love him from scratch.*

He closed his eyes as the minutes ticked by. Someone brought him a cup of coffee in a plastic cup, but it lay untouched in front of him. And when eventually the doctor came into the waiting room with a ward sister beside him—a different one this time—he sprang to his feet and felt the true meaning of fear. His hands were clammy and cold. His heart was pounding in his chest.

'How is she?' he demanded.

'She's fine—a little shocked and a little scared, but she's had a scan—'

'A scan?' For a second he felt confused. He realised that he'd been thinking in Greek instead of English and the word sounded alien to him.

'We needed to check that the pregnancy is still viable, and I'm delighted to tell you that it is.'

'Still *viable*?' he repeated stupidly.

'The baby is fine,' said the medic gently as if he were speaking to a child. 'Your wife has had a slight bleed, which is not uncommon in early pregnancy—but she's going to have to take it easy from now on. That means no more rushing around. No horse riding.' He smiled gently, as if to prepare him for some kind of blow. 'And no sex, I'm afraid.'

They took him to Ellie's room, where she lay on the narrow hospital bed, looking almost as white as the sheets. Her eyes were closed and her pale fringe was damp with sweat, so that her dark, winged eyebrows looked dramatic against her milky brow.

She didn't stir and, mindful of the doctor's words, he sat down noiselessly in the chair beside the bed, his hand reaching out to cover hers. He didn't know how long he sat there for—only that the rest of the world seemed to have retreated. He measured time by the slow drip of the intravenous bag which was hooked up to her arm. And he must have been looking at that when she eventually woke up, because he turned his head to find her grey eyes fixed steadily on him. He tried to read the expression in them, but he could see nothing.

'Hi,' he said.

She didn't answer, just tugged her hand away from

his as she tried to sit up, reaching down to touch her belly, her gaze lifting to his in agonised question.

'The baby?'

He nodded. 'It's okay. The baby's fine.'

She made a choked kind of sob as she slumped back against the pillows, her mouth trembling in relief. 'I didn't dream it, then.'

'Dream what?'

'Someone came.' She licked her lips and paused, as if the effort of speaking was too much. 'They were putting something cold on my stomach. Circling it round and round. They said it was going to be okay, but I thought...'

He felt completely inadequate as her words tailed off and he thought: *You have only yourself to blame. If you hadn't pushed her away, if you hadn't tried to impose your own stupid rules, then you would be able to comfort her now. You'd be able take her in your arms and tell her that everything was going to be all right.*

But he couldn't do that, could he? He couldn't make guarantees he couldn't possibly keep. Promises she'd never believe. All he could do was to make sure she had everything she needed.

'Shh,' he said in as gentle a voice as he'd ever used and she shut her eyes tightly closed, as if she couldn't bear to meet his gaze any longer. 'The doctor says you're going to have to take it easy.'

'I know,' she said as tears began to slide from beneath her lashes.

They kept her in overnight and she was discharged into his care the following day. She tried refusing his offer of a wheelchair, telling him that she was perfectly capable of walking to the car.

'They said to take it easy,' she told him tartly. 'Not to spend the next six months behaving like an invalid.'

'I'm not taking any chances,' came his even response, but his tone was underpinned with steel. 'And if you won't get in the wheelchair, then I shall be forced to pick you up and carry you across the car park—which might cause something of a stir. Up to you, Ellie.'

She glowered but made no further protest as he wheeled her to the car, and she didn't say anything else until they were back at the apartment, when he'd sat her down on one of the squashy sofas and made her the ginger tea she loved.

She glanced up as he walked in with the tray. Her expression was steady and very calm. She drew a deep breath. 'So what are you intending to do about your brother?'

His throat constricted. She'd gone straight for the jugular, hadn't she? 'My brother?' he repeated as if it were the first time he'd ever heard that word. As if he hadn't spent the past twenty-four hours trying to purge his mind of its existence. 'It's you and the baby which are on my mind right now.'

'You're avoiding the subject,' she pointed out. 'Which is par for the course for you. But I'm not going to let this drop, Alek. I'm just not. Before I went into hospital, we discovered something pretty momentous about your—'

'I don't have a brother,' he cut in harshly. 'Understand?'

Frustratedly, she shook her head. 'I understand that you're pig-headed and stubborn! You might not like the journalist, or the message she left—but that doesn't mean it isn't true. Why would she lie?'

He clenched his hands into fists and another wave

of powerlessness washed over him, only this he could do something about. 'I'm not prepared to discuss it any further.'

She shrugged, a look of resignation turning her expression stony. 'Have it your own way. And I'm sure you'll understand that I'm no longer prepared to share my bed with you. I'm moving back into my own bedroom.'

Alek flinched. It hurt more than it should have done, even though it came as no big surprise. Yet something made him want to try to hang on to what they had—and briefly he wondered whether it was a fear of losing her, or just a fear of losing. 'I know the doctor advised no sex, but I can live with that,' he said. 'But that doesn't mean we can't sleep together. I can be there for you in the night if you need anything.'

She stared at him as if he'd taken leave of his senses. 'I can call you if I *need* anything, Alek.'

'But—'

'The charade is over Alek,' she said. 'I'm not sleeping with a stranger any more.'

He looked at her in disbelief. 'How can we possibly be strangers, when you know more about me than anyone else?'

'I only know because I wore you down until you told me—and it was like getting blood from a stone. And I understand why. I realise how painful it was for you to tell me, and that what happened to you is the reason you don't do intimacy. I get all that. But I've also realised that I *want* intimacy. Actually, I crave it. And I can't do sex for sex's sake. I can't do cuddling up together at night-time either. It's too confusing. It blurs the boundaries. It will make me start thinking we're getting closer, but of course we won't be and we never will.'

'Ellie—'

'No,' she said firmly. 'It's important that I say this, so hear me out. I don't blame you for your attitude. I understand why you are the way you are. I think I can almost understand why you don't want to stir up all the emotional stuff of reuniting with the brother you say you don't have—I just can't live with it. If I were one hundred per cent fit, I think I'd be able to get you to change your mind about wanting to stay with me until after the baby is born. Because I think we both recognise that's no longer really important, and I hope you know me well enough to realise that I'll give you as much contact with your child as you want.' She gave a sad sort of smile, like someone waving goodbye to a ship they knew they would never see again. 'Ideally, I'd like to go back to the New Forest and find myself a little cottage there and live a simple life and look after myself. But obviously I can't do that, because the doctors won't let me and because you're based in London.'

'Ellie—'

'No. Please. Let me finish. I want you to know that I'm grateful to be here and to know you're looking out for me and the baby, because this is all about the baby now. And only the baby.' Her voice was trembling now. 'Because I don't ever want to get physically close to you again, Alek. I can't risk all the fallout and the potential heartbreak. Do you understand?'

And the terrible thing was that he did. He agreed with every reasoned word she'd said. He accepted each hurtful point she made, even though something unfamiliar was bubbling inside him which was urging him to challenge her. To talk her round.

But he couldn't. One of the reasons for his outstanding achievements in the world of commerce was an ability to see things as they really were. His vision was X-ray clear whenever he looked at a run-down business, with the intention of turning it around to make a profit. And he realised that he must apply the same kind of logic now. It was what it was. He had destroyed any kind of future with the mother of his child and he must live with her decision and accept it. She was better off without someone like him, anyway. A man who couldn't do feelings. Who was too afraid to try.

A pain like a cold and remorseless wind swept through him.

'Yes, I understand,' he said.

CHAPTER THIRTEEN

So why was he so damned restless?

Alek stared out of his office window and drummed his fingers impatiently on his desk. Why couldn't he accept a life which—despite having a pregnant wife living in his apartment—was still tailored to fit his needs? He told himself that things weren't *really* that different. Why should it bother him so much that he and Ellie were now back in separate rooms?

He still went to work each morning just the way he'd always done, although Ellie had taken to sleeping late these days instead of joining him for tea before he went to the office. At least, he was assuming she was sleeping. She might have been wide awake, doing naked yoga moves as the sun rose for all he knew. Or submerging her rapidly growing bump beneath a bath filled to the brim with sensual bubbles. He had no idea what went on behind her bedroom door once it was closed, although he'd fantasised about it often enough. Hell, yes.

He wondered if his frustration showed in his face. Whether he'd given himself away the other morning, when he'd unexpectedly seen her padding back from the kitchen clutching a mug of ginger tea as he'd been about to take an early morning conference call. Her hair had been tumbling in glorious disarray around her shoulders and the floaty, flowery robe she wore had managed to conceal her changing shape while somehow emphasising it. Her skin had been fresh and her eyes bright, despite the earliness of the hour. She'd looked more like a teenager than a woman of twenty-five and he'd felt a pang of something like regret. Just the day before, the doctor had given her a glowing bill of health. Mother and baby were ticking all the right boxes, and Alek told himself that at least something good had come out of all this.

But wasn't it funny how you always wanted what you hadn't got? Why else would he be craving more of her company and wishing she'd linger longer over dinner? Wanting her to say something—anything—other than make those polite little observations about what kind of day she'd had. He'd made quite a few concessions to fit in with her pregnancy, but even they hadn't softened her resolve. Hadn't he eaten his words and joined that wretched antenatal class, where they were expected to lie on the floor—puffing like a bunch of whales? Yet still she kept her distance. He felt a stab of conscience. Wasn't that how he used to be with her? And wasn't he discovering that he didn't much like being pushed away? And in the meantime, he was aching for her. Aching in ways which were nothing to do with sex.

He'd been brooding about it all week and not coming up with any answers about how he could change things, when on Saturday night she looked at him across the dinner table with an odd expression on her face.

'I want you to know,' she said in the careful way people did when they'd been practising saying something, 'that if you decide you want to start seeing other… women, I shan't mind.'

His fork fell to his plate with a clatter. His heart pounded. Rarely had he been more shocked. Or outraged. 'Say that again,' he breathed.

'You heard me perfectly well, Alek. I'm just asking you to be discreet about it, that's all. I don't particularly want—'

'No, wait a minute.' Ruthlessly he cut across her words in a way he'd avoided doing of late, leaning across the table and glaring at her. 'Are you telling me that you *want* me to start dating other women?'

Ellie didn't reply, not immediately. She fiddled around with her napkin for just long enough to hang on to her composure—telling herself that this was the only solution. She couldn't keep him chained up like a tame lion. 'I don't know if *want* is the right word—'

'Maybe you want to watch?' he suggested crudely. 'Perhaps that's one of your fantasises. Does the thought of me having sex with somebody else turn you on, Ellie?'

'Don't be so disgusting!' she snapped, feeling her cheeks growing hot. 'That's not what I meant at all and you know it.'

'Do I?' he demanded furiously. 'What am I supposed to think, when you give me your blessing to have sex with someone else, while you're still living under my roof?'

She glared back. 'I wasn't giving you my *blessing*. I'm trying to be fair!'

'Fair?' he echoed, furiously.

'Yes, fair.' She took a shaky sip of water. 'I know you're a virile man with a healthy sexual appetite and I shouldn't expect you to have to curtail that, just because…'

'Because you no longer want me?'

Ellie swallowed as she met the accusation spitting from his blue eyes. Oh, if only. If only it were as simple as that. 'It's not that I don't want you.'

'You just take masochistic pleasure in us sleeping apart? In me lying wide-eyed for most of the night knowing you're in the room next door?'

'I told you before. I can't do fake intimacy. And I didn't start this conversation to discuss the reasons why I won't sleep with you.'

'Then why *did* you start it?'

'Because I'm trying to be kind.'

'*Kind?*' He stared at her incredulously. 'How does that work?'

'I'm just suggesting that if you want to relieve your frustrations, then feel free—but please be discreet about it. I just don't want it in my face, that's all.'

There was silence for a moment while he stared down at his clenched fists and when he looked up again, there was something in his eyes she didn't recognise.

'Why not you?' he questioned simply. 'When you're the only woman I want? When we both know that if I came round to the other side of that table and started kissing you, you'd go up in flames—the way you always do when I touch you.'

'So why don't you?' she challenged. 'Why don't you take control, as you're so good at doing? Take the choice away from me?'

He shook his head and gave a short laugh. 'Because that would make it too easy. A short-term fix, not a

long-term solution. You have to be with me because
you want to, Ellie—and not just because your body is
reacting to something I do to you.'

She stared at her napkin. She stared at her water
glass. But when she looked up, she shook her head. 'I
can't,' she said. 'It would be insane to even try. We're
planning a divorce before too long and I want to accli-
matise myself to the situation. I'm trying to get used to
the separate lives we've agreed to lead.'

For a minute there was silence.

'And what if I told you I don't want separate lives, or
a divorce?' he said at last. 'That I wanted to start over,
only this time to do it differently? We'll take it as slow
as you like, Ellie. I'll court you, if that's what you want.
I'll woo you with flowers. I won't take business calls
when we're away. I'll do whatever it takes, if you just
give me another chance.'

His bright eyes bored into her and for a moment
Ellie couldn't speak, because she got the feeling that
Alek didn't often ask questions like that. And hadn't she
sometimes dreamt of a moment like this—even though
she'd told herself it would never happen? But it *was* happening. He was sitting there and saying things she'd
longed to hear and temptation was tugging at her—
because Alek in a peace-making mood was pretty irresistible. His blue eyes were blazing and his lips were
parted, as if already anticipating her kiss—and didn't
she want to kiss him so badly? She could go into his
arms and they could just lose themselves in each other,
and...

And what?

How long before domesticity bored him? Before the
emotional demands *she would inevitably make* became

too tedious for him to bear? Because he still didn't do communication, did he? Not about the things that really mattered. He was still denying that he had a brother. He was only talking this way because he was bargaining with her. Because it was probably frustrating the life out of him that she wasn't falling into his arms with gratitude.

She shook her head. 'I can't.'

'Why not?'

She realised that his pride was going to be hurt—and maybe that wasn't a bad thing. But she needed to show him that this was about more than pride. She had to summon up enough courage and strength to present him with a few harsh home truths.

'Because I can't contemplate life with a man who keeps running away.'

'Running away?' he echoed and she heard the anger building in his voice. 'Are you accusing me of cowardice, Ellie?'

'It's up to you to make the diagnosis, not me.' She stared at the little vase of blue flowers which sat at the centre of the table. She thought how delicate the petals were. How most things in life were delicate, when you stopped to think about it. She lifted her gaze to his, trying not to react to his anger. 'When you told me all about your family—about your mother walking out on you and the effect it had on you—I could understand why you never tried to get in touch with her. I understood that you'd taken your pain and turned it into success and that it was easier to turn your back on the past. But you're an adult now, with the world at your fingertips—the most successful man I've ever met. You're intelligent and resourceful and yet you've just heard that you've got a brother and you're acting like nothing's happened!'

His dark head was bent and there was silence, and when at last he looked at her she flinched from the pain she saw written in his eyes.

'Not just a brother,' he said. 'I think I could have dealt with that. But a twin brother? Do you know what that means, if it's true? Have you thought about it, Ellie? She didn't have another baby with another man. She had one who was exactly the same age. *She took him with her and left me behind.* I was the one she rejected. I was the one she didn't want. How do you think that makes me feel?'

'I don't think it makes you *feel* anything,' she whispered back. 'Because you're blocking out your feelings, the way you've always done. You're ignoring it and pretending it isn't there and hoping it will go away. But it won't go away. It will just fester and fester and make you bitter. And I don't want a man like that. I want someone who can face up to reality. Who can accept how it's making him feel—even if it hurts—and who isn't afraid to show it.'

She leant forward and her voice was fervent. 'The stuff you imagine is always worse than the real thing,' she said. 'I know that. When I met my father—all the dreams I'd nurtured about us becoming one big happy family were destroyed the moment he pushed the table away and my cappuccino spilt everywhere. And of course I was upset. But afterwards I felt…well, free, I suppose. I could let go of all those foolish fantasies. Because it's better to deal with reality, than with dreams. Or nightmares,' she finished as she rose to her feet. She looked into his face and saw the pain which was written there. Such raw and bitter pain that it made her instinctively want to reach out and comfort him.

But she knew she couldn't rid him of his nightmares. She couldn't *fix* Alek. He had to do that all by himself.

CHAPTER FOURTEEN

HE DIDN'T TELL her he was leaving until the morning of
his departure, when Ellie walked into the kitchen and
saw him drinking coffee, a leather bag on the floor beside his feet. He turned as she entered the room and,
although his hooded eyes gave nothing away, his powerful body was stiff with tension. A trickle of apprehension began to whisper down her spine.

'You're going away on a business trip?' she questioned.

He shook his head. 'I'm going to Paris.'

Fear and dread punched at her heart in rapid succes-
sion. Paris. The city of romance. She looked down. An
overnight bag. The fear grew. 'You've decided to take
me up on my offer?' she breathed in horror.

He frowned. 'What offer?'

'You're seeing someone else?'

His brow darkened. She saw a pulse flicker at his
temple. 'Are you crazy? I'm going to meet my brother.
I phoned the journalist and spoke to her. She gave me
his details and I emailed him. We're having lunch at
the Paris Ritz later.'

Ellie's heart flooded with a complex mixture of emotions. There was relief that he hadn't taken her up on

her foolish suggestion and joy that he'd taken the step of arranging to meet his brother. But there was disappointment, too. He was facing up to his demons—but he hadn't stopped to think that she might like to be involved, too. She was curious to meet her baby's uncle, yes—and wasn't it possible she could be a support to her husband if she was there at his side? She took an eager step towards him, but the emphatic shake of his head halted her.

'Please don't,' he said. 'Elaborate displays of emotion are the last thing I want to deal with right now.'

It wasn't an unreasonable reaction in the circumstances, but that didn't stop it from hurting. Ellie's arms hung uselessly by her sides as she pursed her lips. Yet, why *should* he accept her comfort or her help when she'd spent weeks pushing him away?

She nodded. 'Good luck,' she said quietly, though never had she wanted to kiss him quite so much.

She spent the day trying not to think about what might be happening in France. She told herself that Alek wouldn't ring and she was right. Every time she glanced at her phone—too often—there were no texts or missed calls and the small screen remained infuriatingly blank. She'd been due to meet Alannah for lunch, but she cancelled—afraid she would end up doing something stupid, like crying. Or even worse, that she would blurt out the whole story. And she couldn't do that. It wasn't her story to tell. She'd already broken Alek's confidence once and to do so again—wittingly this time—would be unforgivable.

She tried to keep herself occupied as best she could. There was a subtle nip to the air, so she slipped on a jacket and walked across a park with leaves showing the distinct bronzed brushstrokes of autumn. She went shopping for food in the little deli she'd discovered, which was hidden unexpectedly in a narrow road behind the smart Knightsbridge shops, and she bought all the things she knew Alek liked best to eat.

But no matter what she did, she couldn't clear her mind of nagging questions which couldn't be answered until he arrived home. Though it occurred to her at some point that he might not want to tell her anything. He was naturally secretive and that wouldn't necessarily have changed. Discovering something about his past wasn't necessarily going to transform him into someone who was comfortable with disclosure.

She went to bed at around eleven and it was sometime later that she heard the sound of a key in the lock and a door quietly closing. Her throat dried. He was home. She could hear him moving around, as if he didn't want to wake her, but as the footsteps passed her door she called out to him.

'Alek.'

The footsteps halted. The floor creaked and there was silence.

'Alek?' she said again.

The door opened and a powerful shaft of light slanted across the room to shine on her bed, like a spotlight. She blinked a little in the fierce gleam and sat up, pushing her hair out of her eyes. She tried to search his face, but his eyes were in shadow and all she could see was his powerful body silhouetted against the bright light.

'Are you okay?' she said.

'I didn't want to wake you.'

'Won't you…come in?' Her voice gave a nervous

wobble as she switched on the bedside lamp. 'And tell me what happened.'

She'd been half expecting him to refuse, to coolly inform her that he'd tell her everything—well, maybe not quite everything—in the morning. That would be much more characteristic of the Alek she knew. But he didn't. He walked into the room and sat down on the edge of the bed, only she noticed he kept his distance— as if ensuring that he was nowhere within touching range. And stupidly—because it wasn't very appropriate in the circumstances—she found herself wishing she were wearing some provocative little excuse for a nightie, instead of an oversized T-shirt which had nothing but comfort to commend it.

'So,' she said nervously. 'What happened?'

Alek looked at the way she was biting her lip. At the shiny hair spilling over her shoulders and the anxiousness she couldn't quite keep from her eyes. He thought that she loved him, but he couldn't be sure. His mouth hardened. How could you tell if a woman really loved you? He had no baseline to work from.

'We met,' he said. 'And after a while he showed me some photos. The first—' His voice cracked slightly. 'The first photos I'd ever seen of her.'

She nodded. Swallowed. 'What were they like?'

He tipped his head and looked up at the ceiling. 'She was very beautiful—even in the later shots. She had this thick black hair and the most amazing blue eyes.'

'Like yours, you mean?'

He gave a wry smile as he looked at her again. 'That's right. Just like mine.' It had been beyond strange to see the physical evidence of somebody he'd only ever heard about in the most negative terms. A woman in a cotton dress, glinting at the sun—her face filled with an unmistakable sadness.

'And what was your brother like?'

Ellie's words broke into his thoughts and Alek opened his mouth to answer but the most articulate person in the world would've had difficulty expressing the conflicting feelings which had torn through him when he'd seen his twin brother for the first time.

'He looks like me,' he said, at last.

'Your twin brother looks like you? You don't say!'

And unexpectedly, he began to laugh—her quip doing the impossible and taking some of the heat out of the situation. He thought about how he'd felt when he'd walked into the famous hotel and seen a black-haired man with a face so scarily like his own, staring back at him from the other side of the restaurant. He remembered the overpowering sense of recognition which had rocked him and momentarily robbed him of breath.

'His name is Loukas but his eyes are black,' he said. 'Not blue.'

And that had been the only physical difference he'd been able to see, although after the second bottle of wine Loukas had told him about the scars which tracked over his back, and what had caused them. He'd told him a lot of stuff. Some of which was hard to hear. Some he'd wanted instantly to forget. About a mother who had been a congenitally bad picker of men, and the sorry way that had influenced her life. About his poverty-stricken childhood—so different from Alek's, but not without its own problems. Dark problems which Loukas had told him he would save for another day.

'Had he been trying to find you for a long time?' Ellie whispered.

He shook his head. 'He only discovered that I existed last year, when his…our…mother died.'

'Oh, Alek.'

He shook his head, unprepared for the rush of emotion, wanting to stem it, in case it made him do what he'd been trying very hard not to do all day. He cleared his throat and concentrated on the facts.

'She left behind a long letter, explaining why she'd done what she'd done. She said she knew she couldn't live with my father any more—that his rages and infidelities were becoming intolerable. She had no money and no power—she was essentially trapped on his island. She thought he would blight the lives of all three of us if she stayed, but she also knew that there was no way she could cope with two babies. And so she…she chose Loukas.'

She nodded, not saying anything and for a moment he thought she wasn't going to ask it, but of course she asked it. This was Ellie, after all.

'How did she choose?'

Another silence. 'She tossed a coin.'

'Oh.' Her voice was very quiet. 'Oh, I see.'

He gave a bitter laugh. He wasn't a man given to flights of fancy but he'd vividly imagined that moment just before she'd walked out of the house for good. He'd wanted his brother to lie; to invent a fairy story. To tell him that she'd chosen Loukas because he had been weaker, or because she thought that Alek would fare better because he was two minutes older and a pound heavier. Or because Loukas had cried at the last minute and it had torn at her heartstrings. But no. It was something much more prosaic than that. His fate and the fate of his brother being decided by a coin spinning in the air, until it landed on the back of her hand and she covered it with her palm. What had she thought as she'd lifted her hand to see which boy would be going with her, and which boy would be left behind? Did she find it easy to walk away from him?

'My mother flipped a coin and I lost out,' he said.

Another silence. A much longer one this time.

'You know she did it because she loved you?' she said suddenly. 'You do realise that?'

He raised his head, barely noticing the salty prickling at the backs of his eyes. 'What the hell are you talking about?'

'She did it because she loved you,' she repeated, more fiercely. 'She must have done. She must have been out of her head with worry—knowing that she could barely look after one baby, let alone two. And if she'd taken you both, he would have come after you. He definitely would. She must have thought your father would be glad to have been left with one son, and that he'd love you as best he could. But he couldn't. He just couldn't— for reasons you'll probably never know. But what you have to do, is to stop thinking that because of what happened you're unlovable—because you aren't. You need to accept that you're very lovable indeed, if only you'd stop shutting people out. Our baby is going to love you, that's for sure. And I've got so much love in my heart that I'm bursting to give you—if only you'll let me. Oh, darling. Darling. It's all right. It's all right. Oh, Alek—come here.' Her eyes began to blur. 'Everything's going to be all right.'

She put her arms around him and he did what he'd

been trying not to do all day, which was to cry. He cried the tears he'd never cried before. Tears of loneliness and pain, which eventually gave way to the realisation that he was free at last. Free of the past and all its dark tentacles. He had let it go and Ellie had helped him do that.

His hand was shaking as he smoothed the pale hair away from her face and looked at her.

'You would never do that,' he said.

She turned her head slightly, so that she could kiss the hand which was still cupping the side of her face. 'Do what?'

'Leave our baby.'

She turned her head back, biting her lip, her grey eyes darkening. 'I don't want to judge your mother, or to compare—'

'That wasn't my aim,' he said quietly. 'I'm just stating a fact and letting myself be grateful for that fact. I've given you a hard time, Ellie, and a lot of women might have lost patience with me before now. Yet you didn't. You hung on in there. You gave me strength and showed me the way.'

His question shimmered on the air as she looked into his eyes.

'Because I love you,' she said simply. 'You must have realised that by now? But love sometimes means having to take a step back, because it can never flourish if there are darknesses or secrets, or things which never dare be spoken about.'

'And I love you,' he said, his free hand reaching out to lie possessively over the bump of their unborn child. A lump rose in his throat as he felt the powerful ripple of movement beneath. 'I love you and our baby and I will love you both for ever. I will nurture and care for you both and never let you down. Be very certain of that, *poulaki mou*. I will never let you down.'

He could taste the salt from her own tears as he kissed her and did what he'd been wanting to do for so long. He lay down beside her and put his arms around her, gathering her close against his beating heart.

EPILOGUE

'SO WHAT'S IT LIKE, being back?' Ellie's words seemed to float through the warm night air towards her husband. 'Is it weird?'

Shining brightly through the unshuttered windows, the moon had turned the room into a fantasy setting of indigo and silver. Over their heads whirled a big old-fashioned fan and the sheets were rumpled around their gleaming bodies. The faint scent of sex hung in the air and mingled with the tang of the lemons squeezed into the water jug which stood beside the bed.

Ellie turned onto her side and looked at Alek, who lay beside her with his arms stretched above his head, looking a picture of blissful contentment.

This journey to Kristalothos was one they'd waited a while to make, until both of them were certain they were ready. A trip to the island home of Alek's childhood—a place which symbolised so much of the darkness and horror of his past—was never going to be at the top of their bucket list. In fact, Ellie had been surprised when Alek had first suggested it because although their life had been hectic, it was pretty close to perfect. The birth of their son two years previously had put the seal on their happiness and Ellie had been...

She swallowed.

Frightened that going back would test their happiness and threaten to destroy it? Scared he might go back to being the secretive Alek of old who had locked her out of his heart—or that the reality of confronting his past might bring renewed bitterness?

Yes, she had thought all those things—and more. But she'd quashed her fears and entered into his plans with enthusiasm, because she'd sensed it was something he'd needed to do. Hadn't she been the one who'd insisted you had to face your fears instead of running away from them? And perhaps there was some truth in the idea that you could never go forward until you were properly at peace with your past.

After much discussion, they had decided to leave their little boy behind in England. Young Loukas— their adored son, who they'd named after Alek's twin brother and who had given them so much more than joy. It was the tiny tot more than anything who had been responsible for Alek's growing ability to show emotion. Because children loved unconditionally and Alek had learnt to do the same. He had learnt that real love knew no boundaries and sometimes Ellie just sat watching him play with their little boy and her heart swelled up with so much pride and affection.

But a lively two-year-old was not an ideal companion for a cathartic trip which might be emotionally painful, which was why they'd left him behind with Bridget— who had become his honorary grandmother.

Ellie and Alek had chartered a boat from Athens, which had taken them out to his childhood island home of Kristalothos, with the vessel making a foamy trail through the wine-dark sea as they journeyed. They had arrived on a spring morning, when the wild flowers were massed over the gentle hills and the sea was crystal clear as it lapped gently against the fine white sand.

As he had looked around him with slightly dazed eyes, Alek had told her the place had changed beyond recognition. Some of the changes he'd discovered when he was making plans for their trip but seeing them with his own eyes had really driven home the fact that nothing ever stayed the same. A Greek-born hotelier named Zak Constantides had bought his father's old fortress and razed it to the ground, putting in its place a boutique hotel, which was fast becoming as famous as his iconic London Granchester.

But Alek had chosen to rent a villa instead of staying there and Ellie was glad, because she didn't want to spend a single night on the spot where a young boy had spent so many miserable years.

She leant across the rumpled bed and stroked her fingertips over his bronzed cheek, and her touch seemed to stir him from his pensive mood. He smiled as he reached for her and thought about her question.

What was it like being back?

Reflectively, he stroked her hair. 'It is a bit weird,' he admitted. 'But it doesn't hurt. Not any more. And I'm glad I came, because it was something I needed to do. Another ghost laid to rest. I like the fact that Zak's hotel has brought work and prosperity to the island and that the place is no longer ruled by fear and oppression.'

'I'm glad, too,' she said, wriggling up closer.

'But I'm glad of so many things,' he said. 'Mainly for my beautiful wife and my equally beautiful son, who provide me with the kind of contentment I never thought existed.' He tilted her chin with the tip of his finger, so he could see the gleam of her eyes in the moonlight. 'I'm even glad that I've got a brother, although—'

'Although Loukas has his own demons,' she finished slowly.

'Yes, he does. But it isn't Loukas I'm thinking about at this moment, *poulaki mou*. It's you.' He rolled on top of her, his fingers playing with the tumble of her hair as he felt the softness of her body beneath him. 'Because without you I would have nothing. I am who I am because of you, Ellie. You made me confront things I'd spent my life avoiding. You made me look at myself, even though I didn't want to. I've learnt…'

'What have you learnt?' she questioned softly as his voice tailed off.

He shrugged. 'That it's better to face up to the truth rather than to block it out. And that feelings don't kill you—even the very toughest ones. Everything that's worth knowing, you have taught me and I love you for that, Ellie Sarantos—and for a million reasons more besides.' He gave a mock glower of a frown. 'Even though you have stubbornly refused to let me announce that particular piece of information to the world.'

He traced a thoughtful finger over the angled line of her collarbone. He had wanted to go through a second marriage ceremony—a big glitzy occasion at the Greek Cathedral in London, intended as a mark of his love for her because he felt she'd been short-changed last time. For a while Ellie had been agreeable—even consulting a wedding planner and hearing about the rival merits of a string quartet versus an old-fashioned bouzouki band for the reception. Until one morning at breakfast, she'd told him she didn't need declarations or lavish gestures. That it was enough to know he cared, and in the private moments of their precious relationship his heartfelt words of love meant more than a truckload of confetti.

And wasn't that another aspect of her personality which made him love her so much? That the things she cared about weren't the *things* which so many people strived for. She didn't need to put on a show or make some kind of statement. She didn't need to prove anything. Diamonds she could take or leave, and, although she wore silky tea dresses because she knew he liked them, she was happiest in a pair of jeans and a T-shirt. She was still Ellie—the same straightforward, uncomplicated woman he'd first fallen for—and he wouldn't want her any other way.

He reached for her breasts and cupped them and she made a purring little sound in the back of her throat, because she liked it. *Theos*, but he liked it, too. But then he liked everything about his soft and beautiful wife.

'Shall I make love to you now?' he questioned.

She touched her fingertips to the dark shadow of his jaw and followed it up with the slow drift of her lips. 'Oh, yes, please,' she whispered.

They were in the place of his birth, but they could have been anywhere. A place which had once symbolised darkness and heartbreak, but not any more. Because Ellie made everywhere feel like the home he'd never really had. Ellie breathed life into *his* life. He bent his head and kissed her as the night herons gathered around the lapping bay outside their window.

* * * * *

AN HEIR TO
BIND THEM

DANI COLLINS

This one's for my kids who managed to turn out amazing despite having a writer for a mum. Or should I say, not having a mum.

I often joke that our daughter has done a marvellous job raising our son. For that, and all the times Delainey made lunch for Sam (and me) so I could write, I am deeply grateful.

I also owe a very special thanks to Sam for his suggestion when I had ten thousand words to go on this manuscript and I was stuck. He said, "Dude." (Yes, he calls me Dude, but this dude looks like a lady.) "Dude, have the brother tell her something she doesn't know about the hero." Post-secondary tuition saved!

Canadian **Dani Collins** knew in high school that she wanted to write romance for a living. Twenty-five years later, after marrying her school sweetheart, having two kids with him, working at several generic office jobs and submitting countless manuscripts, she got The Call. Her first Mills & Boon novel won the Reviewers' Choice Award for Best First in Series from RT Book Reviews. She now works in her own office, writing romance.

PROLOGUE

THEO MAKRICOSTA BLINKED sweat out of his eyes as he glanced between his helicopter's fuel gauge and the approaching shoreline. He was a numbers man so he didn't worry at times like this; he calculated. His habit was to carry twice the fuel needed for any flight. He'd barely touched down on the yacht before he'd been airborne for his return trip. A to B equaled B to A, so he should have enough.

Except in this case *B* stood for *boat,* which was a moving point.

And he'd made a split-second decision as he lifted off the *Makricosta Enchantment* to go to Marseille rather than back to Barcelona. It had been an instinct, the type of impulse that wasn't like him at all, but uncharacteristic panic had snared him in those first few seconds as he took flight. He had wheeled the bird toward what felt like salvation.

It had been a ludicrous urge, but he was committed now.

And soaked in perspiration.

Not that he was worried for his own life. He wouldn't be missed if he dropped out of the sky. But his cargo would. The pressure to safeguard his passengers had him so tense he was liable to snap his stick.

It didn't help that despite the thump of the rotors and his earmuffs plugged into the radio, he could hear both babies screaming their lungs out. He already sucked at being a brother. Now he might literally go down in flames as an uncle. Good thing he'd never tried fatherhood.

Swiping his wet palm on his thigh, he pulled his phone from his pocket. Texting and flying was about as smart as texting while driving, but if he managed to land safely, he would have a fresh host of problems to contend with. His instincts in heading north instead of west weren't *that* far off. The perfect person to help him was in Marseille.

If she'd help him.

He called up the message he should have deleted a long time ago.

This is my new number, in case that's the reason you never called me back. Jaya.

Ignoring the twist of shame the words still wrung out of his conscience, he silently hoped her heart was as soft as he remembered it.

CHAPTER ONE

Eighteen months ago…

JAYA POWERS HEARD the helicopter midmorning, but Theo Makricosta still hadn't called her by five, when she was technically off the clock. Off the payroll in fact, and leaving in twelve hours.

Ignoring the war between giddiness and heartache going on in her middle, she reminded herself that normal hours of work didn't confine Mr. Makricosta. He traveled so much that sometimes he couldn't sleep, so he worked instead. If he wanted files or records or reports, he called despite the time and politely asked her for them. Then he reminded her to put in for lieu or overtime and thanked her for her trouble. He was an exceptionally good man to work for and she was going to miss him way beyond what was appropriate.

Staring at herself in the mirror, packed bags organized behind her, she wondered why she was still dressed in her Makricosta Resort uniform. She gave herself a pitying headshake. Her hair was brushed and restored to its heavy bun, her makeup refreshed, her teeth clean. All in readiness for his call.

After everything that had sent her running from her home in India, she never would have seen herself turning into this: a girl with a monumental crush on her boss.

Did he know she was leaving and didn't care? He'd never

overstepped into personal, ever. If he had any awareness that she was a woman, she'd be shocked.

That thought prompted her to give a mild snort. If she hadn't seen him buy dinner for the occasional single, vacationing woman, always accompanying her back to her room then subsequently writing off her stay against his personal expense account, she'd have surmised he wasn't aware of women at all.

But he hooked up when it suited him and it made her feel...odd. Aware and dismayed and kind of jealous.

Which was odd because *she* didn't want to sleep with him. Did she?

A flutter of anxious tension crept from her middle toward her heart. It wasn't terror and nausea, though. It wasn't the way she typically felt when she thought of sex.

It wasn't fireworks and shooting stars, either, so why did she care that she might not have a chance to say goodbye?

Her entire being deflated. She had to say goodbye. It wasn't logical to feel so attached to someone who'd been nothing but professional and *de*tached, but she did. The promotions and career challenges alone had made him a huge part of her life, whether his encouragement had been personal or not. More importantly, the way he respected her as useful and competent had nurtured her back to feeling safe in her workplace again. He made her feel like maybe, just maybe, she could be a whole woman, rather than one who had severed herself from all but the most basic of her female attributes.

Did she want to tell him that? *No.* So forget it. She would leave for France without seeing him.

But rather than unknotting her red-and-white scarf, her hand scooped up her security card. She pivoted to the door. Stupid, she told herself as she walked to the elevator. What if he was with someone?

A few minutes later she swiped her damp palms on her

skirt before knocking on his door. Technically this fortieth floor villa belonged to the Makricosta family, but the youngest brother, Demitri, wasn't as devoted to duty as Theo, flitting through on a whim and only very seldom. Their sister, Adara, the figurehead of the operation, timed her visits to catch a break from New York winters, not wasting better July weather elsewhere when it was its coolest here in Bali.

Theo—Mr. Makricosta, she reminded herself, even though she thought of him as Theo—was very methodical, inspecting the books of each hotel in the chain at least once a quarter. He was reliable and predictable. She liked that about him.

Licking her lips, she knocked briefly.

The murmur inside might have been "Come in." She couldn't be sure and she had come this far, so she used her card and—

"I said, *Not now,*" he stated from a reclined position on the sofa, shirt sleeves rolled up and one bare forearm over his eyes. In the other hand he held a drink. His jaw was stubbled, his clothes wrinkled. Papers and file folders were strewn messily across the coffee table and fanned in a wide scatter across the floor, as though he'd thrust them away in an uncharacteristic fit. His precious laptop was cocked on its side next to the table, open but dark. Broken?

Blinking at the mess, Jaya told herself to back out. Men in a temper could be dangerous. She knew that.

But there was something so distraught in his body language, in the air even. She immediately hurt for him and she didn't know why.

"Did something happen?" she queried with subdued shock.

"Jaya?" His feet rose in surprise. At the same time he lifted his arm off his eyes. "Did I call you?" Spinning his feet to the floor in a startling snap to attention, he picked up his phone and thumbed across the screen. "I was trying not to."

The apology sounded odd, but sometimes English phrasing sounded funny to her, with its foreign syntax and slang. How could you *try not* to call someone?

"I don't mind finding whatever paperwork you need," she murmured, compelled to rescue the laptop and hearing the door pull itself closed behind her. "Especially if you're dismayed about the way something was handled."

"*Dismayed.* Yeah, that's what I am." He pressed his mouth flat for a moment, elbows braced on his wide-spread thighs. His focus moved through her to a place far in the distance. With a little shudder, he skimmed his hands up to ruffle his hair before staring at her with heartrending bleakness. "You've caught me at a bad time."

For some reason her mouth went dry. She didn't react to men, especially the dark, powerfully built, good-looking ones. Theo was all of those things, his complexion not as dark as her countrymen, but he had Greek swarthiness and dark brown hair and brows. With his short hair on end, he looked younger than his near thirty. For a second, he reminded her of the poorest children in India, the ones old enough to have lost hope.

Her hand twitched to smooth his disheveled hair, instinctively aware he wouldn't like anyone seeing him at less than his most buttoned-down.

He was still incredible. His stubbled jaw was just wide enough to evenly frame his gravely drawn mouth while his cheekbones stood out in a way that hollowed his cheeks. His brows were winged, not too thick, lending a striking intelligence to his keen brown eyes.

They seemed to expand as she looked into them. The world around her receded....

"We'll do this tomorrow. Now's not a good time." The

quiet words carried a husky edge that caused a shiver of something visceral to brush over her.

She didn't understand her reaction, certainly didn't know why she was unable to stop staring into his eyes even when a flush of heat washed through her.

"I can't take advantage of your work ethic," he added. "It could undermine our employer-employee relationship."

Appalled, she jerked her gaze to the floor, blushing anew as she processed that she'd been in the throes of a moment and hadn't even properly recognized it as one until her mooning became so obvious he had to shut her down.

How? In the past few years, any sort of sexual aggression on a man's part had stopped her heart. Terror was her reaction and escape her primary instinct. Wistful thoughts like, *I wonder how his stubble would feel against my lips,* had never happened to her, but for a few seconds she'd gone completely dreamy.

Her body flamed like it was on fire, but not only from mortification. There was something else, a curiosity she barely remembered from a million years ago when she'd been a girl talking to a nice boy at school.

If she had the smarts she always claimed to, she'd let his remark stand. She'd excuse herself to Marseille and never be seen again.

At the same time, as discomfited as she was, her ability to have a moment was so heartening she couldn't help standing in place like someone testing cold waters, trying to decide whether to wade farther in.

Not that she'd come here for that. No, she wanted to say goodbye and he'd given her an opening.

"Actually, we don't have that kind of relationship anymore." With jerky movements she set his laptop on the coffee table and pressed the lid closed. "Today was my last day. I should have changed, but I'm having trouble letting go."

He sat back, hands on his knees, taken aback. "Why

wasn't I informed? If you're moving to the competition, we'll match whatever they're offering."

"That's not it." She sank onto the seat opposite him and grasped her hands together so she could portray more composure than she actually possessed. Emotions rose as she realized this was it, no more uniform, no more career with the Makricosta hotel chain, no more Theo. Her voice grew husky. "You—I—I mean the company—have been so good with training me and offering certifications. I would never throw that in your face and run to the competition."

"We believe in investing in our employees."

"I know, but I never dreamed I could go from chambermaid to the front desk in that kind of time, let alone manage the department." She remembered how frightened she'd been of getting in trouble for leaving her cleaning duties when she'd brought a lost little boy to the office, hovering to translate until his parents were located. Theo happened to be conducting one of his audits and was impressed by her mastery of four languages and ability to keep a little one calm.

"My confidence was at a low when I began working here," she confessed with a tough smile. "If you hadn't asked me if I planned to apply for the night clerk job I wouldn't have thought I'd even be considered. I'm really grateful you did that."

There. She'd said what she had wanted to say.

"My sister would disown me if I turned into a sexist," he dismissed, but his gaze went to his phone. His despondency returned to hover in the room like a cloud off dry ice. She sensed that whatever news was affecting him, Adara Makricosta had delivered it.

"Where are you going, if not two doors down?" he asked abruptly.

She lifted her gaze off the strong hands massaging his knees. He wasn't as collected as he was trying to appear.

For some reason, she wanted to take those hands and hold them still and say, *It'll be okay. You'd be surprised what a person can endure.*

"France," she replied, not wanting to talk about her situation, especially when it appeared he was only looking for distraction from his own troubles. "Marseille. It's a family thing. Very sudden. I'm sorry." She wasn't sure why she tacked on the apology. Habits of a woman, she supposed, but she *was* sorry. Sorry that she had to leave this job, sorry she was inconveniencing him, sorry that her cousin was dying.

She felt her mouth pulling down at the corners and ducked her head.

"You're not getting married, are you? This isn't one of those arranged things?" He sounded so aghast she had to smile. Westerners could be so judgmental, like all *his* relationships were love matches rather than practical arrangements.

"No." She lifted her head and he snagged her into another moment.

It occurred to her why she didn't feel threatened by this. They'd had a million of these brief engagements, all very short-lived. For over four years, she'd been glancing up to catch him watching her and he had been looking back to his work so smoothly she had put the charged seconds down to her imagination, convincing herself he didn't even know she was alive.

Our employer-employee relationship...

Was that what had kept him from showing interest before? It wouldn't surprise her. He held himself to very high standards, never making a false move.

But if that was what had held him back, what did it mean for her right now, when she was alone with him in this suite and he knew she was no longer off limits?

Ingrained caution had her measuring the distance to the door, then flicking a reading glance at him.

The air of masculine interest surrounding him fell away and her boss returned. "This is a blow to the company. I'll provide you a reference, of course, but would a leave of absence be more appropriate? Should we keep your job open for you?"

His sudden switch gave her tense nerves a twang, leaving her unsettled. Men never seemed to get her messages to back off. Having Theo read her so clearly was disturbing.

"I—No." She shook her head, trying to stay on topic, tempted to say she'd return, but Saranya's cancer made it very unlikely. She hated to even think about it, but she'd been through it with Human Resources and had to get used to reality. "I'm moving in with my cousin and her husband. She's very ill, won't survive. I'm close with their daughter and she'll need me."

"I'm sorry. That's rough."

She absorbed the quiet platitude with a nod.

"I don't mean to sound crass, but would money help?" he added.

"Thank you, but that's not the issue. My cousin's husband is very well-off. They were extremely good to me when I left India, taking me in until I was able to support myself. I couldn't live with myself if I wasn't with them through this."

"I understand."

Did he? His family seemed so odd. Estranged almost. His remark about his sister a few minutes ago was as personal as she'd ever heard him speak of her. The few occasions when she'd seen any of them together, none had shown warmth or connection.

Who was she to judge, she thought with a jagged pain? She'd been disowned by her family.

He seemed to have equally dismal thoughts. His gaze

dropped to the papers still scattered across the floor. He picked up his drink, but only let it hang in his loose fingers.

"Do you want to talk about…whatever is troubling you?" she asked.

"I'd rather drink myself unconscious." He sipped and scowled, "But I only have watered down soda, so…" He set it aside and stood, giving her the signal that heart-to-heart confessions were off the table.

She tried not to take it as a slight. He was a private man. This was the most revealing she'd ever seen him.

"I'm sorry we won't be working together any longer, Jaya. Our loss is the hoteliers in Marseille's gain. Please contact me if you're interested in working for Makricosta's again. We have three in France."

"I know. Thank you, I will." She swallowed and wondered if she would turn into a complete fool and start to cry. Standing, she put her hand in his and tried for one firm pump with a clean release.

He kept her hand in his warm one. His thumb grazed over the backs of her knuckles.

Her skin tingled and her stomach took a roller coaster dip and swoop.

She looked at his eyes, but he was looking at their hands. Her fingers quivered in his grip as he turned her palm up. She almost thought he was going to raise it to his lips. He looked up and the swooning dip hit harder. That was a *sex* look.

But it was Theo's eyes, Theo's expression that was always so aloof but now glowed with admiration and something else that was aggressive and hungry. He skimmed his gaze down her cheek to her mouth and sensations like fireworks burst through her. Zinging streaks of heat shot down her limbs and detonated her heart into expansive pumps.

She was experiencing sexual excitement, she interpreted

dazedly, and the sensations grew as he stepped closer and lowered his head. He was going to kiss her!

She stiffened with apprehension and he straightened. Her hand wound up hanging in the air ungrasped as he pulled in a strained breath from the ceiling. "You're right. It's not appropriate." Weary despair returned like a cloak to weigh down his shoulders. "I apologize."

"No, I—" *Please* let her dark skin disguise some of these fervent blushes. "You surprised me. I came in here reminding myself not to call you Theo. I didn't think you thought about me like that. I would—" Was she really going to risk this? She had to. She'd never get another chance. "I'd like it if you kissed me."

CHAPTER TWO

"Jaya—"

The gentle let-down in his tone made her cringe. She'd lost him to her habitual rejection of male closeness, but wanting a man to touch her was so *new*. She couldn't help that it scared her.

He searched her face with his gaze. "You have to know how pretty you are. Of course I've noticed you. I've also noticed you don't party like the rest of your age group. You're not the one-night stand type."

"I said a kiss, not that I wanted to sleep with you."

Her swift disdain amused him. He quirked his mouth and tilted back his head. "So you did. You can see what a philanderer I am, it didn't occur to me you weren't of-fering to stay the night." He made a noise of disparage-ment that seemed self-directed. His wide shoulders sank another notch.

He appeared so tired and in need of comfort. Conflict held her there another minute. She wanted him to see her as available, yet wanted to self-protect. It was frustrating.

"What age group?" she challenged, pushing herself as much as him. "I'm twenty-five. What are you? Thirty?"

"Are you? You look younger." His mouth twitched again as he reassessed her in a way that incited more contradic-tory feelings all through her.

Just go, her timid self said. *It's safer.* Her more deeply buried self, the girl who had grown up determined to make something of herself, believing in things like equal rights and reaching her own potential, stood there and tried to make him see her as someone who shouldn't be dismissed. Someone with value and values.

"Having a career is important to me. Makricosta's has been a second chance to build one and I haven't wanted to do anything to jeopardize it. You won't be surprised to hear I send money to my parents. I can't afford to drop shifts because I'm hung-over."

"I'm not surprised at all. You've always struck me as very loyal. And sweet. Virginal even." It was almost a question.

The backs of her eyes stung and she lowered her gaze to her clenched hands. "I'm not," she admitted in a small voice, not wanting those memories to intrude when she felt so safe with him.

"And you've been judged for that? Men and their double standards. I hate my sex. Judge *me*. I sleep with women and never talk to them again. I really do that, Jaya," he confessed with dark self-disgust.

She heard the warning behind his odd attempt to reassure. She appreciated the effort—even though he had it all wrong. Yes, she had been judged, but for a man's crime against her, not any she'd committed.

"I hate men, too," she admitted. *But not you,* she silently added.

"Ah, some bastard broke your heart. I excel at being the rebound guy, you know." Here was the generous tycoon with the hospitable expression who asked a guest if she was enjoying her stay and wound up sharing her table along with further amenities.

"Is that why you pick up those tourists?" she couldn't help teasing, amused by this side of him in spite of her exasperation. "You're offering first aid?"

"I'm a regular paramedic. 'He cheated? He's a fool.'"
He shook his head in self-deprecation. "I should be shot."

"Are you really that shallow?" She didn't believe it. The
women were always relaxed and euphoric, never morose,
when they checked out. She was envious of that. Curious.

"I'm not very deep." He rubbed his face. "But I don't
lie. They know what they're getting."

"One night," she clarified, wondering why he thought
he had nothing to offer a woman beyond that.

"One night," he agreed with an impactful look. His
hands went into his pockets and he rocked back on his
heels, saying, "And apparently you restrict to one kiss. But
I'll take it if you're still offering."

The craving in his gaze was so naked, she blushed hard
enough her cheeks stung. Covering them, she laughed at
herself and couldn't meet his eyes. "I'm not a certified attendant."

"There's not a woman in the world with enough training to fix me. Don't try." Another warning, his tone a little cooler.

She shook her head. This was about fixing herself, not
him. "I just keep thinking that if I leave without kissing
you, I'll always wonder what it would have been like."

That sounded too ingenuous, too needy, but his quietly
loaded, "Yeah," seemed to put them on the same page,
which was remarkable. He stared at her mouth and hot
tingles made her lips feel plump. She tried to lick the sensation away.

His breath rushed out in a ragged exhale. He loomed
closer, so tall and broad, blocking out her vision, nearly
overwhelming her. But when his fingers lightly caressed
her jaw and his mouth came down, she was paralyzed with
anticipation.

There'd been a few kisses in her life, none very memorable, but when his mouth settled on hers, unhurried and hot, she knew she'd remember this for the rest of her life.

The smooth texture of his lips sealed to hers. He didn't force her mouth open. She softened and welcomed his confident possession, weakening despite the nervous flutters accosting her. He rocked the fit, deepening the kiss so she opened her mouth wider, bathed in delicious waves of heat. Their lips dampened and slid erotically. His tongue was almost there, then not, then—

He licked into her mouth and she moaned, lashed with exquisite delight. This was the kind of kiss she'd only read about and now she knew there was a reason they called it a soul kiss. Her hand went to his shoulder for balance. She lifted on her toes, wanting more pressure, more of him settling into her inner being.

With a groan, he slid his arm around her and pulled her tight against him, softly crushing her mouth while digging his fingers into her bound hair. It was good, so good. She reached her arms around his neck, loving how it felt to be kissed and held so tightly against his hard chest and—

He was hard *everywhere*.

Like hitting a wall, she pushed back, perturbed by how intensely she had been responding and the dicey situation she'd put herself in.

He didn't let her go right away, kind of steadied her first while staggering one step himself, then he ran a hand through his hair and swore under his breath. "Hellfire, Jaya. I suspected it'd be good, but I didn't know it'd be *that* good. Are you sure you don't want to spend the night?"

"I—" Say no. *Go.* But what if he was the one? The man who would get her past the hurdle of burying her sexuality out of fear? "I really wasn't expecting this." *Liar,* an inner vixen accused. "You're right that I don't have affairs. I don't know if that's what I want right now, but…" She found herself wringing her hands like the virgin he'd accused her of being. "I really liked kissing you."

"Are you trying to let me down gently? Because it's not necessary."

"No! I'm genuinely confused about what I want." It was almost a wail of agony she was so frustrated with herself.

His mouth pulled up on one side in a half grin that might have been patronizing if he hadn't softened it by saying, "You're not the one-night stand type, but your life has been derailed and sex would take your mind off things. Believe me, I sympathize."

She cocked her head, intrigued by these glimpses into the man behind the aloof mask. "Is that why you're asking me to stay?"

"That obvious, am I?"

"You're making me worry for my friends. Is there a problem with Makricosta's?" she probed.

"No," he assured promptly, then sighed and scratched at his hair like he could erase whatever was going on inside his skull. "Mine is a personal derailment. A family thing, not an illness like yours. I've been angry with someone for a very long time and learned today that I have no reason to be. I'm running out of people to hate and blame. I don't know what to do about that."

Kiss me, she thought. She couldn't believe he was opening up to her like this and way in the back of her mind, she suspected he would regret it, but right now it softened her into wanting to heal him. Madness. She was more broken than he was.

"You told me not to try fixing you," she reminded gently. "It's good advice. I honestly don't know if I can be what you're looking for tonight." She wanted to be, but the thought of that kind of intimacy opened such a gaping vulnerability in her, she could hardly breathe. "I keep telling myself to leave." She gestured toward the door.

"But you're still here."

She lifted a shoulder. "It sends the wrong message, I know."

Their gazes tangled and all she could think about was the heart-racing kiss they'd just shared. He claimed he was the opposite of a gentleman, but she sensed that despite his rock-hard physical power and authoritative command, he was capable of gentleness.

"Give up on me at any point. It won't bother me a bit," he coaxed with surface nonchalance, but she sensed a tighter intensity beneath. Because he wanted her that badly? Or the mental escape?

"Really?" She folded her arms, highly skeptical.

"It's a lady's prerogative to change her mind," he said with a fatalistic shrug, then grinned with surprising wickedness. "But I'll do my best to keep it interesting."

Her equilibrium rolled and dipped again, making her unsteady on her feet.

"I can't believe I'm having this conversation," she said, shaking her head at her own waffling forwardness and his sexual arrogance. "With *you*."

"I've trained myself not to fantasize about women wearing that uniform. It's pretty surreal for me, too."

She chuckled, then sobered as she met his avid look. He was holding himself under tight control and she suspected she'd always been aware of his ruthless self-discipline, that it was one of his qualities she was most attracted to.

"I really can't decide, Theo."

His expression eased a little. "You don't have to." He snagged her hand and led her to the sofa, his manner laconic. "We'll take it one kiss at a time. See how it goes."

"You *really* want to take your mind off things."

"I really do," he admitted, dropping onto the sofa and bringing her down beside him. "Will you take your hair down for me?"

After a tiny hesitation, she did, feeling incredibly vulnerable, like she was removing her clothing. Her severe appearance was a shield. Freeing her hair invited him to stroke his fingers through it. He fanned it out from her ear, creating tickling sensations in her scalp as he marveled at the length.

"It's so silky," he murmured.

No product or bleach to make it brittle, she almost said, then decided this would go better if she didn't compare herself to other women whose hair he had petted.

His patience surprised her. She didn't know why, seeing as he was the most unflappable man she'd ever met, but his contentment to take his time combing her hair with his fingers when he seemed so intent on getting physical almost made her worry he was changing his mind. Just when she grew restless, however, he flicked the tie at her throat.

"Can we take this off?" He tugged to loosen the bow.

"Are you going to tie me up with it?" she asked, trying to sound light, but filled with trepidation.

"Do you want me to?" His gaze skimmed over her as though he was reassessing all his preconceptions about her.

"No." Firm. Prudish even.

His lips twitched, but when his gaze came up from watching the scarf trail down her lapel, his lids were heavy and his voice laconic. "Good, because I want to feel your hands on me."

The scarf floated away and he moved in, settling a lazy, drawn-out kiss on her mouth that was reassuringly tender and sweet.

And, after a while, a tiny bit frustrating. She wanted more than this slow pace. She wanted the hand climbing her waist to quit stopping at the underside of her breast. *Touch me,* she willed, breasts feeling swollen and achy. She wanted the space where they leaned into each other to close so she could press herself to his wide chest. He'd come out of the private lap pool here once, when she'd arrived with a file. Even though he'd shrugged on a shirt immediately, his washboard abs had been full-on. He was gorgeous and she wanted to see his naked chest again.

She plucked at the buttons on his shirt, not quite nervy enough to tug them open.

He broke away to look down at where her indecisive fingers lifted away from his breastbone. Without a word, he one-handedly yanked, disregarding the exceptional quality by tearing its holes, pulling it free of his waistband at the same time so it hung loose on his shoulders.

Gasping at his near savagery, she touched her fingertips to her sensitized lips.

He caught her hand and bit softly against the plump pad at the base of her thumb. "I'm dying for you to touch me. Don't worry, I won't rip your uniform. We'd have to account for the loss."

His husky comment made her laugh. Half of her dry chuckle was mild terror because he was taking her hand to his chest. She caught her breath as her fingerprints made contact with the heat of his skin, taut over his hard muscles.

He shivered under her touch.

"You're so hot," she murmured.

"Thank you. I've always thought the same about you."

Smiling, she did something she hadn't imagined she could. She leaned in and kissed his mouth while both her hands skimmed over the intriguing ripples of his upper chest, exploring the texture of a light sprinkle of hair and satin skin over muscles that flexed under her caress.

He groaned, but rather than gather her into a tight crush, she felt a tickling graze of fingers between her breasts. A second later, she was the one to draw back and watch as he finished opening her white-and-red Makricosta blouse.

Her ivory bra beneath was practical and almost adolescent. She didn't have much to support and had never seen the point in spending money on something only she would see. An urge to apologize rose to the back of her throat, but the way he traced the top of one small cup, caressing the upper slope of her breast, had her holding her breath.

"I have a wicked addiction to cocoa," he told her as he took his time spreading the shirt wide on her shoulders, patiently tugging it free of her skirt. His returning touch was whisper-soft as he grazed her ribs and found his way to the clasp in the middle of her back.

Her back arched from his caress and her bra loosened. She drew in a breath, hesitant, but his hand came around and cupped her breast. The sensation blanked her mind, holding her in thrall. So much heat. He was like an inferno, and so masculine, but reverent. There was aggression, she could feel the possessiveness in the way he enclosed her like he had every right, his touch firm, but he was gentle at the same time. Softly crushing, as if he knew she would enjoy the sensation of pressure increasing by degrees. He massaged flesh that felt heavy and achy and prickling in one tight spot.

His touch shifted as he leaned in to capture her mouth. Muscle flexed under her hands as she met his searching kiss with welcome. Sensations overwhelmed her, but a particularly sharp one pierced through her psyche. He thumbed her nipple, making it feel knotted and tighter and more sensitive. And so vulnerable, yet excited.

She whimpered, distressed by the rocketing spikes of pleasure going straight through her abdomen into a place that had retreated to hibernation a long time ago.

"God, Jaya, let me taste you."

He pressed her onto her back on the cushions, covering her so smoothly she didn't realize how she'd wound up under him, her bra pushed up and his weight pinning her hips, one leg between his, the other dangling off the edge of the cushions.

A gasp of shock scraped her throat as she pulled in air, trying to catch up to this new circumstance, trying to decide if she was okay with it.

"So gorgeous."

Damp heat closed over the pulsing tip of her breast. Knifing spears of delight pulled upward from her flesh.

Be scared, she told herself, but the scariest thing was how devastating this pleasure was. Her hands couldn't get enough of roaming his back. His bunched shirt kept getting in the way, irritating her. His weight on her should have terrified her, but when she bucked, it was slowly, because she couldn't help herself. Her leg couldn't find purchase alongside his so she let her ankle curl behind his thigh.

And she moaned. Aloud. Even though a distant voice said, *Don't. Don't be sexual, don't encourage him, don't embarrass yourself.* She couldn't help it. He had both her breasts cupped into mounds that he sipped and licked and tortured. It was incredible.

"Theo, I can't stand it."

He lifted to kiss her, swooping like a predator to ravage her mouth as he shifted their position and was fully between her legs. The layers of her wrinkled skirt had climbed so his fly came into firm contact with the cotton of her underpants.

Panic began to edge out her arousal.

She pressed his shoulders and he broke their kiss to set his damp forehead against hers. "I know, I'm pushing it, but this is as far as we're going. I've just realized I don't have any condoms." He smoothed her hair back from what must have been a stunned expression and kissed her once, quite hard. "You have no idea how sorry I am."

She did. Her hips wriggled involuntarily and he shuddered, pressing that most assertive part of himself to her vulnerable softness, pinning her motionless as he released a dry laugh.

"Okay, maybe you do." Kissing her with regret, he grazed his lips over her cheekbones and eyebrow. "You feel so good. You're so pretty. I don't want to stop touching you." His hand skimmed the outside of her thigh, making her trembling muscles contract to tighten her leg against him. "Will you let me make it good for you, at least? Can I know what it feels like to touch you?"

He set a sweet kiss on her chin while his hand climbed under her gathered skirt and learned the style and texture of her mood-killing matronly underpants.

She opened her mouth, thoughts scattering in a dozen directions by arousal and conflicting misgivings. Her mind refused to fix on anything let alone a clear yes or no.

Before she could form words, he shifted enough to cover her mound with a compelling rock of his hand. Stars shot behind the backs of her eyes.

"Like that?" he murmured, licking her neck and easing his touch to a lighter caress through the layer of cotton. Just a soft trace against a very intimate place that made her pulse with need. "Softer? Tell me what you like."

"I didn't come here for this," she managed to whisper, aware that she was becoming completely abandoned, letting her legs fall open to his incredible facility with a woman's body. Wanting whatever he'd give her. "But it feels so good."

"I know. Hate me later, but right now can I keep doing this? You're so incredible…"

He kissed her neck and sidled his touch beneath the cotton, knowing exactly what he was doing in a way that should have alarmed her, but she didn't care. At this moment, she really didn't care about anything except that he keep his attention on that exquisite bunch of nerves tangled into a signal that sent ripples outward through her abdomen. He wasn't in any hurry, seeming to luxuriate in circling and stroking, driving her crazy.

She bit at his lips, dying, wild, loving his touch and him for giving her this amazing build of pleasure, this incessant desire for physical contact with a man.

He said sinful things about what he wanted to do to her, sucked her nipple and said, "Let me kiss you here. I want to lick you. It'll be so good, Jaya—"

"No," she gasped. Her horror was pure, latent shyness, but the idea of him doing that was so wickedly intriguing her arousal spiked to something she couldn't contain. Convulsively trying to close her legs, she could only squeeze his wide, masculine hips, unable to stop what he was doing. She couldn't catch back her uninhibited response. Her only choice was complete surrender to him and her body's sharp need.

Her reward was a deep throb of sheer joy expanding through her in shuddering waves. Her throat filled with a cry of release that was more than just physical. It was emotional triumph. Freedom from the past. Joy at a man's touch.

CHAPTER THREE

INCREDIBLE TENDERNESS MADE her slither in sweet lassitude beneath him, loving the hard strength of him, the disheveled intensity holding him tense as she ran her fingers into his hair. She made him lift his head so she could look at him.

It was painfully intimate to let him look into her eyes when she had just shattered so completely. His hand stilled where he still had it tucked against her mons and an internal ache made her long to beg him to continue stroking her.

"Thank you," she whispered, hoping he put down her shiny eyes to arousal.

A slow, wicked grin spread across his face. "Stick around. There's more where that came from." He punctuated with a gentle, deliberate caress that slid low and penetrated her pulsing channel.

She tightened, part of her reaction instinctual resistance, but the sensation of clasping his thick finger was so delicious she moaned and lifted her hips a little, encouraging more.

"Ah, Jaya..." His hot mouth opened in a wet kiss against her neck and he deepened his possession of her.

"Wait," she gasped, still clasping his head and this time clutching him close with her arms hard on his shoulders while she stared at the back of the sofa. Was she really going to do this? Her body was on fire while her mind was cleaving in all directions.

He removed his hand from her underpants and she moaned in loss.

"It's okay," he murmured, skimming his lips against her jaw before he lifted his head and removed her hand from his hair. "You don't have to rip my hair out. This has gone further than you wanted to, I get it."

"No, I—" Disconcerted, she dropped her twitching fingers to his shoulders, sorry she'd hurt him, sorry she'd lost his exquisite caresses. She didn't want this to end, not yet. This was her chance to get over her past. "I have a pill in my room. One that, um, prevents a pregnancy after, um, unprotected sex." *Please don't ask me why I have it.*

Her voice faded toward the end. She was grossly unsure of herself and given how he'd pulled away, maybe he wasn't all that invested. He became very grave as he pondered what she'd said, making her hold her breath.

"I always wear a condom."

Disappointment sliced surprisingly deep. She swallowed and nodded. "I understand. It's okay. Like you said, this isn't something we intended, so—"

"No, I mean I'm clean. I've never gone bareback so you don't have to worry I'd give you anything."

"I…" *Had tests.* Again, she didn't want to think about Saranya taking her to the doctor once she'd got her out of India. That dark time was being overcome, here, tonight, with this man. "I'm clean, too."

He searched her face. She recognized the glaze of concentration in his eyes as a passionate force. It nearly squeezed the air right out of her.

"Swear to me you'll take that pill." His lips barely moved.

"My family would take out a contract on me if I had a baby outside of marriage."

He held himself in steely control and she could almost hear the computations of risk against desire. "I don't want to be a father. Ever. If you're thinking this might lead to something—"

"No!" she insisted, casting for the right words. "It's like you said about not wanting to think about certain things. I want something different in my mind." *A new memory. A good one.* "A baby would be a disaster. But I want to feel... you," she ended in a whisper.

His nostrils flared as he drew a deep breath, his nod brief and sharp before he pulled away, gathering her up as he found his feet. The strength in him as he lifted her and held her cradled to his chest made bells ring in her ears, but she found herself curling her arm around his neck and burying her face into the masculine scent in the crook near his shoulder.

What she had said was broad enough to be true in many ways. She wanted to think of men differently, but there was a part of her deeply enthralled in the now. She could barely form a thought beyond her need for physical contact with this man.

He set her on the bed and straightened, not turning on the light. Only the faint glimmer from the pool deck through the windows penetrated.

She hugged her knees as she watched him slide his belt free and toss it away, toeing off his shoes at the same time.

"Are we taking turns? Because I'm dying to see you," he said with enough ragged edge on his voice to make her shiver.

She looked down at her crumpled uniform, her shirt open, her bra still loose across her chest. Shyness was the only thing holding her back from undressing, she realized with a glistening lilt of joy. Not fear, just natural self-consciousness about undressing in front of a man.

As she hesitantly drew her shirt off her shoulders she confessed, "You've seen a lot of women. I don't know how I'll compare."

Down to his briefs as he peeled away his socks, he said, "I'm not very sure of my ability to hang on until I've given you everything I want you to have. I do *not* want to be the selfish bastard you compare every future lover to."

He wouldn't be, not by a long shot. And even though a quick coupling was probably better for her, given her hang-ups, she doubted it was a good thing to say. Besides, he stole the shirt she was trying to fold and lifted her bra away, dropping both to the floor. The air-conditioned room made her curl her toes, incredibly self-conscious of her naked breasts and beaded nipples as she forced her hands to remain beside her hips.

Sitting there in the half-light, staring at his muscled frame, she was accosted by a pull in her abdomen, but it wasn't fear or misgivings. It was longing. She wanted his hot, muscled body on hers. She wanted to feel those hard thighs between her own without cloth between them.

He started to remove her sandals and she kicked them off herself, letting him ease her onto her back in a sprawl under him as he loomed over her. The brush of his skin against hers was brand-hot, making her quiver with disconcertion. But the reassuring stroke of his hand up her waist to cup her breast calmed her nerves even as his expert touch sensitized her.

"Did I mention my addiction to cocoa?" he asked huskily. "I could sip these chocolate nipples of yours all night."

He bent to enclose her in wet heat and the return of excitement was like a blow, bringing up one of her knees. Sweet delight flashed through her, rippling waves of pleasure that didn't fade, only increased.

"I want to kiss you," she admitted as he shifted to tease her other breast. A coiled knot of tension pulled in her abdomen. It made her bold, impatient for the build and release of orgasm.

As he lifted his head to look at her, he skimmed a hand

down, silently asking her to lift her hips so he could push her skirt off. When had he lowered the zipper?

She complied and he reared up onto his knees, stealing the last of her clothes. Her thighs twitched, locking closed in nervous tension while she stared at the black briefs hugged tight to his hips and thighs. His erection was a thick, unapologetic ridge behind the stretchy fabric.

He sat back on his heels, knees splayed, hands in loose fists against his thighs. He let out a harsh breath, like he was under strain. "God, you're pretty."

He says it to all of them, she warned herself, but she couldn't help smiling. The way he studied her with the intensity he usually reserved for spreadsheets, but had that light of excitement and wolfish half smile on his face, seemed like genuine admiration. It affected her, relaxing her and making her want to writhe invitingly—if only she knew how.

"Will you kiss me again? Please?" She lifted a hand and he let out a gruff laugh as he stretched out beside her, leaning over her.

"I'll kiss every inch of you." He gathered her up to his muscled body and she felt bruised by the hardness of him. He was so hot, so strong beneath his taut, satiny skin. She couldn't resist stroking his back and shoulders as he kissed her. Their tongues flicked and delved and it felt totally natural. Better than natural. Necessary.

She did writhe then, moved by instinct, body involuntarily lifting into the stroke of his hands, arching to push her breast into his cupped palm, rolling her face into his caressing fingertips when he dragged his mouth to her neck. Then he was laving her nipple again, bringing the ferocious need into her loins. Mother Nature had a plan, quite obviously. She ached for attention between her thighs.

If only she knew how to make love as well as he did. He massaged her belly and grazed fingertips along the seam of her thighs, inciting her to relax them open. Then, finally, he was tracing into her wet heat, penetrating easily into the dampness that welcomed him. His caress was so stunningly *good.* As his thumb rolled over the taut peak of her clitoris, tiny sparks shimmered through her, gathering toward the implosion. She gasped, awed that she could feel this way again, from this deeply intimate touch.

He shifted, licked under her breast and kissed a trail down her abdomen.

"Theo," she panted.

"Every inch, Jaya." He left off caressing her and used his damp hand to crook her knee open, pressing a firm kiss to her inner thigh.

"No, Theo, please don't."

"Don't be shy." He came back onto his elbow beside her, his expression so feral and aroused she ought to have been terrified, but his voice was calm and controlled, his hand on her navel soothing. "I am seriously worried about not being able to last once I get my skivvies off. Let me make it good for you."

While a nervous giggle bubbled in her at his blunt remark, she knew her limits.

"This *is* good for me." Her voice hitched with deep emotion and she glanced up through stinging eyes, hoping he couldn't see in the shadowed light how out of sorts she was—enthralled and uneasy, but resolved. "I want to feel you inside me."

He muttered a curse, closing his eyes and averting his face.

Pressing into the mattress, she asked warily, "Are you angry?"

"What? No. But you're not helping my control with talk like that. Do you have any idea how long I've wanted to be inside you? Years. Since the first time I saw you."

He jackknifed off the bed, giving her space as he continued his grumbling tirade while stripping his briefs.

"You said earlier that you didn't know I thought about you this way. Well, you've never once hinted you did, either. Do you know how sexy it is to hear you want me?"

As he straightened, she thought, *"want" is debatable*. She wanted to feel normal. She wanted to feel close to Theo. But that aggressive thrust of masculine power made her apprehensive.

He came back to cover her, a practiced knee pressing her legs open as he settled on her. She stiffened, waiting for the breach, but he only cupped her face and set a soft kiss on her upper lip.

"Did I kill the mood? I didn't mean to. This is the most bizarre night of my life."

"That sort of flattery restores it," she teased, because this was the considerate Theo she recognized. Even so, she was hyperaware of the hard, thick muscle pressed so close to her vulnerable folds.

Rather than laugh, he released a sigh that was hot and damp against her cheek. "I'm grateful you're here, Jaya. All the crap outside these walls…It can't touch us right now. I hope you feel like that, too. I don't want to be the only one finding escape."

"You're not," she assured him, shivering in nervousness, but certain this was what she wanted: escape from her past. "I'm using you, too."

"Good." He kissed her, the familiar press and pull drawing her back toward the arousal that had been simmering under her last-minute nerves. When he rocked his hips he furrowed open the softness of her, finding and reawakening her to pleasure, she jerked, surprised by the spike of desire.

His big body overwhelmed hers, but there was a sense of safety here, too. His chest rubbed hers, stimulating her nipples. His thighs were tense and abrasive, but she couldn't help stroking his legs with hers, oddly entranced by the sensation, inadvertently parting her legs and opening herself with the movement.

Her undulations brought him to her entrance. A whimper of mixed emotion escaped her, but she cradled his head and stroked the back of his neck and lifted her hips into the pressure, making this happen.

She braced for pain, but there was only a tremendous sense of fullness as he slid into her. Her muscles tightened instinctually, but that only heightened the friction— the sweet, delicious friction—of his burying himself deep into her body.

A shudder of reaction took her.

He squeezed her in constrictor arms, rocking himself deep and tight against her body, sending glittering sensations through her as he whispered, "Already? That's okay, I'm really close, too. Come for me. Let me feel it."

She caught back a sob, not hurt, not ready to orgasm, but shattered emotionally by how complete she felt. Pride in herself almost burst her apart, making her cling to him, wanting this moment of perfection to imprint in her mind forever.

After a few seconds, when she only stayed very still beneath him, he murmured, "Together then?" against her temple. His hard arms caged her as he withdrew and returned. "Tell me when."

Pure white light seemed to expand in her as he fit himself to her depths.

"Oh, Theo."

"Yeah." He thrust again, deeper. Like he wanted to lock himself into her forever.

It was fantastic. Sweet and primal and delicious.

And not enough.

"Don't stop," she gasped.

"Never." He kept moving, his hips meeting hers with more force.

Sensations danced with giddy promise through her. She couldn't speak, could only brace for another pulse as he returned again, his muscled tension a gathered force over and around her. Like a storm building.

She panted, greeting each thrust with an arching welcome of her hips. Thought receded and she embraced pure womanhood, primitive and earthy and natural as they mated. His scent was perfume, his groans behind his gritted teeth music. She smiled at her power over him and herself, reveling in the dance. Cries built in her throat as the silver threads of crisis gathered. Her hand went to his buttock, nails digging in as she tried to push him deeper, needing just a little more. She was so close.

Sweat adhered them and they struggled in ecstatic perfection, almost there, almost there…

Orgasm ripped through her and her ragged cry was pure liberation. Absolute completion as her body shuddered and clasped at his.

He let out a fierce shout of his own. In her trembling sheathe, his thick shaft pulsed, filling her with volcanic heat. She closed her arms and legs around him and willed this union to last forever.

CHAPTER FOUR

Present day...

AS HE SETTLED onto the tarmac Theo eyed the waiting limo. Jaya was smart enough to wait for the blades to slow before leaving the car, but he was anxious to see her. He told himself it was the babies he was worried about, and whether he'd have the help he needed in caring for them. It had nothing to do with the gnawing ache that had stayed with him during the eighteen months since he'd made love to her for hours before she'd hurriedly dressed so she wouldn't miss her flight.

His gut knotted. She'd seen him with his defenses blown apart by the family strife he'd been trying all his life to wall off. He'd never been as unguarded with a woman as he'd been that night, usually focusing strictly on the physical pleasure of his encounters and saying as little as possible.

With her, he'd reveled in the cessation of emotional pain. When she'd left him to the silence of the suite, he'd blamed his plummet back into misery on the return of his dark memories from childhood, but there was more to it. He used to look forward to Bali; he hated it there now. He missed her.

And he couldn't imagine how she'd react to this. He glanced back to the passenger cabin, able to see through the open door that his nephew had fallen asleep. His niece stared wide-eyed from a tear-stained face, startled into silence by the return to solid ground and the new noises of shutting down the chopper.

"I'll be right back," he told her, not sure if his words had any impact. He dropped outside to tether the machine. He'd fueled here in the past, so the hangar wasn't unknown. He still didn't like leaving his machine without prior arrangements. Choice, however, had been pitched into the Med when he'd flown out to the new Makricosta cruise ship only to see a gunner boat approaching from the horizon.

His brother-in-law, Gideon, had been all smiles on his arrival, bringing the babies to have a look at uncle's helicopter. The second Theo had delivered the news he hadn't wanted to share over the radio, Gideon's hand had bit into his arm. "You have to get them off this ship."

Not only did Theo have no idea what would happen to his sister and older brother, or their spouses, but what in *hell* would he do with two babies? Especially if this turned into a permanent situation?

Forget the worst-case scenarios, he reminded himself. Deal with the moment at hand. By his estimation, he had to perform triage for twelve to twenty-four hours before he'd receive new information that would allow him to make a fresh decision.

The limo driver came around to open the back door. Jaya emerged.

Until he saw her and his tension bled away, he hadn't realized how fearful he'd been that she wouldn't come.

The rotors had slowed to listless circles, but he was still struck by a sensation of wind gusting him off his feet. She was wearing her hair shorter, just long enough to touch her shoulders and it had a wave in it he'd never seen before. He liked it better than the tight, sleek bun. She looked younger and more carefree.

Sexy.

Not to say she wasn't looking professional and confident at the same time. Her suit was tailored and chic, the scarf at her throat familiar. A deliberately distancing touch, he wondered, since it was *not* Makricosta colors?

Are you going to tie me up with it?

Do you want me to?

She'd run her fingers through his hair and he'd almost died. Hell, he'd been so needy it was demoralizing.

She smoothed her hands down her jacket, the navy and ice-yellow smart and flattering on her slender figure. Her big, round sunglasses stayed firmly in place as she waited by the open door of the car, not approaching.

He motioned her to come into the interior of the helicopter. After a brief hesitation, she walked forward.

"Mr. Makricosta—"

He paused with one foot on the step and looked back at her, his ghostly reflection in her lenses a picture of one shielded face confronting another.

"Theo," he corrected, tempted to stand here until she said it, which was inane. If he'd had one plan when—*if* he ever saw her again, it was that he'd pretend they'd never slept together. Unfortunately, he kept hearing her whispery gasps of his name, lightly accented, in his dreams and wanted to know if he remembered it right.

"Would you please tell me what is going on?" A hitch of panic entered her tone as he let her question launch him up the steps and into the helicopter. She followed, protesting, "I can't go anywhere. I have commitments. Work and…."

She didn't finish, making him wonder what other commitments, but he didn't press her. "You got my text. You know I need a room. Somewhere no one will expect me to hole up. When I said this was an emergency—"

He indicated the two babies. He'd had the white leather seats outfitted with child harnesses so he could transport his siblings and their children, but the babies looked ridiculously tiny in the first-class armchairs.

"*You have kids?*" she screeched, standing taller in the low-ceilinged inner lounge of the Eurocopter.

Androu jerked awake and began to wail. Evie broke down into renewed tears.

"Nice going," he shot at Jaya.

She stared at Androu, seeming to go yellow beneath her natural mocha tone. "How old is he?" she hissed.

"They're not mine," he ground out, resisting a weird guilt attack even though he'd taken pains—and it had been painful—to ignore her messages and reinforce to her that she didn't have any claim on him. "Help me get them into the car." He handed her Androu and turned to unstrap Evie.

She took the boy into her arms like a natural, which he'd known she would be, even though her lips were so pale and frozen he wondered if she'd ever smile again.

It wasn't in her to take out her feelings on a child, though. The first time he'd seen her, a blond German boy's pale hand clutched in hers, he'd recognized her strong maternal instinct and liked her for it. Today she soothed Androu as she carried him outside where the change of scenery calmed him.

Evie remained stiff in his arms, inconsolable. They slid into the limo like bank robbers after a heist and the driver pulled away.

"You might have told me so I could have had proper car seats installed. This is dangerous, Theo."

Damn. His name sounded better than he remembered and made him hunger to hear it against his ear.

"So?" she prompted. "Who are they?"

"Can he be trusted?" he asked in a murmur, nodding at the driver. "Because I couldn't risk a phone call that might have been heard over the radio. I was texting one-handed—" He was interrupted by Jaya's sudden query to Evie.

"*Pyaari beti,* do you have to use the potty?"

Evie's distressed face nodded vigorously.

For the second time today, Theo's mind blanked with panic. She was on his knee!

"Oscar—" Jaya turned to say, but the driver was ahead of her, already slowing outside the terminal building.

"Wait—" Theo said as Jaya plunked Androu onto the cushion beside her and scooped up Evie.

"There's no waiting at her age. What is she, two?" She was out the door as the limo halted, the little girl wrapped onto her hip like a monkey.

Theo clenched his teeth and did the math on discoverability. He didn't dare let himself calculate the odds on Jaya stealing the toddler. He made himself believe he knew her better, even though he didn't. Not really. Not when he'd treated her the way he had.

Sleeping with Jaya had been wrong.

He wasn't a man who got anything wrong. Mistakes were a luxury he had never been able to afford.

Something about Jaya eroded his discipline, however. Two years ago, he'd started allowing himself to fantasize about an employee. Then he'd begun finding reasons to stay an extra day in Bali, to review reports he could generate himself. He'd rationalized a one-night affair and taken her to bed knowing it was not just unwise and bordering on unethical, it was downright stupid. She was sweet and generous, not the worldly, here-for-a-good-time kind of woman who would forget him as quickly as he forgot her.

God, he wished he could forget her.

The best he'd managed was not to return her tentative few calls. It had been a cruel-to-be-kind favor in her best interest. Not that he expected her to see it that way, but he had warned her they had no future. Surely she wouldn't hold a grudge when he'd been honest about that much?

Skipping his gaze between Androu, who was turning himself and scooting backward off the opposite seat, and the terminal doors that remained closed and reflected the black windows of the limo, he evaluated how much of a chance he was taking letting Jaya whisk Evie into public.

This airstrip catered to private aircraft belonging to celebrities and Europe's high society, which meant most people would have very little interest in anyone but themselves. It was a tempting place for paparazzi to hang around looking for the shot of their career, though. Evie's parents were scrupulous about keeping her out of the limelight. Dressed in her hotel uniform, Jaya would be dismissed as a flight attendant or a nanny. Since Evie's almond eyes and black pigtails didn't match either her adoptive father's blond hair or her mother's green eyes, the chances of anyone recognizing her were narrow.

It was still an interminable wait as Androu rocked his still learning feet across the short expanse to clutch at Theo's knee. "Mama," he said.

Oh, hell. Theo stared into innocent eyes that could have belonged to his little brother, Demitri, at that age. "I know, buddy," he said, even though he didn't know a damned thing except that Adara had done this surrogate parenting at a far younger age than he was, so he had to man up and make this work.

Adara had had Jaya's instincts, though. Somehow she'd hung on to them through the war ground that was their childhood and look what she'd made: Androu was a happy little cub who'd eaten fistfuls of his first birthday cake a few months ago.

"Papa," Androu said, making his request in that polite yet firm way his father had.

"Not here, either, sport." Theo eyed the driver who was

circumspectly keeping his eyes forward. *Discreet,* he'd said in his text to Jaya. *Emergency. I need discreet transport and accommodation.* He'd told her where and when to pick him up and she'd come through for him. Surely that meant she'd bring back his niece.

Androu picked at the seam on Theo's jeans, absorbed, allowing Theo to train his X-ray vision on the terminal doors, willing them to open.

What in hell was taking so long? A tiny thing like Evie couldn't have much liquid in her, especially when she'd cried most of it out. Thank goodness he'd had the sense to call Jaya. Putting a little girl on a potty was not something he would think to do, let alone know how to make happen. He was completely unprepared for this situation, like he'd been dropped on a deserted island with two little gremlins.

And Jaya.

God, she looked more incredible than ever. He still dreamed of that mouth, wide and full and feminine. Her body was better than ever. If he wasn't mistaken, she was holding onto a few more pounds, filling out her slender figure to voluptuous perfection. Her breast would probably overflow his hand when—

If.

Hell, *never.*

It couldn't happen. Best to cut those thoughts short now. Seriously, what was she *doing?*

He couldn't go after her, no matter how much he was tempted. He wasn't a movie star, but the Makricosta siblings had been featured in upscale magazines recently, promoting the cruise ship currently being taken over by pirates. Was it targeted? Were high seas criminals after a hefty ransom by kidnapping some of the richest people in the world? The inaugural cruise had drawn a very elite crowd.

One thing at a time, he ordered himself. Gideon would protect Adara at all costs and he, Theo, had removed the only distraction Gideon might have had. Once the tots were safely stationed, he'd check in with Gideon and the authorities Gideon had raced off to advise.

A sharp pain in his thigh had him jerking his knee from the source, jostling the boy who'd bent to taste denim with his newly cut teeth. Startled by his near fall, the corners of Androu's mouth went down and his eyes filled again.

"Wait. It's fine. Go ahead and use me as a chew toy. You just startled me."

Outside, the terminal doors slid open and Jaya appeared with Evie still on her hip. She clutched an overstuffed bag in her free hand and wore a harried look.

Theo moved faster than the driver, pushing open the door as she reached the car.

"Seriously? Shopping?" He took the bag and steadied her under an elbow as she crawled in, catching a full inhale of her exotic sandalwood and almond scent. It hit him like a drug that weakened his muscles and teased him with euphoria.

Unless he was very careful, coming to her would turn into another mistake. He couldn't let it happen. He released her to pull the door shut behind her.

"Funny," Jaya said tartly, then, "Thank you, Oscar. Directly to the hotel now, please. The underground entrance." She pressed a button to close the privacy window and steadied Evie beside her on the seat as the car began to glide forward.

Theo picked up Androu and settled him on his thigh, catching a look on Jaya's face that might have been stunned hurt, but she looked away. Better that she was hurt and hated him. It would be easier for both of them.

Turning a gentle smile to Evie, she said, "You've been very patient. Would you like your drink now?" She brought a bottle of water out of the bag and opened it, helping Evie to sip.

Androu put out a hand and made a noise of imperative.

"I bought one for him, too. Do you know if they have any allergies?"

"I don't think so." Not Androu anyway. Adara was always prattling on about every little thing Androu ate, touched or said. Theo only listened with half an ear, but he would remember if she was worried about something like that.

There were bananas in the bag with yoghurt cups and a bag of vanilla cookies. Food. Right.

"Good call," he told her as he spilled water all over himself trying to keep the greedy Androu from drowning. The kid didn't have the first clue about the physics of tipping a water bottle and ended up coughing it all down his chin. "I think he uses a special cup for this."

"Really? Perhaps you should have stolen it when you kidnapped him." She brought out a banana and broke off pieces, making everyone sticky but quiet and happy.

"This is Androu, my nephew, Adara and Gideon's boy."

"Oh, of course." Everything in Jaya changed, softening as her gaze hooked onto Androu's little face with as much fixation as her first stare, but with a touch of wistfulness now. "I'd heard gossip about a miscarriage when I was in Bali. I'm happy for them. He's beautiful."

Her tone was sincere, moved almost. Or maybe he was reading into it. His emotions had been stripped to their rawest form the last time he'd been with her. Today wasn't much better. He hadn't planned ever to see her again and when he had indulged in imagining he might, he'd pulled himself together.

"It's been an eventful couple of years," he couched, trying to gloss over all the inner tearing down and rebuilding he'd been forced to do without betraying how brutal it had been. "Look, Jaya. I came to you because I figured I could trust you. We've kept some family business out of the papers for my mother's sake and even though she's gone now, we prefer not to air our dirty laundry, but..." He shrugged. "Are you aware that Nic Marcussen is my older brother?"

"No, I didn't even know your mother had died. I'm so sor— Wait. Marcussen Media? *That* Nic Marcussen?"

"Yes."

"Married to Rowan Davidson, the actress? Who adopted a baby from—" She looked at Evie who tilted her almond-shaped eyes up curiously.

"Where's Mama?"

"She's coming to get you soon," Jaya reassured her, handing Evie another piece of banana. "Isn't she?" she prompted Theo.

"I sincerely hope so, but from what I saw from the air, they have to evade pirates first."

"Where? On the Med? You can't be serious!"

"I know what I saw and the authorities have been notified, but there's every chance we'll be looking at ransom negotiations. The last thing we need is a media circus, especially around the babies. Hell, they're kidnap targets. You were the closest person I could think of who could provide me a place to stay that was off the radar."

Completely practical, exactly as it was supposed to be, he assured himself.

"You knew where I was working?" Her clipped challenge held dual notes of hurt and ire, suggesting that if he had known, he should have called.

He bit back a sigh. "I was contacted as a reference," he lied, adding politely, "Congratulations."

"Oh, um, thanks," she dismissed with a self-conscious shrug. "It's a boutique hotel, very well respected even before the upgrades. They're looking to bring in a higher clientele and hired me because of my experience with Makricosta's. I guess I'm indebted to you...again." Her voice trailed off. The way she bit her lips together suggested she would rather be run over by this limo than face him after referencing their night together.

He pretended they'd left it at the point where she'd thanked him, as if the rest hadn't happened. "As I said then, the hoteliers here got lucky."

Her eyelashes flinched in a way that seemed to say, *Did you really just say that?*

He had. It was unkind, but he wasn't about to acknowledge how lucky he'd been that night. If his insensitivity toward her made his gut knot with sick self-hatred, so be it. He was here for only one reason.

Jaya visibly pulled herself together. "I've arranged the Presidential Suite. It's yours as long as you need it. I'll talk to the staff, keep housekeeping out of there, tell them you're antisocial." Her tight smile said, *It's not even a lie,* and the churning rolled in his stomach again. "My new boss isn't nearly as hands-on as you were. You'll be long gone before he asks who was in there."

Hands-on?

Her cool delivery let him know that two could play this game.

Androu curled his banana-coated fingers into Theo's shirtfront and tried to wriggle down to his feet, forcing Theo to break their stare.

"I need more than a safe place to hide," Theo said, tentative in his struggle with Androu, afraid of hurting his tiny body, but not wanting him hurting himself by trying to walk around in a moving vehicle. Androu grew frustrated and started arching with temper. "I don't know what to do with babies. I need your help."

"Like a nanny? I can call an agen—"

He shook his head, impatient that she was being obtuse. "I can't trust strangers. That chauffeur hearing my name is bad enough. I need complete discretion, at least until I know the situation on the ship. Twenty-four hours, maybe forty-eight, then we can reassess."

"We? You're suggesting me? No." She shook her head. "Definitely not. I can't." Her eyes grew big, panicked maybe, but she shielded them with a downward sweep of her lashes. "I really can't. It's impossible. No. Sorry."

Because of their history. Because he'd just been a bastard about it. *Damn it.* There was a reason he didn't make promises to women: he couldn't keep them, not the emotional kind. He didn't have it in him to fulfill and make happy. Not in a romantic way. In other ways...

He thought fast. "Look at what you gain. This is the son of the Makricosta chain of hotels and resorts. Do you recognize how much favor will be bestowed on the person who keeps him from harm? How do you feel about working cruise lines? Gideon has another ship launching next fall. You're climbing ladders so I assume your career is still very important to you. You'll be able to write your own ticket, Jaya. Anything you can't do, Adara will pay for you to learn. Hell, name your price and I'll pay it to know that I've got someone I can trust for the next few days."

"To babysit." Her mouth stayed in a flat, grim line of disgust.

"They're the toughest guests to please. Free dinner goes nowhere with them."

"Am I supposed to be laughing? Because I don't find this funny."

"Look, I know it sounds sexist. That's not why I'm asking. You're good with kids. Or does it bother you that I'd offer you money to help me?"

"Your being here bothers me, Theo," she snapped, turning her face away. "This is..." Her brow flinched into anguish.

Her anxiety was a kick in the chest, especially as he sensed that her refusal wasn't coming entirely from being scorned. There was a fear component. Something more emotional. It occurred to him there might be a man in her life making her hold back.

His insides shrunk to knotted pieces of rawhide. He couldn't bring himself to ask if that was the problem. He didn't want to know.

"It's a big favor, I realize that," he managed.

She choked out a laugh. "Is that what this is? A favor? A professional courtesy?"

"It's an appeal to your better nature. Think of the children."

"Are you serious right now?" She pursed her mouth in a furious white line.

"Jaya, I can't afford mistakes. Letting a stranger look after these kids would be wrong. I need *you*. Tell me what it will cost. I'll pay it."

CHAPTER FIVE

JAYA'S EMOTIONS ROSE and fell on his words along with her temper. *Think of the children*. Really. *Really?*

As for mistakes, he obviously thought they'd made one. The truth was the complete opposite.

Her eyes kept gravitating to Androu. The resemblance was startling. Her family was supposed to be the one with the cookie-cutter genetics that stamped out cousins who could ride each other's passports. To see so much of Theo in his nephew threw her for a loop and she was already in a tailspin at seeing the man himself.

One glimpse of the sky pilot with his broody expression behind mirrored aviators and she'd turned into a lovestruck schoolgirl again. Never mind that she'd spent the past year and a half taking on responsibilities she'd never dreamed herself capable of shouldering. Men had been completely off her radar, given her being needed so much at home. She'd shut down thoughts of a future with Theo when he had neglected to return her few calls. She hadn't felt sexy and romantic anyway. She'd been tired and grief-stricken and determined to continue her career for the sake of her pride.

Finally, in the past few months, things had begun to settle into a routine. She'd felt good, if wistful, at the way things had turned out. She was empowered and in control: the independent, worldly, modern woman she'd always longed to be.

And yet she'd leaped to respond to Theo's text and had grown breathless watching his athletic frame tether his helicopter. Her eyes kept stealing glances at his leather bomber jacket and black jeans that were old enough to be scuffed gray in all the right places, accenting the muscles of his thighs. He was tough and aloof and as quietly commanding as always, framing his demands with that polite, *I need. I need a file, I need lunch at one, I need you, Jaya. I need you to care for my babies.*

Her heart lurched.

"I need to think," she mumbled, even though this situation was beyond comprehension. Her mind was going a mile a minute, trying to figure out what to do. Where was Saranya when she needed her cousin's sensible advice? *Why did life have to keep throwing such hard curves in front of her?*

No time for a pity party, she reminded herself as Oscar turned into the underground parking garage and stopped next to the elevators.

They'd arrived at Theo's *discreet* accommodation. She hadn't known what to think of that text, but she hadn't been able to ignore it. You didn't slam doors in this business no matter how badly you wanted to. He was right about her interest in her professional development. She had plans and one affair eighteen months ago wouldn't derail them—no matter how life-altering the consequences had turned out to be.

Besides, she had told herself when the text had popped up, *he was probably making the request on behalf of a favored guest.* When she'd climbed into the limo, she'd told herself not to expect Theo at the private airstrip. She'd braced herself for a mistress.

Talk about special guests who needed personal attention!

As they rode up the elevator, she sent him yet another glance of exasperation. They each carried a child. He had the bag of minimal groceries in his hand and was looking at her. His narrowed brown eyes sent a prickle of heat into her center.

No. They weren't starting that again. She'd learned her lesson, thanks. Looking away was like ripping off a bandage, but she mentally scoffed, *Think of the children.*

Although, when it came to advancing your career through favors for influential guests, he was right that they didn't come bigger than this. Managing this gorgeous hotel on the Mediterranean coast was fun and fulfilling, but if she pulled off keeping both the Marcussen Media and Makricosta Resort heirs off the paparazzi radar, she'd have it made in the shade. Paris, London, New York… She could name her price.

As they entered her hotel's best suite, she automatically searched for flaws that needed correction, but the eclectic mix of 1960s reproduction furniture, pop art, and ultramodern amenities awaited judgment with quiet perfection. Where many of France's oldest hotels were rabbit warrens of tiny rooms with even tinier beds, this one had been upgraded into chic suites of fewer rooms that catered to a very affluent clientele. An open space in the middle of the sitting room would be perfect for the babies to play. Since a curved breakfast bar was the only partition to divide the kitchenette from the adjoining dining area, they'd be in sight while their meals were made.

She couldn't have planned it better, she decided, glancing at the impossible-to-scale glass fencing around the pool deck. There were even child safety locks on the glass doors that led to the pool's edge.

If only she didn't have the sense she was approaching one of those crossroads she and Theo had talked about that night in Bali.

Don't think about it, she warned herself. He obviously didn't reminisce about what they'd shared. The memories twinkling through her like fairy dust needed to be blown off, swept up and dumped in the bin.

"This kid stinks," Theo said, pulling her back to the present and brutal reality.

"I'll order some diapers and show you how to change him," she said, refusing to be moved by the kicked puppy look he sent her.

He tried to put Androu down, but the tyke clung on, demanding to be held.

"Seriously kid, you stink."

"He's scared," Jaya provided. "Almost as scared as you."

His head went back and a mask of aloof dismissal fell over his features.

Oh, had that penetrated his thick shell? Rather than bask in satisfaction, she suffered a twinge of conscience. Deliberately insulting people wasn't her thing. She'd been on the end of too many bullying tactics herself.

And Theo's discomfort with having care of these two babies wasn't funny. It broke her heart. He really wasn't keen on children.

Still, she couldn't help noticing with a pang, "He trusts you. Do you spend a lot of time with him?"

"Whenever I'm in New York," he shrugged. "Adara's always inviting me to dinner and handing him off to me. I copy what Gideon does and we get along okay. Airplane rides, right, sport?"

Androu grinned, put out his arms and tipped forward into space, trusting he'd be caught with a firm hand under his chest. He made a raspberry noise with his mouth as Theo did a slow circle and dive with him.

Jaya took it like a punch in the stomach. Turning away from the heart-wrenching sight of Theo playing with the boy, she carried Evie to the sofa and started an animated movie on the television for her.

"Think you can handle them while I make a few calls?"

"You'll stay then," he said as though it was a done deal, but she read the underlying tension in his intense stare.

She wavered, still annoyed that he was only here because he wanted a favor, not because he wanted to see her, but a little voice inside her said, *Quit pretending you have a choice.* All the safe, secure blocks and fences and supports she'd put under and around herself trembled in warning of a bigger shake-up, but it had been destined to happen sometime. Today was as good an opportunity as any.

It was so hard to be near him, though. He still got to her, so handsome despite being stubbled and rumpled and smelling faintly of leather and fuel and sweat. Maybe because he looked so nonplussed and human. Like he genuinely needed her. Again.

He wasn't interested in her, she reminded herself, hurt even though she shouldn't be. He'd warned her not to expect more than their one night. She hadn't. It wasn't like she'd been in love with him. Not deeply, anyway. Just tentatively.

No, it was the fact he hadn't called when she'd had a serious reason to reach out to him. He shouldn't have dismissed her like some ditzy woman who didn't understand the rules. When he had texted her today with his cryptic message, she had responded. She expected that same consideration from him. He should have called her back.

He should know that he had his own baby who liked airplane rides.

Theo spoke to Gideon while Jaya chattered in French, ordering supplies to be delivered to their suite. When she began speaking Punjabi, she lost him, which irritated him further than he already was.

Forcing himself to pay attention to his own call, he heard

Gideon say, "It's a stunt. The son of an African prince. He's chasing down his runaway wife, although the guns are real and so are the consequences. We're stationary while the French and Spanish navies draw straws on whose jurisdiction we're in. Of course the FBI wants a say because we have so many Americans on board. Meanwhile, our pirate is threatening to draw all of North Africa into the fight if we don't turn over his wife, but if she's stowing away, we haven't found her. The ladies are having kittens that I sent the babies off the ship. Are they all right?"

"Safe," Theo replied, eyeing Jaya as she toed off her shoes and shrunk by a couple of inches. Something in her expression seemed disturbingly vulnerable as she spoke with a lilt of persuasion into her phone. Her tone riled up oddly protective instincts in him when, on the surface, she looked more self-assured than ever.

Again he wondered if there was a man in her life, then cut off his speculation. The thought of her with a lover made him nauseous.

"Can you keep them out of sight?" Gideon continued. "Nic's planning a broadcast from his cabin—man can't stand to be scooped—but we want to leave the impression they're still here, otherwise…"

"Understood. We're off the grid."

"Excellent. We're a day from shore once we can move again and may have to wait for a slip in Marseilles. I'll be in touch with an arrival time."

Theo ended the call, mind eased that his siblings and spouses weren't in immediate danger. Now he just had to—

A knock sounded and Jaya lowered her phone to motion at Theo. "That will be the bellman with the things I asked him to bring up. Take Androu to the bedroom while he brings everything in."

Evie was rapt with her princess movie, dark head below the sofa back. He stepped out of the main room and continued to watch her as he listened to Jaya direct a pair of young men to leave everything inside the door. She continued her call as they left.

After hanging up a moment later, she walked him through his first diaper change, then briskly began moving objects to higher ground and double checking that doors were locked, particularly the one to the pool deck.

"We could swim with them later. They'd like that," she murmured, sounding distracted, her nervous tension palpable. Maybe because he was hovering, but he couldn't help himself. He told himself it was the new experience of child-minding. Androu still clung with determined little fists and tight legs which was a disturbing feeling that reinforced to him how inadequate he was with the task of reassurance. All Theo could do was hold him and follow Jaya around.

He wasn't used to her taking an avoidance tack, though. In Bali, she had looked him in the eye and smiled every time he caught her eye, then blushed and shied maybe, but she'd never refused to meet his gaze. Her brisk movements around the flat were as much about putting distance between them as securing the space for the children.

Aware he was seeking his own sort of reassurance, he made himself halt in one spot and quit tagging after her like a lost puppy, but he couldn't stop himself from watching her slender limbs and smooth efficiency. He couldn't help remembering that her skin had smelled like cloves and almonds and her hair had been a cool weight of silk that had warmed against his bare chest.

She paused to scan the equipment littering the entrance.

"That seems like a lot of stuff. Two highchairs and a booster?" It looked like there were three portable cots, not that he was an expert on baby furniture.

"We can deal with this later. What did your brother-in-law say?"

He brought her up to speed and she nodded jerkily. "So

a couple of days. You're really sure you want me here? I'll have to spend the night. That means—"

"It's an imposition, I realize. Do you—" He swore under his breath, unable to put off asking. He didn't even want to know, but it might help control his still thriving attraction. "Is there someone in your life this will affect?" he forced himself to ask.

She stilled, not looking at him. After a long second, she nodded. Then she lifted an expression that was frozen between tortured and fretful.

He swallowed, surprised how deeply the knife thrust and twisted even though he'd braced for it. Even though she had every right to get on with her life. He certainly had no right to possessiveness. This situation was going to be unbearable.

Let her call an agency.

Before he could work up the will to make the concession, soft, pitiful whimpers rose over a lullaby being sung on screen. Evie's sobs turned into a heart-wrenching wail that made Jaya's eyes pop. She rushed toward the girl.

"Baby, what happened? Did you hurt yourself?"

Theo lowered his lids in a wince. "I didn't realize what you'd put on. That's Rowan's voice as the fairy godmother."

Jaya gathered up the toddler in a cuddle and murmured words of comfort. Her swift loving care to a child she barely knew struck into his toughened heart like an axe, leaving a wound that gaped and ached. He'd just realized how perfect Jaya was on the heels of learning she belonged to another man. She *should* be with someone. She deserved to be happy.

He still hated himself for never calling her back. He'd never felt so alone and lonely—and he knew loneliness like other people knew the lyrics to a favorite song.

With his breath burning his lungs, he asked, "What should we do?"

He meant, *Should we call in someone else?* But she only rocked Evie and said, "There's nothing we can do. Little ones need their mamas." Her brow flinched before she tried to distract Evie with a cheerful, "But we could go swimming. Do you like to swim?"

The bait and switch worked and after waiting for swimsuits and special diapers, they all climbed into the pool. Again Jaya was a natural, showing him how to hold Androu and coach him to kick while Evie proved to be part mermaid, pushing herself free of Jaya's grip and swimming to the edge where she came up to grin proudly.

It was a surprisingly conflict-free hour as he shifted his focus onto the moment and the safety of the children. Okay, he was also pretty damned aware of Jaya's nipples poking against the wet cups of her modest one-piece black swimsuit, but thankfully the cool water kept his libido from responding too wildly. She was *way* off-limits, even further than when she'd worked for him, so he suppressed his interest as best he could.

They were back to their Bali roles, polite and capable of basic camaraderie as they discussed neutral topics like the children, the weather, and Marseilles.

Until she said, "Theo," with surprising gravity behind him.

"Yes?" he prompted, keeping his back to her as he boosted Evie toward the edge.

Ah, hell, he had his back to her. Inner tension came on so fast he felt like he solidified and fractured in the same breath.

The scars should have become less of an issue for him in the last year. His whole family had started coming to terms with their childhood, but he'd spent so many years clenching his teeth against it all that he couldn't bring himself to open up to any of his siblings about what was plain as the stripes on his back. There didn't seem any point and they were still so awkward with each other. He wanted to be friends with his older brother, but making that happen was easier if they both pretended the ugliness in their early lives hadn't happened. Maybe it was counterproductive, but all of them had been raised to be polite and ignore. They very easily fell back on that coping strategy.

Jaya was private and quiet, but she was soft. Anything that moved her started at heart level. If she asked him about this, it would be because she was concerned.

Knowing that made the cracks in him extend to even deeper places, touching into areas that were raw and sensitive. Thank God he had a baby to keep an eye on and didn't have to turn and face her pointed silence. He waited with ears that felt stretched and hollow, not ready for this conversation, not imagining he could ever be ready, but he didn't know how to avoid it.

After a long interminable moment, she asked, "What happened to your back?"

Ensuring Evie was out of the water and sitting safely on the edge, he kept a hand on her tiny frame and glanced at Jaya, dreading her pity.

Her anxious frown was so kind it made him want to shudder, like he'd had too big a taste of sugar. He swallowed back a thickness in his throat and was left with the bitter residue of a bleak time when he'd been insignificant and helpless.

"Exactly what you imagine happened," he answered in as controlled a tone as he could manage. Maybe he should have seen a counselor by now, but why? The emotional scars were as permanent as the physical ones. All he could do was accept them and try not to feel ashamed. He was smart enough to know it wasn't his fault, even if he'd grown up believing he must have done something to deserve all that abuse.

"Who—? When…? *Why?*" she choked.

"My father." A shadow of chagrin touched him. Shame that he had been so reviled by his own flesh and blood. Surely that meant there was something wrong with him.

Swallowing, he tried to find his equilibrium. He stepped back and nodded at Evie, inviting her to jump and swim toward him. Once he'd caught her up safe against his chest, he forced himself to look into Jaya's appalled face again.

"He was drunk." He tried to say it matter-of-factly, but a taut line inside him vibrated, making him unsteady. "I didn't keep my brother in his room as I'd been told."

"That's…" She shook her head and he could imagine someone as tenderhearted toward children as she was couldn't comprehend such cruelty. "How old were you?"

He reached for his well-practiced technique of shutting down, wanting to shrug off the details, but he couldn't seem to make it happen. No one had ever invited him to talk about this.

His body shivered as though the water he stood in was full of ice. "Eight. That's why I don't drink. That's why…"

He didn't want to apologize for Bali. They'd been using each other, she'd said so, but she had wound up expecting more after all. He'd let her down. He hated failure, but he didn't have anything else to offer. Maybe if she understood that, she wouldn't hate him so much.

Squinting into the sunlight reflected off the water, he spoke in a graveled voice. "That night in Bali…Adara had called me earlier that day to tell me she'd contacted Nic. We hadn't seen him in years, not since we were kids. Before he left home, our lives were pretty normal and decent. After Nic was gone, both our parents drank. Our father became violent. I blamed Nic because I never paused to think about how we were all kids when it happened. He hadn't had a choice, either. I hadn't considered that he might have suffered in his own way. When Adara told me he had…"

He shook his head, remembering how everything had

skewed in his mind, falling in a jumble he couldn't make sense of. Then Jaya had arrived, sweet Jaya, soothing and earnest and warm, wanting to say goodbye. He hadn't been able to bear the idea of her leaving. All he'd wanted was to keep her close.

"It was a lot to process," he said, hoping his strong dose of self-deprecation hid the impact her sharing herself had had on him.

"I understand."

"Do you?" he asked gruffly.

He wasn't a talkative man. He didn't have drinking buddies or squash partners. Men didn't typically share their personal garbage anyway. Not with each other, but he'd entrusted Jaya with his emotional safety that night. Maybe he hadn't shared his inner dialogue, but when she'd lain against him, naked and soft, her breath caressing his neck and her hair tickling his arm, he'd wanted to.

He wanted that emotional safety net again. Craved it like air.

Bending her dark head over Androu, she said, "I'm lying. I don't understand how anyone can be cruel to someone smaller than they are. It upsets me."

She looked up and the unprecedented connection he'd felt with her in Bali manifested like a beam between them, pulling them toward each other. The urge to move close and cover her mouth with his own was almost irresistible. He could practically taste her papaya flavor, could almost feel the cool mango smoothness of her lips against his.

A buzzer broke the spell.

Jaya's expression fell to one that was appalled and startled before she buckled her shoulders in a cringe. She wasn't given to swearing as far as he knew, but she muttered something in Punjabi that might have been a curse.

"Who is it?" he asked, worried they'd suffered a leak to the press.

"Quentin. I asked him to bring…" Her look of remorseful appeal made all the sharp edges in him abrade against each other.

"Your things?" he guessed. "Understandable."

A ripping sensation went through him nonetheless, tearing away the paper walls he used to disguise the fact his childhood still affected him. He thought, *Lucky, lucky man,* and hated his rival for being smart enough to win her heart and keep it. The bastard had better be good to her.

He waved her to climb the stairs before him then had to avert his gaze from her ass and the backs of her long slender thighs. "Is he staying?" *There'll be a murder-suicide in tomorrow's papers.*

"I thought we'd have more time to talk before he arrived," she said, handing him a towel before wrapping Androu like a Mexican burrito.

"What else is there to say?"

Her flashing glance was loaded as a hot pistol, but she only carried Androu inside. He followed on heavy feet, reluctant to meet her…what was the beau's label? She wasn't wearing a ring so they weren't married or engaged. Maybe they were only dating.

"We'll swim more later," he promised Evie as she protested leaving the pool to come inside. He paused to reach up and lock the door behind him as he entered, then forced himself into the foyer where more bags had landed among the flotsam there.

A stocky blond man chopped his German tirade short as he spied Theo over Jaya's shoulder. His blue eyes were sharp, his manner too damned proprietary.

Every male instinct came alive in Theo, despite having no claim on Jaya. He looked right into the man's eyes with challenge, mentally aware it was wrong, but he couldn't help himself. If the guy wanted her, he could damn well fight for her.

"So. You finally turn up," the German gruffed.

"Quentin, please." Jaya murmured as she turned to look at Theo. Her imploring eyes filled with compunction while she kept a hand in the middle of her paramour's chest. No, not on his chest. As she shifted, Theo saw the baby trustingly clutched in the man's curved arm.

Don't drop Evie, Theo reminded himself, but the sight of that mite with black hair, dusky skin and curious brown eyes was a kick in the gut. He was Jaya's. There was no mistaking the maternal protectiveness in her hand on the baby boy's tiny blue T-shirt.

Time stood still as he processed all of them standing there with babies in their arms, Quentin with his rumpled suit and grim expression, he and Jaya practically naked with towels around their waists. Yes, this was good and humiliating to meet the father of her child with his pants proverbially around his ankles and his ineptness with children on full display.

"Quentin is my cousin's husband. I told you about Saranya when I was leaving Bali. Do you remember?" Jaya asked.

"Of course." Not the father then. His mind cycloned as he attempted to process this new information. If Quentin wasn't the father, who was? To hide his inner chaos, he fell back on the scrupulous manners drilled into him as a child. "How is she?"

"Dead," Quentin said flatly.

Nice. Theo surprised himself by thinking he might understand Quentin's bitterness a little, given how agonized he was at the mere thought of Jaya not being available to him. He couldn't imagine how he'd react if she were beyond his reach in a grave.

"I'm sorry," he offered, aware how useless the words were, but it's what you said.

"You should be," the German growled.

I didn't kill her, Theo bit back, able to curb the desire to be cruel because Quentin wasn't involved with Jaya, but if he wasn't the man in her life, who was?

His gaze returned to the bright brown eyes that were almost familiar, yet not like Jaya's nearly black irises. A hit of déjà vu accosted him because he could have sworn he'd looked into those eyes earlier today...

The air dried up around him. His heart began to pound with thick hammer blows inside his chest. The kicked feeling in his gut tightened around a serrated blade that turned low and without mercy. If he had bones, they'd vaporized.

Don't. Drop. Evie. He rather desperately tried to recollect if Demitri had been to Bali or had business in Marseille last year.

"Will you please let me handle this?" Jaya's voice seemed to come from far away. She tried to take the baby from Quentin, but she already held Androu.

For the life of him, Theo couldn't approach and take his nephew, even though he knew he should.

"Let you play house?" the German grumbled. "For how long? There's a reason you and Saranya were always railroaded by the men in your family. You *let* them."

"So if I tell you to butt out and leave, you will?"

Quentin gave her a stern look, but followed it with a resigned sigh that ended in a kiss on her cheek. He transferred the baby into her arms and straightened to throw another bitter glare at Theo.

The animosity in that look told Theo who the father was. Not Demitri. Hell, he didn't know if he should be relieved or not. How he stayed on his feet, he'd never know.

"Call me if you need me," Quentin said to Jaya and walked out.

Jaya took a shaken breath as the door closed, then turned to face him. The two boys she held weren't far apart in age and despite the slightly darker skin tone on the smaller one,

and the black hair where Androu's was brown, their eyes
and mouth were mirror images.

The sensation of dissolving from the inside out continued to assault Theo. He couldn't form a proper thought. He
tried, but this was more than he could grasp. More than he
wanted to believe.

"This is Zephyr," Jaya said, voice strained, but firm and
a trifle defiant. "My...*our*...son."

CHAPTER SIX

THEO STARED AT her like she was a stranger. His wide tanned chest didn't seem to rise and fall at all where he clutched Evie in a towel against it. His lips were white and severe, his stillness frightening.

Accusation sharpened his level glare.

"I tried to tell you," she began, then thought, *No*. No remorse. He hadn't returned her calls. That's why this was a shock to him. If she hadn't found the right time to bring it up in the past hour, well, he'd had plenty of opportunities in the past year.

Nevertheless, a vision of the striped scars on his back flashed into her mind's eye. Her indignation deflated and their situation became a tangle again. How had they even got here, staring like a pair of cowboys waiting for the other to draw?

Her arms ached worse than her head, but not as bad as her heart.

"They're heavy," she said. "Can we move into the lounge?"

"Of course." He stepped forward and lifted Androu from her, averting his gaze from Zephyr's shy smile.

Zephyr was an engaging little chap, happy as anything, and Theo's turning away from him struck at the very core of her, setting her blood to boil.

Hugging her baby's tiny frame into her wet swimsuit,

she told herself to turn around and walk out, leave Theo to his "real" family.

Zephyr's connection to the other children stopped her. Without her own cousin's love and support, her life would be very different right now. Those sorts of ties were sacred to her and Zephyr wasn't likely to enjoy many of them with her side of the family. Her parents and siblings were even less inclined to speak to her now that she had a bastard soiling the family name.

Was Theo really as narrow-minded as they were, capable of rejecting a boy who hadn't done anything except have the gall to come to life inside her?

"Did you seriously just wet through this towel onto my arm?" Theo asked Androu in an aggrieved tone. "This kid hates me."

"He's a baby. They don't know how to be malicious." *So don't blame Zephyr if you're angry at me,* she added in a silent bite.

A tense twenty minutes passed as she took Evie and Zephyr into her bedroom to dress the girl and herself, leaving Theo charged with Androu. When she emerged, Theo wore a more truculent expression than any toddler. He held a naked Androu and a disposable diaper that looked worse for wear.

"This is why I'm not cut out to be a father," he charged. "I can't even manage the basics."

"Well, you are a father, so I guess you'll have to learn, won't you?" she shot back, heart wobbling in her chest at her own audacity. But this was one thing she wouldn't let the implacable Theo Makricosta block out. It was too important, and not just to Zephyr.

"I wasn't supposed to be. You *promised*. You said it would be a disaster—"

"Zephyr is not a disaster. Do *not*—" She cut herself off from raising her voice, looking away for a second to gather herself, afraid she'd frighten the children if she gave in to the press of emotions strangling her. Tears were right behind the anger so she swallowed hard, trying to keep it all from releasing.

"We're all frazzled and hungry," she managed in a croaking voice. "I called room service while we were changing. I'll dress Androu and once we feed the little ones and they're settled, I'll explain. All right?"

He glared, but didn't argue. An hour later, as she scrubbed faces and hands, he washed his own hands and grumbled, "I'm wearing more than they ate."

"It's better than wearing *what* they ate," she countered, not sure how they'd managed to be such a well-coordinated team when they were barely speaking. He'd let her lead, which surprised her, copying her actions with great care and concentration, as if there was a perfect system for feeding a baby.

It was such a contradictory vision of him and did funny things to her heart. He was so gloriously inept, but so determined to master these little child-care tasks. Like he'd suffer terribly if he failed to do it right.

Get smacked, maybe. With a belt.

Oh, Theo. Her throat filled with words she couldn't voice.

"That's gross," he replied after taking a moment to get her meaning about what the kids ate.

"It's reality," she murmured, lifting Zephyr from his chair and adding, "Do you want to watch them in the other room or finish cleaning up in here?"

As the older pair toddled off in two directions, he gave her a boggled look. "Maybe we should call an agency."

She tensed. So much for their tentative accord. "You don't want me and Zephyr here after all then." It was all she could do to pretend his rejection of their son didn't shatter her.

"No, I mean we need more help. This is a lot of work! Has either of us sat down since we walked in here four hours ago?" He skimmed a hand over his dry but uncombed hair and stabbed a look at Zephyr. "But now we've got this development to manage, too. Discretion is more important than ever, so I guess that leaves us stuck doing it ourselves."

"Development?" she repeated, hysterical laughter competing with outrage. *Stuck?*

"Who else besides your cousin's husband knows I'm— That you and I—"

"Made a baby?" she provided tartly. She tried to remember that he wasn't the most verbal person alive and this was all quite a shock for him, but honestly, why was it so hard for him to acknowledge his son? "Are you ashamed of Zephyr?" she guessed in a tone that thinned to outrage as the possibility sank in. It was the worst thing he could throw at her, striking directly into her Achilles heel. Into her soul.

"I'm shocked! You had to know I would be." He'd changed into a basic white T-shirt that strained across his chest as he gestured toward the view of the sea. "I can't have my family finding out through some cheap sensationalism on the internet. We've suffered enough secrets and lies as it is." He pinched the bridge of his nose.

Unwillingly, she felt sorry for him, which was crazy. He didn't deserve it, but, "I did try to call you when I first realized I was pregnant," she reminded.

He sighed, brows coming together in a pensive frown. "I debated calling you back, I did, but Adara turned up pregnant and given her previous miscarriages Demitri and I had to take over her workload. Then our mother died. By the time the dust settled, there didn't seem any point in contacting you."

They'd both been going through a lot. She supposed she couldn't fault him too much for not returning her calls under those circumstances.

"But I trusted you to take that pill, Jaya. What happened?"

The blame in his tone stabbed her, even though she'd tried to prepare herself for it every time she'd mentally walked through this conversation. Yes, she'd failed to protect both of them from the consequences of their night together and she was willing to own that, but his anger and disappointment filled her with umbrage. She didn't want to feel defensive and solely responsible. He knew what could happen from unprotected sex. It didn't matter that she had a better understanding of what had driven him that night. He had still chosen to sleep with her to satisfy his own selfish needs.

Just as, when it came down to it, she'd kept their baby for her own selfish reasons.

"The pill was expired," she explained with as much dignity as she could scrape together. "I thought I'd be able to get a fresh one once I landed in France, but with the time change and Saranya being so ill, it was days before I came up for air. By then I'd missed the window. Then I thought I'd wait to see if I had anything to worry about."

She flinched from the intensity of his judgmental stare, sinking bleakly back into that time of despair, feeling again the torn sensation of having said goodbye to her life in Bali, and Theo, then facing an even more brutal goodbye with her cousin.

Lifting her chin, she finished without apology, "When it turned out I was pregnant, I couldn't take steps to end it. I just couldn't, not with Saranya dying in front of me. I needed something to look forward to. The promise of life and love."

Scanning the lounge to ensure the older kids were staying out of trouble, she tried to hide that she'd also needed her connection to Theo to continue. Her conscience had tortured her over not keeping her word, but she wasn't sorry. Not one bit.

"I tried to tell you because you deserved to know." She cleared her throat. "I didn't, and don't, expect anything from you. Not money. Not marriage. He was my decision. He's my responsibility."

There. That's all she'd ever wanted to say, even though she had ached every day to share her pregnancy and baby with Theo. Zephyr was such a little miracle. She wanted Theo to love him as much as she did.

"Oh, sweetie, don't eat that—" she blurted, realizing Androu had picked lint out of the carpet.

Rushing forward was a much-needed break from the weight of Theo's gaze. She couldn't face him after what she'd just said and didn't want to see his relief at being absolved of any duty or involvement with his son.

Theo tried to find comfort in her letting him off the hook. God knew he didn't want to explore the miasma of primordial goo that bubbled inside him as he considered what it meant to be a father.

Inexplicably he was hurt, however. Stinging with rejection at her wanting nothing to do with him.

Fortunately, he was too busy to dwell on whether he should feel sorry for himself or not. Once the kitchenette was tidied, there were beds to set up and pajamas to be ordered, then everyone had to be threaded into them—which was like pushing a rope up a staircase.

"I'm thinking we need bedtime stories and some stuffies. Do they have special blankets or sleeping toys? This could be a rough night," Jaya warned as she placed a call to a nearby shop before it closed.

"Unlike the day it's been?" he drawled, waving agreement to whatever she wanted to charge to the room.

He wasn't trying to fuel a fight. It struck him how painfully familiar this tension was, like a typical Makricosta gathering. They had a full-grown elephant between them in the shape of a dark-haired baby boy, but they remained civil, only speaking about the logistics of what needed to be done as they ran their mini-hotel. It should have been a relief, but he found the circumventing and pretending frustrating.

Was this his punishment for the mistake of not wearing a condom? Because he was feeling castigated, chastised and rebuked. Slapped around, knocked down and kicked to the curb.

Why? he found himself wanting to demand. *Why don't you want anything from me? Because you're afraid I'll screw up?*

He'd never been able to challenge his father, not without suffering worse for it, and he wasn't sure how to act around Jaya when he felt this abused. His primary instinct when his emotions were churned up was to isolate himself, but no luck on that score. It was all hands on deck and he was about as frayed and tired as the toddlers, barely keeping it together as he counted down the minutes to their bedtime.

If only Jaya would offer the same quiet reassurance she kept giving to the homesick tykes. He watched her adeptly keep them from shedding more than a few sniffles, relieved to know he'd made the right choice in tracking her down, but he was damned jealous of each cuddle and kiss she offered.

His gaze fell on Zephyr and he experienced the crack between the eyes that was his own egocentric vulnerability eighteen months ago. If only he could go back to the ignorance that had been bliss yesterday.

Not all the way back to Bali, though. He didn't regret making love to her.

Disturbed, he shifted his gaze to Jaya, worried she could read his betraying thoughts.

He wanted to resent her for letting him down, but after what she'd told him about her cousin, he couldn't find it in him to hate her for failing to take the pill. Maybe the promise of love and life hadn't been uppermost in his mind when his mother had been dying, but he had an inkling how helpless and hopeless she must have felt.

He couldn't judge her for using procreation as a coping strategy, either, could he? Not when he'd employed it with her—in a rather shortsighted manner—when he'd been under the duress of Adara's confession about Nic.

And where was the point in being angry about what she should have done? It couldn't be undone. The child was here.

Still, he couldn't face this, couldn't face fatherhood. What kind of an example had been set for him? Look at his back.

Not that the children had any idea how useless he was. Once they'd scattered their new toys across the blanket Jaya had spread on the floor of the lounge, Evie brought him a book.

"Jaya's the reader. I'm the sentry," he said, motioning to his sprawled body acting as a fence between the corner of a chair and the length of the sofa to keep them corralled.

"Peas," she implored with a heart-stealing smile, reeling him in an inch. Until today he hadn't spent much time with her, but she was the most gentle, tender thing he'd ever seen, enchanted with Baby Zepper, chattering like old friends to Androu, missing her parents and thus taking to Jaya with impulsive hugs and embraces.

"Sure, I'll read," Jaya said breezily. "If Uncle takes the next dirty bottom."

"Never mind. I got this." Theo sat up so his back was against the edge of the sofa.

Evie wormed herself into his side, making him lift his

elbow in surprise. The weight of her head felt surprisingly endearing as she let it droop against his rib cage.

He imagined she was just getting sleepy, but it still felt like a very trusting gesture, one that gave him a funny sensation of fullness around his heart.

As he started to read, Androu toddled over with a car clutched in his fist, drool glossing his chin. As he plopped down on Theo's other side, a drip fell to slide down Theo's wrist.

"Seriously, dude, I'm going to talk to your parents about your manners."

"He can't help teething," Jaya scolded, coming across with a tissue to dry the boy's face.

As she bent, Theo raised his hand so she could wipe the spit off his arm. Zephyr, balanced on her hip, read some kind of invitation from their body language and tilted out of her grip, reaching out with his short arms for Theo.

Jaya gasped, so caught by surprise she almost dropped the boy.

Theo had no choice but to catch him one-handed, guiding the boy into a safe landing against his chest. The tot flipped and slid into his lap like an otter down a log.

Distant base instincts cautioned him about the tiny feet kicking near his jewels, but a stronger, less easy to define reaction took over. He was shaken by the natural way Zephyr relaxed into him. It was passive aggression at its best, clashing into his protective inner walls with unseen yet gong-like reverberations. He'd been avoiding touching the boy, thinking he'd decide later whether he'd take an active part in the boy's life, after he'd figured out what to make of the situation and how many options he had.

He didn't want this puppy warmth sitting in his center, thawing the tight frozen pillars he used to brace himself against the world.

But when he looked up at Jaya, thinking to ask her to

take him, her expression was so vulnerable, so fearful of rejection on the boy's behalf, he couldn't do that to her. Hell, he couldn't do it to a child. To his *son*.

This situation was the most perplexing, dumbfounding circumstance of his life, but these little creatures were incredibly defenseless. Like her, he couldn't understand how anyone could hurt a child. He certainly couldn't do it himself.

Which didn't make him father material, he reminded himself, ignoring the clenched sensation around his heart. Kids needed a lot more than the basics of food and shelter and a soft place to sit. Nascent things like love were beyond him so she was setting him up for failure with Zephyr. That was not something he could easily forgive, but he couldn't hurt the boy out of anger with her.

Aware of Jaya standing over him, arms hugged across her middle, he refused to look up to see how she reacted to his playing human recliner.

"There was a farm up the road from my mother's house in Chatham," he said, trying for dismissive when he could hear the rattled edge in his tone. "I saw a sow there once, knocked over by her own piglets because they wanted to nurse. Now I know how she felt." He wasn't doing this because he wanted to, he implied. He had no choice.

He began to read aloud, silently willing her to go away. It was one thing to have his emotions hanging by a thread while children listened to him struggle through a story. They wouldn't know the difference, but Jaya was perceptive. He hated knowing she could tell how confused and defenseless this made him.

After a few seconds, she drew a hitched breath.

"Do you know if Androu has a bottle before bed? I'm going to make one for Zeph." Her voice was blessedly lacking in inflection.

"Text Adara and ask."

"Okay, but—" She started across to her phone. "What have you told her? Does she know I'm here?"

"I told Gideon I'd recruited you, but that was when we first got here. They don't know about…" He looked down at the dark head turning against his breastbone, more interested in the older babies and chewing his fist than the picture book.

Jaya didn't answer. He thought she was texting until he heard the familiar shutter-click of the camera app. He glanced up in dismay.

She shrugged. "This might never happen again." Her trim figure, encased in three-quarter length jeans and a lime-green shirt, disappeared toward the kitchenette.

He drew in a breath that burned his lungs, suddenly wondering whether he had any choice when it came to involvement in his son's life. Jaya might have made up her mind that *this might never happen again.*

CHAPTER SEVEN

"I CAN HONESTLY say this has been the most grueling day of my life," Theo said, flopping onto the sofa when he and Jaya came back to the lounge after settling all the babies.

"Try nineteen hours of labor," she chirped, picking up toys rather than sitting.

Guilt assailed him. He'd put his sister's pregnancy ahead of Jaya's. Unknowingly, sure, but at the time he'd convinced himself he was putting both women's best interests ahead of his own. Somehow he didn't think saying so would be an easy sell to the woman who'd struggled through childbirth alone.

"Was it bad?" he asked, bracing inwardly while leaning to gather the toys within reach.

"It wasn't a picnic, but it was fairly typical. He was worth it."

"That's what my sister says. I don't know how women do it." He searched her expression, awed that she wasn't berating him.

"You just do. There's no time to figure out how." Clenching a stuffed panda between her tense brown hands, she said, "Kind of like the way I sprang him on you. There wasn't any opportunity to prepare you, but you still seem furious so let's have it. Don't keep giving me the robot mode of being terribly polite. If you want to yell, yell. Except, don't wake the babies, but—" She sighed sharply. "I know you feel lied to, but I swear I didn't do it for money or to take advantage of you."

His heart turned over in his chest. He wished he could dismiss her as conniving. It would be so much easier to keep his own emotions out of it if she had none, but one of her main attractions for him beyond the physical had always been her earnest sincerity.

"I believe that money was the last thing on your mind."

Her smile of relief made him wish they could leave it there, but she needed to fully comprehend the rest. Leaning his elbows on his knees, he rubbed his face, trying to erase any sign of the turmoil still blowing like a hurricane inside him.

"But whether you want money or not, it's the only thing you'll ever get from me."

Her lips slacked in surprise, then pursed. Her brows drew together and she shifted her gaze to the darkened windows. "I don't want any."

"No, you want me to be a father, I can tell. But Jaya, that stuff I told you earlier about my lousy childhood. That's why I never wanted to be one." He looked past her knees, jaw clenching, seeing nothing but a blur of his past. "It's not just fear that I'll turn out like the old man and raise my hand—"

"You wouldn't," she said.

He lifted his gaze to focus on her face, trying to read her meaning. Was it a challenging, *You wouldn't dare?* Or an expression of confidence in him?

He mentally stepped away from trying to decipher her words, disturbed by how badly he wanted her to believe in him when he didn't know if he could believe in himself.

"I'd like to think I wouldn't, but if my life fell apart the way my dad's did and I tried to cope by drinking…" He rubbed the hard tension from his jaw, needing her to understand that whether she wanted something from him or not, there was nothing here. "Beyond that, though, is the lack of substance in me. I told you what kind of man I was that night in Bali. I'd make a terrible father. I don't make strong connections, ever. Kids need something better than what I'm capable of offering."

It was the hard truth, but he still searched her expression, wanting her to argue.

"Aren't you underestimating yourself?" Hope wound through her question like a strand of gold, catching at him, filling him with bittersweet satisfaction at how predictable she was. He wished he could live up to her view of him, he really did.

He shook his head. "The closest connection I have is with my sister and we don't talk about personal things." Well, he didn't. Adara had opened up about her marriage when it had almost fallen apart, but he'd only had to listen and stand by her. No reciprocation required.

"What about your brother? You said you talked to Adara about Nic that night we—I mean in Bali."

Inexplicably, he found himself rising, finding himself verging on retreat because her question stood on his toes and leaned into his space, but he couldn't walk out. He owed her some kind of explanation.

He tried to pace off his discomfort. "Adara talked, I listened. Since then I've told you more about how that has impacted me than I've ever admitted to anyone else."

"Really?" She cocked her head in surprise.

"This is what I'm saying, Jaya. I don't connect on a meaningful level. To be honest, I wish I *could* take a page from Nic's book. He grew up isolated and neglected and he's made a really good life for himself. A nice family with Ro and Evie. So has Adara with Gideon. I look at the way they dote on their kids and I'm envious, but I don't even know what words describe those things they demonstrate so how could I become like they are?"

She pressed her drawn lips together and swallowed like she was fighting back deep feelings. Her unblinking eyes glittered before she dropped her lashes to hide them.

"Not every man falls in love at first sight with his child," she allowed in a voice that made his heart shrivel. "It's different for a woman, especially when she carries the baby for nine months. The attachment is there from the minute she holds the baby."

"What if the attachment never arrives?" His worst nightmare was producing that same feeling of being unwanted and unloved that he'd grown up with. "What would that do to Zephyr if he expects it and it isn't there? Don't bother trying to answer that because I know how it feels. I thought I had an attachment to my father and he wound up attacking me with his belt."

She flinched like he'd struck her and he wanted to kick himself.

"I shouldn't talk to you about it." He paced away across the room. This was why he didn't talk about his personal life. "It upsets you to hear it and it doesn't do a damned thing to resolve it for me, but that's what I'm trying to get across. He broke that part of me. I don't know how to be what a child would need. I only know what not to be."

"That's a start."

"A very pitiful one. Zephyr deserves better. Be the mother I know you are and admit that. You wouldn't settle for anything less than the best for him."

She didn't say anything, only pressed her knuckles to her mouth and kept her head bent. She might even have nodded.

That hurt. It hurt so bad he couldn't breathe, even though—maybe especially because—it was the honesty he'd demanded.

"So let's talk about money," he said.

Her gaze came up, dagger sharp with disbelief. "I was

dead serious when I said the last thing I'd ever do is use him to extort anything from you."

"That doesn't mean you'll never struggle. He's the only progeny I'll have." He certainly wouldn't take any woman's word and play roulette with his sperm again. He should look into a vasectomy, he supposed, filing that thought for later because right now he couldn't imagine sleeping with anyone but the woman in this room.

Weird how he could be having this incredibly uncomfortable conversation and still be aroused by the way her breasts moved in the confines of her bra or her pants clung to her backside as she bent.

Forcing himself to set down thoughts too hot to entertain, he said, "Whether you want it or not, I'll set up a portfolio for both of you. You might as well have a say in it."

"Oh, Theo! I was going to leave Zephyr with Quentin tonight." She sprang into action again, tossing soft bears and cloth books into a box that groceries had been delivered in. "Then I saw how much poor Evie and Androu were missing their mamas and I couldn't deprive Zephyr of a night with his own. And I was mad at you! I was mad that you ignored my calls because I never wanted your stupid money or a relationship or anything for *me.* I only wanted to be decent and let you know you have a son. And now what are you doing? Offering me money and trying to pretend your child doesn't exist."

"I didn't say that," he growled, pushing angry fists into his pockets, slouching as he turned his back on her. "That's not what I said."

"Then take part in his life!"

"How? I've just explained that I don't want to hurt him, physically or mentally, but I very likely would!"

"But that's it, that's the vital piece you think you don't have. You already care about him. Don't you? A little?" *Don't beg,* she warned herself. He might be right. It might be better to buffer Zephyr against indifference if that's all Theo was capable of.

She really didn't want to believe that, though. She didn't want her son growing up feeling as she had, dismissed and unimportant. For heaven's sake, didn't he realize what a gift she'd given him? A *son*. That was supposed to elevate *her* value in his eyes.

Congratulations, Jaya. Modern women raise their children alone and *nobody* regards her as special. The clash of cultural mores made her furious.

"Don't write Zephyr off without even trying to get to know him. That's callous. It's cowardly. You be a better man than that," she demanded with a point of her finger. "I never would have slept with you if I believed you lacked compassion and the ability to respect someone for their worth."

"Really." He spun to confront her, head thrown back in challenge as he stared down his nose at her. "I thought we were using each other for escape that night."

And he was getting his back up because he thought she'd been after a deeper relationship after all. Maybe, yes, way down she had feelings for him that longed to be requited, but she shook her head vehemently.

"No. I mean yes, I was using you. But I wouldn't have used a man less decent than you are."

He barked out a disbelieving laugh. "Nice."

"That didn't come out right. I'm saying that I didn't expect to have sex with you, but it happened because I respect you. And I'm not sorry. I'm happy we made Zephyr. I was resigned to not having children so…" She was saying too much. With a pleat stressing her brow, she clammed her mouth and decided they'd talked enough for one night.

"Really?" He tucked in his chin. "You're the most natural person I've ever seen with kids. Was there something wrong that made you think you couldn't have any?"

They'd definitely talked enough.

"I told you my career was important to me," she mumbled, casting about for the last of the toys, but they'd tidied up all of them.

"And you still have a career despite being a single parent. Not always an ideal situation, I'm sure, but I can't believe you didn't see before Zephyr that kids and career can coexist. You must have considered it an option. You didn't say you weren't *planning* to have kids, but that you resigned yourself not to, like you didn't think it was possible. Are you okay, Jaya? Because my sister may not have confided all the trauma of her miscarriages, but I'm aware there can be complications with any pregnancy. It makes me a real bastard for not protecting you that night if I put your life at risk."

"Have you listened at all? I was textbook normal. I'm made to have babies and I'm not sorry I had him. Not one bit. That's all I meant. Now we should get some rest. Even if they sleep through the night—which they won't—they'll be up early." She tried to scoot past him.

He caught her arm.

She caught her breath.

Silly, silly Jaya. Still flushing like a preteen at this man's touch. Shyness kept her face averted. She didn't want him to see how much he still affected her.

His thumb brushed her bare skin, hot palm leaving an imprint of his firm but gentle grip. *Those hands.* Knowledge burned in a trail from the light caress of his thumb to the pit of her stomach and lower, flooding her inner thighs with tingling warmth. Her face stung with the pressure of a hard blush.

He cleared his throat and pulled his touch away like he felt the scald. When he spoke, he didn't pursue the other topic, but floored her with something else.

"When I asked if there was someone in your life, I meant

a man. Is Zephyr it, or is there someone else I should be worried about?"

"Would you be?" she asked, snapping her head up then regretting it. He must be able to read the flush of awareness savaging her, but he looked his old, contained self.

"This is complicated enough without navigating some other man's sense of claim." So aloof. So hands-off. She was back in Bali, heart tattooing her breastbone like a moth against a window, trying to reach the light.

She looked away and rubbed the feel of his touch from her arm. "No, there's not. What about you?" The question escaped as the horrifying thought occurred.

"Are you kidding? No."

"Still playing concierge for the Lonely Hearts Club?" she sniped, annoyed.

"Open to new members. Always."

Ouch. She set her jaw, trying not to let his flippancy bother her. He was only trying to prove his shallowness. Maybe he is that shallow, Jaya. *There's not a woman in the world with enough training to fix me. Don't try.*

She needed to believe he was better than what he was pretending though, she needed it like oxygen. It was how she had let down her guard with him that night. Yes, his rakish ability to give her pleasure had made the memories he'd given her particularly delicious, but her trust in him had been the groundwork. She had believed him to be a good, honorable man, which had allowed her to put herself in his care.

"Don't be less than you are, Theo."

"Don't imagine I'm more."

"I'm only expecting you to be you, the man who saw potential in me and gave me a chance to develop it. You're fair. You're kind. Sometimes you're funny. This isn't a test. You don't have to pass it right now. We have a few days. Apparently," she added with a jerky shrug. "Can't we use this time to figure out how to proceed? Do we have to spit out a settlement contract this evening so you can run out the door tomorrow? Maybe the reason you don't have close relationships is because you don't stick around to nurture them."

He rocked back on his heels. "Touché."

"Was that harsh?" she asked, not as repentant as she could have been.

"No, it's true. I'm as much of a moving target as I can make myself."

The reasons behind that coping strategy put a lump in her throat. She tried to swallow it back with little success.

"Well, this is a safe place," she reminded in a strained tone. "You made sure. No one can hurt you here."

For a few seconds she thought she might have gone too far, appealing to the frightened child in him.

His dry chuckle had a coarse edge. "Okay, sure. I suppose we're stuck here," he said without inflection. "No need to rush to act."

Stuck again. Reacting to that awful word, she said, "There are worse things than taking a day off to play with children, you know."

"I know." His shoulders slumped heavily.

Now she really did feel sorry, but he walked away before the apologetic hand she reached out could touch him.

It was a sleepless night and not just because he had to walk Androu twice. Theo's mind wouldn't stop so he was grateful to have a reason to pace. The boy's warm weight on his arm was oddly comforting as he patted his little back to soothe him.

Jaya had to show him how, of course, demonstrating on Zephyr. "He might be with me, but it's still a strange place," she whispered in explanation of the boy's restlessness. She settled him with expert swiftness and disappeared into her room.

He dragged his eyes off the way her hotel-issued robe draped the curve of her hips and showcased her slender calves. No man in her life and whose fault was that? His. He'd taken a chance with unprotected sex because he'd been anxious to lose himself and his problems in an orgasm.

Which wasn't entirely true. As he stared across the twinkling lights of Marseille to the dark expanse of the Med, he allowed that Jaya had never been like the other women he pursued. She was special. His need that night had been as much about a desire to be with her as it had been to escape his emotional turmoil. Her announcement she was leaving Bali had lit a torch of panic in him. He'd needed, quite literally, to hold onto her.

Maybe some primitive part of him had even been seeking the permanent connection of a blood tie. As much as he'd like to dismiss his failing to protect her as a state of crisis and thoughtlessness, he'd never neglected a condom in his life. He *always* thought ahead to consequences. Fear of a beating had predisposed him to it.

So he couldn't pretend he'd simply been carried away. He'd made a conscious decision to take a risk.

Creating a child without due care and attention seemed like the kind of enormous mistake he ought to be punished severely for. His body was reacting with the same tense anticipation of hell he'd grown up trying to ignore. The clogged chest, clogged throat and anxiety ought to be far behind him, but he could hardly breathe. Sleep had never been a safe escape. Voices could rise in the next room, furniture could topple. Babies could wake and nightmares became real.

The troubling memories kept him tossing and turning even after Androu settled. Then Evie woke like a five alarm fire, jarring him and making his heart pound.

No male voice shouted, though. No impossible demands were made of children barely old enough to reach a toaster.

Jaya worked her magic and scooped up the sad little girl, murmuring reassurances.

Androu wasn't happy about being woken from a sound sleep, but Jaya distracted him with a bottle then cuddled the pair into a nest of pillows and blankets on the floor in the lounge, a cartoon of sleepy baby animals flickering at low volume on the television.

"Maybe they'll fall back asleep. Listen for Zephyr while I have a quick shower?"

He was used to starting his day shortchanged on sleep because of a time zone shift, but he'd barely slept and it wasn't even six o'clock yet. No wonder new parents were so irritable.

A few minutes later, as he searched out the coffee in the kitchen, he heard a cry. It wasn't from either of the toddlers. As he moved into the hall, the unhappy sounds grew louder. Pushing into Jaya's room, he found Zephyr sitting up in his cot with big tears on his cheeks, eyes wide and lost.

It's not a test, Jaya had said, but it was. Not just of his fatherly instincts, of which he had none, but of his ability to keep his emotional blocks from damaging this baby.

Therefore, inadequate as he felt, he couldn't leave the tyke wet and scared to wait for his mother just because she knew how to reassure with affection and he didn't.

At least a diaper change was his first priority. Funny how that seemed like a reprieve from more demanding tasks. Surprisingly, he nailed it in one go. Even got the kid back into his jammies without misaligning any snaps.

Zephyr seemed to want to keep his blanket with him, so Theo wrapped it around the boy's tiny body and snugged him closer to the warmth of his own chest, concerned that the air conditioning was set too low in the lounge.

Whether it was the warmth of his body or he was still sleepy, he seemed content enough to be carried into the lounge.

The older babies had both dropped off and Theo found himself standing over them, Zephyr's silky hair under his chin smelling familiar even though it wasn't anything he really knew.

Babies were unwieldy responsibilities that were so great, they were to be run from, far and fast. That's what he'd believed and it was true, if you were five.

He was an adult, though, perfectly capable of things like changing a diaper and making a proper meal and laundering clothes. Fearing the responsibilities of fatherhood was irrational. Millions did it every day and no one would hold him accountable with a beating if he missed getting a bit of food out of a kid's hair during a bath.

Nevertheless, after his talk with Jaya last night, his terror at taking on the role of a father was worse, not better. He knew why, too. He still feared failing, but not because of the threat of violence. He couldn't stand the idea of disappointing Jaya.

Jaya came out of her bathroom to find Zephyr's cot empty and rushed out to the main room where she found Theo cradling their son like he'd been doing it all his life.

Her blood thickened to such sweet molasses, she couldn't move. Her limbs ached and felt weak.

She must have gasped because he glanced up and touched a finger to his lips, then tilted his head to see into Zephyr's tranquil face. In slow motion, like he was handling a chemical bomb, he tucked Zephyr next to his sleeping cousins on the floor and drew their blanket over him.

She was done. Finished. Melted into a puddle on the floor that housekeeping would have to mop up and wring out of the strings.

He added a final blow by fetching his phone off the dining table and snapping a picture of the children piled together like a litter of kittens.

Removing the hand she'd pressed to her mouth, she accused in a whisper, "You're sentimental."

He shrugged, striding toward the kitchenette where he set his phone on the table and began making coffee. "We're not likely to catch them all together like that again, are we? Not all asleep."

The breath she took was coated in powdered glass. "I thought about sending the photo from last night to your sister, but you haven't told her, have you? Will you?"

He slowed his movements. "Since she's my boss and it starts with explaining that I slept with an employee—"

"Not technically."

He kicked up a brow, unimpressed with the fine line. "Still not the best example." He pushed the button that started the espresso maker. "And I'm still wrapping my head around it. I'd rather keep things simple until I know how we're going to proceed."

She tried to hide her disappointment, then thought, *Why should I?*

"That's not really fair to Zephyr, is it? I mean, they're his cousins." She waved at the bumps under the blanket. "My relationship with Saranya was the most important of my life." Not an understatement. "We grew up together and when I needed her, she was there. You don't just call a cousin out of the blue when your life implodes. Not unless you've been close all along."

She braced against his asking her how her life had imploded, but he only folded his arms and hitched a hip against the counter.

"I didn't think of it like that. I keep thinking how much they're like us. The age mix is different, of course. I'm barely a year younger than Adara and Demitri is almost four years younger than me, but we were only a few years older than Evie and practically left to raise ourselves. Adara was all I had for a mother figure and she was looking after

Demitri. I guess some part of me thought it was too much to ask of Evie and Androu to take on Zephyr, but they have functioning parents."

"So does he," she reminded, wishing she could be amused by his almost naïve misreading of the situation, but it was so tragic. "Is that why Adara always seems so…" She searched for the right word to describe her former boss that wouldn't insult the whole family. "I always thought you and she seemed very introspective."

He snorted. "You mean aloof? Distant? Cold? I've been called worse and yeah, we're not the most demonstrative family, but Adara did the best she could. I can't fault her. I'd do anything for her."

Ignoring the pang of jealousy that struck, she listened deeper, hearing exactly how far he was willing to go on his sister's behalf.

"Did you step in to protect her from your father?" Part of her knew she shouldn't ask. She didn't want to open up her own wounds and show them off so she couldn't expect him to, but her heart ached for the boy he'd been.

He flinched and turned away to set a tiny cup on a silver saucer. "Not that it did much good. She still caught her share. Demitri was the one we worried about. He was so little."

"Oh, Theo. And you think you're not cut out to be a father?"

"Have you seen how Demitri turned out? If that's my work, I'd be scared. The man's a menace." He offered her the first coffee.

"You have that one. I like mine with steamed milk." She stepped into place before the machine and filled the receptacles. "And yes, I have met your brother. Thank goodness for the repellant that is the Makricosta uniform because we all would have been pregnant. He's very adept with the ladies."

"Were you attracted to him?" His sharp gaze made her very aware of her nakedness under the robe she'd pulled on when she'd realized Zephyr had been stolen from his cot.

"I can't deny he's good-looking, but no, not really attracted." *Not the same way I'm attracted to you.* She pretended that the spurt of coffee and steamed milk required close attention, using it to hide the betraying longing she shouldn't be feeling toward him.

"A year and a half ago you weren't dating because your career was too important. Now Zephyr's in the way, isn't he?"

"I wouldn't put it like that, but he's definitely a factor. I'm not about to introduce a string of men into his life. So yes, between him and what's been going on at home and starting my new job I haven't had time to date. But dating has never been a priority so I don't miss it." There, that glossed nicely over her reasons for still avoiding men.

Yet here she stood, vulnerable in a thin robe held closed by a slippery tie, in the presence of a virile man who could overwhelm her without even trying.

Would he try? She sidled her gaze over his broad chest. He was wearing yesterday's shirt that still had some of his nephew's supper on it. That made him seem very human and normal. If he crushed her against that stained cotton, her heart would sing.

When she glanced up, she found him staring into the part of her lapels where her upper chest was exposed. Behind the light satin of the robe, her nipples tightened. Why him, she wondered, but didn't actually care. It was just such a delightfully good sensation to react to a man.

With a harsh inhale, he visibly pulled himself together and looked away. "Are you still sending money home?"

Her sensual curiosity drained away.

"Yes." She didn't elaborate and deliberately put space between them, taking her coffee to the breakfast bar and positioning herself so she could see the kids if they moved. Partly it was decent child minding, but at a deeper level, she was confused and trying to figure out why she longed for Theo to make a move on her when she was still stinging from his dropping her from his life.

"Have you told *your* family about Zephyr?" he asked.

A spike of grief pierced her as fresh as the day her family had first shunned her, hanging up on her because she had dared to run away to live with Saranya, rather than stay in the ruin they all considered her life had become. "Put it this way. If you don't acknowledge him, my cousin's daughter and Quentin are his only support after me."

Silence. When she glanced back, he was scowling toward the lounge, arms folded in frustration. "There are plenty of people with old-fashioned views in America, but it still surprises me they'd ostracize you for having a baby out of wedlock."

She sipped her coffee, ignoring the opening to tell him it was more than that. She shouldn't feel ashamed, but there was also the bit where she'd have to explain that the steps she'd taken to leave India weren't entirely legal.

"Would—"

He didn't continue so she dragged her gaze to his again, finding him looking something like he had that night in Bali: slightly defensive, rumpled but gorgeous in spite of it. His jaw was stubbled, his hair disheveled, but his proud bearing and those hollow cheeks above a strong jawline made him one of those men who would get better looking with age.

There was no sign of uncertainty in his tall, solid stillness. His expression was impassive, as if he was asking after her plans for the day.

"Would it mend fences with your family if we married?"

He couldn't have hurt her more if he'd walked right by her yesterday at the hangar and pretended he didn't see her.

She wasn't a romantic. After being sexually assaulted, she had quit dreaming of the perfect man sweeping her off her feet with a proposal that made her cry happy tears—except possibly if it came from him.

Seriously, Jaya, you have to let this infatuation die.

But one thing she knew she wanted in any marriage proposal was for love to form the underpinning of it.

"Probably," she answered, forcing herself to reply honestly, but the word choked her. She had to sip at her coffee to clear her voice into working order. Eyes on the sleeping cherubs, she added, "But my country is full of women who married because they felt they had no other choice. I do have a choice and I'm not interested."

Another thick silence.

He had to be relieved, but she didn't glance over to interpret what he might be thinking. Her insides ached too much, especially near her heart. If he saw it, he'd know how much she longed for something deeper from him and that could send him running again, making Zephyr suffer for her foolishness.

For such a powerful, confident man, he was awfully gun-shy about being close to people. Given what she'd learned about him, she could see how he'd fear betrayal of the worst kind lurked behind the slightest show of warmth. His warnings against trying to fix him burned bright in her mind. It added up to a hopeless basis for a marriage so she felt compelled to douse any spark of that talk.

"I should answer some emails while I have the chance," she murmured, pushing herself into motion. "I won't have much chance to work through the rest of the day."

Theo watched her walk away, his tired body stirred by the graceful way she moved while the rest of him throbbed with rejection. Funny how he'd got used to women at least wanting to marry him for his money.

Not that he'd asked Jaya to marry him. He'd been careful

to phrase his question as a broad request for information, not sure why he'd brought it up when she'd said last night that she wasn't looking for money or a ring.

Still, the fact she wasn't even nibbling at the possibility of sharing her life with him was quite a slap.

But why would she want to tie herself to him? What did he offer besides money? He circled the globe every quarter, could barely change a diaper and was incapable of love. She was right to dismiss the mention of marriage.

It still left him hollow and empty.

Which was probably exaggerated by the fact he hadn't slept. As Jaya disappeared into her room, he moved to stand over the sleeping babies. They looked pretty zonked, but he couldn't take the chance of lying down on the sofa and failing to wake if they stirred. Androu was sprawled like a starfish, but Zephyr had rolled himself close to Evie.

Stealing a cushion from the sofa as a pillow, Theo settled on his side behind Zephyr then gently rested his arm across Evie's legs and settled one hand on Androu's knee. Reassured he'd hear and feel them if they woke, he let himself doze.

CHAPTER EIGHT

FEED, PLAY, CHANGE, swim, nap, change, read, play, change...
The day was eaten up quickly with the wash, rinse, spin
cycle of baby-wrangling.

"How do parents of twins manage?" he asked when Jaya
returned from taking a phone call in her room. Technically
he was on vacation, although his boss would definitely get
an earful over how relaxing this particular one had been,
but Jaya was putting out fires from downstairs at the rate
of two or three an hour while minding children at the same
time. "What if they have triplets? Or more? How do *you*
manage?"

He'd given so many horsey-rides on his ankle, he would
need a knee replacement, but Zephyr showed no sign of
tiring.

Jaya smiled. "I wasn't working when I first left Bali.
Saranya needed me and so did her daughter. Saranya tried
to hang on until I delivered, but..."

She ducked her head, taking a moment. Obviously talking about it was difficult and he had an unexpected urge to
physically reach out to her. It hurt him to see her hurting,
but he had his hands full and had never been one to act on
impulses, especially touchy-feely ones.

Still, he was sorry he couldn't somehow comfort her
when he saw how she struggled to lift a brave face.

"By the time she passed, I was so pregnant there was

no point in applying for a job. I landed this one about six months ago, but I still live with Quentin. He and I pay a neighbor to watch Bina and Zeph and spell each other off if she's not available. Quentin's been home for most of the year, doing research, so his schedule has been flexible. He'll be starting a new film soon, though. He makes documentaries and the next one will take him to South America. Bina is pressing me to go with them. Saranya and Bina always lived on location with him. I'm pleased with my life here, though, and Quentin doesn't need the money. I wish he'd stay, but he keeps saying work will take his mind off his grief." She shrugged and added in a pained tone, "They loved each other very much."

Theo had never wanted to fall in love and she'd just showcased another reason why it was a bad idea. Quentin's barely suppressed rage came back to him and he felt damned sorry for the bastard.

Nevertheless, he couldn't quit thinking about marriage.

"I'm surprised you're not plugged into the mother ship," Jaya teased, obviously trying to deflect from her own pain and lighten the mood. "I've never seen you go so long without at least one electronic device in hand."

"Haven't you?" he asked, taking a less than subtle stab at testing their shared memory. He was still raw from her rejection and wanted to remind her there had been something really good between them once. He wanted to know if this attraction was still burning as brightly on her side as it was on his.

She stalled in swiping across her tablet. Her cheeks, tanned to semi-sweet chocolate by their hour in the pool, seemed to darken. Her tongue flicked along her bottom lip in a betrayal of discomfiture that otherwise remained hidden behind her impassive expression and lowered lashes.

One of the unique things about Jaya was her subtlety. Where other women threw themselves at his money and

position, she'd always seemed unimpressed. Not repelled
or disgusted, but not moved, either. From things she'd said,
he'd deduced that her cousin's husband had supported her
to a degree, but she supported herself now and sent money
to her family in India. She'd started at the bottom in Makricosta's, changing bedding and scrubbing toilets. She knew
what it was to make do on a limited income, but she'd never
tried to flirt or use her body to lift her circumstances or
gain financial favors.

When it came to her womanly wiles, she didn't project
any of her hidden depths of passion. Despite being pretty
and keeping herself well-groomed, she made no effort to
lure a man. Her sexuality was understated, not obvious
at all.

He appreciated that about her, not because he was a man
who thought women should hide their sexuality, but because
he was a circumspect man all around. He admired anyone
capable of controlling his or her basic, animal urges.

On the other hand, being one of the few people who
knew firsthand her capacity for passion was an erotic secret that strained his control. Every time the word *marriage*
whispered through his mind, the most masculine parts of
him relived holding her. There'd been a couple of women
since—he'd been convinced he'd never see her again and
had almost been trying to inoculate himself against going
after her. It hadn't worked and seeing her again was induc-
ing the opposite: he kept imagining a lifetime of stroking
smooth, warm skin, licking dark nipples that only grew
more taut and firm against his tongue, pushing naked into
hot, tight depths so wet and welcoming he'd nearly died
on the first thrust.

"I, um, just wondered if your sister gave you the day
off so you could watch her son," she finally said, not looking at him.

No outward acknowledgment of his leading comment.

He'd pretend that wasn't a sharp kick in the ego, even though they were long past pretending Bali hadn't happened. Hell, he was holding the proof.

"The cruise was supposed to be a family reunion of sorts," he explained. "Adara's idea. All the siblings were together at my mother's funeral, but it was hardly the time to catch up after not seeing Nic for twenty years. The cruise liner is a Makricosta hotel on a Vozaras ship so it would have been a working vacation, which is probably why Demitri was dragging his heels about showing up."

"He's quite the black sheep at times, isn't he?"

"And yet our father liked him. Which is why he gets away with what he does, I suppose. No one ever told him he couldn't."

"He didn't…I mean, your father never—?"

"Took a swing at him? No, I told you. Adara and I protected him. Kept him quiet when they were fighting, snuck food for him. Turned him into a spoiled brat, I suppose, but that's better than what we went through."

"You don't resent him?"

"Why would I? He was a kid. It wasn't his fault our father was a bastard."

"No," she agreed, eyes so liquid and dark he had to look away. "Only…"

Don't say it, he thought, giving all his attention to where Zephyr was now using his belly as a trampoline. Being able to see that a grown man ought to have more control over his actions than a little boy didn't make him empathetic. Being happy his brother hadn't been knocked around didn't make him paternal. It was common decency, that's all.

She came into his periphery, but only to stroke a soft hand over her son's head.

"He's having fun. Would it be an imposition to leave him with you while I do a bit more work, just while the other two are sleeping?"

An imposition? He was truly pathetic if that's how she thought he regarded holding a happy baby.

"It's fine," he said, disgusted with himself for giving off such an impression, but having a child was still a shock. And he was still so worried about damaging him he preferred to keep her close. If she wasn't hovering, how would he know he was doing everything right?

She must have read something in his tone. She glanced toward her laptop with indecision.

"Go ahead," he insisted, refusing to be frightened of a kid who couldn't even stand up on his own. "From what I've overheard, this place is still transitioning from good to excellent. You're doing a stellar job in pushing them gently, by the way. Obviously in your element. They're lucky to have you."

She checked and looked back at him. "Do you mean that?"

"Of course. I'm not surprised, either. Your knack with this kind of work was obvious to me the first time we met."

She cleared her throat. "Thank you. You're not just anyone. You know what it takes, what the pressures are. Your saying that means a lot." She gave a tiny sniff and wiped under one eye as she scooped up her laptop and moved into the bedroom.

Women. He'd like to see a male manager get all soupy from a pat on the back.

Of course, he was just as bad, still basking in her praise that he was giving his son some enjoyment. The boy had spring-loaded legs, seemingly incapable of tiring.

His son.

His chest walls gave an internal shudder as he faced a grinning countenance that seemed both foreign yet familiar. All the babies were crawling their way under his skin, but Zephyr was different. With the other two, it was easier to let himself develop some affection. There wasn't the same depth of responsibility. He imagined he'd be a fall-back for the rest of their lives, attached by bonds that nature cast like a spell for exactly this circumstance: to keep little ones alive if their primary caregiver was absent, but he wouldn't have to worry about Evie and Androu 24/7 the way he'd worry about Zephyr.

He took a moment to examine that nagging, anxious sensation. For all his concern that he'd crush this boy's confidence, the what-ifs about his future were worse. What if he was wet and this neighbor lady didn't notice? What if Quentin talked Jaya into taking the boy to some third-world country with exotic parasites and deadly spiders? What if something happened to Jaya?

The way Zephyr chewed a finger and thumb while staring deeply into his eyes—much the same disconcerting way his mother had, as if he trusted him implicitly—was a heart punch. It was as if the little guy was already relying on Theo to make sure all the what-ifs were mitigated. Who else would do it? Theo had a lot of faults, but shirking responsibility was not one of them.

His guts wobbled, like he'd taken a misstep on a high wire.

No, he didn't shirk responsibility. If Jaya had said *that* to him last night, rather than trying to prod him into admitting an emotional connection to the boy, she might have had him.

But who *would* look after Zephyr if something happened to Jaya? He'd seen what babies were like when Mama wasn't near. They were distressed. He wouldn't want Zephyr to go through that. Hell, *he* didn't want to go through missing Jaya again and he was a full-grown man.

Swearing under his breath, he tried to take back that thought, but it was acknowledged now. Was that why he was stressing out about Zephyr's future, he asked himself? Because the tyke was his best excuse to hang on to the mother?

No. He did not just see Zephyr as a means to an end. When he contemplated walking away from Jaya *or* Zephyr, everything in him went bleak and gray. His sense of responsibility toward the boy was quickly shifting beyond the desire to provide food and shelter. Quentin might be the better father figure, but Theo couldn't shake Jaya's comment that maybe he'd never developed any deep relationships because he didn't cultivate them.

It wasn't fair to Zephyr to not even *try,* was it?

Zephyr stopped bouncing and gave an exhausted sigh, like he'd finished chopping a cord of wood. Theo found himself grinning in amusement.

"Finally worn out?" He settled the boy against his chest where Zephyr let his head droop, fingers still in his mouth and eyelids heavy.

He wasn't a man who cuddled, preferring his own space unless he was busy with a woman between the sheets, but there was an addictive quality to a baby's snuggled warmth against his shoulder. It was a sense of all-powerfulness. Success at creating a moment of contentment for another human being. After a childhood of being found wanting, he wallowed in Zephyr's unconditional appreciation of having his simplest needs met.

It's just Mother Nature's plan, he tried to dismiss, but a very tiny voice—feminine and lilting with an Indian accent—whispered that maybe it was a father's nature to be happy when his child was happy.

Stunned, he swallowed a lump of emotion, hands cradling his son tenderly as the connection between them wound through him like a creeping vine, hooking into his vital organs in such a way there'd be damage to both of them if they were pulled apart.

Jaya's quiet voice grew louder, speaking to Evie as she appeared with the girl. Her eyes went soft when she saw him holding Zephyr so close, making Theo feel as though he was out on that high wire again, a brisk gale cutting up the canyon toward him.

He lowered his gaze. This was too personal a moment to have even Jaya witness.

"Trade?" he asked in a voice like sandpaper, reluctant to let the boy go, but he was so shaken by his flood of primal instinct to protect and nurture, he let her steal the sleepy baby and tried to distract himself by coaxing a smile from Evie with a promise of a swim later.

It was soon back to chaos, Androu waking shortly after Evie and both of them hungry. He was washing mashed banana out of Androu's hair, using the wet cloth to spike it into a Mohawk, wondering if he was getting the hang of this parenting thing after all, when a knock at the door interrupted them.

Jaya was in her room, answering emails while Zephyr napped in there with her. He sidled to the peephole and saw Nic, Rowan and Adara distorted by the fisheye lens.

Never one to appreciate unexpected visitors, he snapped open the door. "Why didn't you call?"

"Are they okay? Where are they?" The women rushed past him like fans into a rock concert, invading his space.

Nic entered at a more laconic pace, scanning the suite in the way of someone who made his living by sharp observations.

Theo suppressed a prickle of irritability. The place was littered in toys and dirty dishes. Much as he didn't really care about being judged over something like that, he also made it a habit to keep from providing opportunities to be judged.

"They were anxious so I chartered a helicopter," Nic said. "Gideon had to stay with the ship. Everyone is okay, but what a mess. I don't envy him. There's my girl." He broke into a wide smile as he caught Evie reaching from Rowan's arms into his.

"It's not that we didn't trust you, Theo. We just missed them so much," Rowan said, her light touch on his arm apologetic.

He gave a jerky shrug, subtly removing himself from her uninvited touch even though he didn't hate it. She was nice enough and being sincere. It was just he wasn't at his best, accosted by a lot right now with their unexpected visit and a distant, illogical disappointment he didn't want to examine. He didn't need her standing too close, sensing his tension, reading his vibe for him.

"It's fine, I understand," he said, and strangely, kind of did. His chest filled with pressure at the way his sister was smothering the life out of Androu. Her eyes were closed, her lashes wet. He had a new understanding of how precious their babies were to them and was suffused with a weird self-conscious pride that he'd been able to keep their offspring safe for them, whether they had really trusted him to do so or not.

"I knew he'd be fine. He knows you," Adara said, voice thick. "But Gideon threw you into the deep end with both of them. I'm glad you called Jaya—she's perfect—but what made you think of her? How did you know she was here? Where *is* she?"

Before Theo could get past the suffocation provoked by questions about Jaya, she said, "I'm here."

They all turned toward her voice.

"Sorry," she said with a flash of anxious eyes at Theo. "The commotion woke him and he needs a drink."

Zephyr looked sweaty and flushed, hair damp and pushed up in tufts around the face he buried in Jaya's neck to hide.

Theo moved to fetch the boy's cup, distancing himself from something he didn't want to face, then kicked himself just as quickly. This was exactly the kind of abandonment he would hate himself for inflicting on his son. Or Jaya, for that matter.

"I'm sorry we spoiled his nap," he heard Rowan say and glanced across to see her peeking at the boy over his mother's shoulder. "What's your name?"

"Baby Zepper," Evie provided from her happy perch on Nic's bent arm.

"Zephyr," Jaya corrected softly, smiling at Evie. "You've been my best little helper, haven't you? She's been very sweet with both of them."

"Zephyr," Rowan repeated. "That's lovely. Greek god of wind, right?"

Theo absorbed the meaning, wondering if it was a deliberate reference to his love of piloting, thinking, *I really don't deserve her,* as he crossed with Zephyr's sipping cup.

"Thanks," Jaya said with a flickering gaze of apprehension as he approached. She rubbed Zephyr's back to get his attention. "Want your cup, sweetie?"

Zephyr lifted his head and spied the cup, but rather than wait for Jaya to take it, he leaned out for Theo.

Theo was getting used to the boy's impulsive launches. He caught him in what was becoming a practiced scoop and hitched him up against his chest. The air in his lungs stopped moving as he held the cup for the boy, aware of how telling his actions were, how much like a father he must appear. How close a copy of Androu Zephyr was.

Zephyr's little hands settled over his big one while profound silence fell over the room like a dome.

Theo forced himself to lift his gaze and meet each pair of stunned eyes. They had to be reading guilt in him. It sprang from ignoring Jaya's attempts to contact him and thinking he could ignore someone as important as his son. He was ashamed of himself, not Zephyr.

Disgust with himself made him blurt, "He's mine," aware that it was the clumsiest possible way he could have announced it, but he couldn't dance around it. Not when Nic was drilling him a look that said, *You lucky bastard.*

His half brother blinked and the envy was gone, replaced by a doting smile at Evie, but it was the reinforcement Theo needed to keep inching across the hot coals cooking him from the soles of his feet to his collar. Maybe he wasn't doing this well, but he'd figured out what was right and he'd do that much.

In his periphery, he saw Jaya lift an uncertain hand then fold her arms defensively. *Don't,* he wanted to say. *Don't be embarrassed for me. I don't care how stupid I look, only that I not fail where it counts.*

Over Zephyr's loud gulps, Androu made a noise and put out his hand.

"I told you before, sport," Theo said, trying to sound normal while emotions log-jammed in his throat. "Yours is the green one. It's on his tray," he told Adara, nodding to the high chair where Androu had been sitting before she arrived.

He hoped she'd move away and begin to defuse this charged moment, but she didn't. Her gaze was fixed on Zephyr's face.

The boy looked at her with his unblinking brown eyes. Makricosta eyes.

"Theo." She spoke his name with myriad inflections. Shock, awe, surprise, approval. Exasperated *dis*approval.

As he braced himself for whatever she would say, he felt a feminine hand rest on his biceps. Jaya. If he'd had a free hand, he would have wrapped it around her waist and pulled her in close. He might be willing to face the scrutiny of his family without apology, but it wasn't easy. How such a slight woman could be his shield against them, he didn't understand, but he had an intense need to wield her in just that way.

"He didn't know," Jaya said. The tips of her fingers dug into his tense arm. "Not until I told him yesterday."

Had it only been a day?

He drew in a breath, realizing he'd neglected to take in air for several seconds. Looking into Jaya's eyes, he let her know she didn't have to protect him *that* much. It was his own damned fault he hadn't known about his son.

It's okay, she seemed to reassure with a softening of her touch on his arm. *Our secret.* And therein lay her appeal. He feared every stumble, too used to being knocked down a second time for daring to err. She was a forgiving person, though. She was so softhearted, she'd help him to his feet after a face-plant. He wanted to kiss her for it.

Hell, he wanted to kiss her, period. He dragged himself free of their locked stare in time to hear Rowan ask Nic, "Will it be a full Indian wedding, do you think? I've always wanted to go to one."

Jaya's touch on his arm fell away.

Theo stiffened, struck anew by rejection.

"I'm making assumptions, aren't I?" Rowan said with a blush and a reach for her daughter. "Come on, Evie, let's find Androu's cup for him."

"I'll help," Nic said, taking Androu as he passed Adara. "Drink, champ?"

Jaya watched the Viking blond media mogul and his petite wife distance themselves toward the kitchen, leaving Adara staring at their ill at ease vignette.

Zephyr was comfortable enough, she supposed, taking a break from draining his cup to huff a breath and stare after his cousins, but she was hyper-conscious of Theo statue-stiff next to her.

"Will he come to me?" Adara asked, approaching with hands raised.

Her intense focus, the way she caught her breath as Zephyr went to her, the way she enfolded him and pressed

her smile into his hair, all made Jaya want to turn her crin-
kling forehead into Theo's chest.

Having Zephyr accepted by Theo's sister was beyond her
dreams. She wished she'd known it would go this well or
she might have tried harder to reach him. She might have
gone directly to Adara.

"I should have—" Jaya began.

"Don't." He caught her wrist. "*I* should have," he said,
as if he knew what she'd been about to say. His hand slid
to mesh with hers, palm to palm, fingers entwined.

It was such a startling gesture she could only cling to
him, at sea as to how to react. He'd surprised her by claiming Zephyr so openly when she'd been expecting to be
treated like a dirty little secret. Having him hold her hand
as if there was something between them besides a baby
was a kind of magic she knew she shouldn't believe in,
but she wanted to.

"I never thought I'd hold your baby," Adara said with a
misty smile. "I hoped Androu would rub off on you, but—
Wait a minute. How old is he?" She pulled back to study
the boy, eyes narrow as she lifted them to Theo's culpable
swallow.

"It was—" Jaya started to excuse, but Theo squeezed
her hand. Her entire being was warmed by his firm grip,
radiating heat up her arm and into her chest.

"I'm not going to offer excuses—or details. Fire me if
you have to," Theo said.

Adara gave him a look between stern and maddened.
"I'll assume that if you deserved to be fired, you'd say so.
Demitri is the one that needs reminders about employees
being off-limits. Besides, I can't be mad. We have a nephew.
Gideon will be over the moon." She smiled at Zephyr as
the boy reached for Jaya, letting him go.

Jaya had to pull her hand free of Theo's to take Zephyr
and secure him on her hip.

In the carefully emotionless way that Jaya was more familiar seeing in Adara she heard her ask Theo, "What *are* your plans?"

In the blink of one glance, a lot of teeming undercurrents were exchanged between brother and sister. It niggled at Jaya in a way she couldn't interpret. They seemed almost telepathic and it made her feel left out.

She imagined there were considerations with regards to the Makricosta fortune, though. Publicity to finesse and old-fashioned concern for family. Given Theo's dismay at learning he was a father, she expected him to request Zephyr's existence be kept quiet.

With an impactful look at Jaya, Theo became super tall, his posture and air very authoritative. She'd seen him take a hard line when it came to accounting rules, but had never seen him turn such an uncompromising look on her.

"I don't want to miss any more of Zephyr's life than I have," he said.

Oh. Jaya's heart fluttered, surprised by this evolution in his attitude. He'd been tentative yesterday, but she supposed that had been shock. This morning he'd seemed to accept he had a son, even if it had still been a perplexing addition to his life.

Now she could see acknowledgment had moved into something more implacable that was both heartening and threatening. It had never occurred to her that she might have to fight him for her child, but she saw something in his eyes that was resolute and possessive. Something that told her Zephyr had taken up residence inside him in a way she'd been dreaming of doing since Day One.

Why did that make her jealous? She ought to be happy.

"We haven't agreed on how we're moving forward," Theo continued. "But whether it's a big wedding or not— I'll be pushing for marriage."

CHAPTER NINE

THE WORDS CAME between them in an eclipse-like flash. For a second Jaya couldn't breathe, couldn't see.

No. She'd already told him no. Hadn't he heard her? But what she'd really been refusing was a marriage of convenience. If he loved her… Did he?

And how could he just announce it like that to his sister without consulting—without even *asking* her first?

"I haven't convinced Jaya yet," Theo said, taking the weight of his penetrating stare back to his sister.

Oh, sure, put it all on me, Jaya thought, working to keep a scowl off her face. Her instinct was to protest, but she didn't want to draw Adara into it. Given the look exchanged between Nic and Rowan as they returned from the kitchen, they'd heard Theo, adding to her feeling of being outnumbered.

No one needed to know her reasons for refusing to marry except maybe Theo and she'd share that only if and when it felt right.

"We haven't had much time to talk about anything except whose turn it is to change a bottom," Jaya murmured, stroking a hand over Androu's tousled hair as he toddled after Evie to their play area in the lounge.

"Understood," Nic said. "And we're incredibly grateful for your help. If you ever need anything, please let us know."

"I expect we'll be seeing a lot of each other regardless," Rowan said with a warm smile. "Evie's forever begging for Androu and seems equally rapt with Zephyr. I expect a few tears when we leave, to be honest. Brace yourself. She has a tender little heart."

It was true. After thirty minutes of letting the children have a last play together while the adults gathered up toys and clothes, they congregated at the door. Evie broke into pieces when she realized the other children wouldn't be coming with her to Greece.

"Peas, Papa," she begged through her tears.

"I'm sorry, but they have to live with their own mamas."

She wasn't trying to manipulate; she was genuinely heartbroken, weeping into his shoulder with loss.

Her suffering twisted Jaya's heart so badly she found herself promising to bring Zephyr for a visit.

After a tearful kiss and hug from the girl, she said goodbye and was emotionally wrung out as she and Theo moved into the quiet lounge.

"Did I just promise a two-year-old I'd fly to Greece to see her?" Jaya collapsed into a chair. "I can't afford that."

Theo gave her a dry, are-you-kidding look. "Nic has his own plane and so do I." He leaned back on the sofa, hands behind his head, gaze lifting from where Zephyr sat on the floor rattling the stuffing out of a toy bear. "I'll take you as soon as we work out a convenient time."

Her heart lifted while her stomach swooped. The word *honeymoon* blinked like a lighthouse flash in her mind, but she turned away from it. She stared at their baby rather than looking at Theo, nervous of the masculine energy he was projecting. He might appear relaxed, but they were alone now, the buffer of activity gone. The full force of his male magnetism was blasting into her, stronger than she remembered it.

"You're assuming a lot," she said, leaning forward to

remove a hard toy from behind Zephyr. "I'm not quitting my job. I'm not marrying you."

Silence, then, "I realize I threw that at you from left field."

"You did," she snapped. "That wasn't fair."

"I didn't mean to, but…" He sat forward, swearing as he rubbed his face. "Both Adara and Rowan had fertility issues. I could see Nic was thinking anyone who would turn away from the chance to be a father—"

"Are you seriously saying that the only reason you want to be in Zephyr's life is to avoid being judged by your family?" She *lived* that hell, but it was because she was determined to stay true to herself. For him to buckle to their expectations was a very dishonest start to his relationship with Zephyr, something she wouldn't tolerate no matter the consequences.

"No, it reinforced to me what a gift he is. Not everyone has the luxury of one night producing a baby. Yes, this has been hard for me to come to terms with." He waved a confounded hand at their son, but a subtle tenderness crept beneath his hard visage as he watched Zephyr discover his own toes and try to catch them in his waving hand. "I'm still not convinced I'm father material, but Nic figured it out. Maybe I've got a shot. And if there's one thing my childhood taught me, it's how to avoid making mistakes, especially big ones. Turning my back on my son would be a terrible one."

He was saying all the right things, but rather than creating a sense of relief in her, he was undermining her defenses. She needed resentment to keep her from tumbling back into the depths of her crazy crush on him. That sort of weakness would complicate things. She'd start thinking about what she wanted, rather than what she and Zephyr needed.

"We still don't have to marry," she mumbled.

"What would living together do to your relationship with your family?"

"You want to live together?" The words dissolved everything around her so nothing had substance. She was falling, unable to grasp anything that would ground her.

"Yesterday you pointed out that I don't stick around to develop relationships. It's true. If I want to know my son, I have to be near him. Physically." He frowned as he said it, like he wasn't sure, but would give it a try.

That's all she needed, to let him become a daily part of her life then have him quit on her. "I don't want to live with you," she insisted.

"Why not? You live with Quentin. I'll pay for everything."

Back to money. Was there a problem in his world that he wouldn't try to buy his way out of?

"I value my independence," she said.

"But you're not independent," he countered. "You have a son. You and I are connected through him and that makes us interdependent." He pointed between them, as if running lines of webbing that stitched them together. He didn't seem any happier about it than she was. "We have to compromise for his best interest. We'll have to do that for the rest of our lives. There's no getting around that."

Hurt that he was only trying to make a life with her because he thought it was the ethical thing to do, she rose to pace, winding up facing a window, arms folded.

"I grew up fighting tooth and nail for every decision I wanted to make for myself. I won't have the same fight with you. I won't give up and do as I'm told. You're making me feel like I have to live with you. That I have to marry you. I already live with a lot of have-to's as a result of my choosing to have Zephyr."

"You think I don't know how it feels to live under someone else's rules?" he countered. "You think I enjoy calculating interest rates and double-checking the inventory of hand towels? There's a difference between being subjugated and placing duty to family above self-interest. My father isn't around to disinherit me if I quit my job. I stay for Adara's sake, because I want her to succeed. Although we'll have to make adjustments to my duties if I'm going to spend any time with you and Zephyr."

He muffled a curse behind his hand, glowering while his gaze turned inward.

Her stomach did a flip flop, latching too tightly onto his *with you*. She shook it off, not wanting to be so easily drawn in by him. Turning, she considered the dual notes of frustration and sincerity in his voice.

"You hate your job?" she prompted.

He quirked the tight line of his lips before saying, "Don't tell Adara." He shrugged that off. "I don't really hate it, not anymore, but it's not what I would have chosen for myself. My father pushed me into it. He would have taken it out on Adara if I'd rebelled so I kept the peace and took an Econ degree. The work is more enjoyable now that she trusts my numbers and makes the kinds of decisions we always knew were the better ones. We actually see the profits we're looking for. I was constantly set up for failure while my father was alive. That was hell."

She came back to sit across from him. Linking her hands, she pressed her knuckles to her mouth. "I think I hate your father," she admitted in a muted voice. The man bore a lot of blame for Theo's inability to give her what she wanted from him.

"Join the club," he retorted, then expelled a tired breath. "But he's gone so do what I do. Forget him."

Releasing her inner lip from the bite of her teeth, she added, "He is gone, so don't turn me into something you think you have to do. You have a choice, too, Theo."

"I do," he agreed and hitched forward on the edge of the

sofa. "That's what I'm saying. I'm not acting from a sense of duty, although I feel a pretty strong one toward both of you. It's a different kind of 'have to.' The kind that means I wouldn't be able to live with myself if I didn't do what's right by the two of you."

Which framed her refusal to marry him as inexcusable selfishness.

"I can appreciate that you want to be part of Zephyr's life." She couldn't countenance anything less herself. "But live together? Like as roommates?"

"If that's what you prefer." He blinked once, keeping his expression neutral so she couldn't tell what he really thought of the arrangement.

"For how long? Until he's in school? Until he's grown? And what are you doing all this time? Bringing women home?"

"No," he dismissed flatly and cast a gaze toward the pool, one that was stark and seemed rather isolated and lonely.

Her heart shook. She willed it to still, not wanting to be affected. *Don't try to fix him.*

"Is there nothing on your side, Jaya? Of what we had before?" he asked quietly.

She caught her breath, plunged into the deep end, sinking and sinking, pressure gathering in her ears and pressing outward in her lungs. Her vision blurred because she forgot to blink.

"What did we have?" she asked in a thin voice, reminding herself that neither of them had been seeking a long term relationship that night. Her motives had been, if not emotionless, at least not as simple as his.

"More chemistry than I've ever felt for anyone else, before or since." His blunt words detonated a terrific blush in her, making her cover her hot cheeks and look anywhere but at him.

"I didn't mean to behave that way," she moaned, still embarrassed that once hadn't been enough. Twice had been decadent self-indulgence. The third time had been outright greed, stolen against the hands of the clock.

"I loved how you behaved," he said, voice low and taut with sweet memory.

Her heart tripped as he began speaking and stumbled into the dust as she realized it wasn't a declaration of deep feeling. She was still affected, still transported back to a night when touching a man had seemed the most natural, perfect thing in the world to do.

The glint of masculine interest in his eye sparked a depth of need in her she had worried she'd never feel again.

"Okay, then," he said in a satisfied growl, his fixed gaze weighted with lazy approval.

"Theo, don't!" She pushed the heels of her hands into her eyes. Her history with him, especially their night together, had stolen a lot of power from her darkest memories, but, "Don't make assumptions about me and sex. Please. Saying I'm attracted to you doesn't mean I want to have sex with you. It's not that simple for me. Ever."

"Hey, I'm not taking anything for granted," he admonished. "I realize sex could be a hindrance to our working out a good long-term solution. Much as I want to have an affair with you, if we burn out it would have consequences for Zephyr. I get that."

Did he? Because she hadn't got that far. All she could think was that she hadn't expected to have another shot at sharing Theo's bed and really didn't know how she felt about climbing into it again, especially long-term. Talk about assumptions. That would create a lot. All her conflicting yes-no signals were firing, making her cautious even as she found herself literally warming to the idea.

"But you have to admit, we're a good team, Jaya. That's all Adara and Gideon had going for them when they married. Maybe they had sexual attraction, I don't know. I would never ask," he said with a dismissing sweep of his hand and an expression of juvenile repugnance that would have been laughable if her thoughts weren't exploding like popcorn kernels in oil.

"You and I have as good a base as they had," he insisted. "Maybe a better one. We know each other a lot better than they did. An affair, living together… Those are too easy to walk away from. Marriage would force us to work out whatever differences came up. Zephyr needs that kind of stability and commitment. Doesn't he?"

Here was the clarity he'd told her he was capable of. He could see the right course of action even if he didn't know whether he could perform it. Even when he wasn't terribly keen to embrace it.

Still, she was half persuaded by his rationale. He was right and talking about it like they were negotiating a merger kept her from being swept away, allowing her to view the situation objectively.

That's what she told herself anyway, to counter the thick knot of disappointment sitting in her throat.

"Are you hesitating because of what I told you about my father? You're worried I'll resort to abuse?"

"No!" she blurted, heartfelt and sincere. Her waffling feelings were more about having her heart suffer from un-requited attraction than worrying about physical harm.

"If that's what's worrying you, admit it. I'll forget the whole thing. I totally understand." He stood and caught up Zephyr, repositioning him in the middle of the blanket, his movements hiding his face, but she thought she caught a glint of profound hurt. Maybe something else. A sort of hopeless defeat.

"Theo, I don't think you could hurt me or Zephyr even if you wanted to. If we needed a snakebite carved out of us, you probably couldn't do it."

His glance flickered toward her in acknowledgment, colored with ironic humor, but he moved to stand looking through the glass at the pool. He pushed his hands into his pockets, shoulders slumped.

"You've been so willing to listen to everything I've told you I let myself believe it didn't matter, but of course it matters. Of course you have to take time to consider what it means and decide whether you can trust me."

She was going to have to tell him. She could see his back tensed against the same kind of betrayal and injury he'd already suffered. She couldn't leave him thinking something as far out of his control as his childhood abuse would cause her to fear him.

Still, her abdomen tightened as if clenching to accept a blow.

"Theo, it's not you, it's me."

He barked out a laugh and sent an askance look over his shoulder. "Okay."

Not in front of Zephyr, she thought, but their son had tipped onto his side and was contentedly chewing a finger and pedaling his feet. And wasn't he the manifestation of the goodness that had come out of her bad experience? If she hadn't been assaulted, she would have stayed in India and married under her uncle's dictate. Instead, she'd left and wound up meeting Theo and he had changed her life profoundly, giving her this gift.

"I trust you, Theo. I wouldn't have slept with you in Bali if I didn't."

"That's different. One night is not a lifetime. A pair of lost souls finding comfort in physical pleasure is not marriage. It takes a lot more faith in a person to share every aspect of your life with him. I understand."

"No, that's not—" She sighed. "That's not what Bali was for me. Not all it was."

He came around a half step, body still in profile, his grave expression watchful. "What do you mean?"

She took a shaky breath. "The reason I left India…" She pinched her lip, trying to stay focused. "I should back up to explain. I've told you Saranya and I grew up very close? When I was six, my father had an accident on the tractor and was forced to sign our land over to my uncle. We moved in with them. Our mothers are twins. It's a big house, not a bad arrangement except that my uncle is quite controlling. He has very traditional views where women are concerned."

She set the jungle gym over Zephyr so he could swat at the dangling toys.

"Saranya grew up dreaming of being in Bollywood films. Uncle was fit to be tied. He was arranging a marriage for her when Quentin's crew came into the next village. Saranya was convinced this was her break. In a way it was. They fell in love and she eloped with him."

"And you were left with her angry, thwarted father."

She nodded. "And her two brothers and my younger brother and sister. Uncle became more domineering than ever, dictating to my parents how we should behave. It was one of the reasons I was so resolved to get a job, to give my parents money so they wouldn't be so dependent on him. He objected to me working, saying I should marry, but there were other young people going into call centers, bringing money home. A friend recommended me for a position and it was good work. I improved my English, used their lines to speak with Saranya," she confessed with a sheepish grin. "Uncle had disowned her, but I missed her."

"Are you trying to tell me you're afraid I won't let you work?"

"There is that, but no, that's not where I'm going." Rising to try to escape the cloying sense of helplessness that still managed to smother her at times, she paced across the room then halted, arms wrapped around herself.

What would he think of her? Would he blame her as her family had?

"The problem with my job was… There was a man there. My supervisor. He was older, in his forties. I wasn't even twenty yet. He flirted with me, but it wasn't flirting."

"Sexual harassment," Theo concluded flatly, his voice low and chill.

"One night, before I went home, it was sexual assault." Her voice faded into a whisper, but she knew he heard her because the silence took on a thick, heavy quality.

She smoothed a hand over the glossy hardwood of a side table, accidentally lifting her eyes to the reflection in the mirror above it.

Theo was arrested, pale under his swarthy tan, lips tight and outlined with a white ring. When their gazes clashed in the pool of silver, he flinched his glance away.

She caught back a gasp of pain.

"I never should have pressured you that night," he said from between his teeth.

"You didn't. I wanted to," she assured him, swinging around to face him even though her whole body suffused with self-conscious heat. Memories burned through her, sweet and hot. Hands knotting together at her navel, she said in a strained voice, "You know I enjoyed it."

She was dying over here, embarrassed that she had to be so bald in her confession. It was incredibly hard to practically beg him to remember how uninhibited she'd been by the time she'd slipped naked from his bed and reluctantly dressed, but she had faced him proudly in the dawn light, enjoying his admiring gaze as he watched her dress.

"That night was the first time since it happened that I wanted to be with a man. To let anyone touch me," she confided.

"I was your employer."

"No, you weren't. And remember how shocked I was

that you were attracted to me? As an employee I never once felt threatened by you, especially sexually. I was as grateful for that as everything else. I mean, I started out in housekeeping because it was all women, even the supervisors. Moving to the front desk, night clerk, those were all huge risks that I took because I knew I had to move past what had happened to me if I wanted to advance, but I was able to do it because you had this quiet command of everything. I felt like no one would dare touch me because I could go to you. I didn't have any recourse the first time."

He frowned. "You didn't tell your family? What about the police?"

Thick painful tears welled in her eyes and she had to look away to hold on to her composure. "My uncle was ashamed that I went to the police. He called me a slut and my parents weren't in a position to argue in my defense. They wanted me to marry the man, but he was already married."

Theo swore and started toward her only to bring himself up short. "Jaya…" His tone was one of deep shock and struggle.

She wished he'd make this easy and take her in his strong arms, but at the same time she could only stare at the floor feeling the tears drop from her eyes. The assault had been a nightmare, but the time afterward had been the darkest, most bleak and isolated of her life.

Forcing herself to remember it was over and she was safe, she swiped at her wet cheeks and lifted her head, lashes matted and eyes still bleary. Swallowing back the lump in her throat, she managed to say, "Fortunately I had Saranya."

"She came for you?"

"Couriered her passport. My uncle had learned his lesson about leaving them where the children could find them. We're only a year apart and always looked remarkably alike. People mistook us all the time. Quentin was filming in Malaysia so she sent me a ticket to Kuala Lumpur. She'd just had Bina. They took me in and she went with me for all the doctor checks… I look back and think it's such a miracle I didn't get pregnant, given you and I managed it in one go." She gave a weak smile.

"I can't believe you still send them money."

"For my mother's sake, and my sister's. And even though Quentin is quite successful, I don't want to be a burden. I lived too long on my uncle's good graces. Earning my own keep is important to me so I applied at a few hotels, ones that overlooked my lack of paperwork. Having good English was an asset. I picked up Quentin's German and a local dialect. When he began filming in Bali, I got on at Makricosta's. After, um, claiming to the Indian embassy that I'd lost my passport and needed it replaced." She cleared her throat. "I know that was wrong—"

"Hell, Jaya, I'm not judging you. Your uncle, yeah, but not you." He swore again and ran a hand down his face.

Zephyr squawked at that point and she realized he was probably hungry. It was a much-needed few minutes of distraction that allowed her to collect herself. Her hands shook as she moved around the kitchenette and she was aware of Theo standing in one spot the whole time, staring out to the pool.

The sense of being flayed raw stayed with her, making her attempts to be natural and smile at her baby feel forced. Her cheeks were stiff, her brow hooking and pulling. Everything in her wanted to move into Theo's reach and hope he'd take her in his arms, so he might smooth away all the jagged edges and reassure her that what she'd told him hadn't changed his view of her.

He didn't even look her way, which choked her throat with a helpless ache.

The buzz of her phone, which was on vibrate, jangled

her nerves. She thought, *Work,* and it was the most vile four-letter word right now.

Except it would also be a healthy retreat. It suddenly hit her that she *could* leave. Theo didn't need her here. The babies were gone.

Oh. An even more profoundly bereft emotion enveloped her, but she needed distance from him. While her emotions were twining and growing around his return to her life, she couldn't tell what he was thinking. That marriage idea of his certainly wasn't being thrown at her any longer.

Against the ominous plane of his back, she said, "I'll take Zephyr home after he finishes eating. A lot has piled up here. I need to get into my office downstairs."

Theo turned and the withdrawal in him was almost frightening. He was the aloof man she'd first met, not dismissive, but giving the impression he didn't see a woman at all. Just a fellow robot.

The shift crushed her with disappointment. No, something worse. She was devastated. It was like all the accord they'd developed had evaporated and she was a stranger to him. He would be polite, but really, he didn't want to know her ugly secrets. She'd told him too much and now she felt small and soiled.

"Why don't you leave him with me?" he said.

"Wh-what?"

"I'm not going anywhere. We'll be close by if he needs you. You and I still have to figure out how we're going to proceed. I've heard all you've said, I understand why you don't want to marry me, but I'm not flying out of here to forget this ever happened. At some point word will get out beyond my siblings that I have a child. He's every bit as vulnerable as Evie and Androu, security-wise. We have a lot to work out."

He spoke from across the canyon that was the lounge, his words seeming to echo around her, but they weren't quite as empty as she'd begun to fear. She stood on uncertain footing, but this connection he'd talked about, their interdependence, was real. It was a thin thread, delicate as a dew-covered string of spider silk, but she stayed very still, wanting it to stick and endure.

"Okay." She had to clear huskiness from her throat and now her smile at Zephyr was soft and easy and relieved. She felt like she could breathe again. *She would keep seeing Theo a little longer.*

"If you don't mind a late dinner, we could talk then," she offered as she wiped Zephyr's face and hands.

"Downstairs? That's fine. What time shall I make the reservation?"

She had meant room service, but, "I can book it. I'll text you." Feeling gauche and self-conscious, she walked Zephyr across to Theo's tense presence and escaped to gather her composure.

Theo closed his eyes as the door shut behind Jaya.

It wasn't fair to look to an infant for comfort, but he snugged the boy close against him and pressed his unsteady lips against hair dark and silky smooth as his mother's.

The surge of emotions in him was almost too much to bear, certainly near impossible to contain while Jaya had been in the room. Lovely Jaya who wouldn't crush a spider, brutalized by a man she'd trusted. He hadn't had the courage to ask for details. They only mattered if she felt a need to get them off her chest. He certainly didn't want to hear them. As far as he was concerned, the fact it had happened at all was infuriating and heartbreaking enough, but to then not even be supported by her family…

It was unthinkable, blasting him to overflowing with a need to insist—demand—that she marry him and be forevermore under his protection. He wasn't superhuman, but he had resources the average person couldn't touch. The proverbial shields he could place around her were near bullet-proof and his blood raced with the need to affix them. Now.

But she didn't want to rely on him, didn't want to marry him.

If her assailant had reached into his chest and clawed out his heart he couldn't have stolen anything more vital to him than Jaya's trust. Theo had suggested they eat in the public dining room because he was convinced she wouldn't want to be alone with him, and she'd agreed. What did that say?

And here he'd been fantasizing—not taking for granted, only indulging himself—that the sexual attraction was still ripe and strong between them. That it could form the basis of a marriage that stood half a chance.

His fury at the injustice made him want to scream, but he had a child in his arms. A tiny boy who had somehow come to life after Jaya had suffered one of the worst types of betrayal.

He brought the boy up so they were eye to eye. Zephyr's wide grin caused a crack to zigzag across his heart. Not one of damage, but as if the shell that encased it was breaking open. Tender hunger for more of those smiles, more time with Jaya, leaked out.

Never one to believe the Christmas present he wanted would actually be under the tree, he still let a nascent thought form: Maybe if he was very careful with her, there would be hope.

CHAPTER TEN

WHEN JAYA WAS called to the front desk because Bina was asking for her there, her first instinct was to send her cousin home. Quentin had sent the girl with her sitter to check up on her, acting like an interfering, if somewhat endearing, overbearing male relative.

But Bina had a genuine connection to Zephyr that helped the girl cope with the loss she was still grieving. Jaya didn't have the heart to send her away without a visit with her cherished baby cousin. Plus, an uninterrupted conversation with Theo for the first time since she'd seen him again held a lot of appeal.

She texted him that Bina and her nanny were coming up to stay with Zephyr and she'd meet him at the bell desk to go for dinner. Then, in a minor fit of vanity, she visited one of the hotel's boutiques, using her employee discount to buy a new dress and shoes.

Studying herself in the mirror of the staff washroom, she asked herself what she was trying to prove. Her hair was brushed, her makeup refreshed. The only pair of shoes she could find to go with this dress were much taller than she'd normally wear. They had bling. A line of sequins decorated the heel and a jazzy buckle drew attention to the toes Bina had painted a neon pink when they'd been having girls' night a week ago.

The dress was more feminine than sexy with its ruffled

layers of sheer red and orange and pink and fluttering split cut sleeves, but gave her a moment of sober second thought.

She refused to dress like a frump, though. Her confession this afternoon had been difficult. Part of her wanted to crawl into a cave now that her secret was revealed, but she knew better than to let her past cow her. She wouldn't deny the fact she was a woman. She wouldn't pretend to be ugly or asexual. That would only feed her shame and she had nothing to be ashamed of. Being pretty wasn't a crime. Wanting to please the eye of a man wasn't a broad invitation to be abused by all of them.

Still, it was an act of bravery to swipe a final layer of gloss onto her lips and take herself to the bell desk. The bellman was engaged and only Theo stood there.

He stared broodingly at the bobbing lights against the dark backdrop of water beyond the windows, his demeanor the quietly compelling man she'd so admired from afar in Bali. Pausing, she allowed herself a few seconds to take in his profile of statue stillness. He projected casual wealth with his gold watch and tailored shirt over crisp pants with their break in the cuff where they landed on his Italian loafers. Since he took these things for granted, he emanated power. And he was so *attractive* with his fit body and neat haircut and perfectly hewn, freshly shaved jaw.

She had always thought he had it all, had so much he was bored with the world, but she knew him so much better now. He held himself remote as a self-protective thing and that made her see him with new eyes. She realized he must be terribly lonely.

He glanced abstractly toward her, then started with a flash of surprised recognition. Maybe something else. She wasn't sure what she saw between his raking gaze from her lashes to her fancy shoes. He quickly masked his expression.

"No uniform," he commented.

No compliment, either.

"I didn't want to start any rumors if the Makricosta CFO was recognized having dinner with our general manager. I made reservations across the road."

He nodded without reaction and held the door for her as they walked across to *La Fumée Blanche,* The White Mist. She'd secretly wanted to try the dinner and dance restaurant forever, but it was a place for couples, not singles or a woman and her preadolescent niece.

They were shown through a dining room surrounding a small dance floor. On a dais, a trio played French jazz, filling the room with the Pink Panther sound of a brush against a cymbal. Their table had fresh roses, plush velvet chairs and a spectacular view of the Med.

It would have been perfect if she didn't feel like Theo was wearing his CFO hat and picturing her in her Makricosta blouse.

"Wine?" he asked.

"I thought you don't drink?"

"I thought you might."

"Sometimes." She flushed at how awkward this was. Maybe they needed Zephyr between them after all. "If it's a special occasion, but I don't need anything tonight."

This wasn't special, even though the candle glinted flecks of golden light off the silver and touched sparks in the crystal wine goblets. Even though a pianist tickled keys, accompanying a bassist who stroked sensual notes from her instrument.

Even though she was with the only man who'd ever melted her frigid libido and still managed to kindle heat in her when he seemed completely oblivious to her presence.

He ordered starters and painful silence ensued.

"Bina got to the room all right?" Of course she had or he wouldn't have left Zephyr. *Try harder, Jaya.*

"She looks like you," he said with a lift of his brows. "It

was startling. Made me think that's what our—your daughter could look like, if you had one. People must make that mistake often?"

"All the time." She swallowed, trying not to latch onto what she thought he'd meant to say. *Our.*

More silence. This dress, coming out, it was a huge mistake. He wasn't comfortable so she couldn't relax.

Theo eyed Jaya's tense posture. His own prickling tension was at maximum. She couldn't relax, probably because she felt threatened by his mood.

A pile of ferocious curses piled up in the back of his throat. He was so angry, he could barely think straight. Damn it, why did this exquisite woman keep winding up beyond his reach?

He wished he could take back his confession of his desire. He'd come on strong, had taken a lot of heart from her saying she was still attracted to him, but the rest... Hell, no, nothing between them was simple anymore. What had seemed like an obvious solution, marriage, was now a minefield.

And yet...

Bloody hell, he had to let it go. Maybe if he hadn't told her *before* she explained about her past that he was still hot for her. Maybe if he wasn't currently simmering with insane want, but wow, *that dress*.

Ah, hell, it wasn't the dress. He'd seen a thousand scraps of silk and sequins on a thousand beautiful women and this wasn't the most elaborate or provocative. It was exactly Jaya's style: pretty and feminine, accented with fine metallic strands, but rather sweet overall.

It wasn't the dress that smelled so good he felt drugged. He didn't want to run his hands over sheer fabric and frilly ruffles. He didn't want to taste stitching.

Her skin called out to him. Her lips.

He forced himself to look away and sip his ice water.

Cool his head. Somehow he had to kill off this attraction so he wasn't scaring or intimidating her.

"I shouldn't have told you," she said so softly he wasn't sure he heard her. When he glanced at her, her delectable mouth was pouted in misery. "It changes how you see me, doesn't it?"

"Yes," he allowed with brutal honesty, distantly aware that wasn't the right thing to say, but he struggled with emotions at the best of times and these were some of the worst he'd ever encountered.

Her deep brown eyes widened in a flinch of stark pain, gaze not lifting from the tabletop. Then she struggled to regain her composure, brow working not to wrinkle, mouth trembling until she caught her bottom lip with her teeth.

"For God's sake, Jaya. I don't think *less* of you. I hate myself. I shouldn't have taken advantage of you the way I did. You deserved better." His voice came out low and jagged, as if he'd smoked ten packs of cigarettes and was hardly breathing through the thickness clogging his lungs.

"Better than the first real pleasure I've known with a man? Better than Zephyr?" she challenged shakily.

He was rarely shocked speechless. When he pinned his lips, it was because he was prudent, not because he couldn't think of what to say, but her words blanked his mind. Bali had been a mistake, he kept telling himself, but she seemed to be lifting his actions out of reprehensible into something that was almost exalted. He didn't know how to process that.

"It's like your back, Theo. I'll always have scars, but they fade a little more each year. If you make enough good memories, they push the bad ones away."

He sat back, startled by her insight. He snorted. "I guess that's my problem," he admitted as realization dawned. "I've never made any good memories. Well, maybe one." He couldn't help the significance in the cut of his glance toward her. She was so beguiling. Their night together eclipsed every other memory he had.

Even in the low candlelight, he could tell that her brown skin darkened. Her flustered hands moved into her lap and she ducked her head.

"You know I wouldn't—" he began, catching himself from reaching for her. She was such a panacea for him. He wanted to eat her up. Drown in her. She was everything good that could ever be for him, but he couldn't be greedy about it. He had to hang on to his control.

Her reserve was more than natural modesty, he reminded himself. Her sexual inhibitions were well founded and he'd take a thousand beltings before he'd frighten her with his desire. If she had used him that one night, because she was having a brave moment, well, lucky him.

"I'm glad if our night is a good memory for you, but I don't expect it to happen again. If that's why you're reluctant to marry me, we can keep it platonic." He couldn't believe those words had left his mouth, but having even a small part of her in his life seemed like better than nothing.

Again her eyes widened like she was enduring a wave of agony. "Because now you know I'm soiled goods and don't want—"

"What? No!" His hand went onto her arm involuntarily. He had to hiss in a breath as he strove for control and lifted his touch away, but only managed to transfer it to the back of her chair. Leaning in close, he said, "If you think I'm not aching to make more first-class memories with you, then you are even more naïve than I've always feared. The appeal you have for me... It scares *me,* Jaya. You'd be terrified if you knew how intense my desire is."

He forced himself to retreat into his own space. A deep gulp of ice water did nothing to clear his head. The glossy window reflected his iron hard expression back to him as he braced himself for her to bolt. He should have kept all that to himself.

She sat in quiet contemplation, then confessed softly, "I don't know why you're the only man who makes me feel... well, *anything,* but you are. *That* scares me. I feel like I could be at your mercy, not because of your will. It would be lack of my own."

Excitement pierced him, the arrow so thickly coated in desire he had to close his eyes and concentrate on his breathing. Swearing under his breath, he opened his eyes and let her see the hunger in him, just for a second.

"You're killing me. You know that," he accused, voice buried in a chest.

Her lashes flickered and she quivered like one of those plucked strings that were trying to set a calm mood while he was a werewolf fighting to stay inside his human skin.

"I don't mean to," she whispered. "I just want to be honest."

A bleak laugh escaped him. "It would be a helluva better foundation for a marriage than my parents had."

She cocked her head. "They lied to each other?"

"My mother did, yeah," he said, distaste curling his lip. "She said Nic was my father's. When the truth came out, things turned ugly. The only way any of us coped was to pretend. We acted like we didn't remember Nic, like we didn't hate our mother, like we weren't scared of our father." He clenched his teeth, startled by the ugly truths that poured like fresh blood from a new wound. "Your honesty isn't comfortable for me. I'm not used to it, but... It's reassuring."

She offered a crooked smile.

His heart tipped on its edge, making him bold enough to add, "So whatever you're thinking about how I might be thinking of you differently, it's only that I'm trying to offer you reassurance as well. I won't force you into anything, Jaya. Not marriage, not my bed."

Her watchful gaze wasn't easy to bear. He felt like his entire future hung in the balance.

"I believe you," she murmured, leaning on her elbows. "And I don't feel coerced. I know that marriage is probably best for Zephyr, but a lifetime is a long time, Theo. I can't just leap in. I need to know what it would look like first."

"I have no idea," he admitted, tensing against the million ways he could fail her without even being aware of it. "What do you want it to look like?"

She sat back to consider that and her gaze snagged on the couple at the next table as they rose and moved onto the dance floor. Her face became younger, cast with the yearning of a woman who loved to move to music.

"Would you dance with me?" she queried.

"Of course." He stood and held out his hand while calling himself a shameless ass for seizing the excuse to touch her. Maybe it was even a small test to see if she would accept his hands on her. He could live within just about any limit, so long as he knew what it was. He was going crazy not knowing where his lines were with her.

"I meant, you know, are you the kind of man who would dance with his wife?"

"You weren't asking? Then I am. Will you dance with me, Jaya?" He picked up her hand, oddly pleased with the shy smile she hid with a dip of her chin.

He'd learned early that the guy who was willing to dance got laid. He was proficient at most of the ballroom moves, but she made him hyperaware of himself as he fit them together, especially because he was on guard against being too aggressive. He wasn't quite as smooth as he'd wish, but he wasn't standing on her painted toes, either.

She was awkward, her hesitation seeming more from surprise and unfamiliarity with formal dancing than apprehension. After settling her hand on his shoulder and her fingers into his palm, she took a step forward instead of back, then cringed in horror.

He grinned. "It's fine, just follow my lead."

She did and because she was naturally graceful and rhythmic, they moved well together—not unlike the way they'd meshed in Bali. It was her same quiet trust that made it possible, heating him to his core as he absorbed it, solidifying his need to take great care with her, stoking his need.

"Question answered?" he managed to say, trying to keep things light.

"You're sneaky," she accused. "Maybe you don't bully or pressure, but you're not above seduction, are you?"

He stopped dancing and drew in a deep breath, harking back to when he'd done everything he could to lure her by her own desire into his bed. "Jaya—"

"It's okay, Theo. I don't know what I'm doing when it comes to men." She nudged him back into leading. "I've never danced like this, never been on a real date. If you don't make advances nothing will happen because I don't know how. That's really why I'm scared to say I'll marry you. You're the first man who's asked."

Reservations paralyzed him, but when he used the excuse of an approaching pair of dancers to pull her close, his misgivings slipped from his mind. The contact of her abdomen hitting his hips detonated a subdued explosion that drained his thoughts.

Her lips parted as they held the pose for an extended few seconds, eyes locked.

She took a sudden step back, but didn't release his hand when he relaxed his hold on hers. Chewing her lip, she seemed to debate whether to continue their dance.

"I'm always like this around you," he admitted under his breath, throwing his ego into the wind. It might be the dumbest thing in the world to think this would reassure her, but if they had agreed on nothing else, they were being honest with each other. Maybe, just maybe, if she knew she could trust him, he could have her in his bed again some-day. "Every time I saw you in Bali, I was aroused. Just knowing I would see you would do this to me. I've only ever acted on it the once, Jaya, when you wanted me to."

They still weren't moving, only holding the half em-brace while music and couples swirled around them. He searched for uneasiness in her, but her eyes were clouding with confusion and... Was it desire?

If he cupped her breast right now, he wondered, would he find her nipple pebbled and sensitive, aching for the pull of his mouth?

He swallowed, dying as he balanced on the knife's edge between hell and ecstasy.

"Would you kiss me, please?" she asked softly. "I've been wondering—"

He did, not debating, just grasping at permission to cap-ture her parted lips with his. Deep in the back of his mind he reminded himself, *Easy. Go slow.*

It was agonizing to hold himself back. She was so ex-quisite, her mouth the pillowy satin welcome that tortured his dreams. By some feat of inhuman discipline, he kept his hand light when he clasped the side of her neck where she was warm and soft. He raked his mouth across hers in gentle ravishment, drinking in the clove and nutmeg taste of her.

Jaya liked these extra high heels. Her neck didn't hurt from tilting up to Theo's kiss. Her arms rose of their own accord to curl behind his neck. She opened to the tip of his tongue with a hitch of her breath and started to arch into him.

His hands hardened on her hips, pressing her into her shoes as he lifted his head.

"I was wondering, too." His voice sounded like it origi-nated in the bottom of his chest and came out in a purr like a high-performance engine. "We're still incredible together. Make sure you take that into consideration." He circled his thumbs on her hips.

She ducked her laugh into his collarbone, hand pressed to where his heart slammed in the tense cage of his ribs. *Oh, Theo.* She had missed him so much. In this second, all she could think was that she wanted to spend the rest of her life with him, feeling like this.

It reminded her of that fearful moment in Bali when she'd closed her eyes and grasped at her own future. There had been consequences to her actions that she hadn't foreseen. She ought to show a little more sense this time. Marriage was the oldest form of subjugation in history.

But she didn't believe it would be that way with him. Perhaps she was fooling herself, but she felt more like a mammal with the mate she was meant for. Whether she said yes today or years from now, no man was ever going to have this same effect on her. In her heart she was already tied to Theo. Hesitating to make it official seemed like fighting the inevitable.

On the other hand, was money and sex enough? Could Theo ever give her the things she really craved from a lifetime with a man?

"Our food has arrived," he said, nudging her back to their table.

Her pulse jittered from his touch as she sat down and tried to take in the scorched scallops atop crunchy potato cakes.

When they were alone she asked, "Where would we live?"

"With me," he deadpanned. "That's the point."

She laughed, but he only scowled as he chewed and swallowed.

"I need to talk to Adara about curtailing the worst of my travel. Whether you marry me or not, I have to be available to Zephyr, but I'll always have to do some globe-trotting. I don't particularly care for Paris as a base, but it's closer to India than New York. Could you stand it?"

"Could you?" she challenged, taking in the tight grip he had on his fork with a tilt of her equilibrium into caution. "I'm actually quite flexible. I've started over in new places several times. You live in your helicopter. You're used to doing what you like. Having a wife and child would turn your life upside down, Theo."

"I'm aware," he stated flatly, setting down his utensils to stroke restless hands up and down his thighs. "And I won't claim that I'd be easy to live with, especially in the beginning, but I keep coming back to what I can offer you in terms of security and protection. Marriage is the simplest way to accomplish that."

She ought to be flattered, she supposed. There was a type of caring in his bland statement, even if it was the kind one usually showed to, say, an expensive boat or maybe a herd of cattle. On some level he valued her, she deduced. That was nice, but it wasn't enough to sustain a marriage.

Their conversation drifted to what kind of placement she could have with Makricosta's, as his wife or not, and they didn't talk about marriage again until they'd returned to the suite.

First they had to release the matronly Madame Begnoche and Theo had to negotiate a peace treaty with Bina. She was very sad to learn that Theo wanted Zephyr living with him rather than coming to South America with her and Quentin.

"Pyaari beti," Jaya reminded gently, "You know I was going to stay in France and not come with you and your papa."

"I know, but, but…" Her voice threatened to crack into sobs.

Theo extracted a business card and wrote on it before he

handed it to Bina. "This is my personal mobile. Call any-time you are missing Zephyr. We probably won't be able to come to you that day, but we'll try to visit within the week. Or, if your father agrees, I'll bring you to visit him. We'll work it out, I promise."

"Thank you," she said in a heavy but mollified voice, blinking her damp doe eyes.

When she held up her arms, Theo didn't get it. Jaya had to touch his shoulder and nod. "She wants to hug you."

"Oh, um." Clearing his throat, he went down on one knee so Bina could squeeze his neck with her spindly arms. He patted her back awkwardly and deflated with a heavy exhale after she left to meet Oscar and the limo, Theo's treat.

"Thank you," Jaya said to him. "But you can't keep of-fering to fly me and my family around the world."

"Why not?"

Because I haven't agreed to marry you, she almost said, but she suspected it didn't matter. He'd do it regardless. "You're a soft touch when it comes to kids, aren't you?"

"I don't know what that means, but having Nic disappear on us was a trauma I don't want to drop on my own son."

Oh, right. She swallowed, watching him run a fingertip along his eyebrow. She wondered if he was looking for an-other argument to persuade her to marry him.

"Theo." She sat heavily in the middle of the sofa.

His head came up, expression patient.

Her heart grew achy and she had to look at her finger-nails. "I don't want to string you along wondering what you have to do to convince me to marry you. I'm not hesitating because I'm afraid of going to bed with you."

She bit her lips, keeping her head down while stealing a quick peek upward, noting that she had his attention, one thousand percent. He was virility personified, all his masculine features sharpened, his wide shoulders tense and defined beneath his crisp white shirt.

"Actually, I am a little nervous about that. I've had a baby since the last time and it's not like I've had a lot of practice…" She swallowed.

"We'll be amazing, Jaya. Just like last time." His voice reverberated deep in his chest.

If she hadn't been sitting, she would have fallen, he made her so weak. She grasped for the words she needed to say. "I'm not afraid you'd be violent or disrespectful, either. I know I could trust you about most things."

"But not all things." Tone cracked with a jag of disbelief, he recoiled in hurt.

She swallowed, knowing this would be difficult.

"You didn't call me back," she said in a small voice. "I know you said you wouldn't, but…" She tried to shrug off how foolish she felt, how bare this fantasy of hers left her. "I thought I was different. I thought you liked me."

His face transformed in slow degrees, falling from intense focus on her to inward comprehension, into lost hope and finally, self-hatred.

"I don't expect you to love me," she rushed to say, even though it tore open something inside her. "But I always wanted to marry for love." Such a girlish dream, so romantic and silly. That's the message she'd always received, but she still wanted it. "I need something between us that's not just practicality and hormones. Those things aren't a real bond. They're not something you fight for. But if you had any feelings for me at all…"

He did his thing where he froze. Not shrinking. He didn't cringe, but he braced himself. Like he refused to show how vulnerable he felt, while at the same time expected great pain. "I don't understand why you'd want me to."

Careful, she urged herself. He wasn't being arrogant or callous. He probably, genuinely didn't understand. She heard the barest inflection on *me* in his statement and knew this was more about his low opinion of himself than lack of regard for her.

Licking her lips, choosing her words with care, she said, "Everyone wants to be liked. Don't you?"

He shook his head. "It doesn't matter to me either way." Because he'd been reviled by someone who was supposed to love him. The abraded edges of her heart frayed and stung.

"What about your sister? Surely it matters to you that she loves you?"

His shoulder jerked, almost like he was deflecting a blow. "I'm sure she values my loyalty. I take satisfaction in knowing she can count on me."

He only took what pride he gave himself, would never ask for a smidgen more even from a woman he'd take a bullet to protect. How utterly abandoned he must have felt to mold himself into someone so inaccessible.

"Well, I want to be liked," Jaya said with one hand cupped in the palm of the other, trying to project calm control when emotion tore at her throat. "I'd like whatever attraction you feel toward me to be for more than whatever parts of me fit into lingerie. Because I think you're a very good-looking man, but when I say I'm attracted to you, I mean that I *like* you, Theo." *Love,* a voice inside her contradicted, but it was such a huge admission to be in love that she pressed it back into her subconscious, not quite ready to be that vulnerable.

Still, as she lifted her gaze, she was absolutely defenseless, like he must be able to read that her feelings were so much stronger than she was admitting, but she didn't want to scare him, only let him see she was sincere.

"Jesus, Jaya," he whispered in a ragged breath, looking away.

His image swam before her brimming eyes, but she

thought she'd seen a flinch of great anguish, like her words had touched a very raw part of him. He rubbed his hand across his jaw.

"For God's sake, why?" he expelled with disbelief.

Oh, you poor, poor man. She rose and went to him, unable to sit so far from him when he was hurting so much. Cupping his head, she forced his tortured expression to face hers.

"Why do I like you? You're a good man, Theo. When I told you about my assault, you didn't ask what I was wearing or whether I did something to encourage it. You never once lost patience with those babies even though they kept us up half the night. You protected your little brother when you were barely old enough to—"

"Shh, don't." He pulled her into his chest, crushing her so tight she could barely draw breath. His heart pounded against her breast and she felt his swallow where his damp throat was pressed to her temple. His breaths moved harshly in his nostrils as he tried to regain control, holding her against the rise and fall of his shaken breaths.

She let herself soften into him, hoping her signal of acceptance would penetrate.

His own arms loosened a fraction and she wound her arms around his chest. Their embrace became mutual. Tight and close, man and woman. He cupped the back of her head and rubbed his chin on her hair.

"People hate to see me coming," he said after a long time. "I criticize how they're doing things, ask for paperwork they can't find, make them account for items they think are insignificant. You always smiled at me, no matter what I asked for. I was never an imposition to you. That's so rare for me."

He combed his fingers through her hair while she closed her eyes against a sharp sting, feeling dampness gather on her lashes and keeping them hidden in his shirt, certain he'd stop holding her if he knew how moved she was.

"Do I *like* you?" he continued. "I don't have friends. I don't know how that works. I wish I could say I loved you, that I could give you everything you want from a man. Knowing you want love tells me I don't deserve you."

She hitched in a breath of protest, but he was continuing, arms tightening a fraction to keep her in place.

"But I'm not selfless enough to give you up. I want you in my life. Not just because my mouth waters when I think of you naked. Hell, you can feel how I'm reacting now, but there are a lot of beautiful women out there. There's only one you. You *are* special, Jaya."

She hugged him hard, biting her lips because they were quivering. "Thank you for saying that."

"But it's not enough, is it?" He slid heavy hands to her shoulders and eased her back a step. "You do deserve better."

Here was the crossroads again. She couldn't know if marrying him was the right choice unless she made it and looked back on having lived with it, but she couldn't hurt him by rejecting him. All she could do was remember how perfect they had been once and believe that, with time, they could surpass it.

Without breathing, courage gathered into a tight knot in her middle, she picked up his hand to cradle it against her cheek. "You're going to have to trust me when I say that I would be honored and privileged to be your wife," she quavered.

He searched her gaze, a small frown pulling his brows. "Are you saying—"

She nodded, unable to help smiling when he was so plainly taken by surprise. "I would like to marry you, Theo."

The flash of male triumph that streaked into his fierce

visage might have frightened her if there wasn't a helping of relief beneath it, endearingly softening his ruthless expression. In the next instant, he shuttered himself so thoroughly, she wondered if she had seen any reaction at all.

"Thank you. We'll get a ring in the morning."

And the CFO was back, armed with his tasks. Nevertheless, she'd seen behind the curtain and knew there was something there, even if it wasn't very clearly defined.

"I don't need a ring," she dismissed, and reluctantly let her hands drop. She didn't know how to bring herself out from intense emotional intimacy to distance with the swiftness that he did. A chill made her cross her arms and self-protect.

"I want to do this properly," he insisted, then grimaced. "I suppose that means we should wait until our wedding night. How long does it take to plan a wedding?"

"Wait for what? Oh." She ducked her head to hide that she was blushing, partly because she was dense enough not to have got his meaning right away, but also because she was disappointed. "We don't have to," she murmured.

"I want you to be sure." He pushed his hands into his pockets, but she could see he was still aroused. He was trying not to touch her, she realized, and glittering delight bounced through her at her effect on him.

"I am sure." She lifted her face so he could see she wasn't teasing, but she didn't know how to flirt or invite. Arousal was still too new.

"Sure about all of it," he clarified with a rueful look. "Given our track record, I'd knock you up by midnight. As you said, this is your first proposal. I won't trap you."

A small smile touch her lips at the prospect of him forcing a shotgun wedding, but another thought occurred and it was a big one. "Do you want more children?"

His expression blanked in surprise. "I haven't given it any thought. Hell, last week I didn't want any. Today...I don't know. Being a single child sounds lonely for Zephyr, doesn't it? I mean, Demitri is a complete pain in the ass, but I can't imagine not having him around."

"It's open for discussion, then?" she confirmed. This was a deal-breaker for her.

"Yes," he said firmly. "But let's give ourselves a chance to get to know one another again first." His gaze feathered over her cheek and lit on her mouth.

He knew how to say things that both flattered and intrigued. Despite his sweetly suggestive remark, however, a very somber mood came over him.

Her smile faded. "What's wrong?"

"Not one thing." He cupped her face and kissed her with startling tenderness. "You're very lovely, Jaya. How long until I can call you my wife?"

"I don't know." Her heart turned over and already she wondered if she'd done the right thing. "A few months?"

He grimaced.

"Unless you want a small wedding," she rushed to say. "That could be arranged in a week or two."

"I want to do this right." His hands fell to her shoulders and he looked over her head, his expression weighted by heavy thoughts. His hands massaged, but distractedly. Like he'd slipped miles away from her. "You'll want your family to come."

"My parents, yes, but it doesn't have to be a big deal. I've never dreamed of being the center of a society wedding. I can't imagine you have, either." She nudged his stomach playfully.

"More like suffered nightmares." His mouth twisted with aversion. "But we have business associates in New York and relatives in Greece who should be invited."

"Big weddings are expensive."

"Do *not* worry about the cost." He stepped away to state

decisively, "We should be able to make a strong statement in six weeks."

"A statement?" she repeated.

"As opposed to a splash."

"Okay." She tried to read his inscrutable expression.

"You should get some sleep. I'll listen for Zephyr," he said.

"You're staying up to work?" The way he shut her out was not the way she thought an engagement should start.

"I need to think. I'm used to having more time with my own thoughts than I've had in the last few days."

"Oh. Of course." She tried not to take that as a slight. *She* hadn't initiated this chain of events. If only he'd kiss her again, so the fragile bond between them would grow another layer, rather than fade. But he didn't.

"Good night," she said, confidence dwindling as she went to her room.

CHAPTER ELEVEN

As SOMEONE WHOSE life had changed overnight before, Jaya had learned to prefer a gradual, thoughtful approach to making shifts in her world. After her abrupt departure from India, she'd had months of notice before her move to Bali. Once settled, she'd dug in, comfortable in her role there. France had been a culture shock, but she'd had family to cushion the blow.

Nothing could have prepared her, probably not even time, for being pulled into the Makricostas' world. First she'd had to quit her job, which had been a tough decision even though Adara emailed with three job offers "to consider when the time is right." Then there was the travel, flitting up to London for two nights because Theo had a meeting and a thing.

"What kind of thing?" she'd asked when he'd requested she accompany him.

"A presentation. We paid to refurbish a historical building. One of the royals will be there so I've been elected to represent."

One of the royals. Like this was normal.

Which meant an upgrade to her wardrobe. No longer did she own a few nice outfits. Every time she turned around, Theo was bringing in a designer or a stylist or squiring her into a shop where the *prêt-à-porters* didn't even have price tags.

"I thought women enjoyed shopping," he said at one point.

"But the cost! I'm not even working."

He quirked a brow at her. "Do you have any idea how much money I make? How well I invest it? I never spend any."

Except on his fleet of airplanes and helicopters. He did some flitting of his own in those, disappearing to South America and Japan for a couple of days without her. She couldn't complain. She put off her separation from Bina as long as she could and needed the time to pack up her life, plan a wedding and look for a suitable home in New York.

The city was incredible. They spent a week there and she looked forward to living there permanently. However, the bit where Theo ensconced her in the family suite at the Makricosta Grand and visited his apartment without her bothered her immensely. It was too small for them, even in the interim, she agreed. She also understood he was a private man who liked his own space. Plus, as he pointed out oh-so-reasonably, here at the hotel she had help on tap— boy, did she have help. She used to be the one who jumped when a Makricosta rang. It was bizarre to be on the receiving end of that level of service from people a lot further up the corporate food chain than she'd ever been.

Then, just when her insecurities began to get the best of her and she convinced herself he'd be the most hands-off, distant husband, that this whole thing was a terrible mistake, he reassured her. After practically ignoring her all day in front of the real estate agent, he drew her into his arms as they closed the door of the hotel suite and kissed her breathless, saying when they came up for air, "I've been wanting to do that all day. You look amazing." She happened to be wearing one of her own modest navy skirts with a canary lace top over a lemon-colored cami. Nothing flashy or fantastic.

Then, when they'd decided on a penthouse apartment a few blocks from Adara and Gideon's, with a view of the park and a rooftop patio and pool, she'd watched him close the deal with an emotionless handshake. When the agent left them alone, an ominous silence descended, worrying her.

She rocked Zephyr on her hip. "Are you sure? You don't look pleased."

"You said you loved it." He snapped his head around.

"I do! You're the one who went into lockdown when I said I thought this was the one and could we have one more look."

He didn't like it when she called him on his standoffishness. She was learning his tells and noted the tick in his brow and the muscle that clenched in his jaw. But being blunt was the only way to get him to open up enough for her to understand him and not feel closed out.

"I didn't mean to." He kept one hand fisted in his pocket, his mouth tense and outlined in white.

The look he flashed at her was both impatient with himself and...not distrustful, but like he wasn't sure of her. With a cross noise, he shrugged. He kept a proud bearing, but it was like he was headed to the gallows, he was so stiff and withdrawn as he pulled his hand from his pocket.

"You know I'm the furthest thing from a romantic," he said gruffly. "But I thought if we decided this would be home, it would be a good time to give you this, as a sort of... Hell, I don't know." He showed her the sparkle he held. "An official start?"

She gasped. "You picked up the ring?" They'd chosen the stones two weeks ago, but she hadn't expected to see the finished setting until right before the wedding.

"I figured if you said yes to the apartment, you were probably going through with the wedding so..."

He was nervous!

Too awed to laugh, she rushed forward to kiss him.
Zephyr got in the way, of course, little fists grabbing at
Theo and catching a chest hair so he winced and pulled
away long enough to take him. Then he pulled her back into
him like a pirate grabbing a wench, angling her over his
arm as he kissed her like he really meant it. Like he wanted
to devour her because he desired her so much.

Jaya straightened her ring on her finger now, the memory of their kiss embedded into the piece as irrevocably as
the oval cut sapphire. The goldsmith had created a setting
that looked as if he'd cut a blond band open then twisted
it, setting the rare purple stone between the scrolled ends.
He'd finished the tails with ever shrinking pink diamonds.
The result a piece with such femininity, it made the extrav-
agance subtle and elegant.

Much like the stunning mini-villa behind her, she
thought ruefully, lifting her gaze to the view of the Parthenon lit yellow-gold by the fading sun. They'd decided
on Athens for the wedding. It was a less grueling flight for
her family and worked for his.

It was like a fairy tale, but she'd had another run of
doubts as recently as last night. They'd had dinner with
Adara and Gideon. Nic and Rowan had their own apartment in the city, but had joined them in the family suite. The
babies had reunited into a loud, happy flock that Theo had
stood apart from while the others dove in with quick hands
to retrieve a dropped toy or change a bottom. Gideon, as
Adara had predicted, took to Zephyr like he'd made him,
rolling on the floor with all the children, far more relaxed
than she'd ever expected the cool, stern Director of the
Board for the Makricosta empire to be.

Theo, on the other hand, wasn't as forward with his affection, waiting for the little ones to come to him, saying
something about them probably not remembering him.

After a night of agonizing whether he shared her dream

for a loving family, she'd woken to find Theo on his back on
the lounge floor, Zephyr lifted like a superhero above him,
both of them laughing as Theo lowered him to make growl-
ing noises against his little belly. It was exactly the game
Gideon had played with all the children the night before.

She'd pretended she needed her phone to hide her moved
tears.

He just needs someone to show him how to love, she
reasoned. She was that person. Somehow she'd overcome
her mistrust and was falling for him. It was only fair to believe he had the capacity to love her back, given time and
enough trust between them.

A door opened and closed in the suite behind her.

Her ruminations fell away and she smiled with anticipation, expecting him to come to her. Sometimes he checked
on Zephyr first, if he was napping, which he was. Then
they'd neck until they were breathless and oh, why weren't
they married yet? She was growing impatient to feel his
skin, his hands, *him.*

Swallowing the rush of feeling, she blinked the smeared
colors of the Parthenon from her eyes and turned with a
beaming smile.

And saw Theo making out with a woman against the
wall, just inside the entry doors of the penthouse.

No.

Squinching the wetness from her eyes, she swiped her
forearm over them as she stumbled on bare feet across
the marble tiles of the rooftop garden, around the end of
the pool and up to the point where the air-conditioning
of the interior blended with the heat of the outdoors.

Maybe that was her own body causing the hot and cold
baffling through her as she stared with disbelief at a familiar back. His shoulders flexed beneath his white shirt as he
guided a woman's leg to his hip then slid his hand under

the edge of her polka dot skirt. Sharp pink talons poked through his brown hair as they kissed.

A million thoughts whirled like tornado debris in her mind. He had said he was going for a haircut. That wasn't the shirt he was wearing this morning. Where did he think she was that he would bring some floozy back to where they were staying?

Nothing in the world could have prepared her for this. Except a senior chambermaid had taught her what to do in exactly this situation on her first day of work ten years ago.

"Housekeeping!" Jaya blurted in a shrill voice.

With a squeal, the woman's platform sandal clapped to the floor.

He barely lifted his head. "Come back another time." He chased another kiss.

It was Theo's voice, but the way he ignored her wasn't Theo.

"Demitri?" she hazarded.

His head came up again and he sent a laconic glance over his shoulder. "Jaya?"

"You're married?" the woman gasped.

"Hell, no. My brother's fiancée. Jaya, we're going to need some privacy. Can you…?" He gave her a "shove-off" motion.

"Of course." She grasped for her wits and searched for her purse. "I've been waiting for the baby to wake so I could go shopping, but if you'll listen for him—"

Demitri released his partner and reached for the door-knob, blocking Jaya's exit as he pressed his mate through it. "Wait for me at the elevator," he told her as he kissed her pout and gave her a pat on the behind before closing her out.

Jaya returned her purse to the side table and folded her arms, waiting for his next move with her brows in her hair-line.

He turned to her with an amused smile. "Well played."

Now she saw him properly, she could see the resemblance was strong, but not identical. He was obviously younger and not quite as handsome as Theo. *Too* devilish.

"I thought leaving babies with bachelor uncles was how your family does things."

He snorted. "I remembered you as shy and quiet. Made me wonder where Theo found the…"

His pause prompted her to fill in one of the thousand slang words men used to describe the source of their fertility and courage. She held her breath, waiting to hear which vulgar term he would pick.

"…temerity," he provided with a wicked tilt of his grin, "to date you."

He was a brat, through and through. She'd known it from her few interactions with him and now that Theo had explained about their family she even understood why. Demitri got away with his cheeky, outrageous behavior because no one stopped him.

"Speaking of dates, is that yours for the wedding? Because your family is staying in another suite. I'm expecting mine here shortly."

He shrugged off the information. "No, I don't even know her name. I picked her up in the bar." He was utterly without shame or consideration for others.

Genuinely curious about that, she cocked her head. "Why do you like to take people so off guard? Does it give you a sense of power to introduce chaos?"

He barely blinked, but narrowed his eyes in reassessment. "Here I thought I was behaving. The last time Theo was engaged, I picked up his bride."

When she caught a shocked breath, he smiled.

"He never mentioned that?"

She could have kicked him in his temerities, she was so infuriated by his smug air at having disarmed her. How could he do something so awful as seduce his brother's intended? And be proud of it?

Why hadn't Theo told her?

"He knows you're not my type," was the best retort she could manage.

The door lock hummed then opened.

Theo paused to take in Demitri slouched beside the door and Jaya standing across the other side of the lounge, arms crossed in dismay.

"Jaya was just reminding me I'm not her type," Demitri said flippantly. "Good thing I've been preapproved down the hall."

Theo stopped Demitri's exit with two straight fingers poked into his chest.

Jaya found herself holding her breath, never having seen him angry, not like that. Instant and icy cold, completely ready to be aggressive and deadly. His mood was doubly volatile because he didn't lash out, only asked with deadly flatness, "Did he make a move on you?" He didn't take his eyes off his brother.

"N-no," she managed, arms aching where she had them wrapped around herself.

"Don't," Theo said to Demitri. "Ever. I have my limits. You've just found one."

Jaya's insides trembled, all of her shaken by Theo's possessive, protective words. She wanted to be reassured it proved he cared for her, but she was still reeling from the news that he'd been engaged once before and hadn't told her. Had he loved that other woman? Was that the real reason he couldn't love her?

The thought was as bad as those poisoned few seconds when she'd thought it was him in the clinch against the wall.

Demitri calmly moved Theo's hand aside, like he was opening a gate. He walked out without a word.

Theo watched him for a split second, the muscle in his

jaw pulsing, before he stepped in and closed the door. "I'll assume it was garden variety obnoxiousness on his part that has you looking so peeved?"

"Actually it was learning you were engaged before. Were you going to tell me?"

CHAPTER TWELVE

THEO SAW THE hurt Jaya made no effort to disguise and suppressed a flinch of guilt. At the same time, his heart pounded like a pile driver. He and Demitri had their moments, but he'd never been as close to getting physical with his little brother as a few seconds ago. Violence was wrong, but if Demitri had touched Jaya, had scared her...

Such a rush of complex emotions strangled him, his instinct was to turn around and walk out, find somewhere private to pull himself together and come back when he felt in control again.

Maybe if Jaya had been angry and accusing he could have walked away from her. Instead she had that vulnerable look about her, the one that wrenched his heart. Like she was exposing her throat and it was up to him to prove he wouldn't rip it out.

"Zeph sleeping?" he asked.

"He went down twenty minutes ago."

His wingman wouldn't provide a distraction then.

He rubbed his face, trying to push his expression back into stoic when he was still unsettled by what he'd walked into. Amazing how he'd become addicted to entering cheerful disarray where a woman and baby greeted him with smiles, maybe some homey smells, and he had to pick a path across scattered toys, but always found a reward of physical affection at the end.

"Theo?" she prompted.

He squeezed the back of his neck. This was why he'd kept to superficial relationships for so long. One-night lovers asked surface questions with easy answers.

Still, the more time he spent with Jaya and Zeph, the more he craved. He liked hearing her sing in Punjabi to their son, liked the homemade food she cooked, liked the way she drew attention when they were out, pulling it off him as people took in her exotic beauty. She'd always been pretty, but with the professional styling taking her appearance up a notch, he had himself a knockout of a fiancée and couldn't wait to have her legally tied to him as his wife.

He was surprisingly impatient to lock in that life and now realized what had subconsciously been driving him.

But to admit it all to her? *Hell.*

"It's humiliating," he said, tossing his key card on a side table and moving into the suite a few steps, then halting in frustration. He could feel her rebuff from here. An invisible wall sat between them, dense as lead and heavy enough to compress his chest.

"When?" she asked in a strained voice. "Since Bali? Because I never heard anything about you getting married while I was working there. I'm sure I would have."

"It was years before that," he dismissed

That detail seemed to relieve a fraction of her distress, but she still stared at him, willing him to provide more details.

"My father arranged it," he forced himself to say.

"Arranged. But you were so disparaging when you thought I was quitting to go to France for an arranged marriage."

"That's why." Everything in him ached for distance and privacy, but a different, unfamiliar compulsion kept him frozen here, longing to close the gap between them. He was learning the only way was to pick his path through the minefield of his past. He hated it, but for her, he did it.

"Did you love her?" The tentative edge in her voice told him how hard that was for her to ask.

"No," he assured with a disgusted exhale. "She was a socialite, a party girl, the daughter of a well-respected New York businessman who was down on his luck. They wanted the connection to our family, my father wanted an heir…"

"You said you never wanted to be a father!"

"I didn't," he said, recalling such heavy dread it had stuck with him until he'd learned how it really was to have his own child. "But I didn't have a choice."

"Men always have a choice," she said with resentment. "They're never as helpless as women in these situations. She was probably under more pressure to go through with it than you were."

"No, I don't believe that." He never went back over those memories, they made him feel too pathetic, but she forced him to with her accusation. "You're right that I could have walked away from my inheritance," he allowed, "but I couldn't do that to Adara. Not after what happened to us once Nic was gone."

No one would ever know how close he'd come despite that. He'd forgotten how his sister had been the tipping point for him. He'd been scared for her. If he hadn't been there to protect her, no one would have been. His unhappiness with a marriage to a woman he didn't care about had seemed like nothing against Adara's safety.

Somehow, remembering his motive loosed the old shame off him. Yes, he'd been browbeaten and yes, it had been his choice to allow it. But he'd had a good reason.

"Demitri said he slept with her," Jaya said.

"He did." He felt nothing making that admission because the act had become the mortar he used to thicken and heighten the walls he used to protect himself. From then on, he'd held everyone even more firmly at a distance, even his siblings. Why in hell would anyone want to be close to him? He was second best to his outgoing, funny younger brother. Everyone preferred Demitri, given the choice.

Except Jaya. Maybe the seeds of his deep admiration had been born in seeing her deflection of men who came onto her, especially the ones who took for granted they could impress with a grin and a flash of money. She had smiles for everyone, but she reserved her warmest for grandfathers with arthritis or little boys who got off the elevator on the wrong floor.

"Why would he do that? Just to prove he could or…?" She shook her head in bafflement. "To hurt you?"

He drew in a breath that burned. "It wasn't just once for bragging rights. They had an affair. I don't know who started it and God knows I won't make excuses for him, but he was nineteen to her twenty-three. She happily drove to Manhattan and paraded herself through the lobby so all our staff could see them carrying on."

And his father had berated him, like it was his fault when he'd been half a state away finishing exams. *Such* impossible expectations. He swore if Zephyr never aspired to anything more ambitious than flipping burgers in a fast food shack, he'd make sure the boy knew he was proud of him.

"What did she say when you broke it off?"

Here came the degradation, but it was losing its potency as they talked of this. For too many years, he'd let this make him feel weak. He been strong. Enduring. "I didn't."

"Didn't break it off? But…Why not?"

The easy answer was, "I didn't have to. Adara convinced our father the publicity was too damaging to go through with it. By then Gideon was on the scene. Her engagement let me off the hook."

"You would have gone through with it?" She sounded appalled.

He was equally galled with himself, which is why he never revisited this ugly time, but he'd been a different man then. One who merely survived, not one who cared about thriving or his own happiness or anyone else beyond the one person who had always been there for him. Looking back, he barely recognized himself.

The turning point had been Bali, he saw now, and not because of Adara's call—even though that had been a catalyst. No, he'd begun thawing toward his siblings after that, but he couldn't have managed it if he hadn't had that night with Jaya. She'd begun the melt in him with her kind acceptance of his weakness that night. He only recognized now that it was her influence because he'd changed so much since he'd seen her again.

Shaking himself out of the stunning realization, he tried to answer.

"All of my options were terrible. If I'd broken it off, my father would have done anything to hurt me, including going after my mother and Adara." He'd make a different choice today. He was stronger. Because he had someone else in his corner.

Didn't he? She was still struggling to understand why he'd kept this from her.

"But not Demitri," she said. "I can see why you're so loyal to Adara. She's always had your back, but I don't know how you tolerate your brother. Or is that your normal interaction with him? Are you two always hostile?" She nodded toward the door.

"No, we get along. The past is water under the bridge." He forced himself to open hands that had clenched into fists as he recalled his anger when he'd come in to find Demitri with Jaya, her expression cross and distressed. "I wanted him to know there will never be any forgiveness where you're concerned." He leveled a stern glance at her.

"You'll tell me if he crosses any lines. I'm serious about this being a red one."

"Because he did it once before." She looked to her linked fingers.

"Because you have entrusted me to keep you safe. I'd die before I'd let you feel threatened by him or anyone." He'd take on anyone for her, he realized. Not because he approved of violence, but because she was that precious to him.

"Theo." Her head came up in alarm. "Don't talk about dying."

"Hey," he deflected with a snort. "I hope it doesn't come to anything drastic like that, but I bring so little to this relationship, Jaya." The tiny flame in him that he barely acknowledged would never be enough for her. "At least let me give you this much."

"That's not true." Tension distended her neck as she took his remark like a knife to the throat. Could she blame him for not bringing his heart to their marriage though, when his own had been so chronically kicked around? "You bring yourself. Stop thinking that's not enough."

The silence was so profound she couldn't look up. Then, even from across the room, she heard his swallow.

"Is it?" he asked in a ragged voice. "Because you brought Zeph and he's pretty damned incredible."

"He is, isn't he?" she said shamelessly. "But he's half yours so—" She took a few faltering steps toward him, then hesitated, not sure if he was ready to close the distance. The things he'd shared had been hard for him. She'd had to pull the details like teeth and there wasn't any anesthetic for things like this.

He met her halfway, his strong hands reaching out to take hers in a gentle grip. Her own clenched convulsively, grasping for something more than his steady strength, even though she knew she should be satisfied with that. It should be enough.

Pressing her trembling lips into a line, she searched his face.

He didn't like it and looked away, obviously not comfortable with her need for reassurance. She dipped her head, suffering another wave of doubt that he'd ever open his heart to her.

"I'm sorry," he said gruffly. "I should have told you myself, not left it so you'd find out like that. It was like what happened last night, when Gideon told Androu not to touch the light socket and that just made him more aware of them. I didn't want to put the idea into your head."

"That I could have an affair with Demitri? He floated that balloon years ago and I stabbed it with a pen."

Theo snorted, thumbs stroking over her knuckles. "I don't know why he has to behave like such an ass."

"You and Adara hold your lives under tight control. If he turns things upside down he gains the upper hand."

"Now how did you see that and I never have?" He leaned back to absorb that.

"You've spent so many years putting up shields, you can't always see past them."

He blinked in surprise, seeming disconcerted. "But you can."

"Sometimes," she said warily. "Does that bother you?"

He drew a deep breath. "It's not comfortable." His hands tightened on hers and he looked into her eyes, even though he winced as he did it, like it was a kind of torture to let her see inside him. "But…" He swallowed, then, "I trust you, Jaya. I know you're not going to use anything I tell you to hurt me."

His grip crushed her hands, but she didn't think he was aware of it. She squeezed back, feeling they stood on a precipice that, if they took this leap of faith, they could land in new, rich, broad territory.

"I would never want to hurt you. Not ever," she promised, then held her breath.

Bringing her hand to his mouth, he ran the knuckle of her ring finger along his lips. His breath clouded warmly against her skin as he spoke, making her wrist tingle.

"I think half the reason I still speak to Demitri after what he did is gratitude. Ultimately he got me out of a situation I didn't want."

"Really?" This didn't seem the deep confidence she half expected. "Do you think he did it on purpose?" she asked, wondering if that was digging too deep.

"Hell, no. He'd never show that kind of forethought, but he created the excuse and I was glad. Swear to me you'll never reveal that to him."

A giggle escaped her, part relief, part joy that he was confiding in her a little. "Cross my heart and hope to die."

He took a deep breath and looked down on her with something like pride and…affection? His expression had softened into amusement and tenderness. It almost looked like happiness and made her warm all the way to the soles of her feet. He was solemn as he cradled her face and caressed her cheek with the pad of his thumb.

"I can't wait to marry you."

"Really?" She wanted to smile, but she was dissolving under his look and couldn't seem to hold any part of herself steady. "Because I thought it was you at first, when Demitri came in. He made out with that woman right there in front of me and I thought for a horrible second it was you and we were finished. I was devastated," she admitted.

His mellow smile faded. "I'll kill him."

Her turn to set a hand against his smooth cheek, freshly shaved and smelling of something tangy and fresh. "But then I realized it couldn't be you because you'd never do that to me. I never expected I'd be able to trust a man this much, Theo. I wish I could tell you what a gift you've given me with that." She slid her other hand up his chest and around his neck so her breasts pressed into the hardness of his chest and her damp lips touched his ultra-smooth jaw.

He gathered her in, crushing her close in tight arms and releasing a shuddering breath against her ear.

They sought each other's mouths, colliding with practiced alignment, parted lips meeting and sealing, plunging her into a dark jungle of sultry heat and velvet sensations. Combing her fingers up the back of his head, she reveled in the short, freshly cut strands, the new haircut, exactly as he'd promised. The thought made her want to smile but he was kissing her too intently.

He rasped his tongue down her neck, one hand palming her breast, making intense sensations race into her loins. She clenched to contain the deliciousness there.

This was moving fast and a distant part of her wondered if she should be worried about that, but desire flowed through her veins in rivers of lava, making her burn for him.

"God, Jaya," he groaned, stilling her rocking hips against the hard ridge of his erection. "The next two days are going to kill me."

"Oh, Theo, I don't want to wait anymo—*oh!*"

He scooped her up, his strength like a conqueror's as he bounced her into a high clasp against his chest, his arousal evident in the flush on his cheekbones and the sheen on his feral half grin. "If you're not going to stop me, then I won't."

She slid her hand from his shoulder to his ear, pulling herself close enough to kiss where his pulse pounded like a hammer in his throat.

As he started down the hall, two sounds halted him: Zephyr's cry and a knock on the penthouse door.

He swore and she softly wailed, "Nooooo," as he let her feet slide to the floor.

"That's your family, isn't it?" His gruff voice was rueful. "Better now than in five minutes when we would have been naked. I'll get Zeph. I need to pull myself together."

Snickering, she kissed his chin and started to walk away. He yanked her back for another deep swift kiss that included a taste of France. Dazzled, she bounced off the wall on her way to greet her guests.

Despite his sexual frustration, which was more acute than he'd ever thought he could bear, Theo was riding a natural high. Jaya still wanted to marry him.

He hadn't consciously been aware of that niggling concern. She always responded so sweetly to him and even though they had their differences, they always seemed to work through them. Still, a voice inside him had kept harping that he wasn't enough.

She thought he was a gift, though, because she could trust him. He swelled with pride knowing how hard-won that kind of reliance was for her. The determination to protect her ran through him on a current of reverence and resolve. In a few days he would pledge to uphold her faith in him and he'd do it with every fiber of his being.

Speaking of gifts…

Lifting his freshly diapered son to eye level, he took a moment to absorb the awe of fatherhood. While the magnitude of responsibility still scared him, and he wasn't yet a hundred percent confident he'd be everything Zephyr needed, he was learning. For most of his life, he'd been driven by the need to be perfect so he wouldn't catch hell. Now, he yearned to do well so he could be a better father than he'd had.

"That sets the bar pretty low, doesn't it?" he murmured

to his son before he kissed the boy's forehead and carried him out to the main lounge.

Heated voices speaking Punjabi fell into a wall of blistering silence when he appeared. He'd picked up a few words from Jaya and was working on a speech for the wedding, but he wasn't good enough with the language to follow any of what had been said even if he'd properly heard it.

He was the last man to judge a family for dysfunction, but Jaya had seemed to be making progress with them. Her tone had been growing lighter of heart when she'd spoken of them while travel and wedding plans had fallen into place. He had been counting on her finding some emotional fulfillment through her relationship with her mother and sister to compensate for his own lack. It was important to him that he not cheat her of love, that he give her every chance for it since he couldn't provide it himself.

This wasn't love, though. This was a tight army of angry young men backing up a grizzled bear with a thick gray beard. Two older women sat on the sofa, one in green, the other in blue. They bookended a young woman in yellow and a dazed older man. Their clothing seemed extra-colorful against the white leather of the furnishings, their expressions taxed. The women seemed to be trying to make themselves smaller while the young men puffed up their chests under crossed arms.

Jaya stood apart from all of them, her anxiety palpable. The way she dropped her gaze after an initial tense glance at him seemed almost apologetic.

Theo mentally swore. He might have been swimming naked through these sorts of shark-infested undercurrents all his life, but he'd never grown comfortable in them.

"Welcome," he managed in Punjabi, then zeroed in on the woman beside the frail, confused looking man who must be Jaya's father.

"Jaya has been eager to see you all." He hoped that

wasn't overstepping. He hated it when people tried to talk
for him. Forcing himself to move forward even though his
joints felt rusted, he added, "This young man has been waiting to meet his *Naniji,* which is…Gurditta?"

He guessed correctly at the woman in the green sari.

Jaya's mother gasped and stopped dabbing a tissue into
her eye, dropping it away so she could pull Zephyr into her
lap. Her tears turned to joy as she gathered up the wiggling
boy like a bundle of laundry that wanted to drop socks.

Whatever dark cloud had been hovering broke into
beams of sunlight for a second as Jaya drank in the sight
of her mother holding her son. Then she glanced at the
bearded man with a mix of defiance, resentment and—
Theo's heart took it like a stiletto—a remnant of shame.

Before he realized what he was doing, he had moved to
her side and set a firm arm across her back. Belatedly, he
wondered if his hand on her hip might be a familiarity that
would repel someone with traditional views, but he needed
her to know she wasn't alone. They needed to know if they
insulted her, they insulted him, and he was not a naïve girl
working in a call center.

"Thank you for coming," he said, falling back on manners because it was one of his few fail-safe strategies in
a passive-aggressive confrontation like this. "I imagine
you're tired from the flight. My sister has planned a reception for the families to meet this evening, but you have
a few hours to rest."

Jaya's uncle, because that's who the hard-ass old grouch
had to be, said something in Punjabi.

Theo looked to her. She had said they all spoke at least
a little English and that her father would be the toughest
to communicate with because of his injury.

With a level stare that looked through the line of young
men, she said, "They object."

"To sleeping here? Because we're not married? I'm staying in another suite," he assured them. "My family owns the hotel. We have other rooms."

A snort from one of the men almost overrode what Jaya said, her voice quiet and uneven. "It's the marriage they don't support."

A quick blast of Punjabi came at her from her uncle.

She said something back, speaking firmly, but Theo could feel the tension in her was so acute she threatened to shatter.

"You're too rich, man," one of the young men blurted. "Look at my father. We can't pay a dowry that would keep you living like this." He waved at the opulence of the Makricosta Olympus suite. "Jaya should have known better than to agree. Are you that angry with our uncle you'd ruin him?" he demanded of her.

Jaya started to respond, but Theo gently squeezed her into silence, his fury nearly blinding him. It took everything he had to remain calm and civilized. He hated confrontation, but he'd been serious about fighting to the death for her.

"Dowries are illegal. I brought you here because Jaya wished to have her family at our wedding. If you leave, that will hurt her. I can't allow that." He held first her brother's gaze, then her uncle's.

Into the silence, her father said, "Jaya?" He patted Zephyr's leg and smiled.

Jaya drew a sharp breath and said, "Yes, he's mine." She drew Theo forward and crouched to the floor so it would be easier for her father to see her. She spoke slowly in Punjabi to him, something about their wedding and then she introduced Theo as her groom, straightening to stand beside him with pride.

Theo drew her close while the old man studied them. He felt on trial as he used the Punjabi he was still learning to ask her parents for their blessing.

She tilted her smile up to him, her pride in him almost too much to withstand.

When her father nodded, Jaya dissolved into happy tears, first kissing her father then wrapping her arms around Theo so tightly he could barely breathe.

He looked over her head at her brother, still twitching at all the animosity hovering in the room, but bearing it, for her. "I intend to take care of your parents. Leave if you wish, but if you'd like to hear the arrangements you should stay. Now, Jaya." He coaxed her to show her damp face. "Would you please introduce me to the rest of your family?"

As the days of celebration raged, Jaya agonized over whether it was too much for Theo. They hadn't gone with a full-out Indian wedding, but there was enough to be overwhelming.

That's why it surprised her he spent an hour with her male relatives without telling her. Then she was even more annoyed when her brother told her it had been about his arrangements for their parents.

"Every time Uncle raised an objection, Theo said, 'I thought of that, but...' Uncle underestimated him. We all underestimated you." He eyed her like he couldn't imagine how his disreputable sister had landed such a catch.

She quizzed Theo later on when he'd turned into a chauvinist and why he'd kept her from a meeting that impacted her.

"Two reasons," he said without apology. "First, I wanted your uncle to know that he can't manipulate you with guilt or fear any longer. You won't be padding his life with your earnings because I will provide your parents with their own home and income and a care aid for your father. If your uncle finds himself suffering financially, and needs to ask you for help, that will be at your discretion. You have the power now, not him."

"Oh." She was too overwhelmed by the sense of shackles falling off her body to know what else to say. "And the other reason?"

"I'm so angry with the way he treated you, I don't want you in the same room with him."

She didn't cross paths with her uncle much. All of them were so busy with the nearly two hundred guests that swelled the hotel to capacity. Cousins from both sides took over the two lower floors, work associates of the Makricostas' flew in from all four corners, and friends of Jaya's arrived wide-eyed with awe from Bali and Marseilles. Quentin and Bina were the last to arrive and Theo arranged for them to stay with his family, knowing there might be awkwardness with Jaya's.

It was a heart wrenching moment when Jaya's aunt, Saranya's mother, greeted Bina with open arms. Jaya grew tearful during the reception, recalling the way the little girl had broken down in her grandmother's arms, both of them united in grief. Bina had missed out on so much living in Saranya's exile, but her family connections were being restored now. Saranya would have been so happy.

"Jaya," she heard near her ear just before a broad hand settled on her waist and Theo's wide shoulders loomed to block out the Grand Ballroom. "Are you okay?"

She nodded and smiled through her tears. "Just wishing Saranya could be here to see how happy you've made me. You've given me back my family, Theo. They're healing rifts that have broken us apart for years. Thank you."

"I wanted that for you." His smile was so tender, she barely felt the knife of knowing he deliberately surrounded her with love from other sources so she wouldn't miss his.

"But you didn't expect all this, did you?" she said, sheepish at how she'd taken him at his word and put together a wedding that married their two cultures as well as themselves.

He glanced around the room draped in red silk curtains. Gold beads dangled in strings from the ceiling like sunlight caught in raindrops. Children were trying out the bride and groom's thronelike chairs under the floral covered *mandap*. Brilliant saris competed with designer gowns as people danced and stole exotic treats from the circulating waiters.

"This is definitely more socializing than I can typically swallow, but I'm not sorry. Everything is very beautiful." His gaze came back to her, his admiration evident in his slow, studied perusal. "Especially you. I don't know why I never pictured you like this, so exotic. You're breathtaking." His gaze paused on the pendant of her *maang tikka* dangling off the line of pearls in the part in her hair.

"You must feel like you've married a stranger." She lifted a hand to check her red-and-gold headscarf hadn't slipped. His gaze followed the sound of her abundant gold bangles clattering against the red and faux ivory ones anchored on her wrist. She felt like a pack mule, she wore so much heavy, ornate jewelry.

He looked striking himself, not wearing a turban or *pyjama,* but he was carrying a sword over his white morning coat.

"Thank you for including Adara and Rowan in the henna party. When they heard it was supposed to be only for the bride's family, they were devastated."

"They're my friends. Of course I would invite them." In truth, they were quickly becoming as close as sisters to her. "Did they tell you I could barely make it through having my feet painted?" All the women had bonded with laughter when it turned out Jaya's feet were so ticklish, she'd had to keep stopping the artist and making her work on others until she could withstand another few minutes of torture.

"They said my initials are hidden somewhere in the design. I can't wait to look for them." His smoky voice poured a wash of electric tingles over her.

She ducked her head, embarrassed by how badly she was anticipating being alone with him. Naked. It had been almost two years and so much had changed, her body, her feelings for him. They ran so deep now. If the henna artist was right about the color representing how intense her feelings for her husband were, her tattoos should last years.

He caressed the sensitive skin beneath her ear and along her nape, leaning in to ask, "When can we leave?"

A punch of unfettered desire clenched her middle. Her shoulder burned under the weight of his hand resting there. When he grazed his lips against her cheek her throat locked, she was so overcome by hunger.

"You're killing me," he said in a loaded voice. "Tell me. An hour? How much longer?"

She couldn't speak, could only lift her face so he could see how helpless she was to the feelings he incited in her. A muted ringing filled her ears and she realized it was her, trembling amid all this fine gold.

His tormented expression hardened into fierce excitement. *"Now."*

If he had swung her into his arms, she wouldn't have felt more swept away. He turned them toward the room and she wished they could disappear without speaking to anyone. This passion between them was nothing she felt shame over, but it was too personal and concentrated to endure a gauntlet of teasing over it.

Before they could move, Demitri lurched in front of them, unkempt, wearing a smear of lipstick on his cheek. "Hey, I'm ready to claim my dance with the bride."

"Too late," Theo said with only a hint of smugness. He waved away whatever Demitri tried to say. "Redeem yourself by making our excuses. We're leaving."

She thought Demitri might have tried to say something, but Theo stole her out a side exit. From there they broke into a run like schoolchildren and were both laughing and breathless when they tumbled into the elevator.

"We should at least say goodbye to Zephyr," she protested as Theo crowded her into a corner, his grin so boyish and lighthearted she grew dizzy.

"If there's any male getting more attention from women than my brother this week, it's our son. He won't miss us."

Curling his fists against the walls of the elevator, caging her in, he inhaled deeply without actually touching her, then growled in frustration when the elevator stopped, jarring them both into a small stagger.

"I know I'll appreciate the privacy once we get to Rosedale, but right now it's too damned far away." He pushed back and held the doors for her.

The wind had come up and whipped around them as they crossed to the helicopter. A uniformed pilot touched his cap as he helped Jaya up the stairs.

"You're not driving?" she asked Theo.

He gave her a look as he settled beside her in the passenger cabin. "We call it piloting," he drawled, accepting a glass of champagne from the flight attendant that he passed to Jaya, but declined for himself. He picked up her free hand and set a playful bite on the knuckle of her ring finger. "I knew I'd only be thinking of you at this point. Not the right headspace for getting us anywhere alive. This is Nic's crew. They make the trip all the time. Plus, all the pre-flights are done."

She saw the advantage to that as they lifted off the second her seat belt clicked into place. The attendant moved to the copilot's seat and lowered the lights. Minutes later they were high enough and far enough away that the city and sky blended into a blanket of pinprick lights. The moon sat fat and smiling a bluish glow.

Theo touched her chin, bringing her around from staring into the silver-laced waves and captured her mouth with the velvet heat of his. She opened to his pressure, tongue seeking the dampness of his, their union growing deep and wet between one startled breath and the next. Her hand sought the back of his head, urging him to kiss her harder as waves of delicious heat rolled down to the center of her, flooding sensations between her thighs, making her ache.

They were in another world, a bubble of white noise and shadow, straining against their belts as they twisted to be closer. She brushed at the lapel of his jacket, burrowing to his vest and seeking a way past it only to be thwarted by the silk of his shirt.

He groaned and skimmed his hand from her knee up her thigh, over her waist and cupped her breast, thumb circling over silk to tease her nipple. She wriggled in her seat, the erotic sensations building in her loins so intense she gasped and pulled away.

"Please stop."

"Damn, I'm sorry." He sat back, his face stark with self-recrimination as he closed his hands into fists on his arm-rests. "I misread you."

"No, you didn't." She threw her arm across him, face tilted against his shoulder so her whispered words could reach his ear over the din of the helicopter blades. "I'm afraid I'm going to…I can't. Not here, like this, with people right there who might know."

Theo's hands opened to clench into the ends of his arm-rests. She could feel the strain and flex in his biceps and across his chest as he nearly rent the crash-proof seats apart. His head tilted back and the sound he made was animalis-tic, somewhere between fury and helplessness.

When she started to pull back in alarm, he trapped her hand against his chest where his heart slammed. They sat like that until the bird landed on the lawn of a dark estate. An English mansion waited with stately patience, seeming out of place on this Greek island, but who cared? It was

Nic and Rowan's home, a gift of privacy for their wedding night, but Jaya barely saw any of it as Theo whisked her up the steps, past a housekeeper who said something about calling if they needed anything and practically booted her out the door.

"Are you cross? You seem angry," Jaya said, backing away from him in the dimly lit lounge.

"Because I almost lost it up there along with you? Hell, no, I'm going insane." He dragged at his clothes, shedding sword and bowtie and shoes as he stalked her. "Are you afraid of me right now?"

"What? No, not really, but—oh!" She came up against the bottom stair, surprised he'd steered her this way. "You seem really, um… What if the housekeeper comes back and finds your clothes all over the house like this?"

"She won't come back uninvited." His vest hit the floor. "Keep going." He jerked his chin at the upper floor, urging her to back up the stairs.

"You're kind of being, um…" She didn't know what the word was, but he was making her nervous. Not genuinely afraid, but she knew what a small animal felt like when stalked by a cat.

"Aggressive?" he prompted. "Impatient? I'm trusting you, my lovely bride. Keep going. One of these bedrooms is made up for us."

"Trusting me? To what?" She hurried down the hall ahead of him, sending anxious glances over her shoulder as he followed at an implacable pace. "What do you mean? Oh! It's so nice of them to do this…"

She entered an expansive bedroom where the scent of the sea wafted in through open balcony doors with the sensual push of each wave reaching for shore. Tea lights floated in glass globes of colored water, bringing a magical glow to the white sheets and sheer curtains around the canopied bed. An array of treats awaited on a side table beneath silver covers, but she didn't lift the lids, too aware of the half-naked man, his hands lowering his fly as he stepped through the door and left it half-open.

The low light burnished his muscled chest and flat stomach, accentuating his abs. She found herself shaking too much with excitement to be able to remove so much as her grandmother's heavy ring from her forefinger.

Theo moved toward her like he was a missile finding its target. His chest filled her vision and his aggressive masculine scent filled her nostrils, making her dizzy. Without thinking, she impulsively smoothed the narrow line of hair that arrowed down the center of his torso to his navel and lower to the exposed skin behind his loosened fly.

"I, um, don't know what you mean about trusting me," she said.

He sucked in a breath that pulled all his stomach muscles taut. He cupped the side of her face and made her look at him.

"I'm trusting you to tell me if I'm coming on too strong. Have you reached your limit? You're shaking."

"No! I want to touch you and be naked and feel you all over me but look at me! I can't get out of any of this on my own and—"

He kissed her, hard and fierce, the thrust of his tongue forceful, but so welcome, so good. She sucked on him, wanting to eat him alive. They'd been kissing and fondling and teasing for weeks. Her dreams had been full of how he felt thrusting inside her. She couldn't wait any longer. Modesty didn't enter into it. Instinct took over.

With a grunt of hunger he backed toward the bed and sat, pulling her to straddle his legs, gathering her sari and underskirt as he pulled her into his lap. She knelt with her knees parted to hug his hips. The position put her eye to eye with him, mouth to mouth. They never stopped kissing and she couldn't stop soaking in the feel of his skin with her splayed hands. Tiny noises escaped her, like an abandoned kitten then more of a purr when his hot hands slid up to cup the globes of her buttocks. She wriggled in his hold, loving the intimacy of it, wanting him to know how much pleasure his touch gave her.

Her whole body was filling with heat and excitement, blossoming like a flower coated in dew and sunlight.

With a ragged moan, he snapped her underpants, surprising her into gasping and lifting in surprise. He tugged them away and threw them to the floor then freed himself. She reached for the thrusting flesh he revealed, circling him with tentative fingers, reacquainting with the warm satin over hot steel.

The world contracted to this small circle of light where one man and one woman consummated their marriage, harsh breaths mingling as she helped him roll on a condom.

Wordlessly he guided her to lift and be open for him. She let her eyes drift closed as he guided his straining head to rub and tease. Soft gasps of anticipation escaped her and she dug her nails into his shoulders.

When she started to take him in, he gathered her swollen, aching breasts in two hard hands and bit through her sari at her nipples, making her cry out and arch, desperate for penetration. As she let her weight sink down, as her wet, ready sheath swallowed him, he dropped his head back and snarled at the ceiling.

Smiling, she scraped her nails across his chest and worked herself to find the tightest fit against him, heart expanding with joy at each pulse of his hard muscle inside her. He dug his hands through silk to snug her tighter and tighter still, causing delicate explosions as the right place was touched again and again.

They kissed, deep, sumptuous kisses, rocking themselves into ownership of each other's body. Soon their movements exaggerated, pulling away and coming together with more force. She had never ridden a horse, but she rode her husband, using her thigh muscles to rise and fall on exquisite impalement, feeling the strain in him as he balanced on the edge of the mattress, sweaty and strong beneath her, holding himself steady to let her set their pace. His breaths rang with strain and his chest and shoulder muscles bunched with tension. When her stamina began to fail, his hands grasped her hips and kept her rhythm steady so they approached the crisis together.

"Theo! I'm—" Her world was coming apart at the seams.

"Me, too. Now, Jaya. Let me feel you—ah, yes. Like that. Ah, yes, yes!"

She imploded then expanded like a supernova, his pulsing completion within her shooting her into a realm where they were one experience, one person. One.

Draped naked on her stomach across the bed, she lay acquiescent as her husband kissed and stroked his way around the henna on her feet and lower legs. Every few minutes he ran a playful fingertip down the sole of her foot or nuzzled too softly at her ankle—he almost got a reflexive kick in the eye for that one—but he was enjoying himself so she tried to withstand the tickling.

"Here," he finally said, kissing hotly inside her calf.

"Are you sure?" She sat up, scooping the edge of the sheet for a shred of modesty, then studied the scrolled *T.M.* "Should I have it tattooed there permanently?"

"Would you?" he asked. He was so sexy with his rakish stubble and relaxed grin, propped on an elbow and completely at ease in his nudity. He took her breath.

"If you'd like. Unless you have a different favorite spot?" The flirting came naturally after hours of physical contact that bordered on debauchery. They couldn't seem to get enough of each other, whether they were in the bed, against the shower wall, or on the sideboard. Morning was firmly coming alive outside. Birds sang and the air had gone from crisp to soft. The helicopter would be returning them to Athens by late afternoon, but they were very much still on their one-night honeymoon.

Lazy brown eyes perused her from hairline to toenails. "It's all my favorite."

"I never thought I'd be like this," she admitted. "Naked and comfortable with a man. I thought I'd have hang-ups forever. Thank you for making this so good for me." She tilted forward to touch her mouth to his.

"I'm not being too demanding? You would tell me if you're tender, wouldn't you? I look back on our night in Bali and it was incredible, but damn, I was stiff the next day. You should have told me to back off."

"Why didn't you put on the brakes?"

"Because I didn't want that night to end."

She smiled, feeling secretive and womanly and desired. "Neither did I."

"I've never had second chances before." He smoothed her hair behind her ear. The somber gratitude reflected in his eyes warmed her heart. "Don't let me screw this up. Tell me what I need to do to make this work, okay?"

Love me, she thought, feeling a pinch in her heart, but it wasn't something either of them could control. It would happen or not. Still, when he took his time caressing and kissing her, when their bodies writhed together in sensual perfection, she felt loved.

Seeking that, she eased onto her back, pulling him with her. "I'm the inexperienced one," she reminded. "You're supposed to be the one who knows how to make this work."

He flashed a grin, brief and endearingly playful. "If this is all I have to do, our marriage will be a cake walk."

CHAPTER THIRTEEN

FOR A MAN who had never wanted a wife and children, Theo was surprised how quickly he settled into marital bliss. Not that any of it was easy, but it wasn't hard in the way he knew life could be hard. It was little blips of leasing his New York apartment—it was too good an investment to sell outright—being away from Jaya and Zephyr because of a crisis in Sydney and managing child-care until the *au pair* arrived since Jaya was already getting her feet wet in her new job.

The flip side of these minor wrinkles was a smart, warm, stunning woman on his arm and in his life.

He wasn't a man who'd ever needed to bring the prettiest woman to the dance. Nevertheless, he'd had a roster of style conscious women who hadn't minded an evening out on short notice. He'd given them a shopping spree and they'd relieved him of the burden of conversation for a few hours.

Jaya elevated what he used to think of as endurance events to a new, very bearable level, bringing personality without getting too personal. Her people management skills made her the perfect hostess when they were forced to entertain. As a result, he found himself in the remarkable position of enjoying this evening's dinner.

Now that they were settled, she'd taken a job with the family business, choosing an upgrade project that would allow her to work closely with him. While some considered that a recipe for disaster, he had more faith. They tended to work like two halves of a whole and today had been no different, despite being a grueling one over all. However, they'd put their team in place and were kicking off the project with a dinner for spouses. It was also a soft opening for the revamped dining room in their centerpiece New York hotel.

"There will be times when we're asking your husband or wife to work late, so we wanted to let you know up front that we appreciate the sacrifice," Jaya was saying, her graceful fingers resting lightly on the edge of the white tablecloth. If she was nervous speaking to the long table of nearly thirty people, her boss included, she didn't betray it.

"We won't always be eating like this. I'm sure there will be sandwiches at midnight more often than not, but today was a very productive meeting and if we can keep up that momentum, we'll be enjoying another celebration like this at the end of a very successful project." With a teasing smile that impacted like a heart punch, she added to Theo, "Provided we're on budget, of course."

"You will be." Maybe he was biased, even a bit dazzled. He certainly wouldn't let her fail, but he had every confidence she'd pull this off beautifully.

"They're so in love," the wife of their IT specialist said, then pressed fingertips to her lips as everyone turned to look at her. "I'm sorry! I didn't mean to say that so loud."

She was mortified and everyone else seemed amused, but Theo felt as though he'd been stripped naked in front of all of them. Was that what this was? Love?

His sense of vulnerability, of having his deepest desire revealed, was so threatening he couldn't look at Jaya. It would only reinforce how much she meant to him, allowing others to wield his feelings for her as a weapon. He cut an instinctive glance to the place he'd always been able to count on for cover when he was at his least guarded.

Adara was already watching him and smoothly drew everyone's attention to her end of the table. "We're very excited about this pairing. Even if they weren't married, I would have wanted Jaya to head this project, but having them so closely connected should help you all get the answers you need so you can keep moving forward."

Gideon made some remark about the newlyweds curtailing their honeymooning to review software code, but Theo didn't absorb it. The luminescent curtain that surrounded them in this private dining area was supposed to give a waterfall effect, but he was drowning under the rapids at the moment. The pressure in his chest suffocated him while he tried to discern which way was up. Pressure in his ears made the room's music sound muted while the clink of crystal tableware was like shattering glass.

He was falling apart internally while he had to maintain an unaffected front, exactly as he always had.

Jaya was pretty sure she'd never be able to eat here again. She couldn't eat now, when an amuse-bouche arrived in the form of a tiny fried noodle nest with a grape tomato egg and a herb leaf feather floating in a spoonful of consume. She wanted to run away and hide from the terrible lie that she was allowing to prevail.

Her husband *didn't* love her. She wished he did. Every morning she woke next to him hoping today would be the day he'd find the words. In six weeks of marriage, no matter how happy they seemed on the surface, he had yet to speak of his feelings.

But she had to sit here and smile at a table of mostly strangers, reminding herself that her life was actually very fulfilling. Theo did care for her in his way. He had overturned his life for her and their child, provided for them in a way that was ridiculously extravagant and always made time for them.

Then there was the sex. As a couple, they might not be

given to public displays of affection, but behind closed doors they were the clichéd newlyweds who couldn't keep their hands off each other. They started most of their days locked in orgasm and fell asleep sweaty and tangled together.

So what did it matter if people assumed they were in love and it was only true on one side? She was still happy, wasn't she?

Don't be impatient, Jaya. Don't ruin it.

That was a bitter imperative to swallow when she'd spent the beginning of her life telling herself, *Go after what you want. Don't settle.*

The evening turned into the longest of her life and only became more intolerable when they said good-night to their guests at the coat room. Theo held her wool wrap and asked near her ear, "You okay?"

This from the man who had become Robot Theo for the last two hours, tense and barely able to string two civil words together, leaving all the talking to her. If she'd found the love remark disconcerting, he'd found it insufferable.

"I'm fine," she mumbled as she clutched the edges of the wrap across her aching breastbone.

Across the room, Gideon lifted Adara's hair out from beneath the collar of her jacket. His gaze on her was tender as he cupped her face to give her a light kiss. Her smile when he drew back was radiant.

Jaya wanted to cry. She'd settled and could never back out now, even if she hadn't loved her husband so much she thought she'd die of it.

"Don't lie to me, Jaya," he said beside her with quiet ferocity. "Even if you think it might be easier for both of us."

She met his gaze, but it was painful to hold. He'd see how much regret filled her. Funny how she'd thought the worst thing in the world had been being a financial burden on her uncle. No, it was far worse to be an emotional burden. She didn't want Theo to know she loved him when he couldn't love her back. It would be more weight on his conscience than he deserved to carry. It wasn't his fault he couldn't love.

"Adara," he called, startling Jaya with his sharp tone.

His sister turned back from exiting with her husband.

"Is something wrong?" she asked as she approached, looking between the two of them. The weird thing was, it was like she already knew. Jaya had a feeling Adara was as aware of how tonight's gaffe had affected Theo as Jaya was.

A gut-wrenching sense of rejection filled her as she saw Theo's not loving her blink larger than the sign in Times Square. Everyone knew.

"Will you swing by our place on your way home and take Zephyr overnight? The sitter can't stay," Theo said. "I'll text her to let her know."

"What? No!" Jaya protested in shock. "Why—?"

"Of course," Gideon cut in smoothly. "Our pleasure."

"But we're going straight home," Jaya insisted. "Aren't we?"

"We'll use the family suite here tonight."

"Theo—" Jaya began.

"Please let us do this." Adara set a light touch on her arm. "Theo never asks me for anything." Leaning in to buss Jaya's cheek with her own, she whispered, "Please don't give up on him." With a tight smile of concern, she and Gideon hurried away.

Speechless, Jaya watched them depart. "This is crazy. Why did you do that?"

"Crazy? We both know we need to talk."

She hugged herself into her wrap, cold despite their staying inside. As he nudged her toward the elevators, she stumbled.

"I don't want to talk," she mumbled. This was her problem, not theirs. She had known what she was marrying.

Maybe he would come to love her eventually, but not if she forced it.

"There's a switch." He eyed her as he brought out his card and got them into the private elevator.

"What is?"

"You being the one who doesn't want to talk. Especially after you taught me it's the only way to fix things. Why are you trying to take that away from me now?"

"I'm not," she protested as they entered the family suite. "I just don't see any use this time."

"Why not?"

"Because I don't want to hear *again* that you don't love me and never will!" The outburst surprised even her. She pulled her wrap tighter around her throat, turning away to hide her hurt.

He drew a long, harsh breath then heavy silence descended.

She waited.

Nothing.

A choking little cry of protest escaped her. "And there you go again, withdrawing—"

"It's not easy for me, Jaya! I don't even know how to love, not properly. I still feel awkward kissing my son, like the more I want and need him in my life, the more likely he'll be snatched away."

"Not by me! I'm not trying to take away your heart either. Love isn't something to *dread*."

"I know that," he cut in. "But people knowing how I feel... When that woman said we were in love tonight, I lost a bit of sanity. I couldn't bear for them to know how much you mean to me. It makes me too vulnerable."

It wasn't the statement she was looking for, but it was close enough to make her turn and look at him. "Do you mean that?"

"The last thing I feel toward you is dread, Jaya. When I

walk through the door, I'm relieved, like some kind of unidentified pain has stopped. I'm so damned happy to see you, it's embarrassing. Is that love? You tell me. I've never felt like this toward anyone. It sure as hell isn't anything like what I feel toward my sister," he growled.

She pressed a hand to her diaphragm, reminding herself to keep breathing because she felt as though the wind had been knocked out of her. Somehow she found her voice. "Each time I see you, I'm filled with intense *joy,* like I'm finally home and safe again, no matter where we are."

Reaction seemed to spasm across his features. "When you say things like that, I almost don't want to believe it. It means too much and I trained myself not to care, not to want, but I crave those things you say, Jaya. They make me start to hope."

"For what?" A fragile bubble of optimism was building in her, but she was afraid to grasp it in case it burst.

He visibly struggled, feet shifting, glance cutting to the door before he hardened his stance and lifted his chin, no defenses anywhere on him as he revealed both somber vulnerability and an achingly tender warmth toward her.

"That you might come to love me one day."

Her own controls fell away, leaving her floating in a void, jaw slack, mind wiped clean by shock. A hot pressure flared in the back of her throat, urging her to speak, but all she could say was, "I'm such an idiot."

Before she could cover her face and absorb how appallingly stupid she'd been, she glimpsed how her words affected him. The tightening and closing, the dimming of his eyes.

"I thought if I told you how much I love you, it would scare you," she blurted, lurching forward a step. "I'd make you feel too much pressure. Like you were failing me because we're not equal, but I shouldn't have held back. I should have told you."

"That you love me," he clarified in a voice that rocked between disbelief and shaken anticipation. He came forward to grasp her arms. "That's what this is? This feeling like if we have a disagreement, I'll die of loneliness? That if I'm hurting I don't want anyone around except you, and if you're there I can bear anything, that's it? That's love?"

She nodded, blinking matted lashes. A tickle of wetness ran onto her cheek. "That's how it is for me. I want to tell you things I'd never admit to another soul."

He cupped her face in gentle fingers, his eyes blazing with heat and admiration and adoration. "Then Jaya, I have loved you for a very long time."

She couldn't breathe. Her heart had grown too big for her chest. Her mouth wouldn't form words because her lips were quivering.

He soothed them with the pressure of his own. The tender kiss deepened by degrees past sweet wonder into heat and passion and a deep need to express their love completely. They knew each other's signals and they were even more evocative now. He cupped her breast and held her heart. She pressed her lips to the pulse in his throat and only a very fine, translucent wall separated her from his lifeblood.

"Oh, Theo, I'm sorry—"

"Shh, I shouldn't have made you wait, either. I just didn't know…"

"I know. I love you." She kissed him again, unable to control the outpouring of emotion, passion, her need to connect.

He slowly drew back, but only to offer a smug smile. "I scored us a free night of babysitting."

"How could I not love you for that?" She was bursting with joy at how carefree he looked. Like he'd fully broken free of his shell and all of him was available to her.

He swooped to whisk her off her feet and into the cradle of his arms, making her gasp in surprise. As he started for the bedroom, she toed off her shoes so they clunked to the floor.

"Are we going to sleep at all tonight?" she teased.

"You say when, you know that." He set her onto the bed and followed her in one motion, his strength and power entwining with hers in the familiar way she'd come to love. "But I'll make it worth staying up if you do," he cajoled.

He did, fulfilling her completely when, hours later, they were trembling with sexual exhaustion. Still panting, damp skin adhered and bodies locked in ecstasy, he smoothed her hair from her cheek with a shaking hand and looked into her eyes. "I love you. I will love you forever. Thank you for being my wife."

* * * * *

THE GREEK'S
TINY MIRACLE

REBECCA WINTERS

Rebecca Winters lives in Salt Lake City, Utah.
With canyons and high alpine meadows full
of wildflowers, she never runs out of places to
explore. They, plus her favourite vacation spots
in Europe, often end up as backgrounds for her
romance novels – because writing is her passion,
along with her family and church. Rebecca loves
to hear from readers. If you wish to email her,
please visit her website at cleanromances.com.

CHAPTER ONE

April 27

EVERY TIME MORE hotel guests entered the beachfront resort restaurant on Grace Bay in the Turks and Caicos Islands in the Caribbean, Stephanie expected to see her black-haired Adonis appear. That was how she thought of Dev Harris.

After their fantastic ninety-foot dive to Elephant Ear Canyon that afternoon to see the huge sponges, the tall, powerfully built New Yorker, who resembled a Greek god, had whispered that he'd meet her in the dining room at eight for dinner. They'd watch the sunset *and later, each other.*

As he'd helped her out of the dive boat, giving her arm a warm squeeze, his eyes, black as jet, conveyed the words he didn't speak in front of the others in their scuba diving group. He was living for another night with her like last night.

She'd reluctantly left him to go to the beachfront condo and get ready for dinner. Her silvery-gold hair needed a shampoo. She'd decided to wear it loose from a side part. Time with the blow dryer and a brush brought out the natural curl, causing it to flow across her shoulders.

With the golden tan she'd picked up, tonight she'd chosen to wear a blue sleeveless sundress. She wanted to look beautiful for him. Last night she'd worn a filmy tangerine-colored dress and had bought a shimmering lip gloss to match. He'd told her that, in the dying rays of the sun, she'd look like a piece of golden fruit he longed to devour very slowly and thoroughly.

Her body trembled just remembering those words. While she waited for him to come, the memory of the way he'd made love to her over and over again made it difficult to breathe. It was her first intimate experience with a man, and had happened so naturally she felt as if she was living in a dream, one from which she never wanted to awaken.

In ten days' time Stephanie had fallen so deeply in love, her whole world had changed. Throughout her dating years she'd had various boyfriends. Just last week she'd gone on a date with a guy named Rob Ferris, who ran an auto parts franchise, but she knew when he took her home after dinner that she really wasn't interested in a second date.

Then she met Dev. The first time she'd seen him walking toward the boat with the dive master, her breath had caught. When their gazes collided, that was it. The feeling she'd been waiting for all her adult life.

Other relationships with past boyfriends had nothing to do with the profound kind of love she felt for the sophisticated thirty-two year-old bachelor, who'd told her he was in the international exporting business. He blew away every other man in existence.

Her three girlfriends who'd arranged their April

vacations to come on this scuba diving trip with her fully agreed he was out-of-this-world gorgeous. Melinda thought he must be one of those frogmen from the military, the way he maneuvered under the water. He was certainly built like one.

Stephanie agreed with her friends, but there was more to Dev than his physical attributes and diving skills. Much more. Everything he said and did revealed that he was well-traveled and educated, making him exceptional, and so charismatic she could hardly breathe when she thought about him.

Where was he? By now it was quarter to nine. Obviously, he'd been held up. The only thing to do was go back to her room and call him on the hotel land line. His beachfront condo, where they'd spent last night, was located on the other side of the restaurant, but she thought she should phone him first.

Stephanie was on her way out when a waiter came toward her with a florist box in his hands. "Ms. Walsh? This is for you, with Mr. Harris's compliments."

Thrilled to have received it, she went back to the table to take off the lid. He was probably on his way to her now. Inside the tissue was a corsage of gardenias with a card.

Thank you for the most memorable ten days and nights of my life, Stephanie. Your sweetness is like these gardenias and I'll never forget you. Unfortunately, I've had to leave the island because of an emergency at my work that couldn't be handled by anyone else. Enjoy the rest of your trip and be safe flying back to Crystal River. I miss you already. Dev.

Stephanie sat there and felt the blood drain from her face.

Her spring idyll was over.

He'd already driven to the airport to catch his flight to New York. *Of course* he hadn't left her a phone number or address, nor had he asked her for the same information. On purpose he hadn't given her a shred of hope that they'd ever see each other again.

She had to be the biggest fool who'd ever lived.

No, there was one other person she knew who shared that honor. Her mother, who'd died from cancer after Stephanie had graduated from college. Twenty-four years ago Ruth Walsh had made the same mistake with an irresistible man. But whoever he was hadn't stuck around once the fun was over, either. Stephanie didn't know his name and had no memories of him, only that her mother had said he was good-looking, exciting and an excellent skier.

He and Dev were two of a kind.

Stephanie closed her eyes tightly. How many females went off on vacation and supposedly met their soul mate, who swept them off their feet, only to abandon them once the excitement wore off? It had to be in the hundreds of thousands, if not the millions. Stephanie, like her mother, was one of those pathetic statistics who'd gotten caught up in the rapture.

White-hot with anger for being in her mid-twenties before learning the lesson she should have had memorized early in life, because of her birth father, Stephanie shot out of the chair. As she passed the waiter, she gave him a couple dollars and told him to get rid of the things she'd left on the table.

Stephanie didn't know about her friends, but she

couldn't possibly stay on the island for the last four days of their trip. Tomorrow morning she'd be on the first plane back to Florida. If a man was too good to be true, then shame on the woman who believed she was the first female to beat the odds.

Dev was so attractive there had to be trails of broken-hearted females around the scuba diving world who knew exactly what it was like to lie in his arms and experience paradise, only to wake up and discover he'd moved on.

He'd told her that scuba diving was his favorite form of recreation. What he hadn't mentioned was that womanizing went hand in hand with his favorite pastime. It was humiliating to think she was one of those imbeciles who didn't have the sense to take one look at him and run far away as fast as possible.

Too furious for tears, she returned to the condo, thankful her roommates were still out. They'd probably gone into town to party with some of the other tourists staying at the resort. That gave Stephanie time to change her flight reservation and pack without them asking a lot of questions.

By tomorrow afternoon she'd be back on the job. Stephanie loved her work. Right now she was planning on it saving her life.

If she let herself think about those long walks with Dev, past the palms and Casuarina trees while they were entwined in each other's arms, she'd go mad.

July 13

"Captain Vassalos?"

Nikos had just finished putting on the jacket of his

uniform—the last time he would wear it. Steadying himself with his crutches, he looked around in time to see Vice Admiral Eugenio Prokopios of the Aegean Sea Naval Command in Piraeus, Greece, enter his hospital room and shut the door. The seasoned Greek naval hero was an old friend of his father and grandfather.

"This is an honor, sir."

"Your parents are outside waiting for you. I told them I wanted to come in first to see you. After your last mission, we can be thankful the injury to your spine didn't paralyze you, after all."

Thankful?

Nikos cringed. His last covert operation with Special Forces had wiped out the target, but his best friend, Kon, had been killed. As for Nikos, his doctor told him he would never be the man he once was. His spine ought to heal in time, but he'd never be 100 percent again, and couldn't stay in the Greek military as a SEAL, not when he would probably suffer episodes of PTSD for a long time, maybe even years.

He'd been getting counseling and was taking a serotonin reuptake inhibitor to help him feel less worried and sad, but he'd had several nightmares. They left him feeling out of control and depressed.

"Now that you're being released from the hospital this morning, it won't be long before you won't need those crutches."

Nikos hated the sight of them. "I'm planning on getting rid of them as soon as possible."

"But not until you've had a good long rest after your ordeal."

"A good long rest" was code for one reality. The part

of his life that had brought challenge and purpose was finished. Only blackness remained.

"I don't expect it to take that much time, sir."

After a two and a half months' hospitalization, Nikos knew exactly why the vice admiral had shown up. This was his father's work. He'd been thwarted when Nikos had joined the military, and expected his son to return to the family business. Now that he was incapacitated, his father had sent his good friend Eugenio to wish him well with a pep talk about getting back in the family fold.

The older man eyed him solemnly. "Our navy is grateful for the heroic service you've rendered in Special Forces. You're a credit to your family and our country. Your father is anxious for you to resume your place with your brother at the head of Vassalos Shipping so he can retire."

His father would never retire.

Vice Admiral Prokopios had just let Nikos know—in the kindest way, of course—that though his military service was over, the family business was waiting to embrace him again. Of course, the older man knew nothing about Nikos's history with his father, or he would never have said what he did.

Until after Nikos was born and turned out to be a Vassalos, after all, his father hadn't believed he was his son, all because of a rumor that turned out to have no substance. The experience had turned him into a bitter, intransigent man. The damage inflicted on the Vassalos marriage carried over to the children, and had blighted Nikos's life.

The navy turned out to be his escape from an impossible situation. But ten years later it was back in triplicate.

He was thirty-two years of age, and everything was over.

Sorrow weighed him down at the loss of Kon Gregerov. Nikos's best friend from childhood, who'd come from a wonderful family on nearby Oinoussa Island, had joined the navy with him. The man had been like a brother, and had helped keep Nikos sane and grounded during those tumultuous years while he fought against his father's domination, among other things.

He and Kon had plans to go into their own business together once they'd retired from the military, but his friend had been blown up in the explosion that almost killed Nikos.

It should have been me.

"I'm sorry you were forced to leave Providenciales unexpectedly to perform your last covert operation. So when you're ready, we'll send you back there for more rest and relaxation."

Nikos's stomach muscles clenched at the mere mention of Providenciales. That experience had been like a fantastic dream, one he'd relived over and over on those nights in the hospital when he wasn't suffering flashbacks. To go back there again without *her* would kill him. After what had happened to him, there could be no Stephanie Walsh in his life. He was going in another direction entirely.

"Nikos?" the vice admiral prodded.

"Thank you for the kind offer, but I'd rather recuperate at home."

"If that's your wish."

"It is."

"Then I'll say goodbye for now. Be assured I'm mighty proud of you. Good luck."

They saluted before he left the room. Moments later one of the hospital staff entered with a wheelchair. As Nikos sat down, his parents swept into the room. They'd been constant visitors, but they hovered until he felt he would choke.

"Darling!" his mother exclaimed, and hugged him before carrying his crutches for him. "You look wonderful despite your weight loss. Once we get you home, we'll fatten you up in no time. Your grandparents are elated and your sister and Timon have already arrived with the children to welcome you back."

"This is a great day, son." His exultant father embraced him before reaching for his luggage. "Leon's eager to talk business with you."

Nikos had no intention of working in the family business like his elder brother, and his father knew it. But his dad never let up about anything, and it had driven a wedge between them that couldn't be breached. However, now wasn't the time to get into it. The three of them moved out of the room and down the corridor.

"How did it go with Eugenio?"

As if his father didn't know. "Fine."

They emerged from the main doors of the hospital under a blue sky. Once they were settled inside the limousine, his father said, "We've been waiting for this day. So has Natasa. She and her parents will be joining us tomorrow evening for a small party."

Nikos's anger flared. "Then *uninvite* them. You might as well know that after tonight, I'll be living on the *Diomedes* while I get my strength back." He was sick of visitors and hospital staff. He needed to be completely alone and didn't want anyone to know his activities. His boat would be his refuge from now on.

"You can't do that to us *or* to her!" his father thundered. "You've put this situation with Natasa on hold for long enough. A marriage between the two of you has been understood for years. She's expecting it now that you're home for good. Your mother and I want you to give us grandchildren. We've waited long enough."

Their families had been best friends for years. His sister, Gia, and Natasa Lander had always been close. It had been an impossible situation he'd been happy to get out of when he'd joined the military.

"Then that's a pity, because I never made love to her or asked her to marry me. She should have moved on years ago." She was attractive enough and would have made a good wife and mother, but he'd never been on fire for her. Thank heaven he hadn't made the mistake of sleeping with her. After meeting Stephanie, the thought of Natasa or any another woman was anathema to him. "Now that I'm out of the hospital, I need to go my own way."

"But that's absurd! She's in love with you."

"It's a moot point, since I'm not in love with her and never have been. Any hope you had for me marrying her is out of the question. I'm deadly serious about this."

His father's cheeks grew ruddy with emotion. "You don't know what you're saying!"

"But I do. Natasa is a lovely person, but not the one for me." Unless she had an agenda of her own, there was something wrong with her for waiting around for him this long. "At this point I'm afraid a marriage between the two of us is only a figment of your and her parents' imagination."

"How dare you say that!" his father muttered furiously.

"How dare *you?*" Nikos retorted back. "You'll be doing her a favor if you tell her and her family that I'm not well enough to see anyone now. Hopefully, they'll finally get the point! Don't turn this into a nightmare for me or you'll wish you hadn't!"

Nikos had suffered too many of them since the fishing vessel with all the surveillance equipment, along with Kon, had been blown out of the water by the enemy. If Nikos hadn't happened to be over the side, checking the hull for damage because of a run earlier in the day, he wouldn't still be alive.

As it was, he'd been found unconscious in the water. The doctors at the hospital hadn't given him a chance of walking again due to the damage to his lower spine, but they'd been proved wrong. He'd come out of it with deep bruising and reduced mobility. No one could say how much he would heal with time.

"We can discuss this later," his mother said, always anxious to mollify his father. For as long as Nikos could remember, she'd tried to keep peace between them. Though he loved her for it, the ugly history with his father had dictated that certain things would never change....

"There's nothing to discuss."

His military career was over. Life as he'd known it was over. Nikos was living for the moment when he could be away from everyone. Both his parents crowded him until he felt stifled, but he knew he had to endure this until tomorrow morning.

He'd already made arrangements with Yannis, who would come to the house and drive him to the marina in Nikos's car. Once on board the *Diomedes,* he intended to stay put. Drinking himself to death sounded better and better.

Silence invaded the vehicle until they reached the small airport in Athens. Nikos took a fortifying breath as he stepped out and reached for his crutches to board his father's private jet. The steward knew him well and nodded to him. "Welcome home, Nikos."

"Thank you, Jeno."

"Are you hungry?"

"No."

"Some tea?"

"How about a beer?"

The other man smiled. "Coming right up."

Nikos found a seat in the club compartment with his parents, who for once had gone quiet. He put the crutches on the floor and fastened himself in. It was a short forty-minute flight across the Aegean to Chios. From there they'd take the helicopter to Vassalos Shipping on Egnoussa, where they'd land and drive home.

He stared blindly out the window until fatigue took over, causing him to lounge back in the seat and close his eyes. The mention of marriage had triggered thoughts of a certain female in another part of the world he'd had to leave two and half months ago—so abruptly he still hadn't recovered from the pain.

Stephanie Walsh would have received the gardenias with his note. It would have sent a dagger straight to her heart. Nikos knew how it felt, because when he'd had his farewell gift delivered to the restaurant, he'd experienced gut-wrenching pain over what he'd been forced to do.

His hand formed a fist, because there hadn't been a damn thing he'd been able to do to comfort her at the time. As a navy SEAL, everything about his life was classified. Since then his whole world had been turned upside down, ensuring he would never seek her out again.

From the second he'd first met the beautiful American woman on the beach, her appeal had been so strong he couldn't find the strength to stay away from her. Knowing his leave was for only two weeks, he hadn't intended to get involved with her. Because he'd be returning shortly to join his unit, there could be no future in it.

Every day he kept telling himself he'd go to another resort on the island to keep his distance, but every day he grew more enamored of her. The night with her before he'd received orders to return to Greece should never have happened.

He loathed himself for allowing things to get that far, but she'd been like a fever in his blood. Intoxicated by her beauty, by everything about her, he'd given in to his desires, and she'd been right there with him. Her loving response had overwhelmed him, setting him on fire.

There'd been other women in his life, but never again would he know a night of passion like that. What he and Stephanie had shared for those ten precious days had been unbelievable. His longing for her was still so real he could taste it.

When he'd awakened on their last morning together, they'd been tangled up in each other's arms. She'd

looked at him with those sapphire eyes, willing him
to love her, and he'd wanted to stay in that bed with her
forever. After their dive that afternoon, it had shredded
him to walk away from her and board the jet for the
flight to Athens, but he'd had his orders. He couldn't
imagine a world that didn't include her.

After meeting up with Kon for their next covert operation, Nikos had confided his deepest feelings, telling him that after this last mission was completed, he
planned to resign his commission and marry her. But
just three days after that, the enemy had struck, and
his best friend was dead. Nikos was no longer a whole
man. Stephanie could be only a memory to him now.

En route to the Caribbean he'd never dreamed he
would meet the woman who would leave her mark on
him. His mind went over the conversation he'd just
had with his father.

You don't know what you're saying!

*But I do. Natasa is a lovely person, but there's some-
thing wrong with a woman who waits around for a
man who's never been interested in her romantically.
I'm afraid a marriage between the two of us is out of
the question.*

Nikos had met the ideal woman meant for him, but
she would have to remain in his dreams. If Kon were
still alive he'd say, "Get in touch with her and tell her
the truth about your condition. You trusted her enough
to spend every living moment with her. It might ease
the pain for both of you if she knew who you really
were, and what happened to you."

A groan escaped Nikos's throat. With his spinal injury, he wasn't the same man she'd met. Part of the collateral damage had rendered him sterile. He'd never be

able to give a woman a child from his own body. Nikos lived in a dark world now. He looked and felt like hell. No woman would want a man whose flashbacks could make him dangerous to himself and others. Stephanie would only hate him for lying to her. For using her for pleasure, then dumping her without explanation.

"Nikos?"

His eyes flew open. "Jeno?"

The steward looked at him with compassion. "Are you feeling ill? Can I get you anything?"

He shook his head. He'd come to a dead end. The woman he loved and desired was permanently beyond his reach now.

"We're getting ready to descend."

"Thank you."

He fastened his seat belt. Jeno was right about one thing: Nikos did feel ill. The meeting with the vice admiral was like the first handful of dirt thrown on top of the coffin. He saw the life he'd once known vanish into the void, leaving him to travel through a tunnel of blackness that had no end....

July 26

Stephanie was going to be a mother.

She ran a hand over her stomach, which had grown fuller, making it harder to fasten the top two buttons of her jeans. It still seemed unbelievable that she was carrying Dev's child. When she'd missed her period last month it hadn't alarmed her, because she'd always been irregular. In college she'd gone six months without a period.

But over the last three weeks she'd felt weak and

nauseated. In her depressed state she'd lost her appetite and thought she had a flu bug. But it didn't go away and then she started noticing other changes to her body. It all added up to one thing, and the home pregnancy test yesterday had turned out positive, shocking the daylights out of her.

The trip to Dr. Sanders today had confirmed that she was three months along with Dev's baby. *Incredible.* Her OB had ordered pills for her nausea, plus iron and prenatal vitamins to build her up.

If she caught up to Dev, would he want to know he was going to be a father?

Deep down, she'd been waiting for him to contact her. He knew she worked for Crystal River Water Tours. It would have been easy enough for him to call and leave a message. But that hadn't happened. He hadn't planned on ever seeing or talking to her again.

Yet she felt certain the man she'd fallen in love with would have wanted to hear the truth about his own baby. But it seemed that man didn't exist. If she were able to find him, would he still tell her he wanted nothing to do with her or the baby, once he found out?

For the next twelve hours she agonized about what to do, vacillating over the decision she needed to make. By morning, one thing overshadowed every consideration. She knew her child would want to know its father. It would be the most important thing in her baby's life.

Stephanie knew all about that, having always longed to meet her birth father and know his name. It took two to make a child, and it was up to her to inform Dev if it was at all possible. What he did with the information was up to him.

But her hand hesitated before she reached for the phone to begin her inquiries at the resort. The two people she knew there might wonder why she needed information. They'd probably deduce she was some obsessed girlfriend.

How humiliating would it be to confide the truth about the baby to them? She just couldn't. But maybe it would work if she explained she'd been worrying about him ever since he'd disappeared, the very night they were going to have dinner together. She felt certain he'd been ill, thus the reason for his swift departure. Did they know any way she might get in touch with him, just to see if he was all right?

With her hand shaking, she called the number on the brochure she'd kept, and waited.

"Dive shop. This is Angelo."

She gripped the cell phone tighter. "Hello, Angelo. I'm glad it's you. I tried to reach you earlier, but you were out. This is Stephanie Walsh. You probably don't remember me. I was there almost three months ago."

"Stephanie? I always remember the pretty girls, you especially."

Her heart beat too fast. "You just made my day."

He laughed. "You had a good time on vacation?"

"Wonderful, thanks to you." *The best of my whole life until the box of gardenias was brought to the table.*

"That's good. How can I help you?"

"I'm trying to reach Dev Harris, the scuba diver from New York I partnered with that first week. Do you have a phone number or an email for him? Anything at all to help me? He left so suddenly, I've worried over the last few months that he might have been taken ill. I have pictures I'd like to send him via email."

"Let me check. Don't hang up."

"No. I won't."

She paced the bedroom of her condo while she waited. There were a lot of Devlin, Devlon or Devlan Harrises listed in New York City, but none she could reach was the man she was trying to find.

When she'd first gotten back to Florida, anger had driven her to phone New York information, but there was no such name listed for him. She'd spent several days phoning exporting companies where he might be working, but she'd turned up nothing.

After exhausting that avenue, she'd called various airlines that had landed planes on the island April 18, but got no help. The resort could tell her only what she already knew, that he was from New York. That was when she'd given up. But her pregnancy had changed everything.

"Stephanie? I'm back. Sorry, but there is no address or phone number. Perhaps one of the shops you visited would know something."

She bit her lip in disappointment. "We didn't do any shopping, but he did have some flowers delivered to me. Would they have come from the resort?"

"No, no. The Plant Shop in town. Just a minute and I'll give you the number." She held her breath while she waited. "Yes. Here it is."

Stephanie wrote it down. "You live up to your name, Angelo. Thank you so much."

"You're welcome. Good luck finding him."

After hanging up, she placed the call. Stephanie had once told him she loved gardenias. Tears stung her eyes. She had to admit his parting gift had been done with a certain style, while at the same time destroying her dreams. If there were no results, then the baby she was carrying would never know its father.

"The Plant Shop."

"Hello. My name is Stephanie Walsh. I'm calling from Florida. On April 27 a box of gardenias from your shop was delivered to me at the Palm Resort. I never did get to thank the gentleman who sent it to me. He left before I realized he'd gone. His name was Dev Harris. Could you give me an address or a phone number, please? He's from New York City. That's all I know."

It was a long shot, but she was desperate.

"I'm sorry, but we can't give out that information."

"Can you at least tell me what time he left the order?"

"Just a moment and I'll check." After a minute, the salesclerk returned. "It was phoned in at 5:00 p.m."

"Thank you for your help."

After she hung up, one more idea flitted through her mind. She called the resort again and asked if she could speak to Delia, the darling girl who'd been the maid for their rooms. Could Delia call Stephanie back collect, please? It was very important.

The front desk said they'd give her the message. Within a half hour, Stephanie's phone rang and it was the resort calling. Delia was on the other end.

"Hello, Stephanie."

"Oh, Delia. Thanks so much for calling me back."

"Of course. How is the handsome Dev?"

I wish I knew. "Actually, I'm not sure. I'm really worried about him. That's why I've phoned you. I'm thinking he must have left the island early because he was ill and didn't want me to know or worry. I thought

I would have heard from him by now, and need your help to find him if it's at all possible."

"Tell you what. My boyfriend works at the airport servicing the planes before takeoff. I'll ask him to find out what planes took off on April 27 after five in the evening. Perhaps he'll learn something that can help you."

"I'll make this worth your while, Delia."

"I would like to do this for you. I never saw two people more in love."

Tears scalded Stephanie's eyes. "Thank you," she whispered. "I just hope he isn't fatally ill."

"I don't blame you for being upset."

Whether Delia believed her excuse for calling or not, Stephanie couldn't worry about that now.

Two hours later her phone rang again. "Stephanie? He couldn't get you names, but there were three flights out that evening, if this helps. One was a nonstop flight to Los Angeles, California, another nonstop to Vancouver, British Columbia. The last was a private jet owned by the Vassalos Corporation, headed for Athens, Greece."

She blinked.

None of the planes had headed due north to New York. Her spirits plunged. If he'd been called back to his work on an emergency, surely he would have taken a direct flight to New York. There were dozens of them leaving the Caribbean for that destination.

"You're an angel for being willing to help me, Delia. Expect a thank-you in the mail for you and your boyfriend from me."

Stephanie rang off, shaking with the knowledge that Dev had lied to her without compunction. *Who are you, mystery man?* Had he pulled a fictitious name out of a hat on the spur of the moment? Was Dev a nickname?

One thing she was convinced of at this point: he was no New Yorker. And he'd been in an enormous hurry when he'd left Providenciales. Thousands of businessmen traveled by private jet. Certainly if he'd needed to leave before they'd even had dinner, it would make sense he had his own special mode of transportation waiting. No long lines...

Before she did anything else, she went to her computer in the den of the condo she'd inherited from her mother, to make a global search of the name Vassalos in Greece. One source came up more prominent than all the rest and drew her attention. *Vassalos Maritime Shipping, Egnoussa, Greece.*

Shipping...

After more searches she discovered the Oinousses, a group of small islands in the eastern Aegean Sea near Turkey. Egnoussa, the largest inhabited one, was fourteen kilometers long. One of Greece's most important naval academies was based there, due to the rich seafaring history of the islands. A smaller island, Oinoussa, was also inhabited.

Reading further, she learned Egnoussa was home to some of the richest shipping magnate families in the world. There were only four hundred or so inhabitants, with some fabulous mansions. A naval commercial academy and museum were located on one part of the island.

She replayed the memories of Dev in her mind. His urbane sophistication and knowledge set him apart from other men she'd known. He'd possessed a natural authority and spoke impeccable English. But when she thought about it, she realized he hadn't sounded like a New Yorker.

Had he come from a Greek island? If so, he would naturally be at home in the water.

He'd told her he worked for an international exporting company in New York. Did that company have an outlet in Greece? Did Dev work for it? Exporting could translate to mean shipping, couldn't it? In her mind it wasn't a far stretch to see where he might have come up with his lie.

What if Egnoussa was his home? Was he from *that* Vassalos family, with the kind of wealth that had opened every door for him? Maybe this was a stab in the dark, but the more she thought about him, the more the shoe seemed to fit. The cliché about looking like a Greek god fit him like a second skin.

She could phone the shipping company and ask questions. But since he obviously didn't want to be found, if he was there or got wind that she was trying to reach him, she might never get answers. Scrolling down farther, she found more information.

After a short flight from Athens to the island of Chios, an hour's boat ride takes you to Egnoussa Island. There's one hotel with only twelve rooms, one taxi. You can walk Egnoussa in a day.

Her mind reeled with ideas. She could take some pictures of him with her and show them to someone at the shipping office. Stephanie would know immediately if that person recognized him. Maybe she was a fool, but for her baby's sake she had to try to find him, and would use some of her savings to get there.

Stephanie called the doctor to make certain it was okay to fly. He told her she'd be all right for twenty-eight weeks. After that, she'd need to check with him about it. Since Greece didn't require immunizations for visitors from the United States, she'd be all right.

Luckily, she already had a passport. When she and her friends had decided to vacation together, they'd applied for passports in case they decided on a vacation along the French or Italian Riviera. But in the end, the Caribbean had won out.

If she traveled to Greece and it turned out to be a fruitless mission, then so be it. Whatever happened, the sooner she went, the better for her state of mind. Unlike her mother, who didn't attempt to tell her lover he was a father, at least Stephanie could explain to her child that she'd done everything humanly possible to locate the man who'd called himself Dev Harris.

Life was going to be difficult enough from here on out. She would have to discuss her condition with her boss. If he could give her a front desk job until after the baby was born, she'd be thankful and grateful. But if not, she'd need to start looking for another kind of job after she got back from Greece. Besides finishing paying off the mortgage, she needed to earn enough money to provide for herself and the baby.

CHAPTER TWO

July 28

NIKOS HAD BEEN out on the *Diomedes* for two weeks, but this afternoon he'd docked at the marina in Egnoussa. As soon as he replenished his food supply, he'd be leaving again. To his chagrin, he still needed support to move around, but had traded in his crutches for a cane. He used it only when he was exceptionally tired.

His right-hand man, Yannis, a seaman who'd worked for the family for over forty years, had just finished tying the ropes when Nikos's silver-haired father approached them.

"Where have you been, Nikos?"

"Where I've been every day and night since I was released from the hospital, exercising and swimming off shore." Battling his PTSD.

Despite taking medication, he'd had two violent episodes flashing back to the explosion. According to his doctor, with the passage of time they'd start to slow down, but it might take months or even years. For the time being Nikos had made the small custom-built yacht his home, where no one except Yannis could be witness.

What his family didn't know was that some of his time had been spent with Kon's grieving parents. He'd also had long talks with Kon's married brother, Tassos, about many things. He was only a year older than Nikos and lived on Oinoussa, an island close to Egnoussa. Before Kon's death the three of them had been close.

Tassos had gone into oil engineering and had recently returned after working on an oil rig in the southern Aegean. He had a brilliant head on his shoulders. He and Nikos had been talking a lot about Greece's financial crisis and the direction of the country. For the time being Nikos mostly listened to Tassos, but he could scarcely concentrate while he felt half-alive.

"I've been phoning you for the last hour! Why didn't you answer?" His father had to be upset to have come down to the dock.

"I was doing some shopping with Yannis, who's bringing things on board from the car. What's wrong?" His father looked flustered.

"You have a visitor."

"If you mean Natasa, you're wasting your time."

"No. Someone else."

"I can't imagine who could be so important it would send you here." Since returning home from the hospital, Nikos had stayed in touch with his family by phone, but he'd seen no one except Kon's family and Yannis.

His father's eyes, dark like his own, studied him speculatively. "Does this woman look familiar to you?"

He reached in his pocket and pulled out two snapshots. One showed Nikos and Stephanie in the dive boat. They'd just removed their gear and were smiling at each other. His breath caught at how beautiful she was. Angelo had taken the picture.

The other photo showed them on the beach with their arms around each other, right after the sun had set. In that sundress she'd looked like a piece of golden fruit. In fact that's what he'd told her, among other things. The girl Delia, in housekeeping, had taken their picture.

"I take it she's the woman who has erased thoughts of Natasa from your mind."

Nikos could hear his father talking, but at the sight of Stephanie in those photos, he reeled so violently he almost fell off the pier into the water. She was here on the island? But that was impossible! There was no way on earth she could have found him.

"You were careless to allow yourself to be photographed in the Caribbean while you were still in active service. What is she to you, Nikos? Answer me."

He couldn't. He was still trying to grasp the fact that she'd flown to Greece and known exactly where to come.

"After looking at these pictures," his father continued, "I've decided you're in much deeper than I thought. Her beauty goes without saying, and she has a breathless innocence that could fool any man. Even *you,* my son."

Nikos closed his eyes tightly.

"You've never looked at Natasa or any woman the way you're looking at this female viper. I admit she's devilishly ravishing in that American way, but she's a mercenary viper nonetheless, one who knows your monetary worth and has come to trap you.

"Surely after what happened to Kon years ago, you realize that getting involved with a foreign woman on vacation in those surroundings can only mean one thing. Don't let her get you any more ensnared. I know you well enough that if she's pregnant, it's someone else's."

His father's words twisted the knife deeper. The mention of Kon's tragedy brought back remembered pain. Was history repeating itself with Nikos? This just wasn't possible! No one in the Caribbean knew Nikos or anything about him. *No one.*

He rubbed the back of his neck. "Do you mean she simply walked into the building?"

"Like she knew the place, according to Ari," his father explained. "After arriving in the taxi, she approached him at the front desk and asked to speak to Mr. Vassalos. When she showed Ari the pictures, he phoned me at home. I told him to have her taken into my office, where she's waiting for word of you."

Nikos still couldn't believe it. For a number of reasons this seemed completely out of character for Stephanie. He could have sworn she was the one woman in his life who gave everything without wanting anything back. While he'd been diving with her, he'd trusted her with his life, and she him. Or so he'd thought. To have been so wrong about her gutted him in an agonizing way.

"Have you made a commitment to her?"

They'd made love all night, transforming his world.

"Though it's none of your business, the answer is no," he muttered in a gravelly voice, poleaxed by this revelation. Not then, and since the explosion that had blown his dreams to hell, *most definitely not now...*

After receiving the gardenias, the Stephanie he thought he'd known would never have come searching for him. She would have understood the gesture meant goodbye, but apparently that hadn't deterred her from what she wanted.

How had she found him? Was it his money she was after? He'd taken precautions, ruling out pregnancy as a factor. But as his father had said, she could be pregnant by someone else. The very accusation he'd turned on Nikos's mother, ruining their lives. The notion that Stephanie had been after Nikos for his money made him feel ill.

"It's little wonder you've displayed such indifference to Natasa. What do you intend to do?"

Just when Nikos thought life couldn't get worse, *it had.*

He stared at his father. "Nothing." He handed him back the photos. "Give Ari instructions to tell her I'm out of the country and won't be back."

"No personal message?"

"None." He bit out the word.

A gleam of satisfaction entered his father's eyes. His parent still had this sick fantasy about Nikos and Natasa. "I'll take care of it."

Stephanie sat in the chair, actually stunned that her intuition had paid off. The second she'd shown the photographs to the man in reception, she'd seen the way his eyes had flared in surprise.

The next thing she knew, he'd made a phone call and said something in Greek she couldn't understand. Before long he'd escorted her to an office down the hall filled with pictures of ships of all kinds, almost like a museum of navigational history. The man told her they were trying to locate Kyrie Vassalos.

Until that moment she'd believed this trip had been

in vain, and that something might be wrong with her mentally to have gone this far to trace a man who didn't want to be found. But a voice inside said he still had the God-given right to know a child of his was on the way.

She'd been waiting close to an hour already. But the longer she waited, the more she expected to be told he wasn't available. If so, she would leave Egnoussa and not look back. He was a member of the Vassalos family. That was all her child needed to know.

One day years from now, it was possible Dev—or whatever he called himself—would be confronted by his son or daughter. That would all depend on whether or not her child was like Stephanie, and wanted to meet the man who'd given him or her life. Some children didn't want to know.

No matter; Stephanie planned to be the best mother in the world. She loved this baby growing inside her with all her heart and soul, and would do everything possible to give it the full, wonderful life it deserved.

After another ten minutes had passed, she couldn't sit there any longer, and decided to tell the man in reception that she would come back. The weather was beautiful, with a temperature in the mid-eighties. The island was so tiny she could walk around the port and then return. The doctor had told her mild exercise like walking would do her good and help bring her out of her depression.

As she got up to leave, the man who'd been at the desk walked into the room. "Ms. Walsh? I'm sorry I took so long. It seems Kyrie Vassalos is out of the country and won't be back in the foreseeable future. I'm sorry." He gave her back the snapshots.

So, it was just as Stephanie had thought. She would

have handed him one of her business cards from Crystal River Water Tours, where she took tourists and groups on swimming tours. But at the last second she thought better of it. For their unborn child's sake, she hoped Dev would be curious enough to find her on his own.

"Thank you for your time."

"You're welcome," he said with a smile.

After putting the pictures in her purse, she left the office and walked down the hallway to the entrance of the building. If she hurried, she'd be in time to make the next boat going back to Chios. Her trip hadn't been wasted. She'd done her duty for her child. That was all that really mattered.

She made her way through picturesque winding streets paved with slabs. En route she passed mansions and villas with tiled roofs built in the Aegean island architectural style. Dev lived in one of those mansions, but she feared she'd never see the home where he'd grown up, and they'd never share anything again.

Stephanie kept going until she arrived at the landing area, where she sat on a bench and raised her face to the sun. This island was its own paradise. Evidently the lure of scuba diving had caused Dev to leave it. Being born here, he would have been a water baby, which explained his natural prowess above and below the surface.

Was he a true playboy? Or maybe a hardworking shipping tycoon who took his pleasure on occasion where he could find it around the world, as in the Caribbean? She knew nothing about him. He might even have a wife and children.

Stephanie shuddered to think she could have been

with a married man. If that were the case, she would never forgive herself for sleeping with someone else's husband. If he had a wife, it could only hurt her to see Stephanie's business card. She was glad she hadn't left it.

Face it. You took a huge risk being with him at all.

Disturbed by her thoughts, she reached in her purse for some food to help abate her nausea. She ate a sandwich and drank some bottled water she'd brought with her. The doctor told her she needed to eat regularly, to maintain her health. For once she *was* hungry, probably because she finally knew Dev Harris was a Vassalos and could be reached here.

After finishing her sandwich, she pulled out a small bag of grapes she'd purchased in a fruit market. On impulse she offered to share them with an older woman who'd just sat down by her.

The woman smiled and took a few. "Thank you," she said in heavily accented English.

"Please take more if you like."

She nodded. "You are a tourist?"

"No. I came to visit someone, but he wasn't here."

"Ah. I wait for a friend."

"Do you live here?"

"Yes."

Stephanie's pulse raced. "Do you know the Vassalos family?"

"Who doesn't! That's one of their boats." She pointed to a beautiful white boat, probably forty-five to fifty feet long, docked in the marina. "Why do you ask?"

"It's their son I came to see."

"They have two sons. One works here. The other I never see. He's always away."

Did that mean he was always doing family business elsewhere?

Unable to sit there after that news, Stephanie got to her feet. Maybe all wasn't lost yet. "It's been very nice talking to you. Keep the grapes. I think I'll take a walk until the boat gets here."

Without wasting another second, she headed in the direction of the moored craft. Maybe one of the crew would tell her where she could reach Dev. She'd come this far....

Closer now, she realized it was a small state-of-the-art recreational yacht, the luxurious kind she occasionally spotted in Florida waters, but she saw no one around. After walking alongside, she called out, "Hello? Is anyone here?" But there was no answer.

Upon further inspection she took in the outdoor lounge with recliners and a sun bed. Beyond it was the transom, with water skis, a rope and scuba gear. The sight of the equipment brought back piercingly sweet pain.

She stepped closer and called out again. Still no answer. Since the boat that would take her back to Chios wasn't in sight yet, she decided to wait a few more minutes for someone to come.

Praying she wouldn't get caught, she sat down facing the open sea and hooked her arms around her upraised knees. Before long she spotted the boat in the distance, headed toward the harbor.

Time to go.

Her spirits reached rock bottom because she'd come to the end of her journey. With her head down, she retraced her steps along the pier. "Oh—" Stephanie cried out in surprise as a hard male body collided with hers. She felt a strong pair of hands catch her by the upper arms to prevent her from falling.

Through the wispy cotton of her white blouson top the grip felt familiar. But when she lifted her head, nothing was familiar about the narrowed pair of glittering black eyes staring into hers as if she were an alien being.

"Dev—"

It *was* him, but he was so changed and forbidding, she couldn't comprehend it. He released her as if she'd scorched him, and kept walking.

"Dev!" she called in utter bewilderment. "Why won't you even say hello? What's happened to you?"

He continued walking, not fast or slow, never turning around.

She thought she'd been in pain when she'd opened the box of gardenias to discover he'd gone, but this pain reached the marrow of her bones.

Let him go, Stephanie. Let it all go.

Turning away from him, she kept walking, and had almost reached the beach area when he called to her in his deep voice. "Stephanie? Come back."

She looked over her shoulder at him. "When you left the Caribbean so fast, I worried you were ill or even dying, but obviously you're fine. Don't worry. I'm leaving and won't venture near again."

"Come back, or I'll be forced to come after you."

She heard the authority in his voice that left her in no doubt he'd do exactly that. With her heart thudding, she started toward him. By the time she reached him, her khaki-clad legs would have buckled if he hadn't helped her onto the nearest padded bench aboard the yacht.

The last time she'd seen him he'd been in his bathing suit after their dive. His eyes had smoldered with desire as he'd kissed her passionately, before they'd parted to get ready for dinner. He'd told her to hurry, then had pressed another long, hot kiss to her mouth. Neither of them could bear to be separated.

Or so she'd thought.

This brooding version of Dev looked formidably gorgeous. He was wearing white cargo pants and a gray crew-necked T-shirt. His black wavy hair had grown longer, setting off the deep bronze of his complexion. With his height and fit physique, he bore the aura of a man in command, just as she and the girls had supposed. But he'd lost weight.

He lounged against the side of the boat, his hands curled around the edge, his long legs extended. *Legs he'd wrapped possessively around hers, whether under the water or in bed.* But there was a gauntness to his handsome, chiseled features that suggested great sorrow or illness. She'd been right about two things: he'd left the Caribbean on some kind of emergency, and was a native Greek down to every black hair on his head.

"I heard you showed up at the shipping office, but I never dreamed I'd find you outside the *Diomedes*. What are you doing here?"

Stephanie could hardly fathom the frigidity of his words. "I told you. After what we shared, you left so fast without an explanation I could live with, I feared something terrible must have happened to you. I—I needed to see for myself," she stammered.

"I thought the card I left with the flowers summed things up."

"It did, but I guess I'm a hard case."

She heard his sharp intake of breath. "I'll ask again. What are you doing here?"

"I came to Greece to find you, and was told you were away on business indefinitely. The man at the desk didn't give me any additional information, so I was trying to find someone on this yacht who might tell me where you were. But no one was about."

"Evidently that didn't stop you from waiting around." He spoke in a low wintry tone so unlike him she shivered in fresh pain. "In your desperation, I'm surprised you didn't come to Egnoussa much sooner."

Her desperation? What on earth was wrong? How could he have changed into a completely different person? He might not like seeing her again, but his demeanor bordered on loathing.

Though terrified at the thought he might be seriously ill, and stung by his hostile behavior, Stephanie still held her ground. "I would have been here the next day if I'd known where you lived. But the note you put with the gardenias didn't tell me where I could find you."

"How remiss of me." Coupled with his sarcasm was an icy smile, devastating her further. "Still, with the help you were given, you managed to track me down easily enough."

"If you're talking about God's help, you're right."

Evidently he didn't like her response, because he straightened to his full height. "Even knowing you as I thought I did, I have to admit I'm surprised you'd use that excuse to cover who you really are."

"Who *I* really am?" Despite being stymied, she lifted her chin proudly. "Then we're on even footing, because I don't know who you are either. The man I met in the Caribbean was named Dev Harris, an international exporter from New York on a scuba diving holiday. A man who made our dive master, Angelo, look like a beginner."

Below black brows, Dev's dark eyes pierced her to the core of her being. This frontal view of his face exposed shadows beneath them, and carved lines around his mouth that hadn't been there before. Despite her anger it grieved her that he could have been suffering all this time.

"And you made quite the seductress."

A gasp escaped her throat over the unexpected remark thrown out at her like that. Incredulous, she shook her head. "Seductress? I don't know what you're talking about."

"Come on, Stephanie. The game is over. Working for Crystal River Water Tours, you don't make the kind of money to send you all over the world, on two occasions in the last three months, without a definite agenda."

For a moment she was so shocked, she couldn't make a sound.

"However, I have to admit you played your hand with such finesse, you almost took me to the cleaners, as you Americans say. I barely got out of there in time."

"In time? For what?" She couldn't begin to understand him. In a slow rage over his indictment of her, she moved closer. "Curious you'd say that, because it seems I flew out of Providenciales too late."

He folded his powerful arms. "And now you're in

trouble up to the last silvery-gold strand of hair on your beautiful head."

"Yes," she answered in a quiet voice, without blinking. Trouble that came wrapped in a baby quilt, with a bottle of formula, among other things.

A white ring encircling his mouth gave evidence of the negative emotion fueling him. "So you're here to continue where you left off."

She swallowed hard. Two could play at this game he'd accused her of. If she could keep him talking, maybe she'd find out what was going on. He wasn't the same Dev. "Only if you still want me."

"That's an interesting proposition. Why don't you make me...*want* you." His voice grated the words. "If you can accomplish that feat, I'll let you name your price."

"What price are you talking about?" she cried in absolute shock.

His eyes narrowed to black slits. "One way or another, money is the reason *you're* here."

"You think?"

In spite of his cruelty to her, his dare emboldened Stephanie to take him up on it. Much as she wished she could turn off her desire for this man whose child she was carrying, it didn't work that way. With her only thought being to get to the bottom of this nightmare, she reached for him and slid her arms around his neck.

"I've missed you," she whispered, before pressing her mouth to his, needing to be convincing so he'd listen to her. "You have no idea how much." After three months deprivation, her longing for him was at full strength, despite her pain at being abandoned. She needed to feel his arms around her and be kissed the way he'd done before, as if he was dying for her.

At first she could wring no response from him, and couldn't bear it. Then, suddenly, she felt his groan before he pulled her closer, as if he couldn't help himself. Every remembered memory came flooding back…the rapture, the ecstasy of his mouth and hands doing incredible things to her.

If anything, the flame of heat licked at both of them even more strongly than before. She rejoiced that she'd found him and that he still wanted her. His response couldn't be feigned. He was definitely covering up something. But right this minute intense desire was the one truth between them, and she'd cling to it with every breath she possessed until she knew what had happened to him.

Their bodies swayed due to the intensity of their passion. He clung to her with surprising strength. Voluptuous warmth enveloped them, bringing her inestimable pleasure that was spiraling, taking her over the edge of coherent thought. "Could we go someplace private?" she begged against his lips. "I've needed to feel you like this for so long, but I'm afraid someone will see us."

After a slight hesitation, he tore his lips from hers and released her. Before he pulled away she thought she saw torment in his eyes. "Come with me." He sounded out of breath.

"Wait. I dropped my purse." She retrieved it from the deck floor.

"No luggage?" he asked, falling back into that accusatory tone she hated.

"I only planned to come here for a few hours, so I left it in my hotel room on Chios."

He studied her through veiled eyes, no doubt assessing the validity of her statement before grasping her hand. "We'll go below." Nikos pulled her to the top of the stairs and they descended. He led her down the hallway past the lounge. Beyond it was the galley and a laundry room. The master bedroom was on the end, with its en suite bathroom.

The bed was unmade. Had he slept on board last night? While she stood there, bombarded with questions she needed answers to, he shrugged out of his T-shirt. After throwing it on a chair, he sat on the end of the bed to remove his sandals. She took a quick breath when he stood up to get out of his cargo pants. Despite his weight loss, he was such a striking man her mouth went dry looking at his hard-muscled frame.

"What are you doing?"

He shot her a penetrating glance. "I thought this was what you wanted. I'll pay your price after we're finished. Let me help you." In a lightning move he reached for her purse and tossed it on the chair on top of his shirt, panicking her.

"Wait, Dev—"

But he was beyond listening to her. "Delightful as that blouse is, I'm aching to see you again without any artifice. It's been a long time since our all-nighter. Kissing you has caused me to remember how delightful you are. Do you want to remove it, or shall I?"

Suddenly apprehensive, she stepped away from him. The challenge she'd initiated, to break him down, had backfired and she started to be afraid. "Please don't be like this, Dev. We need to talk." She refused to tell him why she'd come all this way, until she understood the reason he'd changed into someone else. If he made love to her, he'd know what she was hiding.

His smile had a wicked curl. "I don't remember you being this coy with me before. Come here." He inched closer and caressed her cheek. "We were lovers. Why pretend to be shy now when you were—shall we say—so accommodating before?"

Heat flooded her face. He was the most irresistible male alive. She couldn't bear it that there was this awful anger emanating from him. "For one night I slept in your bed, but I wouldn't call us lovers, not when you took off the next day, never to be seen again."

She felt his hands circle her neck, where he rubbed his thumbs over the pulse throbbing in the hollow of her throat. "That must have been a shock, eh?" he taunted. "Didn't you like the flowers I left behind?" he whispered silkily. "You told me gardenias were your favorites."

Stephanie had promised herself she wouldn't break down in front of him, but she had to fight the sting of salt against her eyelids. "I loved them, and would have thanked you if you'd left me a forwarding address or phone number."

His hands slid to her hair, where his fingers curled around the strands of her ponytail. "Since you've found me anyway, come to bed and show me just how much you loved them. Don't worry. You'll get what you came for."

She shook her head. "Don't do this, Dev. Whatever terrible thing you think I've done, those ten days we spent together have to account for something to cherish."

"Cherish?" he mocked, wounding her all over again, before freeing her. His hands went to his hips in a stance of male beauty all its own. "That word connotes fidelity, loyalty. I wonder if an ounce of either quality exists inside that delectable body of yours." His response dripped like acid from his lips.

Dev would be shocked if he knew what existed inside her and was growing with every passing minute. She pressed her arms to her waist, unable to forget for one second that she was carrying his son or daughter.

"It's clear you believe I betrayed you in some way. How could I have done that? We were together constantly at the resort. On that first day you asked *me* to be your diving partner, not the other way around. I spent every waking moment with you instead of the girls who came with me. I never even left the resort to go shopping with them, because you wanted to be with me every second.

"When I read the note left in the flowers, you have no idea what it did to me. I realized I was only a spring fling to you. I—I thought it was more." Her voice caught. Feeling unexpectedly nauseous, she moved over to the bed and sank down to recover.

He pinned her with those jet-black eyes. "Yet even though you got the message that our interlude was over, you came here, anyway."

After what they'd shared, for him to say that it had been over since they'd left the Caribbean caused her spirits to plummet to a new low.

"Yes. It was important for me to see you again, to find out why you had to go back to your work so abruptly. What if you needed help? Possible reasons for your sudden disappearance plagued me, until I couldn't sleep. I feared it might have even been a medical emergency that prompted you to write me that note, and you didn't want me to worry about you.

"All this time I've wondered if something terrible had happened to you or your family, and you couldn't confide in anyone who knew you. I simply didn't know." She bit her lip. "A few days ago I couldn't stand it any longer and decided to search for you."

"How did you manage that? Who told you my name?" He sounded beyond livid.

"No one!" she cried. "At least not in the way you mean."

"Explain that to me."

She stood up again, kneading her hands together. "When I couldn't find a number or address for you in New York, I turned to the employees at the resort to try to get answers." By the time she'd explained everything she'd done, his expression looked thunderous.

His dark head flew back. "Are you telling me you figured out what plane flew me out of the Caribbean?"

"Not at first. Taking you at your word that you had an emergency at work, I thought about the flights. One to Los Angeles and one to Vancouver. Why would you go to either place when you were working in New York? The private jet to Greece made no sense, either, at least not at first.

"I spent all night wondering. By morning I looked the name up on the computer and discovered Vassalos Maritime Shipping located on the island of Egnassou. I didn't know if you were a Vassalos from Vassalos Maritime Shipping or an employee. But since you'd told me you worked for an international export company, I thought it was a close enough connection to find out.

That's why I brought the photographs, in case someone recognized you.

"I thought there might be a chance I could find you here. When the man at the shipping office desk recognized your picture, I knew I'd come to the end of my search. That's when I realized you'd been lying to me the whole time. Undoubtedly, you do that whenever you meet a woman to enjoy for a time before you disappear."

For a full minute he studied every square inch of her, his expression lethal. "Since you've accomplished your objective, let's go to bed for old time's sake, one more time, shall we? Then I'll send you on your way with enough money to have made your trip worthwhile."

Her body stiffened. "I don't want your money and have already gotten what I came for, Dev."

"The name is Nikos, as you damn well know!"

Nikos...

Somehow she'd thought Dev would soften while they were alone, and tell her why he'd lied to her. But the inscrutable man facing her bore little resemblance to her secret Adonis who'd brought her joy every second they'd been together. It hadn't mattered whether they'd been walking on the beach or finding glorious sights in the aqua depths of the sea.

She decided this man didn't deserve to know about the baby until it was born. He wouldn't believe her if she told him now, anyway. In fact, she was beginning to think he'd drummed up this betrayal business on purpose, to get rid of her. He'd probably pulled the same excuse on his other lovers when he was through with them. If that was true, he'd done a stellar job.

Now that she had the main phone number of Vassalos

Shipping, she could always leave a message for him next January. If he cared to answer, he'd learn then that he was a new father, not before.

His smile was beautifully cruel. "You've been playing me for a reason. Now I want to know what it is."

Stephanie drew in a fortifying breath. "I'd hoped to get an honest answer out of you, but you're not Dev Harris. Let's just say I don't want to ruin my memory of him. You, sir, are someone I don't care to know. For all I know you have a wife and children. The thought of committing adultery with you makes me sick."

She would have reached for her purse to leave, but that's when she saw a cane resting against the wall at the side of the closet. Stephanie looked up at Dev, noticing he'd lost a little color and was braced against the door to prevent her escape.

When he'd grabbed her earlier on deck, they'd both weaved a little. She'd thought it was because the impact had caught him totally off guard, but now she knew that wasn't true. He *was* unsteady. Something serious must have happened for a man as fit as he was to need a cane. Why was he being so brutal to her? She couldn't comprehend it.

"What is it you want, if not money?"

"A little honesty. I—I feel like I'm in the middle of a nightmare." Her voice faltered.

"You're part of mine, didn't you know?" he growled. "Can you still stand there and tell me you found me through Delia's boyfriend?"

"It's the truth!"

"Surely you can do better than that." His tone stung like a whiplash.

"Dev... Nikos... Tell me what I've done?" Her cry

rang in the cabin's interior. "Are you truly so devoid of feeling that you can leave me hanging like this without one word of explanation?"

"Isn't this a case of the pot calling the kettle black?"

Stephanie had taken enough of his abuse. "Let me pass." She feared she was going to be sick.

His black brows furrowed. "You're not wanted here, but since you've shown up anyway, you're not going anywhere until I get an honest explanation."

She shook her head. "Why do you continue to accuse me of something I don't understand?"

Anger marred his arresting features. "Who told you about me? How did you know I'd be staying at that particular resort? Where did you get your information?"

"I don't know what you're talking about."

"You were obviously lying in wait for me at the resort."

"You mean like some femme fatale, so I could get you to sleep with me?"

"Were you hoping to get pregnant by a rich man? Is that it? Your latest boyfriend didn't quite live up to your dreams?"

By this time she was fuming. "Let's presume for a minute you guessed it and that was my sin. What about *your* sin? You slept with me, too."

He hunched of his broad shoulders slightly. "So I did."

"Only it seems just one night was all you wanted before you moved on. Now that I've come here, you're disgusted to see me and obviously regret our interlude." With her hair caught back in a short ponytail, and her probable lack of color, she realized she must look dreadful to him.

"But not you." His eyes had become mere slits. "Who told you about me and my family? How did you know about me?"

She couldn't believe her ears. "No one!" *Only an innocent child who doesn't have a voice yet.* "I was foolish enough to come looking for you here b-because I couldn't believe it was over between us," she stammered. That was the truth, just not all of it.

His expression remained implacable.

Stephanie averted her eyes. "It was wrong of me to sleep with you. I was raised to be wiser than that, a lesson I learned too late. But no, Dev. No matter how much you despise me for coming here uninvited, I could never regret anything so beautiful. Now I'm leaving, but I need to use your bathroom first." She was going to be sick.

CHAPTER THREE

STEPHANIE SWEPT PAST him, causing Nikos to bite down hard so hard he almost cracked a tooth. That week in the Caribbean with her had been beautiful. The most beautiful experience of his life. To think it had been a deliberate setup!

Enflamed to realize she'd used him, Nikos snatched her purse from the chair and dumped the contents on the bed, hoping to learn something. Anything!

Among the contents were three vials of pills, a wallet, a phone, a key card for the Persephone Hotel along the waterfront in Chios, an airline ticket and her passport. He examined it but saw no red flag. Her wallet gave no clues except some pictures. Two of them were of her and Nikos. Another was of her friends and still another of a woman who looked to be her mother. He also found her business card from Crystal River Water Tours.

With a grimace he reached for one of the bottles, which contained vitamins. Nikos opened it and could smell them before emptying the pills on the bed. He examined the second vial, of iron pills. The third held a prescription drug issued from the same pharmacy in Florida. Dr. Verl Sanders. Three a day as necessary for nausea and/or vomiting. The date on all three bottles indicated they'd been issued two days ago.

She was pregnant. Just as his father had intimated…

He swung his head in her direction. By now she'd come back out and was sitting on the chair. "Please, Dev." Her blue eyes begged him, out of a face with a slight pallor he hadn't noticed before. Come to think of it, with that wan complexion, she didn't look the same. The glow of health that had radiated off her in the Caribbean was missing. "If I could have one of those small greenish pills with some water?"

She still insisted on using his fictitious name. Nikos picked up one of the pills, then grasped her upper arm and led her back into his bathroom. Her firm flesh, warm from walking on the island in the sun, was a potent reminder of what he'd been torn from at the resort, but that golden quality about her had disappeared.

"Use the cup from the dispenser."

Stephanie took one and put it under the faucet. When he handed her the pill, she swallowed it with half a cup of water. He'd expected resistance, but the eager way she drank and the slight tremor of the hand holding the cup revealed a vulnerability that brought out his protective instincts and caused his mind to reel.

"How far along are you?"

The empty cup fell into the sink. This was no act. She weaved in place, causing him to tighten his grip on her arm so she wouldn't fall. Her eyes stared at him in the mirror. "You do the math."

That comment—just when he'd felt himself softening toward her—caught him on the raw. He gripped her other arm to bring her close to him, and gave her a little shake. "Whose baby is it? Rob's?"

"You can ask me that?" she cried, sounding so wounded it almost got to him.

"Very easily."

Her head fell back on the slender column of her neck. "Rob? The guy I only had one dinner date with? I was never intimate with him or anyone else! I can't believe you brought his name up."

"I used protection, Stephanie."

"That's what I told Dr. Sanders. He said no protection was perfect, and informed me I was going to have a baby. I'm three months along."

She'd already gone through her first trimester? He'd been in absolute hell during that same time period.

"Call him and he'll confirm it. If you can conceive of my being with another man after what we shared on vacation, then your imagination is greater than mine could ever be. After it's born and you're still in doubt, then a simple DNA test will tell you the truth."

The blood hammered in his ears. He searched her eyes, trying to find any trace of duplicity in her, but could see none. His lips twisted. "So your carefully laid plan had the consequence you'd hoped for, and now you're ready to turn this to your advantage?"

"What advantage?" she blurted angrily. "When you were through with me, you sent me flowers and couldn't have made it clearer our interlude was over. But I happen to believe that a man who's a womanizer still deserves to know he's going to be a father. That's the real reason I'm here!"

The *real* reason. *Which truth was the truth?*

"I could have sent you a bouquet with a note congratulating you on your new status. But I had no idea where to send it, so I decided to do the decent thing and come in person, hoping to find Dev Harris. Instead I found *you*."

With her wintry indictment, she jerked herself out of his arms and hurried back to the bedroom. "Now that you've been given the news, I need to catch the boat back to Chios." She started to put the contents of her purse back, but his hand was faster, preventing her.

"I'm afraid not. There won't be another one until tomorrow." He slid her cell phone and passport in a pocket of his pants.

Her head swerved to meet his piercing gaze. "I never wanted or expected anything from you, and that's a good thing, because I don't know who you are."

"Nor I you." His voice grated. "Except in the biblical sense." He saw a glint of pain in her eyes before she started for the doorway. "Go ahead, but without a passport, you won't be allowed to board the plane back to the States."

"You can't keep me here! I have a job to get back to, a condo to take care of. My flight leaves for Florida in the morning."

"You should have thought of that before you ever targeted me."

Her naturally arched brows frowned in puzzlement. "You certainly have an inflated opinion of yourself. I've met men in Florida with a lot of money. Maybe not as much as the Vassalos family, but enough to keep a grasping woman in style for the rest of her life. Since you can't wait for me to be gone, how long do you intend to keep me here?"

"For as long as it takes to get the truth from you."

She sat down on the edge of the bed as if she was too weak to stand. Her pallor convinced him that part of her story was the truth. She was nauseous, but maybe it covered something other than pregnancy. Kon's wife had done a spectacular job of convincing him she was pregnant.

"Dev… We met purely by accident, when I was scuba diving at the resort with my friends from Crystal River."

"Yet you managed to locate me here without any difficulty whatsoever. Now you're telling me you're pregnant with my child. We both know you were already pregnant when you slept with me on vacation. If you're hoping to inveigle your way into my life with this announcement, it won't work."

By now her hands had formed into fists, and she jumped up from the bed. "I don't want to stay here!" she cried, sounding on the verge of hysteria. "I can't! I'm expected back at work. My friends will wonder where I am."

He would never have credited her with being an hysterical woman. It didn't fit with what he knew about her. Yet what did he really know, except what she'd allowed him to see while they were both on vacation? "No problem. You can call them and tell them you've been detained."

"Dev—"

"It's Nikos, remember?"

"All right then. Nikos. Please don't do this. I need to get back to the hotel in Chios for my personal belongings."

"We'll sail there and Yannis will collect them for you."

"Yannis?"

"He's a seaman who worked for my family when I was boy. Now he works for me."

"What do you mean, collect?" she asked in fresh alarm.

"After we leave Chios, we won't be touching land again for at least two weeks."

After letting out a moan, she started pacing, then stopped. "Call my obstetrician in Florida. He'll verify the dates so you'll have your proof."

"That won't prove anything. You could have been with a man the night before we met. Maybe several."

A gasp escaped. "Surely you don't believe that! There was only you. Phone Delia. She'll verify everything."

"How much did you pay her and her boyfriend to tell me a lie if I called her?"

Stephanie paled more. "Nikos…who are you?"

He raked a hand through his hair, wondering the same thing. After living through a hellish childhood with his father, plus the memory of Kon's disastrous marriage and divorce, Nikos had developed a much more cynical outlook on life.

Part of him couldn't help but wonder why Natasa had been waiting around for him all these years, if not to marry money. She'd lived with wealth all her life and needed a rich husband to be kept in that same lifestyle. The thought sickened him.

What if Stephanie was telling him the truth? His black brows furrowed. "Someone who doesn't like being taken advantage of. You were very clever to try and convince me you found me by sheer perseverance. For the time being you'll remain with me on the *Diomedes.*" It was an impulsive decision, one he hadn't had time to examine yet.

She looked frantic. "Please don't do this."

For a moment he was carried back three months in time. She'd begged him not to tease her when he kept kissing her face, but not her mouth. He'd been on the verge of devouring her and couldn't hold back much longer. Just now that same appeal was in her voice, confusing him, when he needed to keep his wits.

"You don't have to worry. I'll let you contact your boss and make it right with him. Tell him your medical condition has made it necessary for you to stay in Greece for an indefinite period. Your boss will have to understand."

"But Nikos—"

"No doubt your friend Melinda will run by your condo for you and check your mail." He put his T-shirt back on and slid into his sandals. "As for you, I'll make sure you're taken care of in your fragile state. Just be grateful I'm not turning you over to the authorities for trespassing on private property. You wouldn't last long in one of our jails."

Her appealing body shuddered.

"It would be interesting to know who told you I was on the yacht. No one knows except my parents."

"I—I met an older woman waiting for the boat that would take me back to Chios," Stephanie stammered. "She pointed to this yacht and said it belonged to the Vassalos family."

"Why would she do that?"

"Because I asked her if she lived here and knew your family."

"What did she say?"

"That everyone knew your family."

"Did you exchange names?"

"No! I simply offered her some of my grapes while we were waiting for the boat."

"So at that point you just decided to walk over to the yacht and see if it met your high expectations, did you?"

"No. My intention was to find out if anyone on board knew where you really were."

"I guess I'm not surprised you decided to use your beauty to sweet-talk the crew into revealing my whereabouts."

She stiffened. "There *was* no crew."

"Yet having been told I was out of the country indefinitely, you still waited for someone to come to the yacht."

She moistened her lips. "I was afraid that if you were at work and knew I was looking for you, you'd pretend to be away. It was my last resort to try and reach you."

"Therefore once again it was pure luck that you didn't take no for an answer and sought me out at the yacht."

"It appears that way," she whispered.

"I'm afraid your luck has run out." Before he walked out of the bedroom, he said, "Go ahead and fix your own meal. There's food and drink in the galley. We just restocked everything. You're paler and weaker than I remember. That couldn't be good for you in your condition."

"I notice you've lost weight and don't look as well, either!"

Touché.

"In fact, you—" Suddenly, she stopped talking.

"I what?" he demanded.

Stephanie averted her eyes. "Nothing."

He'd seen her glance at the cane, and had an idea what she'd intended to say. It angered him further. "Don't try to go up on deck while we're leaving port."

Adrenaline drove him out of the room and down the hall to the stairs. But he paid the price for not taking care because when he reached the top deck, he felt pain at the base of his spine and realized he'd exerted himself too much without support. *Damn it all.*

CHAPTER FOUR

AFTER A FEW minutes of enforced solitude, Stephanie could feel the yacht moving. Good heavens! Nikos had really meant it. They were leaving the port and she was his prisoner! It certainly wasn't because he was enamored of her. She'd changed physically since they'd been together, making her less attractive.

His looks had altered, too, but in his case the weight loss and dark brooding behavior didn't detract from his virulent male charisma. If anything, those changes made him even more appealing, if that was at all possible.

By now she'd passed the stage where she still believed she was having a nightmare. Rage and bewilderment had been warring inside her, but her greatest need at the moment was for food, so she wouldn't throw up again. No matter what was going to happen, she needed to take care of herself and her baby.

Taking him at his word, she walked to the galley. He'd stocked his fridge well in a kitchen that rivaled that of even the most rich and famous yacht owners. Anything she could want was here. But after she'd eaten, she started going crazy with nothing to do, and decided to go up to the top of the stairs for some fresh air.

To her dismay the tough-looking seaman, Yannis, probably in his sixties, barred her way. "Go back down, Ms. Walsh," he told her in a heavily accented voice.

"Just let me stand here for a little while and breathe some fresh air." There was no sign of her baby's father. The sun had fallen below the horizon.

"Nikos doesn't want you up here until we're out on open water. It's for your safety. I promised him that I would take care of you."

There'd be no point in begging his guard dog to let her walk around on deck. "All right." She turned around and went back to the dimly lit passage below, and finally Nikos's bedroom. Stephanie couldn't believe this was the same man she'd fallen madly in love with.

Since he wasn't working at Vassalos Shipping right now, what was he doing on this yacht? Needing to figure out why he was being so cruel and secretive, she opened his closet, but all she found were casual clothes. Nothing that told her anything. The clothes in the dresser didn't reveal anything, either.

Needing answers, she left the bedroom and went along the passageway to the next door, on the left. It was another bedroom, with a queen-size bed and its own bathroom.

She tried the next door, but it was locked. Maybe it was the bedroom of the man who was crewing for Nikos. Stephanie's gaze darted to the lounge across from it. One end contained a couch, table and chairs, and an entertainment center. The other end had been made into a den, equipped with a computer and everything that went with it.

After checking out his desk, she came across sets of

maps and charts with Greek words she couldn't read. Stephanie was afraid she'd be caught snooping and it would intensify his anger. Quickly, she put them back in the drawers and hurried down the corridor to his bedroom.

Once she'd shut the door, she leaned against it with a pounding heart while her mind tried to make sense of what he was doing on the yacht. When she'd calmed down, she was so exhausted she stretched out on the bed. In case he came to check up on her, he would think she'd been sleeping instead of exploring the yacht without his permission.

Emotionally spent, she closed her eyes for a minute, trying desperately to put all the disjointed pieces together. The man at the reception desk had told her Kyrie Vassalos was out of the country and wouldn't be back in the foreseeable future. It was a blatant lie, since Nikos had obviously been living on this yacht for some time. Why?

Stephanie racked her brain for answers until she knew nothing else. When she next became aware of her surroundings, the yacht was still moving. To her surprise Nikos had thrown a blanket over her. How long had she slept? Her watch said it was 11:00 p.m., Greek time.

When she rolled over to get up, she realized he'd removed her sandals. At the end of the bed she saw her suitcase. That meant he'd already sailed to Chios, and had no doubt taken care of her hotel bill.

She started to tremble. No one in the world knew where she was right now. No one would be looking for her yet. Stephanie was being held against her will in the middle of the Aegean Sea by a man she didn't begin to know.

After slipping on her sandals, she left the bedroom and walked down the hall to the stairs. No one met her at the top. She walked to the railing and looked all around. Night had descended. In the distance she could see lights twinkling from land far away. Though the sight was beautiful, she shivered to think she'd been so foolish as to climb aboard the boat of a perfect stranger. In Greek waters, no less...

Didn't Greek mythology tell of Pandora, the first woman on earth? Zeus had given her a beautiful container with instructions not to open it under any circumstances. But her curiosity had prevailed and she did open it, letting out all the evil held inside. For what she'd done, she'd feared Zeus's wrath.

Another shudder rocked Stephanie's body. Today she'd opened that container, knowing she shouldn't have. The action had seemed so small at the time. But what she'd done, in order to find the father of her baby, had turned out to have severe and far-reaching consequences for her, inciting Nikos's wrath.

"You're not supposed to be up here."

At the sound of Nikos's deep voice, a cry escaped her lips and she spun around. The warm night breeze flattened the T-shirt against his well-defined chest, ruffling his black wavy hair. Despite his hostility, his male beauty captivated her.

"I was looking for you."

"It's dangerous to walk around at this time of night. You're lucky I didn't set the wireless security system yet, or you would have received the fright of your life by the noise."

Her hand clutched the railing. "I'm used to being on boats," she said defensively.

His lips tightened into a thin line. "Go back down. *Now.*"

Nikos's mood was too dark and ominous for her to dare defy him. Taking a deep breath, she turned around and walked back to the stairs, which she descended. She felt him following her, all the way to the bedroom.

After he came inside, she looked at him. "Was the alarm set this afternoon while I was waiting to talk to a crew member?"

"Yes, even if that part of the marina is Vassalos private property. There are some people who will trespass no matter what."

She lifted a hand to her throat. She'd considered going on board, but had held back, thank goodness. "You mean all those other boats belong to your company?"

"That's right." His chiseled features stood out in stark relief. "I must admit I'm surprised you didn't step on the *Diomedes* without permission. When we were together on Providenciales, I noticed what an adventurous person you were, unafraid to explore the depths where the others held back. I guess it doesn't really surprise me you would show such tenacity in trying to find me, regardless of the consequences."

Her softly rounded chin lifted. "That's because I was on a sacred mission."

"Sacred?" he queried silkily. "What an interesting choice of words."

Salty tears stung her eyelids. "You wouldn't understand."

"Try me."

Stephanie shook her head. "You'll only mock me, so there's no point."

"You're trying my patience, what little I have left," he said, his voice grating. He lounged against the closed door. The stance looked familiar, but she had an idea he needed the support. Stephanie wished she didn't care about his condition, but the signs of his suffering, both physical and emotional, had gotten to her. "I'm waiting."

"When we were in the Caribbean, you asked me about my father. I told you he and my mother never married and she raised me alone. But I never went into the details."

"Why was that?"

She sank down on the side of the bed. "Because it's such a painful subject for me to talk about, and because I barely knew you. Eventually I would have told you everything, but we ran out of time." Her voice shook.

His jaw hardened. "That must have been a shock to your carefully laid plans."

"I didn't have any plans, Nikos. I don't know why you won't believe me. You say you want answers, so I'm trying to give them to you. Mom met my father on a winter skiing holiday in Colorado. They spent a glorious week together before he said he had to leave, but would fly to Crystal River to see her.

"She worked in hospital administration. He could have found her at any time, but he never called or looked her up. Mom had her pride and waited in vain for him to get in touch with her."

Nikos eyed Stephanie skeptically. "If she knew where he lived, why didn't she seek him out?"

"By the time I was born, she was so ashamed of

what she'd done, she made up her mind that I would never know his name or where I could find him. She felt he didn't deserve to know he was a father. I was put in day care and she raised me with the help of my grandparents until they passed on."

Struggling with the rest, Stephanie sprang to her feet. "Since you left me at the resort, I have a crystal-clear understanding of what my mother went through and why she was so shattered. But she forgot one thing. She didn't realize how important it was for me to know who my father was, if only to see him once and understand my own genes, to gain more of an identity."

Stephanie heard Nikos take an extra breath in reaction.

"Mother robbed me of that. It's the only thing in our lives that caused pain between us. I loved her. Though she was the best mom in the world, I had a hard time forgiving her for that. However, I finally have. Still, her omission has left scars, because I'm my father's flesh and blood, too. When she died, her secret died with her, leaving me in agony and always wondering about him.

"Do I have grandparents who are still alive? A half brother or sister? Does my father like doing the things I like? Do I look like him? Those are questions for which I have no answers. Unfortunately, I'll never be given them."

She clutched her arms to her waist. "Such is the story of the Walsh mother and daughter. We were both open to a good time, until it was over. I can't believe I've repeated my mother's history, but they say experience is the best teacher."

Stephanie threw her head back. "How I've learned! I had to believe it when the doctor told me I was pregnant. He said a good condom hardly ever fails, but it can slip. That's probably what happened with us."

By now Niko's countenance had grown dark and lined.

"Believe it or not, my very first thought when I learned of my pregnancy wasn't about you or money, but about the life we'd created. I felt all the joy of being told I was going to be a mother, and I loved my baby instantly.

"But I have to tell you, I damned myself and you for the weakness that caused us to reach out for pleasure without marriage or commitment of any kind, without really knowing the most basic things about each other. We were both incredibly selfish, Nikos."

"You're right," he admitted, with what sounded like self-loathing.

"In hindsight I realize I don't hate you for what you did, leaving without a personal goodbye. I took a risk with you. We were equal partners in doing what we did. That's why I did everything I could to find you and let you know you're going to be a father. To *not* tell you would be an even more selfish act.

"I wouldn't be honest if I didn't admit that I wanted to be with you the moment we met in the Caribbean, and I made no secret about it. That time was beautiful beyond belief and something I will always treasure. It's the reason I don't want to make something ugly out of something that was sacred to me at the time, even if it was illicit. I still don't know if you have a wife or other children."

"I don't," he whispered in a bleak tone.

"If that's the truth, then I'm glad I don't have to carry that burden, too. You've accused me of coming after you because of the great Vassalos fortune. Let me say now that I wouldn't ask for money or take it under any circumstances. What we had together wasn't love. It couldn't have been, since it was based on a lie."

At her comment his features hardened.

"You owe me nothing, Nikos, but you have the right to know we're going to have a child. When the baby's born, I plan to give it the last name of Walsh. But I did want to be able to tell our daughter or son your true name—that it wasn't Dev Harris, and that you come from a fine established family from Egnoussa, Greece, and not New York.

"That's why I did everything possible to find you and learn your true identity. I realize I've gone where angels fear to tread, even to trying to find out about you from someone working on your yacht. But I've done it for our child, who doesn't deserve such selfish parents."

"It's very noble of you to take on partial blame." But his mocking tone robbed the sentiment of any meaning.

"Once you let me off this luxury vessel, I'm going back to Crystal River, knowing I've done my best for my baby. One day, when our child asks about you, I'll tell him or her all I know and learned about you during those ten days we spent together. They were the happiest days of my whole life.

"It will help satisfy our child's great need to know about his or her beginnings. Every human born wants to know who they are and where they come from. Were they wanted? I want our child to know he or she was wanted from the second I found out that I was pregnant. Once grown, it will be up to him or her if you meet. I'll play no part in it.

"Now if you'll excuse me, I need to use the bathroom again. After I've gotten ready for bed, where do you want me to sleep?"

"Your bedroom is the next one down the hallway, on the left. I'll show you. You can freshen up in your own bathroom."

He picked up her suitcase and took it to the guest bedroom she'd looked in before. "Get a good night's sleep. It appears you need it," he muttered. The unflattering observation shook her to the foundations.

Nikos had told Yannis to drop anchor off Oinoussa Island for the night. Afraid to go below and fall asleep, where he might have one of his flashbacks and Stephanie would hear him, he opted for a lounger beneath the stars, and covered himself with a light blanket.

All was quiet except for the frantic pounding of his heart at every pulse point of his body.

For the rest of the hours before dawn he lay there in torment, going over their conversation in his mind.

Even if he'd used her while on vacation, Stephanie had claimed she wanted him to know in person that he was going to be a father. At the heartbreaking story of having all knowledge of her own father kept from her, Nikos had been moved beyond words.

To go to so much trouble and expense to find Dev Harris—to risk her health in the process—led him to believe she must be telling him the truth. Otherwise she would have sought out the other man she'd been with, *if* there was another man.

But if she'd been with another man before Nikos, no one had proof of paternity. Only a blood test after the baby was born would prove it. Any earlier attempt would be a risk to the unborn baby and possibly cause a miscarriage. He didn't dare insist on it. Much as he wanted to believe he was the father, and that her true reason for coming to Greece was to inform him of the fact, he was still riddled with doubts.

Nikos closed his eyes tightly. When Kon had been confronted with a similar situation, before they'd gone into the military, he'd believed the nineteen-year-old girl who'd told him she was pregnant. Kon had gotten in over his head with an attractive French girl he'd met on vacation in Corsica, but before returning home, he realized he wasn't in love, and had ended it with her while they were still together.

To his chagrin, she'd showed up a month later with a positive result on a home pregnancy test, claiming he was the father. She was terrified of having her parents find out. What should she do?

Kon was an honorable man and had been willing to take responsibility, so they got married privately at the local church, where Nikos stood as one of the witnesses. His parents accepted her into the family and they'd lived with them until Kon could afford to find a place for them to live on their own.

But two months later his friend realized she'd lied to him and there was no baby. He got medical proof from the doctor at the hospital. She was forced to admit she'd made up the fabrication because she loved him and didn't want to lose him. If he thought they were going to have a baby, then they could get married. As it turned out her plan had worked...for a while.

Betrayed to the point he couldn't look at her anymore, he divorced her and put the whole ghastly affair behind him. But there'd been a heavy emotional price to pay, and the divorce had cost him a great deal of money, which Nikos insisted on funding from his own savings account. It was the least he could do for his friend.

After the agony Nikos had seen Kon go through when he'd realized he'd been deceived, the possibility that Stephanie was lying, too, gutted him. He didn't honestly know what to believe.

Short of making love to Stephanie to learn if she was truly pregnant, which wasn't a viable option for too many reasons to consider right now, he could phone her doctor. Yet somehow that idea was repugnant to him.

The only sure thing to do was wait for physical signs of her pregnancy. In order to do that, he would have to keep her close for the time being.

When Nikos thought back to their first meeting, he recalled he'd been the aggressor. Unlike her friends, who worked at a local hotel in Crystal River, Stephanie had done nothing to come on to him. While they'd flirted with him, she'd kept her distance and been totally serious about diving.

It turned out they didn't have her skills and snorkeled only part of each day. Oftentimes they preferred to laze on the beach and go shopping in town. Not Stephanie. Quite the opposite, in fact, which was why he'd asked her if she'd be willing to be his diving partner for the duration. He'd felt her reluctance when she'd said yes, but it was obvious she loved the sport and couldn't go diving without a partner.

Scuba diving wasn't for everyone, but she was a natural. Together they'd experienced the euphoria of discovering the underwater world. Besides her beauty, there was an instant connection between them as they'd signaled each other to look at the wonders exploding with color and life around each gully and crevice.

When they'd had to surface, he hadn't wanted it to end, and had asked her to eat dinner with him. She'd turned down his first invitation, but the second time she'd agreed. That's when he'd learned she'd grown up along Florida's Nature Coast. She'd learned to scuba dive early with her mother. After college she'd gone to work for a water tour company that took tourists scalloping and swimming with the manatees. It explained her prowess beneath the waves.

If he was truly the only man she'd been with, then her news represented a miracle. Nikos was sterile now, the hope of ever having a child from his own body having gone up in flames during the explosion.

Yet he could feel no joy if she'd set him up—no elation that a deceitful woman would be the mother of his child. If indeed he was the father...

But what if you are, Vassalos?

Think about it.

Your own flesh and blood could be growing inside Stephanie. The only son or daughter you'll ever have.

More thoughts bombarded him.

After his last mission he'd hoped to resign his commission and go after her, marry her. What if she truly was innocent of every charge, and he'd totally misread the situation? If that was the case, then one misstep on his part could hurt her emotionally and damage any chance at real happiness, with their baby on the way.

He got up from the lounger and walked over to the railing, watching the moonlight on the water. His training as a SEAL had taught him that you had to set up your perimeter and have everything in place before you mounted an assault. This time Stephanie was the target. Unfortunately, after leaving her behind, he'd unwittingly planted an almost impenetrable field of land mines and booby traps that would destroy him if he wasn't careful.

If his suspicions about her were correct—that she'd calculated every move since meeting him at the resort, in order to trap him—it meant maneuvering through them with surgical precision while he waited to see if she was pregnant, then awaited the DNA results.

How would he begin making it up to her if he was wrong?

In retrospect, Nikos realized he'd accused her of duplicity, when he'd been the one who'd committed a multiple number of sins. Not only had he forsaken her on the island without giving her an honest explanation, he hadn't tried to reach her during his stay in the hospital.

The moment his father had handed him those snapshots, Nikos had been carried away by his own suspicions that she was after his money and the lifestyle he could provide her. His anger had quickly turned to white-hot pain at the thought she'd been only using him during that time on vacation. In retaliation, he'd treated her abominably.

Nikos let out a groan. Was he turning into his father? A man who'd believed the worst about the wife who loved him, because of a rumor? Whose doubts and suspicions had turned him into an impossible man to live with, catching Nikos in the crossfire?

Stephanie's words still rang in his ears. *What we had together wasn't love.*

But what if it *had* been love on her part, and it was

only her anger talking now? Otherwise why would she have gone through all she'd done to find him?

He owed it to both of them to discover the truth. Otherwise he might be dooming himself to repeat his father's history. Until Nikos had proof, he decided he would believe her story, because his entire happiness could depend on it.

By the time the sun had risen above the horizon, he'd made his plans. The first thing he'd do was shower, then fix breakfast for the two of them. *Or the three...*

A knock on her bedroom door brought Stephanie awake. It was ten after eight. She'd slept soundly, likely because of the gentle rocking of the yacht. But it didn't feel as if they were moving now.

"Yes?"

"Your breakfast is waiting for you in the lounge down the hall, whenever you're ready."

She blinked. "Nikos?"

"Of course."

There was no "of course" about it. Last night he'd told her to fix her own food. This morning it seemed he'd decided to be more civil. That was a good sign, since she needed to go home today, and couldn't without his cooperation.

"Thank you. I'll be right there."

She took all her pills with a cup of water she'd put by the bed, and then got out from under the covers. Once in the bathroom she showered quickly, then brushed her hair and left it loose. A little blusher and lipstick and she felt ready to face Nikos.

Stephanie hadn't packed a lot. She'd brought extra undergarments and a smoky-blue knit top she wore loose over her khaki pants, which were uncomfortable now. She needed to buy some maternity clothes the moment she got back to Florida.

In spite of the fact that she would have to go through the entire pregnancy alone, she was looking forward to it. Having found the baby's father, and knowing his real identity, she felt a bit more lighthearted. Soon she'd start getting a nursery ready, and couldn't wait.

After putting on her sandals, she left the bedroom and moved across the hall to the lounge, where she found Nikos at the table, waiting for her. He stood up when she walked in. She detected the scent of the soap he'd used in the shower. Her senses responded to it, though she tried to ignore them.

"It looks like you've made a fabulous breakfast." He'd fixed coffee, too, but so far she hadn't been able to tolerate it. "We could have eaten in the galley and saved you the extra trouble."

"True, but you're a guest, so I thought this might be more enjoyable."

"For a prisoner who has to stay below deck, you mean," she muttered.

He ignored her comment. "Let's hope there's something here that you can keep down." He helped her into a chair before he sat opposite her at the rectangular table.

"Those rolls and fruit look good." So did he…. This morning he was freshly shaved and wearing a white crew neck shirt with jeans. It was sinful how handsome he was!

While he ate eggs and a roll, his jet-black eyes played over her several times. "Your hair is a little longer."

"So's yours." But she refused to tell him how much she liked it.

He appeared to drink his coffee with pleasure. "What did your doctor tell you about swimming and scuba diving in your condition?"

The question was totally unexpected. "I can do some limited swimming, but diving during pregnancy increases the risk to the fetus, so I'm not taking any chances. Why do you ask?"

One black brow lifted. "Your job. Now that you're pregnant, the kind of work you do swimming with the manatees will have to be curtailed."

She munched on a banana. "I realize that and plan to discuss it with my boss when I get back. Which raises the question of when you're going to take me to Chios so I can get a flight home."

"That all depends." He bit into a juicy plum.

Stephanie fought to remain cool-headed. "On what?"

He finished it, then lounged back in the chair, eyeing her for a long moment. "I have a proposition for you."

"I'm not interested."

"Surely after all the trouble you took to find me, can't you admit you're a little curious?"

"That curiosity died when I didn't find Dev. You're the dark side of him, a complete stranger to me with your lies and secrets. I have no desire to listen to anything you have to say, except to hear that you'll let me go."

"Be that as it may, you've convinced me you were an innocent tourist on vacation in the Caribbean. I take full responsibility for finding you attractive and pursuing you. Since you're pregnant, it's only right that I take care of you and the baby you're carrying."

For him to say that to her now… Pain ripped her apart. "For the last time, I don't want your money, just my freedom."

His eyes narrowed on her features. "You can have it in time *if* it's what you want. That's what divorces are for."

Shaken by his words, she sprang from the chair. "What are you talking about?"

"Our marriage, of course. You came all the way from Florida to let me know I'm going to be a father. But that's not all I want. I want my name on the birth certificate along with yours. To a Greek male, it means everything."

"Since when?" she blurted.

"Since learning that you've known nothing about your own father—not even his name. I can see how devastating that has been for you, which makes it more vital than ever that the baby growing inside you has my name so it can take its rightful place in the world."

Stephanie reeled in place, clinging to the back of the chair. "You don't want to marry me." Her tremulous words reverberated in the lounge.

Now Nikos was on his feet. "On the contrary. It's all I thought about during the night."

"Why?" she cried in torment.

"Because this baby is already precious to me."

Her anger flared. "Last night you questioned if it was even yours."

"Last night I was in denial that a miracle had happened."

She shook her head. "What do you mean?"

"A lot has occurred since we last saw each other." He didn't need to tell her that. Her whole world had been turned upside down. "I was in a boating accident that landed me in the hospital with a spinal injury."

Stephanie bit her lip, pained by the news. "I knew something was wrong," she whispered. "Sometimes you're a little unsteady. I noticed it wh-when you were holding me."

"Nothing gets past you, does it? Your unexpected presence on the *Diomedes* gave me away. Fortunately, I'm getting stronger every day and use the cane only when I'm tired. But I'm not the man I once was and never will be. Furthermore, the accident had certain repercussions I can't do anything about."

Her mouth went dry. She was almost afraid to hear. "What are they?"

"For one thing, my injury left me sterile."

Sterile?

A slight gasp escaped her lips, for she knew that kind of news had to be soul wrenching to a man. "Surely it's only a temporary setback?"

"No." His eyes again narrowed to slits. "It's permanent." The throb in his voice carried its own haunting tale.

Stephanie pressed her hand to her mouth to stifle her cry. "I'm so sorry, Nikos. I hardly know what to say."

"Perhaps now you understand why your coming here to tell me you're pregnant, at the very moment I've been dealing with my news, made me go out of my head for a little while. After having to give up all hope of having my own child, I suppose I was afraid to believe you were telling me the truth."

Stephanie's lungs tightened while she tried to absorb

the revelation. "What was the other repercussion?" She feared it was going to be horrible, too.

"My best friend died in the accident."

"Kon Gregerov?"

Nikos nodded gravely.

"Oh, no…" She couldn't hold back the tears. They rolled down her cheeks. He'd mentioned his friend several times while they'd been diving. He'd told her they were closer than he was to his own brother. They'd grown up together and would have done anything for each other.

After such trauma, was it any wonder he'd changed so completely in every way? Other than anger over what life had dealt him, Nikos had to feel dead inside. If their positions were reversed, Stephanie knew her life would look black to her.

"Now that you've heard the truth from me, here's my proposition. I want to marry you as soon as possible, and we'll live here. It will mean having to give up your job. You can either sell or rent your condo, and put your car and furnishings in storage for the time being.

"It's the only way I can protect you and the baby. But it wouldn't have been fair to you if I hadn't told you I can't give you more children. Millions of other men can. You need to think about that very carefully before you commit yourself legally to me."

Stephanie *was* thinking. It was a shock that she was going to have a baby at all. Right now she couldn't contemplate having more children. Though she knew Nikos wasn't in love with her, she had proof he'd been deadly honest with her just now. Knowing the only child he would ever have was on the way might give him a reason to go on living.

But there was a part of him that didn't know if he was the father or not. And she had concerns, too, if a marriage between them was going to take place. She knew so little about him.

"Nikos?" She wiped the moisture off her face. "What is it you do for a living?"

He put his hands in his back pockets. "I used to work for the family shipping business. Now I'm in the process of starting up something new with Kon's elder brother. It's a project we used to talk about a lot."

"What's his name?"

"Tassos. He's a good friend, too, and married, with a child."

"Does it have to do with shipping?"

"No. We're planning to drill for natural gas in this part of the Aegean."

She knew Nikos was extraordinary, but to consider such an undertaking meant he was a man with vision. It took away her fear that he may have lost interest in everything, including life. To know he was working on something so vital for his own well-being, not to mention his country, thrilled her. Suddenly all those maps and charts she'd seen in the desk made sense.

"You don't need to worry that I can't take care of you," he said mockingly.

"Don't be absurd. The thought never crossed my mind. Nikos? Have you ever been married?"

A caustic laugh escaped. "No, although my family has had a girl picked out for me for years now."

Someone he loved? "You mean a beautiful, well-heeled Greek woman of a good family from your social class. Until I showed up yesterday, were you planning to marry her?"

"No. Natasa wants children. That's the one thing I can't give her."

But he's given one to me, his only one. Stephanie's heart rejoiced, despite the fact she knew he wasn't in love with her.

"When the news gets out that you and I are married, she'll have to move on," he muttered.

Nikos hadn't answered her question, but it didn't matter. Having another woman waiting at home, approved of by his family, explained why he'd never made a commitment to Stephanie on the island. She had enough charity in her heart to feel sorry for Natasa. Nikos was a prize who stood out from every male she'd ever met.

"If I were to agree to marry you, I wouldn't want a big wedding, Nikos."

"That's one area we fully agree on. We'll have it take place in private, with only Yannis and the Gregerov family as witnesses."

Alarmed, she turned to him. "Not even your parents?"

"Especially not them." Stephanie cringed, there was so much heat behind his declaration. "My father and I have been at odds for a long time."

"Your mother, too?"

"Let's just say she's loyal to my father and takes his part in most everything, to keep things civil."

That's why Nikos had never spoken of them on vacation. What could have happened to cause such a breach? "I'm sorry."

He eyed her soulfully. "No more sorry than I am for you to have lived with the hurt your mother inflicted, even if she did it for what she believed were the right reasons. My father justifies his decisions in the same way, without considering the damage. You and I share a common bond in that regard."

A world of hurt laced his words.

"After we're married, we'll drop by the house for a visit and tell them. They'll come around after the baby's born. My parents want grandchildren."

Stephanie eyed him carefully. "Do they know that the accident made you s-sterile?" she stammered.

Frown lines marred his face. "No. To them, children are everything. I don't ever want them to know."

She could understand that. If his family pitied him, he'd never be able to handle it. Stephanie was coming to find out what a private person he was. "Have you considered how they'll feel about me when we're introduced? I'm afraid they'll never see a pregnant American woman from a single family, with no father in the picture, as worthy to be your wife."

His features hardened. "You're carrying a Vassalos inside your body. That makes you the worthiest of all."

Her baby was a Walsh, too, but Nikos had his pride, and right now she knew he was clinging to that one bright hope. More than ever Stephanie realized he was planning on the baby being his. Otherwise there'd be no visit to his family, and her marriage to Nikos would be dissolved.

In order to put him out of his pain, she could swear on the Bible that he was the father, so he'd be reassured, but it would do no good. He needed proof.

Last night he'd told her to go below. She'd thought he was just being mean-spirited, because he was angry. But hearing about the boating accident that had cost his friend his life made her realize Nikos was being protective.

He'd been that way with her scuba diving, always watching out for her. It was his nature. She'd found that trait in him particularly reassuring and remarkable, but she still had reservations about marrying him.

"Earlier you mentioned divorce."

"That's because we don't know what the future will bring after the baby is born."

"You mean you might not want to live with me anymore, under the same roof."

He cocked his head. "As I recall, you were the one who said that what we had on vacation wasn't love. I'm just trying to cover every contingency so there won't be any more surprises. I'd say we've both had enough of them since we met in the Caribbean, and need to lay the groundwork if this is going to work."

Pragmatic was the operative word. She could hardly breathe. "Where would we live?"

"Because of my work with Tassos, I prefer the yacht for the time being. We'll dock at various ports so you can go ashore and explore. A little later on I'll buy us a villa on Oinoussa Island, near the Gregerov's, where you can set up a nursery. Tassos's wife, Elianna, and his younger sister, Ariadne, both had babies recently and speak excellent English. They're warm and friendly. You'll like them."

"I'm sure they're very nice."

The problem was, Stephanie didn't speak any Greek. Yesterday she hadn't known if Dev was even in Egnoussa. Last evening he'd turned into Nikos Vassalos; today he was talking marriage to her. But he wasn't the man she'd fallen headlong in love with on vacation.

That time with Dev could never be recaptured, and she found herself grieving all over again.

Unfortunately, she didn't have the luxury of shedding more tears. For the sake of their child, it was Nikos, not Dev, who'd proposed to her, in order to give their baby a legitimate name and legacy.

"Any more questions?"

"I'm sure more will come up, but right now I can't think of any." She clutched the chair railing. "Is there anything else important you haven't confided to me?"

He rubbed the side of his jaw. "Yes. If you agree to marry me, then I'll tell you the rest. But if you would prefer that I set you up on Oinoussa as my pillow friend and a kept woman, so I have access to you when the baby comes, then there's nothing more you need to know."

She'd heard the Greek phrase "pillow friend" before. A woman with no claim to the man who provided for her until he tired of her and sent her away. Stephanie couldn't imagine anything so awful.

"It's either one or the other, Stephanie, because under no circumstances will I let you leave Greece now."

Nikos meant it with every breath of his body. As he'd told her earlier, this baby was doubly precious to him now.

How bizarre that she was hesitating, when she'd come to Greece to find her baby's father and do the right thing for her child. But nothing had gone the way she'd envisioned it. Theirs would be a marriage without love.

"When do you plan for us to be married?"

"Tomorrow."

So soon! "Isn't there a waiting period?"

"Not with my contacts."

Naturally, Nikos knew someone in high places who could move mountains. Of course he did! Stephanie didn't doubt he could make anything happen, if he wanted it enough. "Where will ours take place?"

"At the small church on Oinoussa, with Father Kerykes, the village priest. He performed Kon's marriage. The man can keep a confidence and be trusted to honor my wishes."

Stephanie moistened her lips nervously. At least they would exchange vows in a holy place.

"What's it going to be, Stephanie?"

As a marriage proposal, it lacked all the passion and romance of her dreams. Without looking at him, she said, "For our child's sake, I want to marry you to give it your name."

"In that case, follow me. I have something to show you."

He left the lounge and walked across the corridor to the locked door, which he opened with a key. It was another bedroom, with two twin beds. "You're welcome to look in the closet."

What on earth?

Stephanie stepped past him and opened the double doors. On one side she discovered two military dress uniforms hanging, one was white, the other navy blue with gold buttons and braid. Next to them was a pair of crutches.

When she glanced on the other side, she was startled to discover half a dozen rifles and a special black scuba diving suit, along with a ton of very official looking gear that would be used by someone in the military.

She turned slowly and sought his gaze. "This equipment belongs to you. What does it mean? I thought you worked for your family's company."

"I did until I was twenty-two. By then Kon was divorced and we decided to join the Greek navy, much to my father's chagrin. We were in for ten years, but for the last five we've been Navy SEALs doing covert operations for our government."

That's why he was such an expert scuba diver.... All those years, Nikos had been fighting for his country. So far every minute she'd spent with him since she'd flown here provided one revelation after another.

"While I was on vacation with you, our unit got called up to do another highly classified mission. Since I can never use my own identity when I travel, and had to leave immediately, the note I left you was the best I could do."

The memory of that note flashed through her mind. *Unfortunately, I've had to leave the island because of an emergency at my work that couldn't be handled by anyone else.* Stephanie was so stunned, she sank down on one of the beds for support.

"Two days later the enemy ambushed our underwater demolition team. They bombed out of the water the fishing vessel we were using for surveillance. After it was detonated, I saw one of them swim away, before I could warn everyone. Kon died in the explosion. I was knocked unconscious and would have died if I hadn't been picked up and flown to the hospital."

"Nikos—"

"At first I was told the injury to my spine meant I'd be paralyzed from the waist down, but slowly feeling came back to my limbs."

"Thank heaven," she whispered in a trembling voice.

"The explosion should have taken me out, too!" His own voice shook with despair.

"But it didn't, and you have to believe there was a reason you survived."

His grim expression devastated her. "If you can make me believe that, then you're a saint."

Anger swept through her. "Kon didn't leave a child behind, but you did! Think about the fact that you're not paralyzed. Otherwise your child would grow up knowing you only in a wheelchair."

He bit out a Greek epithet before he murmured, "It turned out I'd been deeply bruised, but I could walk."

"You're one of the lucky vets, Nikos, and it's going to mean the world to your child that you continue to get better and stronger. Are you seeing a doctor regularly?"

"Yes," he whispered.

"What about exercise?"

"Among his many jobs, Yannis helps me do mine up on deck."

"I can help you with them, too."

"That won't be necessary, but since you're going to be my wife, I wanted you to know about my past. Now we don't ever have to speak of it again."

Nikos closed the closet doors and pulled her cell phone from his pocket. "Before we make any plans, you need to talk to your boss and tell him you can't work for him anymore." He handed it to her. "While you do that, I'll be in the galley. Come and find me after you've talked to him. If I'm not there, I'll be in the lounge."

With her heart thudding, she got to her feet. "Nikos?"

He paused in the doorway, darting her a piercing glance. "What is it?"

With that intimidating look, the question she would have asked him never made it past her lips. In fact, she already did have the answer to what would have happened to them if he hadn't had to leave the island to go on a covert operation.

Nothing would have been different. Like her father, when he'd left her mother, Nikos would have said good-bye to Stephanie, telling her the lie that he'd see her again, and that would have been the end of it.

Until his accident, Nikos's future had been tied up with another woman. As he'd told Stephanie a little while ago, Natasa wanted children....

CHAPTER FIVE

WHEN NIKOS BROUGHT the dishes from the lounge into the galley, he found Yannis enjoying breakfast. The balding seaman needed a lot of food to keep going. He looked up. "What are your plans for today, Nikos?"

"After you finish eating, we'll pull up anchor and head for Oinoussas . Once we've docked I won't need you until tomorrow. That ought to give you some time to do what you want with Maria." The widow who ran a small shop had become his love interest.

"She'll like that."

"But not you?" he teased.

Yannis stared at him. "What's going on? You no longer act like you're on the way to your own funeral."

"I'm getting married tomorrow to Kyria Walsh at the church of Agios Dionysios. *That's* what's going on. I need to make preparations."

His longtime widower friend looked shocked. "Married? To her? But what about Kyria Lander?"

Nikos started doing the dishes. He and Yannis took turns cooking and cleaning up. "She's not pregnant with my child, Yannis. Stephanie is."

"Ah..." The older man crossed himself. "This happened while you were on vacation in the Caribbean?"

"Yes."

A huge smile broke out on his weathered face. "Now I understand. I told you the scuba diving there was the finest in the world. I'm glad you listened to me. She's a real beauty, Nikos. It's about time you had some happiness in your life. Does your father know?"

"Not yet." Nikos was functioning on faith that she was pregnant and carrying his baby.

"There will be an explosion when your family finds out."

"It won't matter, because by the time they hear the news, she'll be my wife. You're going to be a witness, like you were for Kon."

"I'll be honored. Are you having a boy?"

"It's too soon to know. Maybe in another month. For the present we'll live on the yacht. Stephanie needs pampering and must eat for two. Since the last time I saw her, she's lost her glow, and needs to take care of herself." He refused to entertain the thought that she wasn't pregnant.

The older man nodded.

"Just so you know, I've told her how I got injured." He turned his head away from Yannis. "We have no secrets."

His friend got up and added his plate and mug to the dishwasher. "That's good. Otherwise, she'll find out soon enough," he said before leaving the galley. Since Nikos knew that, he would take steps to make certain Stephanie remained clueless about his PTSD.

After reaching for another roll, he headed for the lounge to phone Father Kerykes. They talked for a few minutes to settle on a time for the wedding, which was finally arranged to take place at four in the afternoon.

Next Nikos called Tassos, who seemed overjoyed to learn about the imminent marriage. He insisted that his wife and the Gregerov family would all be there to join in the festivities and take pictures. Later they would treat the bridal couple to dinner at their favorite local taverna.

Just as Nikos hung up, Stephanie walked into the lounge. Her closed expression told him little. "Did you reach your boss?"

She nodded.

"How did he take the news?"

"He wasn't happy about it and complained it would be hard to find someone to replace me."

"I don't doubt it. You're an expert diver and swimmer."

"There are enough qualified applicants in the file drawer that he'll have no problem. It's my reason for resigning he doesn't like."

"How so?"

"Grant is the fatherly type and feels I haven't known you long enough to consider getting married."

"Did you tell him you're pregnant?"

"I had to, otherwise he wouldn't let it go. In the end he grudgingly wished me well and told me he was glad I wasn't going to make another flight back to Florida, considering my condition. He's really a wonderful man. I promised him that after the baby was born, I'd send him a picture of the three of us."

Nikos liked the sound of that. But what if none of it turned out to be true? He rubbed the back of his neck. *You can't afford to think like that, Vassalos.*

"He'll send me my final paycheck when I give him an address."

"Good. What about your friends?"

She lowered her head. "I'll phone them after we're married." She'd called Melinda from Chios to let her know she'd arrived safely. "Otherwise they'll tell me to wait. I can't deal with that kind of pressure right now."

Nikos knew all too well about pressure, especially the parental kind. "In that case let's go up on deck, where you can sunbathe on one of the loungers until we dock at Oinoussa. After that we'll enjoy lunch in town. Among other things we'll do some shopping for clothes, since you only packed enough for a day or two."

Her jewel-like blue eyes fastened on him in apprehension. "What other things?"

"When did your doctor want to see you again?"

"In a month."

"Was everything fine?"

"Yes, except that I need to take iron."

"I saw the pills. To be on the safe side I want to stop in at the clinic, so we can meet the doctor who'll be taking care of you from here on out. Dr. Panos looks after Elianna and Ariadne, who both live on Oinoussa and have great faith in him. You'll need to set up your next appointment."

To his surprise she looked relieved. "I'm glad you thought of a good doctor for me. I really like my OB. He was my mother's doctor and has cared for me since my teens. It's hard to gain trust with someone else."

It was hard to gain trust, period, but since she hadn't fought him on this, Nikos was in a better mood than he'd been since leaving the hospital more dead than alive.

They were coming in to dock at Oinoussa. To Stephanie it looked surprisingly large and beautiful. Tranquil.

The town appeared to be draped over green hillsides, with several churches and charming houses displaying more of the local neoclassical style. Nikos told her there were no springs, so the water came from wells and a reservoir.

She looked over the yacht railing to the brilliant blue water beneath them. Everything was so clean and calm, it almost didn't seem real. This heavenly island was going to be her new home. While Nikos talked of the many beaches she could explore, her mind was on her baby who would be born here, a baby whose father wasn't a New Yorker named Dev Harris.

It started to hit her that she'd done something miraculous for her child, something her own mother couldn't bring herself to do for Stephanie. Because she'd found Nikos, this baby would have a full identity from the very moment of its birth.

Experiencing a sensation of euphoria, she turned to Nikos, who'd come to stand next to her. His hard jawline and arresting Greek profile stood out against the white houses and tiled roofs in the distance.

Suddenly, his black-fringed eyes fused with hers. For a moment, the dullness that had robbed them of their vitality since she'd come here vanished, and they shone with that same energy she'd glimpsed on vacation. "What were you going to ask me?" he murmured in a voice an octave lower than normal.

Her heart raced, because there were times when they seemed to be so in sync, they could read each other's minds. "What's your full name?"

She watched his chest slowly rise and fall. "Theodoros Nikolaos Vassalos."

Stephanie blinked. "Is Theodoros your nickname?"

"No. I don't have a nickname. It's my father's name."

"So when our baby is born, it will take your name first?"

"Yes, because it will be our first and only child."

"Are there rules about naming it?"

"You can name our baby whatever you like."

"But what if we follow the rules?"

"Then if it's a boy, we'd name it Alexandros, after my father's father."

She experimented outloud. "Nikolaos Alexandros Vassalos."

"That's right."

"And if it's a girl?"

"After my mother's mother, Melitta."

"I like both names. Are they still alive?"

"Yes."

She smiled up at him. "Our child will have great-grandparents, too. What a blessing," she said as he studied her hair and features.

"Nikos?" Yannis called out.

"I'm coming," he said, still staring at her with an enigmatic expression she couldn't read. "Get what you need to take with you. We're going ashore."

On legs that felt like mush, she hurried downstairs to freshen up and gather her purse. In a few minutes the men had secured the ropes, and Nikos walked her along the dock to a parking area, where he helped her into a dark blue car.

"Feel free to use this whenever you want to come into town. I'll give you a key when we're back on the yacht."

"Thank you."

She noticed he moved a little slower, but considering his horrendous accident, it was miraculous he could walk without most people noticing anything was wrong.

"Are you hungry?" he asked.

"I'm getting there."

"Did you take your pill for nausea?"

"Just a few minutes ago."

"Good. There's a taverna where you eat in the garden at the back. I'll introduce you to some authentic food I love."

Stephanie couldn't wait to see what he chose for them, especially since these islands were home to him and he knew the streets and shops like the back of his hand.

The proprietor of the small restaurant beamed when Nikos escorted her inside. They spoke in rapid Greek before the older man led them through some doors to a charming garden in bloom with fabulous wild hyacinths and orchids.

There were a dozen or so tables filled with tourists and locals. After settling at a table for two, they were brought fruit drinks and appetizers. One dish, something yellow, was prepared with olive oil, onions and fava beans, Nikos told her. Another, called *caciki,* tasted like cream cheese with cucumber and was served with slices of freshly baked, crusty *psomi* bread. It was followed by shrimp risotto and the grilled calamari.

Stephanie made inroads on everything but the octopus. "Maybe another time," she said to him. After his morose, brooding demeanor yesterday, the white smile he suddenly flashed her, the first she'd seen since her arrival, was so unexpected and startling that her breath caught. She found herself praying this side of him wouldn't disappear.

"Dessert?"

He had to be teasing her. She shook her head. "Thank you. The meal was delicious, but I couldn't possibly eat another bite or it might turn on me."

"Since we can't have that, let's go buy you some clothes."

They went back to the car and he drove to the other side of the village, where he stopped in front of a boutique. "Ariadne likes this store. She says it's trendy. I think you'll find something to your taste."

Inside, Stephanie discovered some great short-sleeved tops, pants, skirts, a couple sundresses and several dressy, long-sleeved blouses in filmy material for evening. Along with those she bought more lingerie, sleepwear and a bikini.

An older woman waiting on her spoke excellent English and was very helpful. As she was putting a white sundress and jacket with small purple violets around the hem in a box for Stephanie, she said, "You will look beautiful in this."

"Thank you."

Nikos stood at the counter with her. "It will make a lovely wedding dress, don't you think?"

Stephanie's heart plummeted. She knew Nikos wanted their wedding to be simple, but she'd still hoped to wear something more bridal to her own nuptials. The saleswoman must have seen her reaction, because to Stephanie's surprise she frowned at Nikos.

"A wedding dress? Oh, no. For that you need to go across the street."

"It's all right," she quickly told the woman.

In order not to upset Nikos, Stephanie forced herself to recover from her disappointment in a big hurry. "I love this dress. It will be perfect. Here's my credit card." She'd come to Greece unprepared, and didn't expect him to pay for a new wardrobe.

Too late, she realized her mistake. In front of the other woman he took the card away and replaced it with one from his wallet. Stephanie gave him a covert glance and saw that his dark expression was back. She should have guessed Nikos had too much pride to allow a woman to pay.

There were so many things she needed to learn about him. On the island they hadn't gone anywhere except the resort, rarely interacting with anyone other than the staff. This was a totally different situation.

He collected her purchases and walked her out to the car, putting everything in the backseat. While he did that, she climbed in the front passenger seat, but he held on to her door so she couldn't close it.

Stephanie looked up at him. "Aren't we going to leave?"

His jaw had hardened. "I saw the look on your face in there. You want a traditional wedding dress? We'll get you one. The most elaborate we can find."

She was crushed. "No, Nikos. Please get in the car so we can talk without everyone hearing us."

"There's nothing to discuss. Come."

After she got out, because he'd left her no choice, he locked the car and ushered her across the street to the bridal shop. An elegant, striking young woman, probably in her mid-twenties, caught sight of Nikos and couldn't look anywhere else. When she spoke in Greek, he responded in English.

"We'd like to see your designer bridal gowns for my fiancée."

Fiancée. What a joke.

"Right over here." She led them to a rack of sumptuous-looking dresses with price tags that meant this was a high end shop. "Go ahead and start looking."

Stephanie hated being in this position. The whole time she examined each dress, she could hear the ringless clerk talking to Nikos in Greek instead of waiting on her. The younger woman was deliberately flirting with him. Stephanie had to get a grip. In the mood he was in, she knew he wouldn't leave this shop until she'd found something for their wedding.

Last night, when she'd opened the closet containing his uniforms, she'd imagined him as a groom wearing the navy one with the gold buttons. With his black hair and olive skin, he'd look magnificent in it. Such an outfit required a wedding dress that lived up to it. If he was now intent on her wearing a designer gown, then she expected him to dress accordingly, too.

After some deliberation, she chose the most expensive dress on the rack. It was a simple princess style, but the floor-length veil of Alençon lace gave it elegance. It cost a fortune, but she didn't care. He'd accused her of using him for his money. *So be it.*

She turned to the clerk. "If you have this one in stock, I'll take it. In America I'm a size 4." Of course, Stephanie wouldn't be that size much longer, but she figured she could squeeze into it once she'd worn off her meal.

The clerk looked taken back. "I believe we do."

"Then please ring it up for me. My *fiancé* will carry it out to our car. Thank you."

Once the clerk went into the back room, Stephanie glanced at Nikos, who was leaning against the counter, his face implacable. No doubt he was feeling some pain, but he'd hate it if she drew attention to it. Maybe she could give him an out.

"Do you still want to stop by the clinic before we go back to the yacht? We could go there tomorrow instead."

His black eyes had taken on that glittery cast. "There's still time this afternoon, unless you're not feeling well."

She wasn't. Not exactly. But for once it had nothing to do with nausea. She sensed he still didn't trust her, and could cry her eyes out after the lovely meal at the restaurant, where he'd been more like…like Dev. "I'm fine."

Stephanie turned her back while he dealt with the saleswoman, then they left the shop.

He laid the dress and veil on top of the other packages before they left for the clinic, which appeared to be closer to the port.

When they went inside to Reception, they learned that Dr. Panos was operating and wouldn't be available. Not to be thwarted, Nikos made an appointment for her for September 1, a full workup.

With that accomplished, they drove to the parking area at the dock. He let her take a few bags, but he carried the rest, along with her wedding finery. Nikos should have brought his cane and let her do more to help, but that infernal pride of his got in the way.

Odd how she hadn't seen it manifest itself when they'd been on vacation. He'd been so mellow and easy-going then. She longed for that time to come back, but it never would.

Once he'd carried everything to her bedroom, he told her he'd be on the phone in the lounge if she needed him. For the next little while Stephanie removed the tags from her purchases and put them away in the closet and dresser.

She checked her watch. It was going on five o'clock. By this time tomorrow they would have been married an hour already.

She supposed she should try on her wedding dress, but for the moment she was too tired, and she'd need a shower first. Emotional fatigue had set in. Maybe later, after she got ready for bed, she'd take it out of the plastic cover and see how it looked on her.

With a sigh she removed her jeans, which were too tight, and lay down on the bed for a minute. She turned on her side, while her hand went automatically to the little bulge, which was definitely getting bigger. Tears trickled out of the corners of her eyes.

"All this is for you, my darling. Are you a little Alex who will be impossibly handsome like your father and turn the head of every girl? Or are you a beautiful little Melitta with flashing black eyes and hair like your daddy? Maybe by my next appointment, or the next, I'll know what to call you."

CHAPTER SIX

WHEN IT GOT to be seven, Nikos hung up the phone with the florist who would bring some flowers to the church tomorrow. All he had left to do was buy a ring. He'd do it in the morning, after Yannis came on board and Nikos had done his exercises.

Now that he'd taken care of everything he could, he got up and walked down the corridor to Stephanie's bedroom. He knocked, but couldn't hear any noise. Since he would have noticed if she'd gone up on deck, he knocked again.

Was she sick? She'd eaten more at lunch than he'd expected. Though he was relieved to see she had an appetite, he worried. Being very quiet, he turned the handle and opened the door a crack.

What he saw made his heart fail. Stephanie had removed her jeans and left them on the floor where she'd stepped out of them. Could he hope it was because they were too tight?

She was out for the count, with her long gorgeous legs uncovered. Jet lag had caught up to her. Her gilt-blond hair splayed out on the pillow. He'd seen this sight before, when she hadn't been wearing any clothes.

The memories came rushing back, increasing the

ache for her that had never gone away. Before he lost control, he closed the door and went to the galley to fix himself a cup of coffee and throw a salad together. Anything to keep busy. When she awakened, he assumed she'd want some dinner.

Nikos had just added the feta cheese when she appeared in the doorway. He shot her a glance. She was wearing a new pair of jeans and one of the flowered print blouses she'd picked out, this one in aqua and white. He noticed that she'd brushed her hair. Beneath the light it shone a silvery-gold, and given those dazzling blue eyes of hers, he'd never seen a woman with such fabulous coloring.

"At last."

"I didn't mean to sleep so long."

"You're still catching up. Are you hungry?"

"I am, if you can believe it. I just took another pill to make sure I stay feeling good."

"It seems to be working. Come all the way in and join me."

He'd already set the galley table with fresh fruit and rolls, plus apple juice and water for her. After serving the salad, he poured himself coffee and sat down opposite her. She reached for the water first and drank a full glass before eating a roll.

"The hot weather this time of year will get to you if you don't stay hydrated."

"So I've noticed. I'll start carrying a bottle around with me. Thank you for fixing dinner, but I hope you know I don't expect to be waited on."

"I enjoyed fixing our prenuptial meal."

She ate some of her salad, then rested her fork on the plate. "Speaking of our wedding, I'd like to explain about today. I didn't want to leave the impression that the white sundress wasn't good enough to wear at the church."

"You owe me no explanation."

"Yes, I do." She wiped the corner of her mouth with a napkin. "The clerk at the boutique mirrored my surprise, but she shouldn't have said anything."

"It's fortunate she did. As I understand it, the wedding day is for the bride."

Defeated by his attitude, she said, "You're right. Women are hopeless romantics in that department, but for me it's more than that. I know you wanted to keep the marriage simple, and I would have been perfectly happy with that if I wasn't pregnant, and our situation was different."

"What do you mean, different?" His question came out sounding like ripping silk, alarming her.

"We're not marrying for the normal reason and I've been thinking about the baby. When it's old enough, our child will want to see pictures of the wedding. Blame it on me for wanting to give it everything I was denied.

"I'm sure there are wedding pictures at your parents' home, of them in their finery. A child wants to see what its mother and father looked like on that special day, the way they wore their hair, what they were wearing. The moment I opened the closet in the extra bedroom, I could envision you in the navy blue uniform."

She leaned toward him excitedly. "Think what it would mean to our child to see you in it on your wedding day. He or she will know about your injury and why you had to leave the service earlier than you'd planned. It'll be preserving a piece of history.

"I have no history from my father, but you can leave some for our child. That's why I chose the dress in the bridal shop with the long lace veil. I know it was expensive, but the sundress wouldn't do justice to your uniform. There's nothing like a handsome man in his dress blues. Any woman would tell you the same thing."

"Stephanie—"

She took a quick breath. "Don't deny it. You *are* exceptional, Nikos. My friends on the island never did get over you. The girl in the bridal shop couldn't take her eyes off you, either. Our son or daughter will be so proud of you and the honorable way you served your country."

Nikos jumped up from the table, too full of conflicting emotions to sit there any longer. He'd leaped to the wrong conclusion after she'd chosen the most expensive gown in the shop. How easily his trust had worn thin. But he'd been remembering the conversation with his father.

You've never looked at Natasa or any woman the way you're looking at this female viper. I admit she's devilishly ravishing in that American way, but she's a mercenary viper nonetheless, one who knows your monetary worth and has come to trap you.

"Don't make me out to be a hero, Stephanie."

"Any man or woman who serves in the military is a hero, Nikos. I'll make two albums to preserve our wedding day. One for our child and one for your parents. Maybe Yannis will take pictures for us." After a pause, she added, "And perhaps the day will come when you'll tell me what they did to you that was so terrible you don't want them at the wedding."

Without looking at her he said, "My reasons run

fathoms deep, but they have nothing to do with you."
He doubted he could ever talk about it.

"Still, they *are* your parents and our baby's grandparents. I know an album of our wedding day will
mean everything to them, too. Please tell me you'll
wear the uniform."

"I'll think about it," he muttered. "I have to go
ashore again. When I leave, I'll set the security system. If it goes off, the harbor police will be alerted and
a signal will be sent to my cell phone. You'll be perfectly safe while I'm gone."

"Where are you going?"

"If you must know, to visit a friend."

"Tassos? Have you told him about the baby?"

"No one knows except Yannis. I'll see you in the
morning."

He left the boat and took off for the cemetery. It
would be his first visit to Kon's grave. Nikos had been
in the hospital when his buddy had been buried in the
Gregerov family plot. They'd always talked over everything important....

At three-thirty the next afternoon, Nikos waited at the
car, ready to take pictures that he knew were so essen-
tial to Stephanie's happiness. After breakfast he'd gone
into town to purchase her ring. When he returned, he'd
discussed the details of the wedding ritual with her.
Now it was time to go.

In a moment she stepped off the yacht. With Yannis's help she started walking along the dock in her
wedding dress. He doubted there'd ever been a sight
like her before, and he started clicking frame after
frame.

The few people around the port watching her would think they were seeing a heavenly vision of femininity in flowing white silk. Angel hair glinted silver and gold through the lace in the late afternoon sun. His throat swelled with emotion to realize this bride was going to be his.

In his gut he wanted the child she was carrying to be his. If it wasn't…

After seeing those jeans lying on the floor at the side of her bed last evening, he was convinced she was pregnant. He couldn't let any more doubts ruin today, which would never come again.

Stephanie's urgent plea had gotten to him and he'd put on his dress blue uniform. With nothing more than a few clues, she'd come all the way from Florida to find him, so he would know he was going to be a father. The least he could do was accede to her desires on this issue. He'd told Kon as much.

Nikos had been thinking a lot about Stephanie's father. Maybe he could be found through the help of a good private investigator. It was worth looking into, but that would have to wait until another day.

Yannis, acting in the place of her father, who would probably have given her away if he'd known of her existence, had worn his best white suit for the occasion. Nikos suspected the older seaman was enjoying this. He and Stephanie seemed to be getting along well already. Yannis was an old softie beneath his gruff looking exterior. It was clear she had already charmed him.

Nikos kept taking pictures until they reached the car. Her eyes, so solemn, met his for an instant before Yannis took over, asking them to pose together before they got inside. After some careful maneuvering to protect her dress, they helped her into the backseat, and Nikos sat in front while Yannis drove.

"Oh, Nikos!" she cried softly when they'd traveled a distance up the hillside. The small domed gray-and-white church of Agios Dionysios stood overlooking the sea. "How beautiful! I can't believe we're going to be married here."

"My wife and I were married in that same church forty years ago," Yannis said over his shoulder.

"Were you childhood sweethearts?"

"How did you know?"

Her gentle chuckle found new areas inside Nikos's body to warm. "Do you have children?"

"Two married sons and six grandchildren. They're fishermen and live here."

"You're a very lucky man."

"It was a lucky day when Nikos met you."

Well, well. Stephanie's takeover of Yannis was now complete.

"Thank you, Yannis."

The next few minutes were a blur as they pulled up to the church's parking area, where the Gregerov family was waiting *en masse* to greet them. Nikos introduced her to Tassos's parents, Castor and Tiana Gregerov, and his pretty wife, Elianna, who had dark blond hair. The other women were various shades of brunette. More pictures were taken. Nikos had hired a professional photographer to film everything.

In the rush he noticed Tassos reach for Stephanie and press something in her hand. Nikos was curious to know what it was, but he would have to wait. He saw her eyes glisten with tears before she kissed him on the cheek.

After embracing Tassos's mother, Nikos reached for Stephanie and they proceeded inside the church. He cupped her elbow, taking care with her veil, and walked to the front, where a dozen sprays of flowers filled the nave with perfume. He'd made certain there were some gardenias among the arrangements.

He had the distinct impression Stephanie was pacing herself carefully in deference to him not being able to move quite so fast. Small courtesies seemed to come naturally to her, another trait he couldn't help but admire.

Father Kerykes chatted with them before asking Tassos and Yannis to take their places on either side of the couple. The others sat in a group. For Stephanie's sake he presided in English, promising to keep it as short as possible. But as Nikos had explained to Stephanie earlier, there was no such thing as a short Greek wedding.

First came the service of the betrothal with the rings. Nikos had bought her a diamond ring, and a gold band for her to give to him, but she produced a ring he immediately recognized as Kon's. Nikos was so moved by Tassos's gesture, he choked up during the marriage sacrament.

It was followed by the crowning and ceremonial walk. Three times around the priest, who at the end removed their flowers. After they kissed the Bible, he pronounced his blessing on them.

"For better or worse, you're Mrs. Vassalos now," Nikos whispered as they walked down the aisle holding hands. "Are you feeling all right?"

"I—I'm fine." Her voice faltered. "Just thirsty."

"There's water in the vestibule, where we'll sign the documents. Then we'll go outside for more pictures."

By the time she emerged from the church with her bouquet, her cheeks looked flushed. Nikos urged everyone to hurry with the well-wishing and the pictures, but all of them were pressing for the bridal kiss. He did it swiftly, noticing Stephanie was fading fast. No wonder there was little response.

"Are you going to be sick?" he asked as he helped her into the car.

"No," she replied, but her voice trembled. "I'm just feeling weak and overheated. I'll be all right in a minute."

"In this weather a wedding like ours is brutal, but it's over now. The taverna will be cool. It's only a mile away. Drive fast, Yannis."

"I feel a fraud, Nikos. I'm a hot weather girl and don't know what happened to me in there."

"You're pregnant and have been through an arduous marriage ritual."

She lay back in the corner with her eyes closed. "Once was enough. I fought so hard not to faint in front of you."

"You made it. I'm very proud of you."

Stephanie started laughing. "I had no idea it would be an endurance test."

"Why do you think I put it off all these years?" he teased.

"Sorry. You must be stifling in your uniform. In hindsight I can see why you wanted me to wear the sundress." She let out a little moan. "I shouldn't have tried to find you in the first place. It forced you to have to go through all this."

With those words he felt as if he'd been rammed in the chest. She had no idea what was going through his mind. *"Don't ever say that again."*

Stephanie groaned. She'd said the wrong thing and had upset him, but it was the truth.

She might not have forced him with a sniper's rifle, like the ones in his closet. But the chance that this baby *could* be his had served as the ultimate weapon. Stephanie wasn't a fool. She knew he had doubts about its true paternity and wouldn't be satisfied until a DNA test was done, thus the reason for bringing up the possibility of divorce.

Over the last three months her heart had been hardened against him for his desertion of her, only to be softened after he'd insisted on either keeping her as his mistress or marrying her for the sake of their unborn child.

The *only* child he would ever have…

Their child, who would know its father and love him.

That's what this whole day had been about. She couldn't lose sight of that pertinent reality. After letting out an anxious sigh, she sat up straighter in the seat. "Forgive me for my show of temper. I can be a crosspatch sometimes. This has been a beautiful day and a wedding every bride dreams of. The flowers were beautiful and I love my ring. Thank you for making it all possible, Nikos."

"As long as you're feeling better and there's no harm to the baby, it's all that matters."

His need to protect had come out. No wonder he'd

snapped. She had to remember that and watch what she said from now on.

"We're headed for the most traditional taverna on the island, where there are few tourists. The owner's family makes their pasta and *dolmadakia* by hand. Besides oven-baked lamb and spit roast with lemon potatoes and garlic, you'll enjoy stuffed zucchini and meatballs, called *keftedes,* that melt in your mouth."

"I love meatballs."

"They're made in a tomato sauce that's out of this world."

Nikos sounded hungry.

Within fifteen minutes they were all assembled inside the authentic Greek restaurant, where everyone laughed and ate with great relish to the accompaniment of music. Stephanie found Kon's family members charming and felt the women's acceptance.

More pictures were taken, and toasts rendered, along with speeches from everyone including Yannis. It was clear they all loved Nikos. At one point he reached for her and kissed her warmly several times on the mouth, to the delight of their wedding party.

She couldn't drink alcohol and instead opted for a spoon sweet, which was a fruit embedded in syrup. "You taste delicious," he murmured as she kissed him back, always telling herself it was for the pictures that would go in the family album.

The evening wore on in a celebration she would always cherish, but when she looked around, she felt an ache in her heart that Nikos's family wasn't a part of it. As for herself, she wished her mother were still alive and could have been here.

If there'd been time, Stephanie would have invited

her friends who'd met Nikos on vacation. But it wasn't meant to be, because this had been pulled together on an emergency basis. Every flash of light from the diamond solitaire on her finger seemed to be sending a warning. *You may have had a wedding with all the trappings, but remember, it's the baby he wants, if it's his....*

She felt Nikos's gaze on her. "It's still too warm in here for you. I can see your eyelids are drooping. It's time to get you back home to bed, where you'll be cooler."

He stood up and announced they were leaving. "Stephanie and I thank you for making this day the most memorable of our lives." On that note he ushered her out of the taverna. Twilight had stolen over the island, giving it a magical feel. Nikos helped her into the car. Once more Yannis drove them down the hillside.

In the distance she saw the yacht. Nikos had called it home. Until he bought them a place here on the island to live, it would be hers, too.

Tassos and Elianna had followed them and brought half a dozen of the flower sprays from the church to decorate the lower lounge. His kindness today had touched her deeply and she gave him a hug before Nikos went up on deck with him. Besides being a good friend, he and her brand-new husband were in business together and had a lot to talk about.

Elianna started to leave, but Stephanie touched her arm. "Before you go, would you mind unbuttoning the back of my dress?" She put her veil on the couch to make it easier.

An odd smile broke out on the other woman's face. "You don't want Nikos to do it?"

Stephanie averted her eyes. "He wants to talk to Tassos right now."

"If you're sure."

"I am."

Elianna got busy. "It's the most beautiful dress I ever saw. How did you get it fastened?"

"Yannis helped me."

She let out a quiet laugh. "With all these buttons, it must have taken quite a while. Nikos didn't mind?"

"Yannis told Nikos to go away so he wouldn't see me until we left for the church."

"You are the envy of every woman in the Oinousses. People here thought he would marry Natasa Lander."

"I understand she's very lovely."

"Yes, and very rich. Her family is in shipping, too. They have the largest mansion on Chios Island. Nikos has surprised everyone."

"Our marriage surprised me, too," Stephanie said in a tremulous voice.

"Tassos tells me you two met on vacation in the Caribbean before the explosion happened."

"Yes. We were both scuba diving and paired up to explore." She was tempted to tell Elianna she was pregnant, but then thought the better of it, since Nikos hadn't chosen to tell Tassos yet.

"Ah. Nikos and Kon tried to teach me, but I got too frightened and couldn't control my breathing. I panicked."

"With more practice, you can overcome your fear of it, Elianna. I'd be happy to work with you if you'd like."

"Tassos wants me to dive with him."

"It's a beautiful world under the sea. If you can shake your fear, you'll learn to love it."

Stephanie felt the last button release and turned around. "What do you say?"

"Maybe I'll try again with your help."

"That's wonderful! I'll call you in a few days. We'll have lunch and make plans. Bring your baby. How old is he?"

"Theo is ten months and trying to walk."

"I can't wait to see him."

Elianna's dark brown eyes widened in surprise. "You won't be on your honeymoon?"

"We already had ours in the Caribbean. Right now Nikos is anxious to get started on the drilling with your husband. Since the accident that killed Kon, Yannis tells me he's been morose and unhappy. Now that he can't be in the navy, he needs to plunge into something else."

The other woman nodded. "Everyone took Kon's death hard, especially Tassos. He's thrilled that Nikos is interested in his ideas to start their own company."

"Then we need to help them. Right?"

They stared at each other for a moment before she nodded. "Yes. I'm glad he married you."

"I'm glad, too." If Elianna only knew the half of it. "Thank you for helping me." She gave her a hug before they parted.

While Tassos's wife disappeared up the stairs, Stephanie reached for the veil and walked down the hall to her bedroom to remove her wedding finery. First she stepped out of her dress and underskirt, which she hung in the closet. What a relief, so her stomach could expand! Another week and she wouldn't have been able to wear a size 4. The shop probably wouldn't have sold that gown any larger.

After a quick shower, she wrapped herself in her plaid flannel robe, then folded the veil with care and put it on the shelf above. Since she had no idea how long Nikos would be, she decided now would be the perfect time to phone Melinda.

With the room pleasantly cool, she lay down on top of the bed to make the call. So much had happened since her arrival in Greece, it felt like a century instead of a few days since she'd talked to her friend, let alone seen her.

After three rings Melinda picked up. "I'm so glad it's you, Steph. I've been worried."

"Don't be. Everything's fine. I have a lot to tell you, but if this is a bad time—"

"No, no. I'm taking a late lunch. Tell me what's going on. I'm dying to know how your hunch is panning out. Are you onto anything?"

Stephanie sat up, almost crushing the phone in her hand. "I found him, Melinda."

"You're kidding…"

"No. His real name is Nikos Vassalos. I don't know how much time I have before he comes to find me, so I'll make this quick."

For the next few minutes she told her what she could, ending with, "We were married a little while ago and now we're back on the yacht."

"Wait, wait, wait. You're *married?*"

"Yes, and I won't be coming back to Florida until after the baby is born and it's safe to fly." A noise in the hall attracted her attention, followed by a tap on the door. "Listen, Melinda— I'm not alone. I'll have to call you tomorrow. *Ciao.*"

She hung up and tightened the belt on her robe before opening the door. Nikos was still dressed in his uniform. His dark gorgeous looks affected her the same way they'd done on the island when she'd first laid eyes on him. She couldn't breathe then, either.

"I take it Tassos and Elianna have gone?"

He nodded. "I could hear your voice just now."

"Yes. I was talking to Melinda."

His black eyes searched the depths of hers. "Elianna told me you've invited her over in a few days."

Nervous, Stephanie clasped the lapels of her robe. "Yes, if that's all right. But if you have other plans for us, I'll phone her and we'll decide on a later time for a visit. I just assumed you would want to get back to work." When he didn't respond, she added, "Ours isn't a conventional marriage, and my coming to Greece interrupted everything. I don't want you to think you have to entertain me."

"Elianna told me you were going to try and help her get over her fear of scuba diving. How did she know you're an expert?"

At the way his brows furrowed, alarm shot through Stephanie's body. "While she was helping me out of my dress, I mentioned that we met scuba diving in the Caribbean. Did I say something wrong?"

He undid his tie and removed it in a way that made her pulse pick up speed. "Have you forgotten you're having a baby? You told me you were giving up diving."

"Nikos…that doesn't mean I can't swim at all. A little exercise for pleasure will be good for me. As for helping her, I won't be descending with her. I'll only work with her on the surface and encourage her until she overcomes her fear. Tassos wants her to do it, but she would probably feel better around someone like me who doesn't intimidate her."

"You mean Tassos *does*," Nikos drawled in a tone with an edge.

"He's her husband. She wants him to be proud of her, not watch her struggle."

In a quick move Nikos unbuttoned the jacket of his uniform. "Anytime you go in the water, I intend to be close by." With that parting remark, he started walking down the corridor.

"Wait…"

He paused midstride and looked back.

"Is Yannis still on board?"

"No. He won't be coming until morning. Why?"

That meant they weren't going out to sea. "I just wanted to thank him for everything he did for me today."

Nikos turned to face her. "It was no penance for him to button you up. He asked my permission, by the way. Yannis was worried you had no one to attend you."

Silly as it was, she felt heat swarm her cheeks. "He was very sweet."

"You can tell him that tomorrow."

She shoved her hands in her robe pockets. "Let me thank you now for making this day perfect. The Gregerov family couldn't have been kinder. I can see why you feel so close to them. I—I wish I'd been able to meet Kon." She stuttered over the words. "Your heart must have been touched to receive his ring."

"You can't imagine. It belonged to his grandfather, who gave it to him before he died. Kon wore it until he entered the military, then put it away to make sure nothing would happen to it until he retired. He planned to give it to a son if he ever had one."

Stephanie heard tears in Nikos's voice. She wasn't at all surprised at the depth of his grief and understood more than ever why she'd found him so broken when she'd first collided with him on board. "I'm sure Kon would have wanted you to have it."

She bit her lip, not knowing what else to say to comfort him. In fact, she feared her talking was irritating him. "Do you mind if I go up on deck for a while?"

He gave an elegant shrug of his shoulders. "This is your home. You can do whatever you like. When I was in town this morning, I bought some English speaking films on disk, which you can watch in the lounge. I won't set the security alarm until we're ready for bed."

"Thank you," she said to his retreating back.

After drinking some water from the galley, Stephanie went up on deck to take in the wonder of the night. She'd always lived by the water, but no place in her experience lived up to the beauty of these isolated islands set like glittering jewels on dark velvet.

Time passed, but Nikos still didn't join her. She had assumed that, in marrying her, he intended to sleep with her. She didn't know and he hadn't spelled out a detail like that, but without love on his part, she wouldn't be able to respond.

The problem was this was their wedding night. The kisses he'd given her at the restaurant had felt like a prelude to making love, but maybe they'd been for show. *For the photographs.*

Deciding not to wait for him any longer, she went below. There was no sign of him in the lounge. She could go down the hall and knock on his door. Was he waiting for her to come to him? Stephanie had no idea what to do. When they'd been together on the island, he'd never left her alone.

But they weren't married then, and he'd never intended to propose to her. They'd found intense pleasure together, but in his mind it had been temporary until he returned to his unit and ultimately to Natasa Lander.

Even leaving the other woman out of it, the more Stephanie thought about the situation, the more she understood that if he still didn't believe she was carrying his child, he wouldn't want to sleep with her. Maybe the thought was distasteful, even repugnant to him. Shivering at the possibility, she made up her mind never to expect a physical relationship with him.

After brushing her teeth, she took a pill and turned out the light. But once she was under the covers another thought came to her, with such force she let out a small cry and sat up. She didn't know why she hadn't considered it before. Since he was sterile, it was more than possible he was impotent, too.

Nikos...

If that was the case, then her heart grieved for him. He was such a proud man, it was only natural that since the explosion he wouldn't want to marry Natasa or *any* woman.

But he'd trusted Stephanie enough to marry her in order to give their child a father. In the process he'd become her husband in name only, to make it legitimate while he waited to find out the results of the DNA test. The dots were lining up.

No wonder he hadn't wanted his family to be a part

of today's nuptials. Everything was based on whether or not he was the father. She fell back and buried her face in the pillow to stifle her tears until oblivion took over.

CHAPTER SEVEN

THERE WAS AN animal suffering in the darkness. Stephanie kept looking for it, but couldn't find it. The whimpering turned into moans, torturing her. If only she could do something to help it. When it let out a piercing cry, the sound brought her awake.

All this time she'd been dreaming!

Trembling, she shot out of bed, incredulous that her mind had conjured anything so terrible. Something she'd eaten at the restaurant must not have agreed with her. Maybe a drink of water would help. She hurried to the bathroom. When she reached for a cup, her watch said 3:30.

After draining it, she went back to bed, but before she could fall asleep again she heard another blood-curdling cry. This time she wasn't dreaming. Without hesitation she threw on her robe and ran down the hall to Nikos's room. Though she knocked several times, he didn't respond. That was odd.

She knocked again before turning the door handle, hoping he wouldn't mind the intrusion. One glance inside the room told her he hadn't been to bed. It was still made. Had he gone to town?

Again she heard a moan, louder this time. It was

coming from the deck. An animal had to be trapped there. Maybe a cat or a dog, but she hadn't heard the security alarm go off. Needing something to protect her, she grabbed a fluffy bath towel from the bathroom and gingerly went up the stairs.

Once she was on deck the cry sounded like human sobbing. It was coming from the area of the transom. She walked toward it, then stopped dead in her tracks. There, crouching on the floor, was a man in a pair of sweats and nothing else. A crumpled blanket and sun bed lay nearby. He was on his knees with his head in his hands. As she got closer, she put a palm over her mouth.

Nikos!

Except it wasn't the man she knew. This version of him wasn't cognizant of the world right now. In a deep sleep, he was heaving great sobs, and fell over on his side. In the moonlight his tortured features glistened with moisture. Greek words broke from his lips. She couldn't make out anything except Kon's name, which he cried over and over again.

He'd been reliving the explosion. She knew about PTSD, but she'd never been with someone who was in the middle of a flashback. Without conscious thought she sank down on the sunbed next to him and put her arms around him.

"Nikos, wake up! This is just a bad dream." She rocked him for a few minutes, but he was too immersed. At one point he grasped her arm and let out a scream that raised the hairs on the back of her neck.

"It's all right, Nikos. It's over. Go back to sleep."

He twisted and turned, but held on while he sobbed on and off for another half hour. His fingers bit into her skin through the thin material of her robe, with such force she knew she'd have bruises. As terrifying as it was to see him like this, she felt a new closeness to him. His cries let her into his psyche, where he suffered. He'd seen the horrors of war, but the explosion that blew up his friend had traumatized him dramatically, and she was a vicarious witness.

Her gaze flew to Kon's ring. The reminder of their friendship must have set him off during his sleep. While she kissed Nikos's face, she put her leg over his to help quiet him, and murmured endearments.

Nothing seemed to help. Not at first. Then slowly, his fingers slid away and he fell quiet. Yannis would know all about this. Tomorrow Stephanie would get him alone and find out the name of Nikos's doctor. He needed help getting through his nightmares.

She held on to him. He'd said this yacht was home to him now. Had he decided to sleep up here? If so, how often did he do that? A few days ago, when she'd explored the lower deck, she'd noticed his unmade bed. The poor darling had probably suffered these incidents since being hospitalized.

Did he have more than one episode a night? She'd read that a flashback could be triggered by something and come on at any time. While he stayed on this yacht, he could be away from people.

It made perfect sense that he didn't want to be with family. But what if he hurt himself while up here on deck? What if he walked in his sleep and fell overboard? She'd heard the military wouldn't take sleepwalkers because they could be a danger to themselves and others.

After a few more minutes she eased away from him

and got to her feet. In his trauma, he'd flung his arm around and his elbow had caught the corner of her jaw. Both it and her arm felt sore, but it didn't matter. She covered him with the blanket, then reached for the towel and sat down in the lounger to watch over him. It was quarter to six. Who knew how long he'd sleep?

Since her arrival, he'd been watching her like a hawk because of the baby. What an irony, since it was *his* welfare she would be worrying about, along with her own, from here on out! He could injure himself without realizing it. She couldn't bear it if anything happened to him.

Before this new day was over, she planned to talk to his doctor. Nikos needed watching. One thing was certain: Stephanie wouldn't let him go to bed without her. Wherever he chose to sleep, that's where she'd be.

She'd sat there for another half hour when she saw Yannis come on board. The second their gazes met, she got up without making a sound and padded across the deck toward him.

"So you know," he whispered with a grave expression.

"Yes. I heard him during the night and came up to investigate. He's resting now, but I need to talk to his doctor."

He nodded. "The one he sees now is at the main clinic here on the island." The same place her new OB practiced. "His name is Dr. Ganis."

"Thank you. I'm glad you're back. I don't want him to know I heard anything until I've talked to the doctor."

"I think that would be best."

"Does he have flashbacks often?"

"Since he got out of the hospital, he had one the first night on the yacht, and last night."

"The wedding must have triggered thoughts of Kon. I'd better go below so he doesn't know I was up here."

"That's a good idea. He'll notice the red mark along your jaw."

Yannis didn't miss much. "I'll cover it with makeup." She patted his arm before hurrying toward the stairs.

The first thing she did on entering her room was get the card for her appointment out of her purse. Once she found it, she phoned the off-hours service at the clinic and left word for Dr. Ganis to call her back ASAP. As soon as she mentioned it was Mrs. Nikos Vassalos calling about her husband, the receptionist said she'd get in touch with the doctor right away.

For the next hour Stephanie got ready for the day. First her pills, then she took a shower and washed her hair. By the time she'd finished blow drying it, marks had come out on her left arm. She'd been afraid of that.

An application of makeup to the small blotch near her chin helped, plus a coating of mango frost lipstick. Then she headed for the closet. Stephanie thanked providence she'd had the foresight to buy a long-sleeved blouse. It was an all-over print in a gauzy fabric that hung just below the waist. She put it on and matched it with a pair of white pleated pants that accommodated her thickening figure.

Stephanie had just put on some lotion when the phone rang. She grabbed for it and clicked on immediately. It was Dr. Ganis's nurse, who indicated he had an opening at 11:00 a.m. if she could make it. Stephanie said she'd be there and hung up.

Things couldn't be working out better. She'd

planned to go into town, anyway, and buy some picture albums. While she was at it, she'd look for a handicraft store in order to start making a quilt for the baby. While Nikos did business, she intended to stay busy and not bother him.

Nikos had told her she could use the car. While she left him alone to work, she would carry on with her new life. Besides loving to explore new places, Stephanie liked to cook. She could shop for food and fix their meals from now on. This evening she planned to prepare a totally American meal and surprise him. She wanted to help him. There was no use kidding herself any longer. She loved him desperately.

Once Nikos had showered and shaved, he got dressed and walked down the hall. Just as he knocked on Stephanie's door, she stepped out of the bedroom and then collided, wringing a small cry from her. He grabbed her arms to steady her. To his surprise he saw her wince. Not only that, he noticed a slight bruise along her jaw that hadn't been there when she'd gone to bed last night.

"You've hurt yourself!"

She averted her eyes. "It's nothing." She tried to ease away, but he prevented her from walking out the door.

"What's wrong with your arms?"

"Not a thing."

"Since you're wearing long sleeves, I'll be the judge of that. Let me see." With care he pushed the sleeve of her blouse up her right arm, but found nothing. When he did the same thing to the left, it was a tug-of-war, but he prevailed and saw bruising both above and below the elbow. "Who did this to you, Stephanie?"

"No one. When I was in the galley, I was clumsy getting something down from the cupboard. It hit my jaw and jammed my arm against the counter by accident."

"I don't believe you. Look at me." When she refused, he said, "These marks were made by someone's hand. You're trembling. Tell me the truth."

Finally, she lifted her eyes to him. Those dark blue pools stared at him in pain. "About three-thirty this morning I heard moaning sounds coming from the deck and thought it was an animal. When I went up to see…"

Nikos drew in a burning breath. "You found *me*."

"Yes. I knelt down to try and comfort you."

He raked a hand through his hair, gutted to think she'd seen him like that and he didn't even remember it. "I could have done real damage to you and the baby. I could have given you a permanent injury, or worse!"

"But you didn't, Nikos. You were jerking, but you weren't violent and didn't walk around. Mostly you were crying Kon's name. I wouldn't have let myself get close to you otherwise."

"I should have told you about my PTSD. The doctor gave me medicine, but sometimes the nightmares come on, anyway. By not saying a word to you, I put you at risk and have done the unforgivable."

"That's not true!" She cupped his face between her hands. "I'm glad I saw you like that. It helped to understand what you've been going through since the explosion. You've suffered so terribly. All I wanted to do was calm you down." She kissed his lips. "After a little while you started to sleep peacefully again. I sat there until Yannis came on board."

Nikos backed away from her. "Forgive me."

"For deserting me on our wedding night?" she teased.

"You know what I mean." He rapped out the words angrily.

"Nikos, there's nothing to forgive. Now that I know, I have a suggestion, because I'm worried about you sleeping up on deck when one of those flashbacks hits. As you told me on the way out of the church, I'm your wife now, for better or worse, so why don't we sleep in the room with the twin beds? That way we can keep an eye on each other. When you have a bad night, you'll be safe and so will I."

"I'm not safe to be around anyone, especially not you when you're pregnant."

"Where did you get an idea like that? Thousands of soldiers come home from war with battle fatigue. They resume their lives with their wives, who are pregnant or not, and they work things out. To be honest, I asked Yannis for the name of your doctor this morning. I have an appointment at eleven. I'd like to hear what he has to say, and want you to come with me. But if you won't, I'm going anyway, because I need to know the best way to help you."

She headed for the galley. Nikos followed her and watched her reach for a roll. She darted him a glance. "Have you had breakfast?"

"I couldn't." He wasn't able to tolerate the thought of food after what he'd done to her. "Stop being so damn brave."

"That's what I've wanted to say to you since I saw that cane you've refused to use in front of me. Why don't we agree that *you've* tried to be brave long enough? Now it's time for us to be totally honest with each other. Otherwise how are we ever going to get through the rest of this pregnancy without losing our minds?"

Totally honest?

Since Stephanie had shown up on board the *Diomedes,* he wasn't sure he was in control of his mind or his fears. Deep down he wanted the baby to be his more than anything in this world.

She poured herself a glass of orange juice and drank it. "I'm planning to do some grocery shopping while we're in town."

"We just stocked up a few days ago."

"Have you forgotten you've picked up an American wife since then? She'd like to make you some of her favorite foods." He blinked. "Oh, and will you bring the camera? We can take it to a print shop and have the pictures downloaded so we can mount them."

He cocked his head, amazed by this unexpected domestic side of her. Being with Stephanie on vacation hadn't prepared him for this aspect of her. "Anything else?"

She flashed him a full, unguarded smile that knocked him sideways, though the sight of the bruise on her jaw tortured him. "Since we don't know the gender of the baby yet, I think I'll work up a white puffy quilt and stencil it with the outline of a lamb. I'd love your input on the materials."

She washed out her glass in the sink. "I'll get my purse and see you at the car. If not, would you give me the keys?"

He ground his teeth. "I'm coming with you." As they left for town it occurred to him he needed to buy them a house, preferably today. The yacht was a great place for him to do business with Tassos, but it was no place for a woman whose nesting instincts had already kicked in.

While Nikos waited for her outside the local photo shop, he called Tassos, who knew of a villa he'd had in mind for Nikos for a while. It was in a more exclusive area of town that would be perfect for them.

With a phone call to a friend who was a Realtor, he made the arrangements and gave Nikos the address. The man agreed to meet Nikos and Stephanie there at one o'clock. That would give them enough time to see the doctor first.

It seemed to make Dr. Ganis's day to find out Nikos was married to a wife who intended to be proactive over his PTSD. He gave them a card they should both read regularly, but all the time he spoke, he couldn't take his eyes off her.

Nikos had already come to learn that with Stephanie's blond beauty and lithe figure, taking her out in public was proving to be a hazard. He could already count one traffic accident because the male driver had taken one look at her and driven right into the back of another car. It served the poor devil right.

Nikos read what was on the card.

Always be truthful with your vet, always keep safety in mind. Don't walk on eggshells. Grieve for what is lost and move on. Stay on top of medications. Short periods of withdrawal to help control anger make sense, but withdrawing from life into a "bunker" is not helpful. Conflict is normal. Focus on the issue at hand and resist bringing up

issues from the past. Exercise, get regular meals,
good nutrition, plenty of rest and time for play.
Enjoy the good times. When bad times come, hang
on. Good times will come again.

As they got up to leave his office, Stephanie won
the doctor over with her final comment. "I consider
these bruises *my* mark of bravery." His laughter followed them out the door.

Unable to help himself, Nikos gave her waist a
squeeze as they left the clinic for the car. "Do you mind
if we put off all the shopping until tomorrow? I have
a surprise for you that could take up most of our day.
Let's grab a bite to eat before we meet Mr. Doukakis."

Stephanie couldn't imagine what it was. However, she
was so happy to see that Nikos had forgiven himself
for the bruises, and seemed to be in a mellower mood,
that she didn't care what they did as long as it was together. When he'd interrogated her in the doorway of
her bedroom earlier that morning, she'd been frightened that irreparable damage had been done to their
relationship.

At one of the sidewalk cafés she ordered a lime
crush drink and discovered she adored the bruschetta
made with apple and goat cheese. Nikos downed a
whole loaf of lamb rolled slices. Taking the doctor's
advice, he passed on caffeine-laden coffee and ordered
decaf. Stephanie made a mental note to buy the same,
so he would sleep better.

When she couldn't eat another bite, he drove them
up a hillside covered with flowering vegetation. They
came to a charming, two-story villa, where he stopped

behind the car parked in front. The man at the wheel had to be this Mr. Doukakis he'd mentioned.

She flicked a glance at Nikos's striking profile. "What are we doing?"

He shut off the engine and turned to her. "Hoping to buy us a house."

What? "But I thought—"

"Let's not go there." He cut her off. "I'll use the yacht for business, but decorating one of the rooms below deck for a nursery is absurd."

"I agree, and have no intention of doing any such thing. As for the quilt, it'll be a gift for our baby. I'm looking forward to making it, that's all."

"You're avoiding the issue, Stephanie, and I know why. If you don't like the looks of this house, we'll find something better."

Just when she'd been on a real high, he'd sprung this on her. Already she could see the writing on the wall. While she was at the house, he'd work late, then call to tell her he was staying on the yacht overnight. No way!

"I don't want a house, not with you coming and going when the mood takes you."

"You mean you don't like *this* one," he thundered. "If you want a mansion, just say so and I'll accommodate you."

Now *she* was angry. "I thought we left that issue in the past, but I can see you won't let it go, about me wanting to marry you for your money. For your information, I *love* living on the water."

She watched his hands grip the wheel tighter. "It's no place for a baby."

"The baby won't be here for months! Why did you bother to marry me, Nikos? Sticking me in a house will make me feel like a kept woman. I thought you'd been honest with me, but you weren't."

His features had turned into a dark mask of anger. Good!

"Since it obviously irritates you to have a woman around, I'll settle for living on my own boat, to stay out of your way. Instead of a house, buy me one of those little one-person sailboats bobbing at the marina on Egnoussa. I'll pay you as much as I can when the condo sells."

"Don't say another word, Stephanie."

"You started this, so I'll say what I like. It would cost only a fraction of what it would take to buy me a mansion I don't want to live in by myself. Or better yet, let me *rent* a sailboat. That would be fair. Yannis could take me to pick one out, and bring it across to moor by the yacht. 'His and hers.' We'll be the talk of the island."

While she was still shaking from their angry clash, he got out of the car and walked to the other one. The two men spoke for a few minutes before Nikos came back and levered himself into the front seat once more.

She sensed he'd love to wheel away on screeching tires, but he controlled himself on the drive back to the dock. By the time they reached the parking area, she'd repented of the way she'd blown up at him.

The doctor's advice came to mind. Conflict was normal. Focus on the issue at hand, not past issues.

"Wait, Nikos," she said as he opened the door. "I apologize for my behavior. Instead of welcoming your gift, I threw it back in your face. I'm so sorry. Please forgive me."

He shifted his gaze to her. "I should have prepared you for what I had in mind."

She shook her head. "I'm afraid my reaction would have been the same. Look, I realize you were happy living by yourself on the yacht with Yannis. Then I came along and disturbed your world. If I promise not to be a nuisance or get in your way, can we start over? But I can't just be a lump around here. Give me a job and I'll do it, besides my share of the cleaning."

One dark brow lifted. "You really want to cook?"

"Yes. As many meals as you'll let me."

"Then so be it. That'll free up me and Yannis to do other work." Nikos closed the door. "Let's drive to the market. Ever since you mentioned American food, I've been relishing the thought of it."

Stephanie sighed in relief that they'd survived another skirmish. "Thank you. I promise you won't regret this."

Following her fried chicken for dinner that evening, both men finished off the apple pie. The fact that there were no leftovers told her she'd hit a home run on her first try.

Yannis got up from the table and winked at her. "If all your meals are this good, I'm going to put on weight."

"I'm glad you liked it."

After he disappeared, Nikos sat back in his chair with the hint of a smile. "I guess you know you're permanently hired. I'd help you with the dishes, but we're headed for Engoussa right now. I need to assist Yannis."

"Do you have business there?"

"Yes. I want my parents to meet you tonight."

Her heart started racing. "Do they know about us?"

"Not yet. I phoned and told them I'd be coming by. They'll send a car. It's time they met their daughter-in-law, before the news of our wedding reaches them."

The surprising revelation filled Stephanie with ambiguous feelings, of relief that their secret would be out, and anxiety because she wanted to make a good impression for Nikos's sake. "I'll wear the long-sleeved blouse with one of my new skirts."

He nodded his dark head. "Stephanie…" The way he said her name made her think he was dead serious. "Follow my lead and don't let my father intimidate you."

After Nikos left the galley, she put their plates in the dishwasher, already feeling intimidated. She wished she knew what kind of deep-seated trouble lay between Nikos and his father. If he'd just given her a hint…

She dressed for the evening, then waited up on deck as the yacht pulled up alongside the dock on Egnoussa. Fairyland at night. Few people were out.

Nikos joined her, looking fabulous in a silky black shirt toned with dark gray trousers. To her surprise he'd brought his cane. This was a first. Using it for support, he reached out with his free hand and grasped hers. They left the yacht and started walking along the pier, toward a black car she could see waiting in the distance.

It appeared the ordeal he was about to face had drained him physically. Stephanie would do everything in her power to help him. As they reached the car, she gave his hand a squeeze. But whatever his reaction might have been was lost when a stunning dark blond woman with appealing brown eyes opened the door and stepped out of the driver's seat.

"Nikolaos. It's been such a long time."

"Natasa." He let go of Stephanie's hand long enough to kiss the woman on both cheeks. "I didn't know you were on the island."

Stephanie felt de trop. This was the woman he would probably have married if Fate hadn't stepped in to change his life.

"When I heard you were coming, I arrived early and asked your parents if I could meet you at the dock so we could talk in private. They assumed you'd be alone. Who's your friend?"

Nikos turned to Stephanie. "This is Stephanie Walsh from Florida, in the States. She arrived a few days ago. Stephanie? This is Natasa Lander, an old friend."

"How do you do, Ms. Lander."

In the semidark, Natasa's face lost color. "Ms. Walsh," she acknowledged. "How is it you know Nikos?"

Stephanie groaned inwardly for this poor woman, who'd carried a torch for him all these years. It was no wonder. How could any other man compare?

"I was on a scuba diving vacation in the Caribbean months ago and we met."

"Why don't I drive?" Nikos offered. "When we reach the house, we can all catch up on each other's news at once."

Nikos... This was a terrible idea, but what could she do? While he helped Natasa into the backseat, Stephanie grabbed his cane and hurried around to the front to get in. As far as she was concerned, this was worse than any nightmare.

En route, Nikos chatted with Natasa the way you'd do with an old friend, drawing her out, until they reached the impressive Vassalos mansion with its cream-and-beige exterior. His ancestral home stood near the top of the hill next to equally imposing ones Stephanie had seen on her first day here. The burnt-orange-tiled roofs added a certain symmetry that gave the town its charm.

He pulled the car around to the rear and parked. Both Stephanie and Natasa moved quickly, not waiting for his help. Natasa went in the rear entrance first. Stephanie handed Nikos his cane, but he put it back in the car, then reached for her hand.

"Ready?" he asked under his breath. That forbidding black glitter in his eyes had returned. It was clear he hadn't been expecting Natasa. Stephanie suspected the other woman's appearance had been orchestrated by Nikos's father. Yet unseen, the older man made an adversary that caused the hairs on the back of her neck to stand up.

When she nodded with reluctance, she heard his sharp intake of breath. "Maybe this will help." He pulled her into his arms and found her mouth, kissing her with a fierceness she wasn't prepared for, almost as if he was expecting her to fight him.

Stephanie clung to him, helpless to do anything else, and met the hunger of his kiss with an eagerness she would find embarrassing later. At last he was giving her a husband's kiss, hot with desire, the one she'd been denied last night. Whether he was doing this to convince himself he was glad he hadn't married Natasa, she didn't know. But right now she didn't care.

The way he was kissing her took her back to that unforgettable night on the island, when they'd given each other everything with a matchless joy she couldn't put into words. He pressed her against the doorjamb to get closer. One kiss after another made her crazy with desire. Stephanie was so in love with Nikos that nothing existed for her but to love him and be loved.

All of a sudden she heard a man's voice delivering a volley of bitter words in Greek. It broke the spell. Gasping for breath, she put her hands against Nikos's chest. He was much slower to react. Eventually, he let her go, with seeming reluctance.

Still staring at her, he said, "Good evening, Papa. Stephanie and I will be right in. Give us a minute more, will you?"

Another blast of angry words greeted her ears.

"She doesn't speak Greek, Papa."

"How dare you bring this gold digging American into our home!"

That was clear enough English for Stephanie, who was thankful Nikos was still holding her. She eyed his father covertly. Except for their height, the formidable older man with gray hair didn't look like Nikos.

"I dare because she's my wife. We were married in a private church service yesterday. I wanted you to be the first to know."

"Then we'll get it annulled," he answered, without taking a breath.

"Not possible, Papa. Father Kerykes officiated. Naturally, I expect you and Mother to welcome Stephanie into the family. If you don't, then you'll never be allowed to see your grandchild."

Stephanie could hardly breathe. Nikos was claiming their child as his own even though he didn't have proof?

"So you *are* pregnant!" his father virtually snarled

at her. "I told Nikos I suspected as much when I heard you'd come to Egnoussa to track him down. Trying to pass off your baby as my son's? There's a word for a woman like you."

The man had just provided part of the source for Nikos's basic distrust of her. She eased away from him and stared at his dad without flinching. "I'm sorry you feel that way, Mr. Vassalos. I've been anxious to meet the father of such a wonderful, honorable man. You're both very lucky. I never knew my father.

"But I have to say I'm sad you're on such bad terms. Our baby is going to want to know its grandparents. I can only hope that one day you'll change your mind about me enough to allow us into your life. Now if you'll excuse me, I'm going to wait in the car while Nikos spends some time with you and your wife. *Kalinihta.*"

Good night was one of the few words in Greek she'd picked up, from listening to Nikos and Yannis.

No sooner had she climbed in the front seat and shut the door than Nikos joined her behind the wheel. He didn't speak the whole time they drove to the port. Stephanie knew better than to talk, but her heart was heavy for him and the tragic situation with his father.

After he pulled around to the parking area of Vassalos Shipping, Nikos left the keys on the floor of the car and they walked back to the yacht. "I want to get to know your family, Nikos, but I couldn't possibly stay in their house, since it would cause too much stress for everyone.

"Much as I want to make things right, I can't tolerate your father's attitude or the way he spoke about me.

Maybe in time things will get better. I could hope for that, but not right now. I trust you understand."

Silence followed her remarks, until he helped her step on the deck. "I owe you an explanation."

She threw her head back, catching sight of his tormented expression. "If you mean that kiss you gave me at the back door was supposed to be an in-your-face gesture for your father's digestion, I already got the message."

"If you think that, you couldn't be more wrong," Nikos grated. "Just when I thought my father had run out of tricks, there he was once again, trying to set me up with Natasa. But this time you were there. No amount of makeup could conceal the bruise on your jaw. It stood out in the moonlight, reminding me that you'd unwisely faced my demons and held me during the night, despite the consequences to you and the baby.

"Tonight I realized how very beautiful you are and how courageous to have forgotten yourself to help me. No one has ever been that self-sacrificing for me. In a rush of emotion I felt the need to show you how I felt. Since my father chose that moment to appear, then he has to live with that picture, because I refuse to apologize for something that had nothing to do with him."

Stephanie swallowed hard. Nikos's sincerity defeated her. "Do you think Natasa saw us?"

He gave an elegant shrug of his shoulders. "If she did, let's hope it was cathartic."

For the other woman's sake, Stephanie hoped so, too, and looked away. "I would have liked to have met your mother."

"One day I'll introduce you to her and the whole family. They're very nice people."

One day. That sounded so lonely.

"Nikos…about the baby—"

The mere mention of it brought a look of anxiety to his dark eyes. "Are you all right?"

"I'm fine!" she assured him, not wanting to add to his worries. "I was just surprised you told your father."

Nikos's hard body tautened. "Hearing the truth from my lips has put an end to his dream of my marrying Natasa in order to consolidate our families. He's been stuck in that groove for a decade. Since I've refused to work in the company, he has lost his hold on me."

Stephanie drew closer to him. "What's he afraid of?"

Nikos studied her for a long moment. "At one time he thought I was Costor Gregerov's son."

It took a second for Stephanie's brain to compute. When it did, she let out a gasp. "Your mother and Kon's father?" Surely she'd misunderstood.

"It's complicated. My mother and Kon's mother were best friends growing up on Oinoussa. My parents married first and had two children before I came along. But Tiana's eventual marriage to Costor brought a lot of grief to her family, because he's part Turkish.

"In some corners of society, the Greeks and Turks refuse to mix. The built-in prejudice against him caused a painful division. For Tiana, it was she against the world once she'd married Costor. They had four children before Kon came along."

As Nikos peeled back the layers, Stephanie's anguish for his pain grew.

"My mother defended Tiana's decision and was always sympathetic to Costor. At one point someone started a rumor that she got too close to him. It wasn't true, and both my mother and Costor always denied it, but my father was a bigoted man. He believed it and there was an ugly falling out that never healed."

Stephanie bit her lip. "DNA testing wasn't available when you were born."

"No, but it wasn't needed. As Tiana once told me, the stamp of a Vassalos was unmistakable. Unfortunately, my parents' marriage suffered. It's a miracle my mother didn't leave him, but she loves him. She remained close friends with Tiana, which threw me and Kon together, but the damage done to both families during those early years was incalculable."

Stephanie clutched the railing. "What a tragedy."

Nikos nodded. "My father became controlling and possessive. He tried to rule my life and choose my associates, making sure I didn't mix with people like Kon's family. By my teens he'd cultivated a friendship with the Lander family, laying the groundwork for the future he envisioned for me. But he went too far when I was forbidden to spend any more time with Kon, who'd become like a brother to me. Naturally, I defied my father, because Kon had done nothing wrong."

Stephanie darted him a glance. "Except to be a constant reminder of the past."

Nikos breathed deeply. "Everything reached a boiling point when Kon needed money for his divorce. I gave him what I'd saved from working. My father found out and threatened to disown me. I told him it wouldn't be necessary, because Kon and I had already joined the navy and would be shipping out."

The night breeze had sprung up, lifting the hair off Stephanie's cheek. "You and Kon shouldn't have had to suffer for your father's paranoia. How long did it take him to beg your forgiveness?"

"His pride won't allow him to beg. For my mother's sake I visited them on leave, but things have never been the same. Underneath he's still a bigot and distrustful."

"Evidently he doesn't like Americans, either," she whispered.

"He's predisposed to dislike anyone whom he imagines might have control over me. I invested my military pay and bought the *Diomedes* so I would never have to be beholden to him."

Heartsick for Nikos, Stephanie looked at her husband through new eyes. Here she'd suffered all her life, wishing she knew anything about her father, while Nikos... Her ache for him grew worse. "I can't tell you how sorry I am."

"You've married into a complicated family. Don't try to sort it all out tonight. You look tired, which comes as no surprise after your wrestling match with me last night."

Stephanie would do it again and again if he'd let her, but after this incident with his father, she sensed he was unreachable. True enough, his next words left her in no doubt.

"You go below. I'll stay up here and wait for Yannis. As soon as he comes, we'll leave port and head back to Oinoussa."

CHAPTER EIGHT

September 1

NIKOS HAD SEEN his wife in a bikini when they swam on one of the isolated beaches. Oftentimes Elianna came with them. With the growing evidence of her pregnancy, there'd been a decided change in her since April, when they'd met. But he broke out in a cold sweat as he watched the doctor spread the gel on Stephanie's tummy to do a Doppler ultrasound.

"Ooh, that's cold."

"All my patients say that."

"Are you all right?"

"Of course she is." Dr. Panos smiled at Nikos. "Sit down, Kyrie Vassalos, and watch the screen. We'll take a peek inside to see how your baby is progressing. This will take about ten minutes."

Nikos couldn't sit. More than his concern about the gender of the baby was the fear that something might show up to indicate a problem. The doctor moved the probe over her belly. Pretty soon the sound of a heartbeat filled the examination room.

"Can you hear that?" Stephanie cried in excitement.

"Your baby has a good, strong heartbeat. Keep watching the screen."

Whether it was his baby or not, Nikos stood there mesmerized by the sight of pictures that gave evidence of the living miracle growing inside her.

The doctor nodded. "I like what I see."

"Then it's healthy?" Stephanie's anxious question echoed that of Nikos.

"At this stage everything looks fine and normal. The baby could fit in the palm of your hand."

Yet you could see it was a perfect baby. Nikos could only shake his head in awe.

"But it needs to turn for me if we're going to find out its gender." Dr. Panos pressed in various spots. "I know you're uncomfortable after drinking all that water, Stephanie. Just a few more minutes, then you can use the bathroom."

She let out a big sigh. "As long as there's nothing wrong, I don't care if it's a boy or a girl."

Since the night she'd held him during a flashback, Nikos had secretly worried he might have damaged the baby in some way. At the good news, exquisite relief swamped him.

Though she'd promised not to come near him at night, that fear had caused him to lock his bedroom door when he went to bed so she wouldn't try to help him during an episode. Much as he desired sleeping with her, even if it would only be in the cabin with twin beds, he didn't dare.

"From the positioning, I don't know if we're going to be successful. I need a better angle. Otherwise we could try another one in eight more weeks, at the end of your second trimester." He continued to move the probe. "This one is active and kicking."

"That sounds good to me," Stephanie told the doctor. "I want to teach it to scuba dive."

"So you're a diver."

"We both are," Nikos volunteered.

After a surprisingly long period of silence, Dr. Panos said, "Then let's hope he shares your interest."

"He?" they exclaimed in unison.

"See that?" He pointed to the baby's anatomy. "There's your boy. Got a name for him yet?"

Her eyes filled with tears as she looked at Nikos. "Nikolaos Alexandros Vassalos!"

Stephanie...

Dr. Panos chuckled. "Well, that sounded definite." He turned off the machine and handed each of them a photo. "You can get up and use the restroom now. Keep taking your iron and vitamin pills, get plenty of rest, and I'll see you in a month. Make your appointment with my receptionist on your way out."

"Thank you!" Stephanie murmured emotionally.

"You're entirely welcome. Congratulations."

Nikos shook his hand, then studied the pictures while he waited for her. He couldn't help remembering the time in the hospital when he'd been told he would never father a child, would never know the joy of hearing those words from a doctor, let alone be given pictures.

Stephanie's glowing face was the first thing he saw when she met him out in reception. With excitement she scheduled her next visit, for early October.

Don't let your doubts drag you down now, Vassalos.

He ushered her outside to the parking lot. "This calls for a celebration. What would you like to do?"

"Go to a furniture store and buy a crib. I've almost finished the lace edge on the quilt and can't wait to see it set up in my room."

"Be honest with me, Stephanie. Wouldn't you rather we went looking for a house first?"

His question brought shadows to her eyes. "I thought we went through this a month ago."

"I was afraid you were humoring me. I thought to give you a little more time."

She put her hands on her hips. "I think it's time you were honest with me. Are you dying to live in a house? Or have you decided you want to deposit me in one before you go crazy? I'm getting the message you need space away from me, while you conduct your business meetings on board. If that's the case, please say so now."

"Space is not the issue."

Color tinted her cheeks. "Then what is?"

"I was only thinking of your happiness while you make preparations for the baby that's coming."

"I'm perfectly happy, but apparently you're not. So I have an idea. While I go back to the yacht, you can look at furnished homes to your heart's content with Mr. Doukakis. Let me know when you find the one you think will suit me best, and I'll move into it."

Damn. On this red letter day he'd mentioned a house only to please her, not to undo all the joy she'd been feeling since her visit to the doctor.

"Not every woman with a baby coming wants to live on the water."

"But I'm not every woman," she retorted. "The yacht

is home to me. From my condo I used to watch ocean-going vessels out on the water and dream about sailing around the world on one. That idea has always intrigued me."

He nodded. "Then I won't mention buying a home again. After we find the right crib, let's have lunch on the island before we return to the *Diomedes*."

Now that she had run out of steam, she seemed to droop a little. "Nikos? Forgive me for snapping at you. I can't believe I talked to you like that when you're always so wonderful to me. The truth is I've been so happy, I haven't wanted anything to change. But that's the selfish part of me talking. I'll go with you to look at a house, and never complain again. The last thing I want to be is a carping wife." Her voice caught.

"Carping?"

"Yes, as in a petty woman who looks for trouble and finds fault at every turn, appreciating nothing. With your command of English, I'm surprised you haven't heard that word."

He cradled her lovely face in his hands, forcing her look at him. She'd picked up a golden glow since living on the yacht. Her eyes shimmered an intense blue. Nikos could easily get lost in them. "You're none of those things and you know it."

"I'm the ball on your chain, holding you back." She was serious.

Laughter rose out of his throat. "From what?"

She averted her eyes. "From whatever you planned to do before I ventured into Vassalos territory without permission. I look back on it now and can't believe I was so audacious."

Right now he couldn't relate to the man who'd

collided with her along the pier. That man had been drowning in despair, without a glimmer of hope. For a moment he'd thought he was hallucinating. But the minute he'd touched her, he'd realized she was no figment of his imagination. Stephanie Walsh had materialized in the flesh.

Nikos slid his hands to her shoulders, covered by her leaf-green top. His fingers played with the ends of her silvery-gold hair. Desire for his pregnant wife was eating him alive. Oh yes, she was pregnant. He had the proof resting in his pocket.

With their mouths so close, it was all he could do not to devour her in front of the people coming and going from the clinic. But he did kiss her very thoroughly, and was shaken by her powerful response.

"I dare you to kiss me like that when we're back on the yacht and no one is watching," she teased.

That's what drew him to Stephanie. Though she could be fiery, she didn't take herself too seriously, and retained a sense of humor lacking in the women he'd known. They'd had a month of togetherness and he still wasn't tired of her. If anything, he couldn't wait to get her back to the yacht. He'd taken the day off work and no one else would be around.

"I'm so glad you know how to put this crib together. I wouldn't have a clue." Stephanie sat propped on her bed, finishing the lace edge of the baby quilt while she watched her husband work. As she studied his dark, handsome features, a feeling of contentment stole through her.

She picked up the ultrasound picture and studied it for the hundredth time. Knowing she was carrying his son made this day unforgettable. How could Nikos possibly not know and feel that this was *his* baby?

But every time she put herself in his shoes, she remembered the horror story about his parents. And not just his parents, but the tragic lie that had bound Kon to the Frenchwoman. Trust was one of the most vital essentials in a relationship, let alone a marriage. Nikos's view of life and women had been flawed because of circumstances, yet there was a part of him that was still giving her a chance. She loved him for that modicum of trust in her, loved him with every fiber of her being.

"It's your fault I feel stuffed after eating lunch." It had been a marvelous lunch of filet of sole with grapes and capers. "I've gained too much weight since my first doctor's appointment, in Florida. Do you realize there's no such a thing as a bad meal on Oinoussa?"

He darted her an all-encompassing glance that sent a shiver of excitement through her body. "Nor on the *Diomedes*. The acquisition of my new cook is putting back the pounds I lost in the hospital. When we were on the island, you never told me you're such a fabulous cook."

"You and Yannis are full of it, but it's nice to hear. Mom was always at work, so my grandmother taught me a lot of her recipes."

"Yannis says you put Maria's cooking to shame."

"It's the butter instead of the olive oil."

"I like both."

"So do I. The blending of two worlds." She let out a sigh. "Nikos? I've started picking up some Greek around you and Yannis, but it's a slow process. I want to be able to talk to the baby in both languages. How would you feel if I found someone on Oinoussa to tutor me for a few hours every day? You speak perfect English. I feel embarrassed that I can't converse in Greek."

"I think it's an excellent idea."

"You do?" She'd been holding her breath in case he told her the future was still uncertain and he didn't think it was necessary.

"I'll look into it." On that satisfying note he got to his feet. "The crib is finished. What do you think?" He'd placed it against the wall opposite the end of her bed.

"I love it! I'm glad we picked the walnut for Alex." She rolled off the bed. Together they added the mattress and padding. When she'd fastened the ties, she reached for the baby quilt and spread it along the railing.

Nikos examined the hand stitching. "You do perfect work. Anyone would think you'd bought this. I'm more impressed than I can say."

"It's full of mistakes, but thanks. I hope he has your black hair. Against the white material, he'll be gorgeous. I can't wait to wrap him in it."

In the next breath Nikos pulled it off the railing and wrapped it around her neck and shoulders. "If he has your blond hair, the effect with this quilt will be sensational." Still holding the material, Nikos drew her close. "All his friends will say he has the most beautiful mother in the Oinousses."

"*Nikos,* I—"

The rest of her words were smothered as he claimed her mouth and slowly savored her as if she were something fragile and precious. Heat began to course through her body, making her legs tremble. She slid her hands up his chest, where she could feel the solid pounding of his heart beneath his sport shirt. For so long Stephanie had been waiting for a sign that he still wanted her. Her great need caused her to respond with an ardor she didn't know herself capable of.

He picked her up and laid her on the bed before stretching out next to her. "Today when I saw the doctor spread the gel and use the probe, I wanted to be the one to feel the baby, Stephanie. Let me feel you now." His voice throbbed.

She responded with a moan as he lifted the hem of her blouse and pulled down the elasticized waist of her skirt. When his hand moved over her belly, sensation after physical sensation swept through her. "Our baby is right there."

As he lowered his mouth to the spot, the shock of his kiss traveled through her womb. Stephanie was filled with indescribable delight and the hope that everything was going to be all right. She let out a helpless cry and once again their mouths sought each other and clung.

There were so many things she'd been wanting to tell him. Now she could show him, without words getting in the way. She'd thought she'd loved him before, but after living together for a month her feelings for him had deepened in new ways and had taken root.

"Don't be afraid you're going to hurt me," she begged, wanting him to crush her in his arms. Though she sensed his growing desire, he held back, kissing her with tenderness rather than the kind of passion she'd once known with him. She wanted more.

He buried his face in her neck. "I don't want to do anything that could injure the baby."

Surely he knew that couldn't happen. Or was he covering for something else she'd secretly worried about from the moment he'd told her he was sterile? "There's no fear of that, unless it's your own injury stopping you."

Nikos lifted his head and looked down at her in confusion. "What do you mean?"

"I'm talking about the deep bruising to your spine from the explosion. When you push yourself too hard, I can tell when you're in pain, but I'm wondering if it's more than that."

To her chagrin he rolled off the bed and got to his feet. "Explain what you mean."

Stephanie sat up, furious with herself for ruining the moment. "I've wondered if your PTSD wasn't the only reason you didn't want to sleep with me in the cabin with the twin beds. If you can't make love, then please tell me. Don't you know it could never matter to me?"

He reared his head in obvious surprise. "There's nothing wrong with me in that department."

For a moment she couldn't breathe, she was so thrilled to hear that news, for his sake. "I—I'm sorry if I jumped to the wrong conclusion," she stammered. "Thank heaven you're all right."

But another part of her was humiliated to have given herself away. It meant he had another reason for not making love to her. Afraid she knew what it was, she got off the bed and put the fallen quilt back on the crib railing.

"Looking back on the explosion, I suppose you could say the collateral damage didn't take everything away," he murmured.

Needing to do something to deflect the pain after that grim assessment, she started cleaning up the mess they'd made. He took the plastic from her hands. "I'll take care of this."

Unable to meet his gaze, she reached for a book she'd been reading, and hurried up on deck to put distance between them. Now that she knew the whole truth of their situation from her husband's lips, she could envision what life had been like after Nikos's father accused his mother of being unfaithful, all of it based on a vicious rumor. The thought that the baby might not be his had changed the dynamics of their marriage.

Was Nikos following the same pattern? Unsure of her still, would he go only so far and no further while he waited for the result in January?

Stephanie had thought her husband was beginning to believe their baby was his. A few minutes ago she'd felt closer to him than she'd thought possible. Though she could shout it to the heavens that the stamp of a Vassalos would be on their little boy, she would never be able to convince Nikos of it until after the delivery.

"Stephanie?"

She wheeled around just as she'd arranged a lounger to sit in while she read. "Yannis! I didn't know you were here. We thought you wouldn't be back until tonight."

"I've got some repair work to do and decided to get at it before dark."

Put on a good face.

She could tell he was dying to know how her doctor's visit went, but he was never one to pry into her business. "We got back a while ago. Nikos set up a crib in my room. You'll be impressed what a good job he did. Our baby boy will be very happy in it."

A grin broke out on the man's bronzed face. "You're going to have a son?"

"That's what the doctor said. We plan to call him Alex."

"That's a fine family name."

"Yes. Ask Nikos to show you a picture."

The older seaman's eyes looked suspiciously bright. "I'm very happy for you."

"We're happy, too." She would keep up the pretense if it killed her. "Thank you for all your kindness to me, Yannis. You do so many things to help me, and I'm grateful."

"It's my pleasure."

"Nikos couldn't get along without you, even if you do put him through torture every day helping him do his exercises. But you already know that, don't you?"

For once she saw him blush.

"He's a slave driver, all right." Nikos had just joined them. "I guess my wife has told you the news."

Yannis clapped him on the shoulder. "She says you have a photo."

"Right here." Nikos pulled it out of his pocket.

The seaman's eyes squinted against the light to get a good look. "He's beautiful, like his mother."

"I was just telling her he'll have the most beautiful woman on the island for his *mana.*"

But you can't take credit for being the father yet, her heart cried.

Stephanie would have to harden herself, because this was going to be the way of it for the next five months.

CHAPTER NINE

December 10

STEPHANIE LOVED HER Greek lessons. For the last four months Yannis had driven her faithfully to and from the school on Oinoussa every weekday after breakfast for her two-hour session with Borus. The forty-year-old was a part-time counselor who was glad for the extra money. He was also a lot of fun.

The closer she drew to her delivery date, the more taciturn and anxious Nikos had become. Whether or not he believed this child was his, she knew he worried. Even though Dr. Panos had assured him at every appointment that she was coming along normally, with no unexpected complications, he didn't seem to quite believe it, and hovered over her until there were times when she wanted to scream.

With the baby due in three weeks, he argued with her that she should stop the lessons. A month ago he'd told her no more swimming with Tassos's wife in order to give her scuba pointers.

While they were eating breakfast this morning, she asked Nikos if he was ordering her to stay home today. The question turned his features into a cool mask before he told her the lessons would end when her teacher left for the Christmas holidays on the seventeenth.

With that pronouncement Nikos got up from the table, taking his coffee with him to the lounge to work. These days the *Diomedes* stayed in port and he used a small cruiser to travel back and forth from the rig erected offshore.

To her joy his business with Tassos was growing, and he'd acquired rights to drill off some of the other uninhabited islands of the Oinousses cluster. His strong concern for the environment made certain there'd be no damage to the local habitat.

As usual when Stephanie came out of class, she tried out what she'd learned on Yannis, who was an excellent teacher himself. But today when he greeted her, she could tell he had something serious on his mind.

"What's wrong? Has something happened to Nikos?" she cried in alarm.

"No, no."

"Thank goodness." She had to wait for her heartbeat to slow down.

"You have a visitor on board. She's very anxious to talk to you."

Stephanie frowned. "Who?"

"Kyria Vassalos, Nikos's mother."

"Oh…" She couldn't believe it. "Is Nikos with her?"

"No. He's gone to the rig. She came when she knew he wouldn't be here."

"How did she know?"

"Because I worked for her when he was just a boy. We've always been friends."

"Which means you've always kept her informed." Stephanie got it.

"Yes. Today Nikos's father is away in Athens on business. It's been her first chance to come and visit. I sent my son to fetch her in his boat. But if you don't want to meet her, I'll tell her to go back to Egnoussa."

"No. Don't do that." More than anything in the world Stephanie had wanted to meet his mother. She just hadn't expected their first meeting to happen when she was in full bloom, with swollen feet and her face marked with chloasma, the pregnancy mask. If she could be thankful for one thing, it was that she could carry on a basic conversation in Greek.

Her nervousness increased as Yannis drove her to the port. Together they walked along the pier to the yacht. Stephanie could see his mother looking out from the rail. Her luxuriant black hair was pulled back in a stylish twist. She was trim, and shorter than Stephanie by several inches. With her white slacks and stunning blue blouse setting off her olive skin, she was a true Grecian beauty. This was where Nikos got his fantastic looks.

As Stephanie stepped on board, the older woman turned, focusing her soft brown eyes on her. "I hope you don't mind," she said in accented English. "I've wanted to meet the woman my son married. I'm sorry it didn't happen when you came to our home. You need to know I'm ashamed of my husband's behavior toward you. My name is—"

"Hestia." Stephanie supplied it for her. "I know your name and I'm so glad you're here now," she said in her best Greek. "You raised a wonderful son. I love him very much."

His mother made a quiet study of her. "For him to

have married you the day after you arrived in Greece, it's obvious how he feels about you."

Stephanie shook her head. "He married me for the sake of the baby." Taking a risk, she added, "He doesn't believe he's the father."

Hestia looked stunned. "I don't understand."

"Come downstairs with me and we'll talk." They went below. "Can I get you something to drink?"

"Nothing, thank you."

"Then come to my room."

A gasp escaped Hestia's lips when she saw the bedroom turned into a nursery. Between Stephanie's bed and everything a mother needed to take care of her new baby, there was barely room to move.

At this point Stephanie's speech was sprinkled with Greek and English. "Please sit down in the rocking chair. I have something to give you." She went over to the dresser and pulled out a photo album. "I wish you had been at the wedding. You should have been there. I made this for you and your husband to keep."

The older woman opened the cover. For the next five minutes she remained speechless as she looked at all the pictures. When she finally lifted her head, tears were rolling down her cheeks. Stephanie saw in those brown eyes all the sorrow a mother could at missing out on her child's wedding day.

"Nikos told me about your husband's distrust when you were pregnant with him. I'm afraid the same thing has happened to me. We had only ten days together on vacation last April. We don't know that much about each other, and so much happened after he had to return to active duty, it raised his doubts about life. About everything."

His mother nodded sadly. "Even though he could walk, he was on the verge of giving up when we took him home from the hospital."

Tears welled in Stephanie's eyes. "He's much better now, but he won't believe this is his baby until after Alexandros is born."

"You can forgive my son for this?"

She smiled. "Didn't you forgive his father?" Stephanie reached for the sonogram picture and showed it to her. "That was at four months. He was only four and half inches long. Now look at him." She placed her hands on top of her big stomach.

Hestia didn't give her a verbal answer, but got to her feet. After setting the album on the dresser, she put her arms around Stephanie and hugged her. "You must come for Christmas and stay the whole day. Everyone wants to meet you. I won't take no for an answer."

Stephanie's heart warmed. "We'll be there. Even if Nikos is still upset with his father, he won't dare refuse to accompany me if I go. He hovers around me constantly these days. Sometimes he follows me when I have to go to the bathroom!"

Laughter bubbled out of her mother-in-law. "That's how my husband was with all three of our children, doubts and all." She wiped her eyes. "I'm going to leave so Nikos won't find me here when he comes home."

"Yannis will see you out to the dock." Stephanie handed her the album to take with her.

"He's a treasure, but I'm sure you've learned that for yourself by now."

"Definitely."

"Take good care of yourself, Stephanie. Your time is close."

"Don't worry. Nikos does it for both of us."

They both laughed as they started up the stairs. Stephanie felt as if she was floating. Already she loved Nikos's mother.

December 17

Nikos lounged against the door of the car while he waited for Stephanie to come out of the school. After going to her doctor's appointment with her, he'd driven her straight here. He was glad this would be her last day of Greek lessons. Her due date was two weeks from tomorrow. Dr. Panos had told her to rest and keep her feet up. Nikos intended to see that she followed his instructions.

Just when his patience had worn thin and he was ready to go in and get her, the school doors opened and his wife emerged with her teacher. Borus Paulos had come highly recommended, but all Nikos could see was that he was enamored of her in the jacketed white sundress she'd bought that first day shopping.

The man gesticulated while he continued talking. Nikos doubted he'd noticed him waiting, but Stephanie saw him. She waved before saying goodbye to her teacher. Then she started walking toward him.

For a moment he was transported back to the Caribbean. He'd been walking along the beach with Angelo when he saw this woman in a wet suit with a fabulous body. Her hair looked gilded in the sun. She was coming to meet Angelo on those long, elegant legs.

When she drew closer, her gaze suddenly switched to Nikos. Her eyes were an impossible blue color, dazzling like rare gems. Her voluptuous mouth curved into a friendly smile. She looked happy and excited because they were going to dive. At that moment the most remarkable sensation had passed through Nikos's body and he was never the same again.

That same electrifying feeling was attacking him now as Stephanie approached the car and their gazes met. He lost his breath. This woman with child was his wife! Whether the baby was his or not, he realized it no longer mattered to him. Somehow over the months they'd become his family. If he'd seen this day while he lay recuperating in the hospital, he would have thought he'd lost his mental faculties along with the ability to walk.

"Sorry it took me so long to get away," she said a little breathlessly. "Borus is a talker when he gets going."

"It wasn't your fault." Her tutor couldn't help his hormones raging in her presence. In fact, the way Nikos himself was feeling at the moment, he didn't dare touch her while they were in front of other people. He opened the passenger door to help her in, seduced by the strawberry-scented shampoo she used in the shower. When her swollen belly brushed against him by accident, his heart gave an extra beat in wonder, while she let out a gentle laugh.

By some miracle she'd stayed incredibly healthy throughout her pregnancy. She'd never developed the serious problems he'd heard various married business associates talk about. Though she complained of swelling and the chloasma she insisted made her resemble a raccoon, he'd never seen her more beautifully feminine.

It had taken control almost beyond his endurance to stay away from her. Because of his injury she'd wrongly assumed he couldn't make love to her as he'd done on the island. But only one thing had held him back. Stark staring fear.

She didn't know what it was like to worry that he might cause harm to her and the baby during a flashback. It was the only force strong enough to keep him locked up in his room night after night. After living together this long without an incident that left bruises on her, he refused to allow anything to go wrong now.

After lunch they were going to do the last of their Christmas shopping. Just a few more presents, nothing taxing. While they were gone, he'd instructed Yannis to put up the little Christmas tree with lights he'd bought and smuggled on board. The lounge was the best place to surprise her. It wasn't a tradition Nikos followed, but he knew Americans were big on it, and such things were important to his wife.

He darted her a glance before he started the car. "Hungry?"

"You know, for once I'm not? But if you want to eat before we shop, that's fine with me."

"What I'd like to do is get the gift buying over with as fast as possible and go back home. I'll cook today and surprise you with something you haven't had before."

She smiled at him. "I'd love that."

"Good."

With the much cooler late autumn temperatures, she appeared to thrive. He could only marvel at her energy.

"Let's shop at the main department store," she suggested. "That way we can find everything we want under one roof."

"I was thinking the same thing." He headed in that direction. "Just so you know, Tassos phoned while I was waiting for you. He and Elianna have invited us to their house for their family's Christmas Day party."

He felt Stephanie stir restlessly in the seat. "That's very nice of them, but we can't go."

He frowned. "Why not?"

When she remained quiet, he slanted her a glance. "Stephanie? What's wrong?"

"Nikos," she began, but her hesitation was plain as day. He saw a guilty look enter her eyes. It surprised him no end.

"You don't want to go?"

"Under other circumstances I would, but that's not it." She shook her head. "I have a confession to make."

Just when he'd been thinking nothing had gone wrong with her pregnancy, he was terrified she was going to tell him something he didn't want to hear. On impulse he pulled over to the side of the street and shut off the engine. Turning in the seat, he slid his arm behind her and tugged on a few strands of her hair.

"Are you ill? Is there something you didn't tell the doctor this morning?"

"This isn't about me. I…it's about us."

In an instant his blood ran cold. "You mean after all this time, you've chosen today instead of Christmas to tell me who the father of your baby is?"

"No! Nikos." Her horrified cry reverberated in the car. "I'm going about this all wrong. Your mother came to see me last week while your father was away in Athens. We had a frank talk about everything. I showed her the sonogram picture. She's wonderful and I love her already. Before she left, I gave her the wedding album I made for them. She has invited us to spend Christmas Day with your family. I accepted for us."

After he'd imagined every horrific thing possible that could destroy life as he knew it, her explanation came as a complete shock. It took a minute for him to assimilate what she'd just said. He waited until he'd calmed down enough to talk. "That won't be a problem. I'll phone and tell her we've made other plans. She'll understand."

"No, I don't think she will. Nikos," Stephanie said in a tremulous whisper. "She adores you and needs to see her son. They've missed out on more than a decade of your life. You can't disappoint them. Life's too short."

He sucked in his breath. "My father's bias against Castor and his children for being who they are has been unconscionable, Stephanie. After what he did to my mother and the way he spoke to you, I can't be in the same room with him."

She put a hand to his cheek. "But she's forgiven him and so have I. As you told me, he's afraid and doesn't know how to make things right. If you don't show him the way, his fear of losing you will send him to the grave a desperately unhappy man. What joy could there be in that for any of us?"

Nikos felt sick to his stomach. "I can't do it. Don't ask that of me."

Stephanie pulled her hand away from him and stared out the window. "Then you go to Tassos's family for Christmas. I'll go to your parents and take your family their gifts."

Seeing black, Nikos started the car and drove straight to the dock.

As Stephanie passed the lounge on her way to the bedroom, she saw a five-foot Christmas tree studded with colored lights set up over by the entertainment center. Yannis had been busy while they'd been gone. She walked over to it and examined some of the ornaments.

After the devastating silence in the car while Nikos drove them back to the yacht, the sight of this brought her immeasurable delight. There was no one like Nikos. But the lights brought pain, too, making a mockery of the peace and joy Christmas was supposed to bring. They'd reached an impasse. His mother's invitation and Stephanie's acceptance had ruined this beautiful day.

Desperate to make things right between them, she hurried to his room before he could lock her out. That's what he'd been doing for months. The night before last she'd heard the gut-wrenching moaning and sobbing that came from his bedroom. So far she'd counted four episodes she knew about since their wedding.

When she discussed this with Yannis, the older man said it was a good sign that they weren't happening as often as they had in the beginning, which could only mean Nikos was slowly getting better. Stephanie wanted that for him more than anything.

He was such an outstanding man; she couldn't reconcile everything she knew about him with the side of his nature that had caused him to shut down just now. She couldn't leave it alone. This was too serious. Without knocking, she opened the door, determined they were going to talk everything out.

She couldn't prevent the cry that escaped when she discovered he'd removed his clothes and had just pulled on his black bathing trunks. With his back still to her, she saw the bruising at the lower part of his spine. Since he'd always worn his wet suit when they went swimming, she hadn't realized how deep and pervasive his injury had been. To think of his lying in that hospital bed broken and in despair... She couldn't bear it.

He wheeled around, a live, breathing, angry Adonis. That awful glittery look in his jet-black eyes impaled her, freezing the breath from her lungs. "I don't recall inviting you in here." The wintry tone he'd once used with her was back in full force.

Stephanie couldn't swallow. "I was afraid I might not get an invitation. I came in to tell you how sorry I am that I didn't let you know about your mother's visit until now. You've suffered years of pain over a situation I haven't fully comprehended until today. I'll call your mother and tell her we can't come."

It was as if he'd turned to stone. She couldn't reach him.

"I should never have attempted to tell you anything about your life or your thoughts," she went on. "I do have an audacious nature and realize it's a glaring flaw in my makeup. So I'll make you a promise now that I'll never keep anything from you again, or try to influence your thinking in any way. I swear it."

Desolate at this point because of his silence, she turned to leave, but paused in the doorway. "I love the Christmas tree. No woman in the world has a better husband than you. I'm sorry you can't say the same thing about your wife. To tell you I'm sorry I came to Greece would be a lie, but I'd give anything if I'd been honest with you after your mother left the other day. I've trespassed on your soul, Nikos. Forgive me. It will never happen again."

She rushed to her room and lay down on her back, pressing the pillow against her face to stifle her sobs. It wasn't long before she heard the familiar sound of the cruiser. Who knew when Nikos would be back? And when he did return, there was no guesstimating how soon he'd speak to her again.

Stephanie knew he couldn't tolerate the sight of her right now. She didn't blame him. That's why he'd taken off. Perhaps the best thing to do was give him some space. The more she thought about it, the more she liked the idea. While she put a plan into action, she ate a substantial lunch and made a phone call.

Once that was done she packed an overnight bag with several days' worth of clothes. On her way out she stopped in the lounge to put some presents under the tree for Nikos. Presents made it look ready for Christmas. After that she wrote him a note, leaving it on his desk where he would see it.

Dear Nikos. We've been together constantly since I barged into your life. What was it Kahlil Gibran once wrote? "There should be spaces in your togetherness." I agree with his philosophy, so I'm taking myself off until the day after Christmas. Don't worry. I won't be far. Please be assured I won't embarrass you by bothering anyone you know or care about. Our business stays our business. I think you know I would never do anything that put me or the baby in danger. I want Alex to know his father. S.

Nikos could be gone for the rest of the day. As for Yannis, he'd said he'd be back at three. She had a half hour to leave without him seeing her.

The town had only two taxis. One of them was waiting for her at the dock. She got in and told the driver to drop her off on a corner where she'd seen used cars for sale. Her passport still showed she was single. The man who sold her the car had no idea she was Kyria Vassalos. That suited her fine. It didn't take long before she was in possession of a clunker that cost only five hundred dollars.

Free to do what she wanted, Stephanie drove to a wonderfully sited convent nestled among pines and ringed with a magnificent garden. The weary traveler was welcome to stay at their hospice, which was located on the west side of the island, about ten minutes from town. During one of their lessons Borus had told her she should visit to learn its history.

En route she passed several quiet coves, enchanted by the scenery and grateful she could use her bank card to draw money from her final paycheck. She still had enough to pay the fee for board and room for a week.

The convent suited her perfectly. For the time being she intended to get some reading done and keep her feet up. But when she got restless, she could take short drives around the island. It helped to know she'd be out of Nikos's hair for a while. He'd been hurtled into a world of pain after he'd left the Caribbean, and deserved a break.

As she'd told him, she was the ball on the end of his chain. By her staying here at the convent, out of sight, he didn't have to drag it around. For the time being he didn't know where to find her and that was good. He hovered too much.

On the plus side, she could give in to her emotions, which were out of control at this stage of her pregnancy. If she wanted to cry her heart out at night, no one would hear her through the thick walls.

Once in her simple room, she sank down on the bed. Right now she was so exhausted she couldn't move. For the last hour she'd had pain in her lower back. It was from all the walking she'd done today. Tomorrow she'd go out in the garden, but not now.

Evening had fallen before Nikos returned to the dock. Yannis was waiting to help him tie up the cruiser. But there was a worried look on the older man's face that raised the hair on the back of Nikos's neck.

"Is Stephanie all right?"

"That's the problem, Nikos. I don't know. When I came back at three she was gone, but she left a note on the desk in the lounge."

Forgetting the pain in his back, Nikos raced along the pier to the yacht and hurried down the stairs. As he read her message, his heart plunged like a boulder crashing down a mountain. "She had to have called for a taxi to take her to one of the tourist lodgings. I'll call and find out which one."

But when he finally reached the driver who'd picked her up, the man was no help. "I dropped her off on a corner by the Pappas Market. She was carrying an overnight bag."

Searing pain ripped Nikos open before he hung up. "I've got to find her tonight!"

Yannis looked grim. "You get dressed and we'll go to every place where she might be staying."

Nikos changed into jeans and a sweater before they took off for town in the car. They combed the whole area for an hour, without results. "I should never have closed up on her like I did earlier. She couldn't help it that Mother came to see her."

"That was my fault, Nikos."

He stared hard at his friend. "No. The fault is all mine for letting old wounds fester until the result caused Stephanie to run away from me. I can't lose her, Yannis." His voice shook. "Where in the hell has she gone?"

"How did she find you?"

The shrewd seaman's question gave Nikos pause. He struggled for breath. "Through sheer persistence and determination." His mind reeled with possibilities. "Since she's not at any local lodgings, she had to get a ride with someone to somewhere else." His turmoil grew worse.

Yannis patted his shoulder. "Perhaps she went to another part of the island."

"Maybe. But there's no place for her to stay, only ruins and churches."

"Could she have gone back to the dock, to take the boat to Chios?"

"Anything's worth looking into." Nikos got the port authority on the line. The captain in charge of the last crossing was emphatic that a blonde, pregnant American woman had not been on board.

Nikos shook his head. "She's here somewhere, Yannis. Maybe she crept on some fishing boat down at the harbor to spend the night."

Yannis scratched his head. "I don't think she'd do that, not in her condition. She's so excited about that baby, she'd never put herself in precarious circumstances. Besides, everyone knows you. I doubt she'd do anything that could embarrass you. She said as much in the note."

Nikos stared blindly at the water in the distance.

"She had to get help from someone, but in my gut I know she wouldn't turn to Tassos or my family. She hasn't made any friends yet."

"That's not exactly true."

His gaze swerved to Yannis. "What do you mean?"

"Bulos."

Though she'd spent ten hours a week for months with her language teacher, Nikos still ruled him out and shook his head. "Let's go home and see if she's back on board the *Diomedes*. If not, I'll think about bringing in the police."

Except that she expected him to trust her enough to take care of herself and come back when she was ready. The police would want to know why she was missing and would figure out she and Nikos were having a domestic quarrel. It would be the talk of the Oinousses.

By three in the morning it was clear she wasn't coming back. Nikos thought he'd been at the end of his rope in the hospital, but this was agony in a new dimension. If anything untoward happened to her or the baby because of him, life wouldn't be worth living.

Yannis made them coffee. Both of them were too wired from anxiety to do anything but pace. They were waiting for morning so they could begin their search all over again.

At five to four Niko's cell phone rang, causing him to almost jump out of his skin. He clicked on. "Stephanie?"

"No, sir. This is Sister Sofia at the Convent of the Holy Virgin on Oinoussa. Are you Kyrie Vassalos?"

Beads of perspiration broke out on his forehead. "Speaking." He couldn't imagine why she'd called.

"Your wife checked into our hospice this afternoon." *The hospice! Of course!* "But she's been in labor ever since and is now at the hospital."

Nikos weaved in place. "God bless you, Sister. You've just saved my life!" He hung up. "Yannis? Stephanie is at the hospital having the baby!"

With Yannis driving, they made it there in record time. Nikos burst inside the emergency entrance. "My wife!" he said to the surprised attendant. "Stephanie Vassalos—"

"She's in the delivery room."

"Has she had the baby?"

"Not yet. Dr. Panos says for you to come with me. I'll get you ready. We need to hurry."

The next few minutes were a blur as Nikos was instructed to sanitize his hands before being led into the delivery room. He was told to sit.

"Nikos!" He heard Stephanie call out to him.

"You're just in time," the doctor said without missing a beat. "Your baby fooled everyone and decided to come a few weeks early. Push, Stephanie. That's it. One more time."

Nikos's wet eyes flew to his brave, beautiful wife, propped on the bed. The strain in her body and the way she worked with the doctor was something he'd never forget.

"Ah, there's the head. This guy's got your husband's black hair."

He heard his wife's shouts of excitement.

"Keep pushing. Here comes Alexandros." Dr. Panos held the baby up in the air by the ankles and Nikos heard a gurgle, followed by a lusty cry.

Stephanie started sobbing for joy. "How does he look?" she begged the doctor.

"You can see for yourself after I've cut the cord." A minute later he laid the baby across her stomach and wiped off the fluid. "Come on over here, Papa. You can examine your son together."

As wonderful as that sounded, Nikos leaned over to kiss Stephanie's dry lips first. "Are you all right? I'm so sorry I wasn't there for you."

Her eyes were a blazing blue. "But you have been, all this time, and I've never been so happy in my life. Isn't he beautiful?"

His gaze flew to the baby, who'd stopped crying and gone quiet. His dark eyes looked at Nikos so seriously, reminding him of the way Stephanie sometimes did. He studied the rest of him. His perfect hands with their long fingers were curled into fists. It was like looking through a kaleidoscope, where all the bits and pieces formed a miraculous design. This one was made from the molds of a Walsh and a Vassalos.

Nikos saw Stephanie's mouth and chin, his brother's ears, his mother's black hair, his own fingers and toes, his father's body shape. *My son. My one and only.*

"He looks exactly like you, Nikos."

He turned his head toward her. "You're in there, too. But I want you to know that even if he didn't look like me, it wouldn't matter, because I fell in love with the two of you a long time ago. A miracle happened on the island."

"I know." Tears gushed from her eyes. "I love you, darling. So much I can't begin to tell you."

"No woman ever fought harder to show her love than you did when you came all the way to this remote island to find me. I'll never forget," he said against her mouth. "I've got to tell Yannis. Then I'm going to call the family and tell them they've become grandparents again."

CHAPTER TEN

January 24

YANNIS WAS WAITING for her at the car outside the clinic. The temperature had to be in the forties. Her sweater felt good. There'd been some light rain that afternoon, but now that the sun had dropped into the sea, it had stopped.

Stephanie had decided to get her six weeks checkup a few days ahead of schedule, without Nikos knowing. The whole point was to surprise him.

"Dr. Panos says I'm 100 percent healthy, but I need to lose weight."

"You look good for a new mother."

"Thank you."

"Now remember our plan."

"Are you sure you want to do this, Yannis?"

He grinned. "Nikos's parents have spent more time on the *Diomedes* than they have at their house. It's my turn."

"Alex is crazy about you."

"I love him. Maria and I have been waiting to tend him. We have it all planned for tonight. Everything's ready for you on the cruiser."

"Do you think Nikos suspects anything?"

"No. Tassos is with him and so are your parents. Between family, the demands of the business and the duties of a new father, he's too exhausted to be doing much thinking."

She took a shaky breath, so nervous and excited at the same time that she couldn't hold still. "Then I'll just keep walking past the yacht to the cruiser, and wait for him to come."

"When he asks where you are, I'll tell him that after you got back from shopping, you went in search of the camcorder, since you couldn't find it in the lounge. In the end he'll come looking for you."

This was the first night they would be away from the baby. "We'll be in that little cove around the point if there's a problem."

"Don't you worry about anything."

"Alex isn't too crazy about formula, but he'll drink it when he gets hungry."

"Of course he will. It's Nikos you should be worried about. He needs some attention."

She had news for him. *So do I.* "You're an angel, Yannis."

After he'd parked the car at the dock, she gave him a hug, then ran along the pier to the cruiser and hurried on board. There was just one bedroom below. She turned on the heat to warm things up. While she waited, she took a quick shower and changed into a new nightgown her mother-in-law had given her for Christmas.

Though she was still missing her little boy, she was dying to be with her big boy. They hadn't been intimate since her vacation on Providenciales. Right now she was horribly nervous. If he still wasn't prepared to make love to her because of his PTSD, she needed to know before she made herself sick with expectations.

For weeks now they'd shared tender, loving moments with the baby, but Nikos went to bed alone every night like clockwork.

Not tonight!

After leaving the light on in the hallway, she brushed out her hair and climbed under the covers with a novel. For fifteen minutes she kept reading the first page, until she heard him call to her.

"Stephanie? What are you doing? The camcorder was in your bedroom. Come on up. The family's waiting for you."

Her heart thudded too hard. "If you don't mind, I'd like to stay down here for a while."

In the silence she could almost hear him thinking. "Why?"

"Because I'd like to have my husband to myself for a little while."

She heard him come down the stairs. "Are you upset about something?" His voice had suddenly deepened. It did that when he suspected trouble.

"Actually, I am."

He burst into the bedroom. The worried look on his handsome face was priceless. "What are you doing in bed?"

She sat up, feasting her eyes on him. "I've been waiting ten months for you. This afternoon Dr. Panos gave me a clean bill of health, so—"

"You've been to see him already?" he interrupted. If she wasn't mistaken, the news seemed to have shaken him.

"Yes. I couldn't stand to wait until next week. Everything's been arranged. Yannis and Maria are taking care of Alex until tomorrow. I told him we'd motor around the point to the cove and stay for the night. I grabbed your medication earlier today. It's in my purse. So there's nothing you need to go back for. Your parents and Tassos will understand."

A haunted look crept over Nikos's features. "Stephanie—"

"If you have a nightmare, you won't have to worry you're hurting the baby. He's safe and sound on the *Diomedes*. I'm tough, Nikos. I can take whatever happens if you'll give me the chance. I want to be your wife. Won't you let me?"

She watched his throat working. It felt like an eternity before he said, "It's cold on deck. Stay right where you are."

"I promise."

In a few minutes she felt the cruiser reversing. After traveling at wake speed, Nikos opened it up and they were flying across the water. It didn't take long to round the point. He eventually slowed down, and she felt them glide onto the sand in the cove.

More waiting while she heard him take a shower.

Before the light went out, she saw his silhouette in the doorway. He'd hitched a towel around his hips. "I have a confession to make, Stephanie."

Not another one. She couldn't take it. "What is it?"

"When I got back to my unit, I told Kon I'd fallen in love with you, and planned to resign my commission after our mission so I could marry you."

With a moan of joy she climbed out of bed and ran to him, throwing her arms around his neck.

He crushed her to him, scattering kisses over her face and hair. "Forgive me for being so horrible to you. You're the most precious thing in my life."

"There was never anything to forgive. Let's not talk anymore, darling. We've said everything there is to say. I want to make love all night, and the same thing every night for the rest of our lives. You have no understanding of how much I love you."

Nikos gripped her shoulders. His black eyes blazed with desire. "Actually, I'm one man who *does* know. And one day soon, I'm going to do everything in my power to help you find your own father. He deserves to know he has the most wonderful daughter a man could ever be blessed with. I adore you."

"And I, you. Love me, darling. Love me."

They were on fire for each other to a degree they hadn't known in the Caribbean.

As he picked her up and followed her body down on the bed, he spoke the Greek words she'd been yearning to hear him say. Over and over again he whispered, *"Agape mou."* My love, my love.

April 26

"Stephanie? Are you ready?" Nikos walked into the nursery they'd made aboard the *Diomedes*. He was so gorgeous, she almost fainted as he approached in a formal gray suit and white shirt.

"We are!" She looked down at their precious four-month-old Alex, who was so excited to see his daddy he kept smiling and lifting his arms. The two were so handsome it brought tears to her eyes to see them together. "Guess what, big boy? Today you're going to get christened."

She expected Nikos to pick him up, but he fooled her and swept her into his arms first. "I need this before we go anywhere." Catching her to him, he gave her a long, passionate kiss reminiscent of their lovemaking earlier that morning, before the baby was awake. It was a good thing her eggshell-colored suit with lace trim was wrinkle proof.

After thinking it over, she and Nikos had decided the ceremony at the church would take place on the date of their baby's conception. It was a secret between the two of them. Knowing Alex was their miracle child, they'd chosen this particular date to commemorate the sacred occasion.

They'd asked Tassos and Elianna to be godparents. Except for the addition of Nikos's mother waiting for them at the church where they'd been married, it was like déjà vu to travel there with Yannis and join their closest friends for the baptism.

Tassos hugged Stephanie before speaking on behalf of their child, then they followed the priest to the font, where Nikos's mother took Alex to undress him and wrap him in a large towel. Stephanie watched in wonder and fascination as they went through the sacrament of baptism.

After the priest gave him the name Alexandros and anointed him, Tassos wrapped the baby in a white sheet and towel. Then Nikos's mother dressed him in his christening clothes, but as she did so, Nikos's father suddenly appeared in their circle. He handed the priest a gold cross and chain to give their baby, the first olive branch toward a reconciliation with his son. At that same moment Tassos lit a candle.

Stephanie slid a covert glance to her husband, whose black eyes filled with liquid. She grasped his hand before they walked around the font three times. Earlier, Nikos had told her it symbolized the dance of joy.

With the circle complete except for Stephanie's mother, who Stephanie felt was watching from heaven, they witnessed their adorable son's first communion. Stephanie followed Nikos's lead and kissed Tassos's hand before he handed her the baby. Everyone murmured, *"Na sas zizi,"* which meant "life to Alexandros."

They'd planned a party back on the yacht afterward, but for Stephanie the real celebrating was going on right here, seeing the beginning of peace for both families after years of turmoil.

On the drive back to the yacht, Nikos pulled her tight against him. "I have two presents for you, my love. One is a home I've bought for us on Oinoussa. Now that we have a son, he needs a place to play besides the deck of the *Diomedes*."

She hugged him hard. "I agree."

"Your other gift is in my pocket. I was planning to show it to you tonight, but after seeing my father show up, I've decided I can't wait."

Nikos sounded exceptionally excited. "What is it?" she whispered against his lips.

"The private investigator I hired has found your father."

"Nikos!"

"This is a picture of him." He reached in his breast pocket and pulled out a small photo. The second she saw the dark blond man, she knew it was her father. "We look so much alike!"

Nikos nodded. "He works at a bank in Cheyenne, Wyoming, where he was born. He's married with a son and daughter, who are both in college. When he met your mother, he was on leave from the army. Like me, he had to go back and serve another tour of duty. Four years later he got out of the army and married."

"D-does he know about me?"

"No."

"Thank heaven!"

A look of confusion entered Nikos's eyes before he kissed her. "Why do you say that?"

"Because he's an honorable man who made a good life for himself." Her voice shook. "I don't want to disrupt it. Since Mother chose not to find him, I want to leave things alone." She grasped Nikos's face in her hands. "It's enough to know what he looks like and who he is."

She crushed her husband in her arms. "Thank you, darling, for such a precious gift. What really matters now is our family, our son. I married the most wonderful man alive and I'm going to spend the rest of my life showing you what you mean to me. I love you, Nikos. *I love you.*"

* * * * *